**Praise for *New York Times* bestselling author
Jillian Hart**

"A tender and highly emotional love story that will
stay with readers for a long time."
—*RT Book Reviews* on *High Country Bride*

"A sweet book with lovable characters that have
problems to overcome with the help of faith and the
power of true love."
—*RT Book Reviews* on *Homespun Bride*

Praise for Victoria Bylin

"*The Bounty Hunter's Bride* is a sweet love story with
rough edges, filled with hope, love, forgiveness
and redemption. Victoria Bylin has written enough
historical novels to know what readers expect, and
she delivers on all levels."
—*RT Book Reviews*

"Those looking for a sweet and heartwarming
romance will want to check this one out."
—*All About Romance* on *The Bounty Hunter's Bride*

Praise for Sara **and**

"This tender love st   blend of
romance and s   *His Arms*

"Mitchell is   or who spins
a tale of gree   ts and keeping the
faith in ones

—   ook Reviews* on *The Widow's Secret*

New York Times Bestselling Author

Jillian Hart

Victoria Bylin
Sara Mitchell

In a Mother's Arms
&
The Widow's Secret

HARLEQUIN® LOVE INSPIRED®CLASSICS

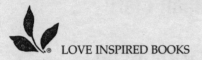

LOVE INSPIRED BOOKS

Recycling programs
for this product may
not exist in your area.

ISBN-13: 978-1-335-45450-8

In a Mother's Arms & The Widow's Secret

Copyright © 2019 by Harlequin Books S.A.

The publisher acknowledges the copyright holders
of the individual works as follows:

Finally a Family
Copyright © 2009 by Jill Strickler

Home Again
Copyright © 2009 by Vicki Scheibel

The Widow's Secret
Copyright © 2009 by Sara Mitchell

www.Harlequin.com

Printed in U.S.A.

CONTENTS

New York Times bestselling author **Jillian Hart** grew up on her family's homestead, where she helped raise cattle, rode horses and scribbled stories in her spare time. After earning her English degree from Whitman College, she worked in travel and advertising before selling her first novel. When Jillian isn't working on her next story, she can be found puttering in her rose garden, curled up with a good book or spending quiet evenings at home with her family.

FINALLY A FAMILY

Jillian Hart

You have turned for me my mourning into dancing;
You have put off my sackcloth
and clothed me with gladness.
—*Psalms* 30:11

Chapter One

Angel County, Montana Territory, 1884

Molly McKaslin felt watched as she sat in her cushioned rocking chair in her cozy little shanty with her favorite book in hand. The story she was reading had taken her far away to the landscape of England, where the rush of fictional rain drowned out the real sounds of the Montana wind breezing through the open windows. Mr. Darcy's offer of marriage to Elizabeth Bennet vanished like mist and Molly blinked, reorienting herself. What had drawn her out of her story?

The lush new-spring green of the Montana prairie spread out before her like a painting, framed by the wooden window. The blue sky was without a single cloud to mar it. Lemony sunshine spilled over the land and through the open windowsill. The crisp scents from the nearby orchard and grass fields filled the cheerful one-room shanty. The door was wedged open, letting the outside noises in—the snap of laundry on the clothesline and the chomping crunch of an animal grazing. My, it sounded terribly close. This was her cousin Aiden's land. Perhaps he had let his live-stock onto the lawn to give the fast growing grass a quick mow?

The peaceful afternoon quiet shattered, right along with a crash. She leaped to her feet, spinning around to see her good—and only—china vase splintered on the newly washed wood floor. The sprays of butter-cups and daisies were tangled amid the shards, water pooling on the polished planks. She stared in shock at the culprit standing at her other window. A golden cow with a white blaze down her face poked her head fur-ther across the sill, obviously curious where the tasty flowers had gone to. The bovine gave a woeful moo, her liquid brown eyes pleading for help. One look told her this was the only animal in the yard.

"And just what are you doing out on your own?" She set her book aside.

The cow lowed again. She was a small heifer with a sweet innocence about her. Still probably more baby than adult. The cow lunged against the sill and wrapped her long tongue around the top rung of the ladder-back chair, straining toward the cookie racks on the table. She was obviously tame. She cast a plain-tive look and mooed softly, perhaps saying the bovine version of "please."

"At least I know how to catch you." Molly had grown up on her family's farm and she knew how flighty cattle could be. This one still might run off on her yet. She grabbed a cookie off the rack and sure enough the heif-er's eyes widened with a doe's sweetness. "I don't rec-ognize you, so I don't think you belong here. Someone is going to be very unhappy with you."

The cow batted her long brown lashes, unafraid.

Molly skirted around the mess on the floor—she would bemoan the loss of her mother's vase later—and headed toward the door. This was the consequence of agreeing to live in the country when she had vowed to never do so again. Life had happened, and her path had led her to this opportunity, living on her cousin's land and helping the family. God had quite a sense of humor, indeed.

Her bare feet puffed up the chalk-dry dust outside her door. Before she could take two steps into the soft, lush grass surrounding her shanty, the cow came running, head down, big brown eyes fastened on the cookie, all four legs blurring in motion. The ground shook.

Uh oh. Molly's heart skipped two beats.

"No, Sukie, no!" High, girlish voices carried on the wind.

Over the cow's head, Molly briefly caught sight of two identical school-aged girls racing down the long dirt road. The animal was too single-minded to respond. The cow's head was down as she pounded the final few yards, her determined gaze fixed on the cookie.

"Stop, Sukie. Whoa." Molly kept her voice low and kindly firm. It may have been a long time since she had managed a cow, but she knew they responded to kindness better than to anything else. She also knew they were not good at stopping, so she dropped the cookie on the ground and neatly stepped out of the way. The cow dug in with all hooves, skidded well past the cookie and the place where Molly had been standing.

"It's right here." She touched the cow's shoulder, showing her where the oatmeal treat was resting in the clean grass. While the animal backed up a foot and nipped up the goody, Molly grabbed the cow's rope halter.

"Good. She didn't stomp you into bits." One of the girls swiped her hand over her forehead, as if in serious relief. "She ran me over real good just last week."

The second girl stood with her head down, sucking in air. "We thought you were a goner. She's real nice, but she doesn't see very well."

"She sees well enough to have found me." Molly studied the girls. They both had identical black braids and golden-hazel eyes and fine-boned porcelain faces. One twin wore a green calico dress with matching sunbonnet, while the other wore blue. She recognized the girls from church and around town. "Don't you live across the main road? Aren't you the doctor's children?"

"Yep, that's us." The first girl offered a beaming, dimpled smile. "I'm Penelope and that's Prudence. We're real glad you found Sukie."

"We wouldn't want a cougar to get her."

"Or a bear."

"Or a wolf."

What adorable children. Molly knew she was staring, she couldn't help it. She drank in details—the faint scattering of freckles across their sun-kissed noses, the glint of trouble in their beautiful eyes, the animated dearness as the twins looked at one another, as if in complete understanding. The place in her soul, the one thirsty for a child of her own, ached painfully. She felt hollow and empty, as if her body would always remember carrying the baby she had lost. For one moment it was as if the sun blinked out, as if the wind died and the earth vanished.

"Hey, what is she eating?" One of the girls—Prudence?—tumbled forward. "It smells like a cookie. You are a bad girl, Sukie."

"Did she walk into your house and eat off the counter?" Penelope wanted to know.

The past slipped back into place, the sun scorched her face and the grass crinkled beneath her feet as the cow tugged her toward the girls. "No, she went through the window."

Penelope went up on tiptoe. "I see them. The cookies. They look real good."

"Yes, real good. The best I've ever seen." Prudence took hold of the cow.

Molly was captivated by the girls and their identically pleading expression, so sweet and innocent. She wasn't fooled. Then again, she was a soft touch. "You two keep a good hold on Sukie, and I'll see what I can do about getting you some cookies."

The girls exchanged happy looks, apparently pleased their plan had worked out so well.

Yep, she was much too soft of a touch. She headed back inside, keeping an eye on them as she went. "Do you girls need help getting the cow home?"

"No. She's real tame. We raised her from a bottle." Penelope and the cow trailed after her, hesitating outside the door. "She loves us. We can lead her anywhere."

"Yeah, she only runs off when she's looking for us."

The girls laughed, the merry sound rising like music on the wind and warming the shadows within her. She tried not to count the years, but she knew. She would always know. Four long years had crept by one day at a time, when she had no longer heard that music of her baby daughter's laughter. Her life had become nothing but silence.

"Thank you so much, Mrs.—" Penelope took the napkin wrapped around the stack of cookies. She tilted her head to one side, puzzled. "We don't know your name."

"This is the McKaslin ranch," Prudence said thoughtfully, enduring affectionate licks from Sukie. "But I know you're not Mrs. McKaslin."

"I'm the cousin. I moved here last winter. You can call me Molly."

"So…" Penelope gave her twin a cookie. Beneath the brim of her sunbonnet, her face crinkled with serious thought. "You don't know our pa?"

"You haven't been sick yet?" Prudence asked as she fed her cookie to the cow.

"No, I only know Dr. Frost by reputation. I hear he's a fine doctor." That was all she knew. Of course she had seen his fancy black buggy with the top up speeding down the country roads at all hours. Other times she had witnessed that same buggy going through town at a more leisurely pace. Sometimes she caught a brief sight of the man driving as the vehicle passed— an impression of a black Stetson, a strong granite profile and impressively wide shoulders.

Although she was on her own and free to marry, she paid little heed to eligible men. All she knew of Doctor Samuel Frost was that he was a widower and a father and a faithful man, for he often appeared very somber and serious in church. She reached through the open door to where her coats hung on wall pegs and worked the sash off her winter woolen.

"Oh, he's a real good doc," Penelope went on, looking entirely innocent as she nibbled on the edge of her cookie, as if debating something.

Likewise, Prudence nibbled, too. "Our pa's nice, and you make good cookies."

"*And* you're awful pretty." Penelope was so excited she didn't notice Sukie stealing her cookie. "Maybe you could like Pa."

"I don't know the man, so I can't like him. I suppose I can't dislike him either." The sash came free and she bent to secure it around Sukie's halter. "Do you want some water before we go?"

"You ought to come home with us." Penelope grinned, happy to take hold of the end of the sash. She no longer looked quite so innocent. No, she looked like nothing but trouble. "Then you can meet our pa."

"Well, I don't know. It's Sunday. A family day." Goodness, why would the twins ask such a thing? "Come on, girls, let's get you home."

"Do you want to get married?" Penelope's feet were planted.

So were Prudence's. "Yes! You could marry Pa. Do you want to?"

"M-marry your pa?" Shock splashed over her like icy water. Had she heard them right?

"Sure. You could be our ma."

"And then Pa wouldn't be cross anymore."

"Or lonely. So, do you want to?"

Molly blinked. The words were starting to sink in. The twins wished so much for a mother that they would take any stranger who was kind to them. The poor things. She froze in place with the tops of the grasses brushing her skirt hem, her eyes blinking from the harsh sun. The girls were adorable. Any woman would be lucky to have the identical set of them to love.

She pushed aside that old longing she felt, one that

could never be satisfied. There would be no children for her. As for stepchildren—well, that was another matter too painful to consider. "No, I certainly cannot marry a perfect stranger, thank you for asking. But I would take you two in a heartbeat."

"You would?" Penelope looked surprised. "Really?"

Prudence lost her last cookie to the cow. "We're an awful lot of trouble. Our housekeeper said that three times this morning, and that was *before* she left for church."

"We would make Pa get you a nice ring. Would that matter?"

"No, sweetie." How did a child understand that marriage was more than a ring and a simple "I do"? Commitment was a lifelong vow, and love was fragile and endlessly complicated. It could not survive without deep devotion and deeper emotional ties. "Does your pa know you propose on his behalf?"

"Now he does." A deep baritone answered. Heavy footsteps crunched in the grass near the house. Dr. Frost marched into sight, rounding the corner of the shanty. His hat brim shaded his face, casting shadows across his chiseled features, giving him an even more imposing appearance. "Girls! Home! Not another word."

"But we had to save Sukie."

"She could have been eaten by a wolf."

Molly watched the good doctor's mouth twitch, as if he were doing his best to keep his foreboding appearance. He spotted her and she couldn't be sure because his eyes were shadowed, but a flash of humor could have twinkled in their depths.

"You must be the cousin." He swept off his hat and

sunshine worshipped his features. The twinkle faded from his eyes and the hint of a grin from his lips. It was clear that while his daughters amused him, she did not. He stiffened, and his deep tone sounded formal. "I had no idea you would be so young."

"And pretty," Penelope, obviously the troublemaker, added mischievously.

Molly's face heated. The poor girl must need glasses. Although she was still young, time and sadness had made its mark on her. She didn't know what to say to that. The imposing man had turned into granite as he faced her. Of course he had overheard his daughters' proposal, so that might explain it. Perhaps he was afraid she would change her mind and accept!

The poor man. She smiled—she hoped not too much—and took a step away from him. "Dr. Frost, I'm glad you found your daughters. I was about ready to bring them back to you."

"I shall save you the trouble." He didn't look happy. "Girls, take that cow home. Get moving while I apologize to Miss McKaslin."

She was a "Mrs." But she didn't correct him. She had put away her black dresses and her grief. Her marriage had mostly been a long string of broken dreams. She did better when she didn't remember. She breathed in the sweet spring sunshine and held its warmth deep inside. "Please don't be too hard on the girls on my behalf. Sukie's arrival livened up my day."

"At least there was no harm done." She winced and he scowled. "There *was* harm? What happened?"

"I didn't say a word."

"No, but I could see it on your face."

Had he been watching her so closely? Or had she

been so unguarded? She blushed, fearing he could see the secrets within her, hiding like shadows. Perhaps it was his nearness. She could see the bronze flecks in his golden eyes and smell the scents of soap and spring clinging to his shirt. A spark of awareness snapped within her like a candle newly lit. "It was a vase. Sukie knocked it off my windowsill when she tried to eat the flowers."

"Was that before the cookies?" His eyes crinkled pleasantly.

"Yes, but it was an accident."

"The girls should take better care of their pet." He drew his broad shoulders into an unyielding line. He turned to check on the twins, who were progressing down the road, passing the bridled horse who stood patiently grazing in the grass between the wagon tracks.

The wind ruffled his dark hair. He seemed distant. Lost. "How much was the vase worth?"

Without price, but how did she tell him? Perhaps it would be best not to open that door to her heart. "It was simply a vase."

"No, it was more." He stared at his hat clutched in both hands. "Was it a gift?"

"No, it was my mother's."

"And is she gone?"

"Yes."

"Then I cannot pay you its true value. I'm sorry." His gaze met hers with startling intimacy. Perhaps a door was open to his heart as well because sadness tilted his eyes and seemed to cover him like a coat. He looked like a man with many regrets.

She knew well the weight of that burden. "Please, don't worry about it."

"The girls will replace it." His tone brooked no argument, but it wasn't harsh. "About what my daughters said to you."

"Do you mean their proposal? Don't worry. It's plain to see they are simply children longing for a mother's love."

"Thank you for understanding. Not many folks do."

"Maybe it's because I know something about longing." It was a living thing within her always yearning, if she would let it, wishing for dreams that could not come true. "Life never turns out the way you plan it."

"No. Life can hand you more sorrow than you can carry." Although he did not move a muscle, he appeared changed. Stronger, somehow. Greater. "I'm sorry the girls troubled you, Miss McKaslin."

Mrs., but again she didn't correct him. It was the sorrow she carried that stopped her from it. She preferred to stand in the present with sunlight on her face. "It was a pleasure, Dr. Frost. What blessings you have in those girls."

"That I know." He tipped his hat to her, perhaps a nod of respect, and left her alone with the restless wind and the place still open in her heart.

Chapter Two

The hot walk on the dusty road beneath the blazing afternoon sun had not put Samuel in a better mood. With every step he took, his emotions strengthened. Even when Miss McKaslin was well out of sight, he could feel the tug of her sadness. One very much like his own.

His feet felt heavy. He had to stop thinking about the woman. She was far too pretty and young for the likes of him. He checked for any signs of traffic on the main road—there were none—and led the horse, his children and their cow across. Dust swirled lazily with the breeze and puffed up in chalky clouds as they went.

"So, Pa." Penelope sidled up to him, as sweet as sunshine and suspiciously innocent. "Wasn't Miss Molly pretty? She's real nice, too. When Sukie almost ran her into bits, she didn't even yell."

Before he could even respond, Prudence chimed in. "She makes good cookies, Pa. That's real important."

He knew about the list the girls had been making, cataloguing desirable traits for a future mother and praying over them every night. It tore him apart. Life was about disappointment and loss, and learning how to face both with acceptance and trust in God. He thought of Miss McKaslin and her sad, soul-filled blue eyes and the tendrils of her golden hair framing her delicate face. No wonder the twins had proposed to her.

He hated to do it, but he had to be practical. He had to teach the girls how to face life. These childish daydreams and wishes were going to break their hearts and their spirits if they didn't stop. He had to do his best to protect them. To teach them how to live. He cleared his throat, to rid his voice of his own turmoil. "What were you girls thinking?"

"Nothing. Not really." Penny, always the leader, was the first to speak. With the scrunch of her face in adorable lines, she was thinking hard on how to explain her actions. "We didn't plan it. Honestly. It was Sukie! She's why we were there. It's *her* fault we met Miss Molly."

"That's true, Pa," Prudy chimed in. "She's not in trouble? You won't punish Sukie, will you?"

"I hardly think sending Sukie to her stall to think about what she's done will help matters." Honestly, those girls. They were too tender-hearted. "But you two are the reason she got out of her pen in the first place."

"She missed us."

"She loves us. That's why she got out."

He bit his lip. Frustration became a burning pressure behind his ribcage. The girls didn't understand. He didn't know if they ever would. His head began to pound, making it harder to figure out what more to say to them.

"It won't happen again, Pa."

"Yep, we'll make sure Sukie doesn't get out again. We promise."

The cow was hardly the issue. Sam thought of all the hard words he could say about life and hardship, but he didn't. The house came into sight along the rutted road. He would have to finish this discussion later. He had responsibilities waiting. "You shut Sukie into her stall this time so she'll be safe. Since Mrs. Finley is at church this afternoon, you girls will have to come with me. I have a house call to make."

"No, Pa. We don't want to go, do we, Prudy?"

"No, Pa." Prudence joined her sister and their identical voices blended in a chorus of dissent. They could stay here. They could take care of themselves. They would stay up high in the tree until he came back.

None of that was going to work. "You girls need to learn to be sensible. You are too young to stay at home without Mrs. Finley. You take care of your pet and come straight to the buggy. I don't want any arguments. You hear?"

"Yes, Pa." The girls' heads bowed together as if to hide their disappointment.

He knew it couldn't be fun for them to sit in the buggy for often more than an hour at a time, but it couldn't be helped. "One more thing. There will be no more talk of Miss Molly. She's Miss McKaslin to you. That's the proper way to address her. I won't have you going across the road to her shanty again. Do you hear me?"

This time there was no answer. The girls merely blew out a quiet sigh. Two identical heads nodded, black braids bobbing up and down. Disappointment hurt, he knew, and he hated it. It was best never to dream. Eventually the girls would figure that out. It was his prayer for them.

He loved his daughters. He wanted what was best for them. And that was a good solid life right here, in this world, with their feet on the ground and their wishes made of practical things, things that had a chance of coming true.

"Don't be long." His warning carried after them on the restless wind as they broke off to lead Sukie to the barn.

"We won't." Penelope's promise sounded far too sad for an eight-year-old girl.

He hated that, too. He kept them in sight as he led Stanley to the buggy and backed him between the traces. The placid gelding stood patiently while he hitched him up. Sam worked fast, keeping both ears on the rustling sounds and lilting voices coming from deep inside the barn. Why he thought of Miss McKaslin and her gentle voice, he couldn't say. He was not a man prone to daydreams of any kind.

"Are you girls ready?" he called out, checking to make sure his medical bag was on the floorboards.

The stampede of their shoes as they came running was answer enough. The little girls, one dressed in green and the other in blue, tumbled into the yard and climbed up onto the bench buggy seat, scooting over to make room for him. He settled down, released the brake and snapped the reins, his mind firmly back where it belonged. On his girls, on his job and on the ill Mrs. Gornecke in need of his help.

Molly tucked the dustpan between her shoes and swept the last of the shards of china off her shanty floor. There. Her last home chore of the day was done. She knelt to retrieve the full pan, and her gaze wandered toward the window. The grass was still slightly trampled from her visitors.

You could marry Pa. Do you want to? The memory of the little girls' voices chased away the silence in her shanty. *You could be our ma.*

How could she feel both sad and sweet in the same breath? She remembered the girls' cute faces, shining with hope and possibility. They could not know how she had once been a mother, or how no other child could fill the emptiness. Still, they were precious, those twins. Remembering the alarm on the good doctor's face when he'd overheard their proposal, she laughed. The poor man! Oh, he'd been friendly enough, but he'd certainly walked away fast as he could. And without a single backward glance as he'd herded the children and the cow down the road.

"Molly! Was that you laughing?" Joanna, her cousin's new wife, padded into sight through the open doorway. She looked lovely as always with her honey-gold hair neatly coiled up and her sensible tan-colored calico. "Why, you are grinning ear to ear. I can't believe my eyes. What has you shining like the sun?"

"It's nothing, nothing at all." Now she was embarrassed. To be caught daydreaming! Good thing she'd only been thinking and not doing something more embarrassing like talking to herself! She set the dustpan on the table, intending to dispose of the broken china later, grabbed the package of wrapped cookies and her sewing basket. A glance at the little mantle clock told her it was later than she'd thought. How much time had she wasted thinking of the Frost twins and their father? "I'm sorry I've held you up. You had to come looking for me."

"It's not like you to be late. You had me worrying. I wanted to make sure you were all right."

"Oh, I'm as fine as can be." She shut the door and checked the lock. The grass rustled against her skirt ruffles as she led the way along the path. "I won't make you wait again, Joanna. I'm grateful for the work and the shanty. I don't want you to think I'm taking advantage."

"I told you, I've been without a home and a job before. I know how hard it is for a widow alone." Joanna's understanding had helped Molly more than she could measure. While Joanna had never buried an infant, she had sympathized gently and wholly. Her compassion had made the first difficult months here much easier to endure, when she had felt so lost. "Am I wrong, or did I see Dr. Frost and his twins at your doorstep?"

"Yes. There was an incident."

"Oh?" A world of hope knelled in that single word.

Molly's face seared once again. The blush had returned, and it had doubled in intensity. What if Joanna realized the reason for her good humor? "It's not what you think. The girls' pet cow found the shanty and the newly baked cookies."

"So, there's nothing sparking between you and Dr. Frost?"

"Goodness! What a thought." She pictured him hurrying down the road. "I doubt I will see him again. At least I hope not. I intend to stay in very good health."

Joanna didn't say a thing, but Molly feared more comments on the subject could be coming at a future time. Oh, joy. Troubling, yes, but she had more pressing concerns to manage. She worked Saturdays and several afternoons for her other cousin, Thad, and his wife. While she was grateful for the shanty on the family land, her job was at times not an easy one. Cousin Noelle, who was blind, needed help around the house and with their new baby. Taking care of little Graham was a joy, but his sweet weight in her arms could bring up a well of sorrow if she let it.

"If you married, you wouldn't have to work three jobs to make ends meet. Something to think about." Joanna was merely being kind, wanting the sort of future for her that Molly wanted for herself. But Joanna didn't understand—she couldn't understand—as they crested the final rise of the trail and the main farm house came into sight.

"Ma!" Sweet, platinum-haired Daisy hopped up from the porch steps and ran toward her mother, her baby doll tucked in the crook of her arm. "See? Lottie loves her new dress we made her."

"I see, precious."

Molly tucked away her own yearnings. It was enough to see that there was good in the world, that children were treasured, and love reigned. Sometimes the fairy tale came true. Storybook endings were possible in real life.

"You aren't feeling poorly, are you, Molly?" Cousin Aiden ambled into sight from the other side of the surrey. The hint of a grin on his granite face did nothing to lessen his intimidating presence. "I spotted Doc Frost and his girls on the road a bit earlier. Thought he might be calling on you."

"Calling on me? Hardly." Did everyone have marriage on their minds? First the twins, then Joanna and now Aiden. Perhaps it was the beautiful May Day. After a long cold winter, folks were naturally optimistic. She breathed in the sweet, warm spring air, determined to find the good in the day and in the blessings of her life. "I'm a very fussy widow. I'm afraid I won't settle for just any doctor who happens along on the road."

That had her cousins laughing as they boarded the stately surrey, and the horse drew them down the driveway, past her little shanty and toward the main road.

She caught herself glancing at the narrow driveway across the way, the one winding through tall new green grasses. She couldn't stop wondering about the handsome doctor with the shadows in his eyes. And his little girls hungering for a mother's love the same way she yearned for a daughter's.

Sometimes there were no ever afters. Sometimes life fell far short of a storybook ending. She vowed to put the Frost twins and their family on her nightly prayer list. After all, they had a lot in common.

"How much longer, doc?" Mrs. Gornecke shifted against her pillows, asked a silent question, one she was probably too afraid to put into words. Hers had been a bad case.

Scarlet fever could be a dangerous illness, that was a sad fact. He'd seen the effects more times than he cared to remember. He snapped his medical bag closed. "I can't honestly say, Mrs. Gornecke. Your fever has been high and persistent. This is of great concern. I'm not unduly worried, but I mean it when I say you must follow my instructions precisely."

"I try to, as much as I can. But my little ones—"

She fell silent, her gaze trailing toward the open window to where her small children often could be seen playing in the lawn of the backyard. Not today. A mother's love shone, transforming her. "Are you sure they are safe?"

"Not a single symptom. As long as they stay away at your parents' place."

"I can't help worrying."

"Of course. If anything changes, I will make sure you know." He left his shirt sleeves rolled up and snatched his jacket off the arm of the nearby chair. He respected Mrs. Gornecke. She was a devoted wife and mother, one who thought of others first, the kind of woman his wife had not been.

And if a quiet voice at the back of his mind wanted to remind him that there were plenty of women in the world with Mrs. Gornecke's integrity and sense of devotion, he refused to listen to that voice. Or the fact that Molly McKaslin came to mind.

"I'll check on you tomorrow, Mrs. Gornecke."

"Thank you kindly for coming on Sunday. We were supposed to be at church this afternoon, me and my little girls."

For the May Day Tea, the Ladies' Aid put on every year. Paula had been the president of the organization years ago. Samuel nodded, anxious to go before the old sorrow could catch up to him. He wanted to keep moving, for it was the best way to cope with long-standing loss and his personal shortcomings. So he grabbed his bag and gestured to the husband, huddling quietly in the corner. He waited until the door was closed and they were in the parlor of the small three-room house before he gave Mr. Gornecke more medicine and detailed instructions on his wife's care.

"I'll do all you say to do, doc." He held open the door. He looked haggard, torn between his work and the important care of his wife. "About the bill—"

"We'll discuss that when your wife is better. Right now, I want you to take care. Or you will likely be the next patient I visit."

Once outside, he rushed down the rickety front steps, hoping his daughters had followed orders and were right where they ought to be. They were in troubled water as it was.

"Pa!" Penelope's green sunbonnet poked out from between the brackets supporting the buggy top. "We're right here. Just like you told us."

Prudence's blue bonnet popped out next to the green. "We hardly moved a muscle. That's what you said to do, and we done it!"

His biggest shortcomings felt enormous when those two pairs of hazel eyes focused on him. He felt their need like the burn of sun on his back. He had failed on his promise to his wife. He could hear the desperate plea of Paula's voice in memory, the guilt increasing with every step he took toward those little girls. *Promise me you will marry again and soon. I know how you feel, but those girls need a mother, someone who is kind. They are so easy to love. Find a gentle lady who will love them as I do.*

Years had passed, and he had yet to keep that promise. He hadn't even tried to make good on it. He could blame it on his work. He'd been overrun with the demands of his job and of the little ones in his care. There hadn't been time for courting and marrying, not even for looking for a kindly woman. The truth was, he hadn't wanted to.

"I'm thrilled to see that you girls behaved for once." Stern, he set the bag on the floor before climbing up. "I almost thought I was dreaming. I thought those finely behaved young ladies couldn't possibly be my daughters."

"But we are, Pa. And we aren't young ladies. Mrs. Finley says we are wildcats." Penny sounded quite pleased as she bounced over on the seat to make room for him. "But I like wild cowboys better."

"Me, too." Prudy quickly agreed. "All we need is a pony. Can we have one, Pa?"

"You know the answer to that." He settled on the seat and reached for the reins, where they lay on the dash. With a snap, Stanley stopped drowsing and gave a mighty pull forward. All he needed was for his girls to be riding wild instead of simply running wild. Yes, that would surely make fathering them easier. "Proper young ladies do not ride horses."

"They do in the dime books."

Bless Mrs. Finley for reading her adventure novels aloud to the girls. "Books are make-believe, not real life. You two ought to know the difference. Now, no more talk about nonsense. When we get home, I want you both to go count up your pennies and figure out how many extra chores it will take to buy Miss McKaslin a new vase."

Penelope sighed. "I *knew* you were going to bring that up eventually."

"Yeah," Prudence agreed. Both girls were downcast again. "We don't gotta lotta pennies, Pa."

"Then I suppose you two have a lot of work ahead

of you." He guided the horse around the bend in the town street, seeing not the road ahead but the image of a blond-haired woman, a vision in a pink calico work dress. For some reason, Molly McKaslin had opened up his emotions and somehow he had to put a stop to them.

"Look at all the pretty things!" The girls' voices rang out in unison, speaking the same thought and drawing his attention back to the road in front of him.

The church with its spire shone pure white in the sunshine, surrounded by lush trees and deep-emerald grass. Cloths in every color of the rainbow draped a dozen tables in the dappled shade. Women and their daughters of all ages relaxed in chairs around the tables, feasting on cake and tea, while others milled in groups on the lawn, deep in pleasant-looking conversation.

"I sure wish we had a ma." Prudy's whisper was little more than a sigh of longing.

A longing he had to ignore. He willed down his feelings, snapped the reins. Stanley obliged by picking up his pace and taking them swiftly away. The lilting rise and fall of women's voices and little girls' laughter carried after them on the wind.

Chapter Three

Three days had passed since the Frost incident, as Molly preferred to think of it. Remembering the little girls and their very naughty cow still warmed her with a chuckle or two. She thought of them this time every day as she guided her trusty mare onto the driveway home. She couldn't see the Frost house from her vantage on the cart seat, and that made her wonder. What sort of trouble were the twins getting into now? Was Sukie securely penned?

There was no sign of girls or heifer as she gave Ruth plenty of rein. The old mare was tender-mouthed and she knew her way home. There was no point in directing her any further. The horse's gait quickened, anticipating a nice restful evening in the shade of the orchard with cool, lush grass for her supper.

Molly didn't blame her one bit. The day's heat was unusual for May, and the hot puff of wind offered not a lick of relief. Wednesday was her toughest day of the week. She'd started at five in the morning at the bakery, helping Mrs. Klaus mix and knead bread dough for hours. A noon stop at the dress shop to work for a few hours and to drop off the piecework she did in the evenings for Cora, the owner. Then off to her cousin Noelle's house to help with the baby and the house chores.

Yes, she had been running for the good part of twelve hours. And it wasn't over yet. She glanced at the two baskets of sewing work she intended to tackle the rest of the week. It would help with the mortgage she had against her dear Ruth, the last of the debt accumulated from her marriage and illnesses. Needless to say, her late husband Fred had not been good with money.

The cart rattled down the lane, bringing her shanty into view. A blur of red and a streak of yellow in the lush green grasses caught her eye. Whatever could that be? She was too far away to see clearly, but it looked like the rounded top of a little girl's sunbonnet. It looked like—

The Frost twins. That could only mean one thing. Sukie was on the loose again.

"Miss Molly!" In tandem, the girls raced through the wild grasses. One in bright yellow calico, the other in bright red, they burst up the rise and through the wildflowers, panting as if they had run a hundred miles. "You're not supposed to be here—"

"—cuz it's supposed to be a surprise—"

"—'cept we had to pick flowers—"

"—and it took longer than we thought."

Molly reined her mare to a stop and set the brake, gazing down at the pair of them. How welcome to see their round button faces shining with goodness and life! Their sweetness refreshed her weary spirit, that was for certain. "I'm worrying about Sukie and you girls are picking wildflowers?"

"Oh, we're not here because of Sukie." One of the twins—Penelope?—swiped an ebony curl from her eyes. "She decided to stay at home."

"We're here because of the surprise." The other twin skipped in place, apparently too excited to stand still.

"Surprise?" Curious, Molly hopped down from the cart, landing with a swish of her skirts. "What on earth have you girls been up to?"

"All sorts of trouble," Penelope assured her as she took Molly's hand.

"Lots of trouble," Prudence concurred as she took Molly's other hand.

Was it her imagination that the sun shone more brightly? Or just her lonely mother's heart delighting in this connection with children—even though they were not hers? Molly felt her loss and loneliness like the shadows cast at her feet, but they were small compared to the great sunlit world around her, shimmering with color. The purple foxglove nodded in greeting along the path, the yellow faces of daisies waved and the buttercups smiled as they skipped by. With small hands tucked in her own, happiness seeped into the cracks of her soul.

"We hope you're not mad we came." Penelope smiled up at her, using both dimples.

How on earth could Dr. Frost deny these girls anything? Molly melted at the sight. "Mad? No, but I am worried about your housekeeper. Does she know you girls are here?"

"She was busy peeling potatoes for supper," Prudence answered.

"Yeah, so we didn't want to bother her with asking."

Molly chuckled; she couldn't help it. "You two are

definitely trouble. You aren't going to worry the poor lady, are you?"

"Nope." Penelope stopped skipping, bringing all three of them to a halt. "Mrs. Finley says we have to tell her where we are, and we did. She can't run after us."

"She's got tired bones," Prudence explained seriously. "But she reads to us and she's nice."

"She's almost like a grandma."

"We like her a lot."

"Since we don't have a ma."

"We sure would like a ma."

They walked the last few yards with the grass rustling their hems and crunching beneath their shoes. One question did happen to bother her. Now seemed like a good time to ask the girls. "Why hasn't your pa remarried?"

"He doesn't want to disappoint some nice lady." Penelope's hand gripped her more tightly.

"It's because of us," Prudence confessed. "Nobody wants so much trouble."

"No, that can't be. Where did you hear such a thing?" How could anyone say that to a precious child? Anger blurred her vision. Sympathy for the girls ached within her. She knelt, so she was level with the girls.

"We're a handful. Everybody says it." Penelope rubbed at her eyes and blew out a brave breath. No tears materialized, but her inner pain showed. "We're awful lucky Pa loves us."

"We're a handful for him, too." Prudence hiccupped. "We don't mean to be trouble, Miss Molly."

"That's why we brought you the surprise." Penelope pointed toward the shanty. "So you wouldn't be mad about the vase."

"An' so you wouldn't think we are a whole lotta trouble."

Both adorable faces gazed up at her, tremulous with hope amid their sorrows. The wind caressed the stray strands that had escaped their braids, giving them a windblown look, like unloved ragamuffins in need of a home.

Tears bunched in her throat, making her voice raw and thin. "I don't think you two are trouble, not in the slightest. What did you bring me?"

She must have said the right thing, because their smiles shone more brightly than their sadness. Dimples flashed, and she was tugged the rest of the way to the shanty.

"Come see," the girls called out in harmony.

There, perched on her top step, was a little vase with a bouquet of hand-picked wildflowers. Daisies bloomed, as if in celebration. What a surprise. "You girls brought me flowers."

"We thought—"

"—you would like 'em."

"I do. I love wildflowers." She willed away the memory of a curly-haired baby sitting up, proud of her ability to do so, gurgling and grabbing at the bobbing daisies while Molly weeded their vegetable garden.

"Did you like the vase?" Penelope ran ahead through the prairie grasses.

Prudence followed, running equally as fast. "We got the one with the most colors."

"We thought you would like it best."

The girls skidded to a halt in front of the bottom step, sunshine kissing them. They vibrated with anticipation. What would it be like to have such energy?

Molly felt wobbly as she joined them, hardly able to see for the burn in her eyes. She blinked hard, trying to bring the blur of colors on her step into focus.

"It's little. It won't hold lots of flowers," Penelope explained as she went up on tiptoe. "But it'll hold some."

"Just enough," Prudence nodded her head in agreement, going up on her toes, too. "Do you like it?"

"Do you?"

She could not believe the beauty of the simple glass vase, hand-painted with sprays of sunflowers, foxglove, daisies and roses. Very fine quality indeed. "I've never owned anything so nice."

The twins beamed, hands clasping, joy chasing away their worries.

Charmed, that's what she was, and utterly sweet on the girls. She blinked until her eyes stopped blurring and lifted the vase with both hands. The glass, warmed from the sun, felt delicate, as if it could be easily broken. She had better not put this on her windowsill, just in case Sukie paid a return visit. "I love it. Thank you. It's mighty thoughtful of you girls to replace the one I lost."

"Pa said to tell you we're bein' responsible for Sukie—"

"—and we're real sorry because it was your ma's." Prudence traced a painted rose with the tip of her forefinger. "Our ma died, too. It hurts real bad, doesn't it?"

"Yes. Very much." All the protection in the world could not save her from the first knell of emotion. Grief for the twins missing their mother. Grief remembering her ma, who would be sad to think of the way Molly's life had turned out. "Come and help me find the right place to put this very special vase."

"It's special?" the girls asked, tromping behind her into the shanty.

"Sure it is, because you two gave it to me." Her shanty was hardly large enough for the three of them to stand side by side in a row. Sunlight streamed pleasantly in through both windows, giving the tidy practical home a golden look. "The table or the bookcase?"

"The table." The two of them trotted over to the small drop leaf table near one window. Two sets of hands reached out to touch the crocheted flowers standing in relief against the lacy runner. "Ooh. It's so pretty."

"Put it right here." Penelope patted the center.

"It's perfect." Prudence sighed in satisfaction after Molly had complied.

"We have a lace bureau cover our ma made." Penelope brushed the petals of the closest daisy. "But that's all."

"Our ma liked to sing songs." Prudence's lightness faded. "She would always be humming and singing."

"Hymns," Penelope clarified, her shoulders hunching with the weight of the memory. "Now all we got is quiet."

"I know just what you mean." Wasn't this the mix of life, the sad and the sweet? "The quiet hurts too, doesn't it?"

"Uh-huh." Both girls nodded gravely. Without their cheer and sparkle, it was easy to see the hardship they had been through.

It was a credit to their father that they still had so much sunlight to them. Thinking of Sam made her feelings sharpen, like a surge in her ability to feel. "It's getting late, girls. Surely you need to be home by supper time?"

"Mostly it's just Mr. and Mrs. Finley—"

"—and us." Prudence traced the edging stitches on one side of the runner.

"What about your father?"

"He comes home late always." Penelope stepped away from the table and out of the bright rays. "He makes sick people better."

Prudence took one last look at the crochet work. "Miss Molly? If you think you can like us now, do you want to think about being our ma again?"

"—now that we fixed things with the vase?"

Molly held out her hands to each girl. "I've never stopped liking you two. I like you both very much."

"We like you, too—"

"—lots and lots."

Small fingers clapped her own, and it was a cozy feeling, like a crackling fire on the coldest day. Like spring after the hardest winter. "You two know why I can't be your mother, right?"

"Cuz Pa hasn't given you a ring?"

"We could get you one."

She laughed, leading them outside. It was the sun tearing her eyes and not the mix of emotions, deeply colored and ranging from bright to dark. "I'm fussy about the man I marry. I want him to love me. That's the reason I want him to propose to me."

"Pa doesn't believe in love."

"He says it's not real, just like a story."

The children's confession troubled Molly all the way to the cart. She remembered the caring father, aware of his blessings in his daughters. Life was endlessly complicated, and she hoped her prayers for him and the girls would make a difference. She wanted

God to especially watch over these broken hearts. Sam Frost might not believe in love's power, but she did.

"You mean they haven't come home from school *yet?*" Sam's head was going to explode. He could feel the pressure building in his cerebellum, sending shooting, red-hot pain into his cerebral cortex. Those girls were going to be the ruin of him. He paced the length of the kitchen, his boot heels striking out his anger on the polished wood planks. "It's after six o'clock. They should have been home hours ago."

"If you're going to get all het up, I'll send Abner out on horseback to look for 'em." Mrs. Finley patted a spray of silver hair from her eyes, reached for a hot pad and checked on the boiling potatoes. "I expect they've gone off to look at the Nevilles' pony for sale. They said they weren't going far. Whoa, there. I hear something outside. Probably those rascals now, bless them."

I sure wish we had a ma. Prudy's words had stuck with him for days, reminding him of all his personal failures. He had been a failure at marriage because he had based the foundation of that union on something as foolish and as impossible as romantic love.

He was going to make certain that his girls did not repeat his mistakes. He strode across the porch, straining to hear their high, merry voices and lilting laughter, but the only sound was the wind whispering through the lilac and rose bushes and the paper-like rustle of the corn stalks in the vegetable garden.

His girls. Other young ladies their ages were stitching samplers and learning to sew. When he'd been on his afternoon rounds, he'd seen several girls doing just that. Tidy and proper, sitting quietly in their parlors, happily practicing their needlework. Wasn't that what little girls were supposed to want to do?

Years went by in a blink. Before long, Penny and Prudy would be young ladies being escorted home by their beaus. One day, they would become wives and mothers. They would need to know how to run a proper household and sew for their families.

But how was he going to teach them? Kathleen suffered terribly from arthritis so she could not, and he had no wish to replace her with a younger housekeeper. He pushed open the gate.

You could marry again. He winced, wishing that thought had remained buried in the recesses of his mind.

The clink of shod horse hooves brought him to a dead halt. With the sun nearly blinding him and the rise of chalky dust from the driveway hazing the view, he couldn't see clearly. His first fear was that the girls had found a way to haggle with the Neville family for their ancient pony. But as he braced his feet on the dirt of the driveway, it was no child he saw but a woman. A beautiful woman dressed all in blue coming toward him, gliding on a yellow sunbeam. Molly McKaslin.

He blinked, hoping his vision would clear. But when he looked again, she smiled at him from beneath her dainty poke bonnet.

The rising clouds of dust and the slant of light gave the illusion. As her horse drew closer, it was plain to see she sat in an ordinary country cart, holding the leather reins in her slender hands. The sun remained behind her, cresting the slim cut of her shoulders and burnishing her golden hair like copper. Making her even more beautiful. Even more poignant.

It had been a long, hard day. He was turning fanciful in his exhaustion. Heaven help him.

"Hi, Pa!" To his surprise, Penelope popped into view from the cart floor behind Molly. An identical sun-bonneted head popped up, too. Prudence. "Hi, Pa!"

Unbelievable. Seeing them safe and sound—not that there was much danger in this peaceful countryside—left him relieved. But seeing them in Molly's cart, that was something else entirely. "You two have clearly been bothering Miss McKaslin, against my express orders."

"No, Pa." In unison, the girls hopped out of the cart the moment it stopped. They spoke, interrupting one another. "We were going to stay out of her way—"

"—but then we remembered what you said about being susponsible—"

"—responsible—"

"—and so we went to the glass shop—"

"—and got a vase for Miss Molly."

"So you would be proud of us."

He drew up, still as steel, so no one could guess at the emotion hitting him. They had *tried* to do the right thing. But in acting on their own, they had made the situation worse. This wasn't only about replacing a broken vase.

It was about the woman beginning to climb down from that cart. The woman who took his offered hand with a subtle smile. The woman whose touch came as softly as spring raindrops against his palm. When her shoes landed on the ground and she moved away, the center of his palm tingled sweetly, as if it would never forget her.

"I brought your wayward girls home." She somehow looked like a story heroine, even with the barn in the background and the old bay mare nibbling at her hat brim. "Thank you for replacing the vase. I know it was costly."

Costly? Normally that would alarm him, but now something like a large bill from the finest shop in town seemed like nothing. Not when compared to how Penny gazed up at Molly as if she'd hung the moon. Prudy, when she sidled next to the woman, did so with clear adoration.

What had come over the two of them? They had never been taken with a lady like this before. It was time to rein in their unruly ways. If he wasn't careful they would have him married by the July Fourth family picnic.

"We owed you a vase, and now our debt is paid." He did his best not to notice the feminine way she pushed a stray curl into place beneath her fashionable bonnet. No, it was best to direct his eyesight to the children ignoring him to cling to her. "The girls will make sure Sukie doesn't bother you again."

"Speaking of which—" She gestured toward the barn, amused. "Unless I'm mistaken, Sukie has gotten loose."

"Sukie!" Penelope held up both hands. "No! Go back to your pen!"

"Bad Sukie!" Prudence scolded, shaking one finger at the cheerful bovine racing across the yard in an ungainly gallop. Her happy moo echoed across the hillside. "She's a runaway stampede!"

"You girls have been influenced by too many novels." That was it. It was decided. These notions of fairy tales, cowgirls and romance had to end. "Put the cow back in her pen—"

The girls were already racing off to intercept their pet, but the heifer turned and led the chase, as if in a merry game. The girls' delighted squeals rose joyfully on the wind.

"You were saying about Sukie?" Molly asked him with a wry tilt to her rosebud mouth.

"I don't know why I try. I'm outnumbered. It's a lost cause."

"Not entirely lost." She laughed, a musical trill that made him think of clear mountain brooks and spring raindrops. "Your girls are delightful. They had me in stitches the entire ride home. I know I've told you before, but they are double blessings. It's a marvel you can keep a straight face."

"It's what I wonder every day." Gazing upon her filled him with questions. Where had she moved from? How old was she? What was she looking for in life? Her fondness for his daughters was unmistakable. Why hadn't she married?

Not that it was any of his business. It was merely curiosity, that was all. As a physician, he knew nearly everyone in Angel County, but he did not know her. This sensible, hardworking lady who watched his daughters race around the field trying to herd their pet cow, who did not cooperate.

"It's an impossible situation. Look at them!" Embraced as she was by the sun, it was hard not to notice her radiant beauty.

A faint, sharp pain arrowed through his chest suspiciously close to his heart. But it couldn't be that organ, since he was not a deep-feeling man. Perhaps his stomach was agitated—he'd been too busy tending a patient to have taken lunch. Surely that was the explanation.

"The more they run, the more Sukie chases them." She laughed, a sound gentler than any hymn. "Now the cow is herding the two of them! What a delightful life you have."

"Yes, delightful." Dryly, the words came off his tongue, but they felt disconnected from his thoughts and his emotions, which for some unexplainable reason centered on her.

She seemed like a responsible, proper lady. He had noticed her before on his rides through town, working in the bakery in the mornings and Sims's dress shop in the afternoons. Hard not to notice her. As lovely as she was, she wasn't terribly young. He would place her somewhere in her twenties and solidly working on becoming a spinster, he reckoned.

Her words came back to him from the first day they met. *Maybe it's because I know something about longing. Life never turns out the way you plan it.* What did she long for? Why hadn't her life turned out according to her plan? As she watched his twins, that same lonely look returned to her face.

Hard not to understand that. Was she as lonesome as he was? Did she have broken dreams too, ones that could never be made whole or found again?

Perhaps it was the doctor in him, always wanting to fix things. Maybe it was something deeper he did not want to understand. The words came off his tongue before he could snatch them back. "What are you doing for supper, Miss McKaslin? Would you consider joining us?"

Chapter Four

Nothing Sam Frost said could have astonished her more. For one second her pulse lurched in her veins as if the earth had vanished from beneath her shoes.

"I have work to do this evening. I—" The words did not come. She wanted to say she had no time for social engagements, but the look of quiet dignity on his granite face stopped her.

This man could open her up like a door into a room. Standing with him on the verdant lawn, listening to the rush of the wind through the field grasses and the squealing joy of the girls, she felt as if the daylight had never been this vibrant or the air so sweet. Awareness of the man glanced through her like dappled sunshine, awareness that was keenly emotional. Lonesomeness, weariness, regret; feelings much like her own.

"A neighborly invitation," he assured her. "Kathleen is probably done boiling the potatoes about now. You may as well stay. There's always plenty."

"I would be imposing." And looking at what she did not have—and probably never would. Men were not tripping over one another to come courting, that was for sure. Sam did not know what he was asking of her.

"It would be doing me a favor." Humor dimpled the corners of his mouth as they slid upward into a spare grin. "Look at the two of them, running wild. It would do them good to see how a real lady behaves. They look up to you."

"Is there a hidden motive in this invitation?"

"No. If they still run wild when the meal is done, you can stay for dessert."

Why was she laughing? She was not about to be charmed by him. This was not love at first sight. Her world hadn't changed when she'd taken his hand to help her from the cart. Love hadn't sparked like a symphony in full crescendo. He was not her Mr. Darcy. That didn't mean she couldn't be neighborly. She drew in a breath of lilac-scented air. "Then I guess it depends on what is being served for dessert."

"I have no idea."

"You make me an offer without knowing all of the facts? I'm shocked at you, Dr. Frost."

"Sam. Please." He raked his fingers through his thick dark hair, laughing a little, too. His reserved nature fled, and this jovial side of him made her see the man he must have been before sadness changed him.

She knew exactly how that was. "Then you must call me Molly. I'm afraid I have a confession to make. I'm a widow. I should have corrected you when we first met, but—"

"—it was too painful," he finished, the humor fading from his face, but he did not close up. He remained as if open to her, a stunning, feeling man of great depth.

At least, that was her impression of him. That was what she felt in the silence as it stretched between them.

"Very." She battled to keep the past where it belonged. "I hope you can forgive me."

"There is nothing to forgive. It was my mistake. I assumed."

"It wouldn't be the first time. I've turned down a few courting men who have done the same."

"So, turning down proposals is a habit for you."

"Yes. Is that relief I hear in your voice?" She liked his chuckle, a low pleasant rumbling, a friendly sound she wanted to hear again. How strange. She sidestepped so a tiny butterfly wouldn't get grounded by her skirts, bringing the children into her line of sight. The girls had caught Sukie and were hanging on her, rubbing her neck and face and giggling when the heifer tried to give them swipes with her tongue. "My marriage was not like a fairy tale."

"Neither was mine." His confession resonated with remorse. She did not need to ask if he had done all he could to make his marriage right. She knew because the cost of it was on his face and a weight, like her own, she could feel.

A bell clanged from somewhere behind her. She whirled around to see a plump elderly lady limping away from the dinner bell. Must be the housekeeper.

"We're having apple crisp for dessert," the woman said matter-of-factly, as if she had overheard every word of their conversation and wasn't ashamed for them to know.

"It's the kitchen window." Sam leaned close, his voice lowered, meant only for her. "Kathleen likes fresh air and to let in the scent of the lilac blooms, but I think she's nosy."

"Good thing for you. If she wasn't, I would be on my way home. Apple crisp is my favorite."

No wonder. Sam tethered the ancient mare in the shade of the barn. A widow. He should have known. She carried a maturity of manner and emotion. She simply appeared so young. Fresh-faced and golden, her features like porcelain. Not that he was noticing.

No, what he noticed was the way she shut the garden gate behind her and disappeared behind purple cones of blossoms, heading to the kitchen to help Kathleen put the meal on the table. He noticed her mare was gentle and white around the muzzle, well groomed and used to kindly care. He noticed the state of the cart—in good repair but not exactly a shining buggy, and the baskets on the floorboards which held pinned up ladies' dresses and petticoats. She must also do piece work in the evenings. A widow's lot could be difficult in these uncertain economic times. Hard not to respect the woman. Hard not to like the first woman in years who had been able to make him laugh.

"Pa?" Penelope skipped into view, a burst of yellow calico in the shady grass. "Where's Miss Molly?"

"I suspect putting the biscuits on the table about now." He gave the mare a pat on the neck and strolled over to the trough pump.

A second calico-wearing girl tumbled into sight. "Is she truly staying to supper?"

"You girls would do well to be more like Molly." He gave the handle a few good pumps. "Do you see her tearing through the pasture like a rampaging cow?

No. She's well pressed and every hair is neatly in place. She's helping Mrs. Finley in the kitchen. You might take a page from her book."

Water splashed into the trough and the mare ambled closer for a sip. She would be cool and comfortable here. He left her, aware of two sets of footsteps tripping after him.

"Do you like her, Pa?"

"Do you like her a lot?"

He caught sight of her through the large kitchen window, where she stood beside the table, pouring milk into glasses. She sure could take a man's breath away. Good thing he wasn't looking for the complications of marriage. Because if anyone could interest him, it would be Molly McKaslin.

Here's where things got tricky. He considered his answer as he led the way across the rutted road and into the grassy side yard. "No, girls, I'm afraid I don't like Miss Molly at all."

"Not the teeniest bit?"

"Not even an eensy bit?"

"Nope. Because you two already have all of my heart. There's no room for anyone else." He endured the twins' groan and moans of disappointment as he swung open the garden gate, stunned by Molly staring at him through the window.

The mysterious smile teasing the rosebud softness of her lips and trouble twinkling like stardust in her dream-blue eyes left no doubt. She had heard him quite clearly. Some females he could think of might be unhappy to hear a marriageable doctor did not like them, but she was obviously no average female.

He opened the back door and let his daughters topple in ahead of him. They ran, shoes beating the floor, grass-stained skirts swishing, flyaway hair trailing out behind them. A striking contrast to the proper, tidy, genteel woman turning from the table with the pitcher in hand to offer them a smile of welcome. "I hope you two were able to get Sukie penned and safe."

"Sort of."

"Mostly."

Sam didn't think anyone noticed as he shut the door behind him. The rise and fall of female conversation may as well have been a different language. He leaned against the wall, folding his arms across his chest, simply watching the twins chatter away without giving Molly a word in edgewise. Funny to watch the girls be so polite. They pulled out Molly's chair. They looked like actual proper girls, standing still without fidgeting, listening intently as Molly spoke to them. Each settled into a chair as close to the woman as they could, mimicking her straight posture and ladylike drape of the napkin across her lap.

"I like her." Kathleen swung close on her way by, with a covered tray to take to their quarters upstairs. She threw over her shoulder, "I'll leave you to your courting. Don't scare her away with that cold manner of yours."

"I don't know what you are talking about." He wasn't a cold man and he wasn't a courting one. He didn't have to worry about scaring Molly away. What he did have to worry about was liking the woman too much. That, he feared, was a very real problem.

"Pa!"

He shook his head, realizing there were three females staring at him. He left his thoughts for another time, crossed the room and took his chair. The kitchen was fragrant with the warm smell of roasted chicken, the rich doughy goodness of buttermilk biscuits, steaming potatoes and buttery green beans. But as hungry as he was, every bit of him from the inside out was aware that this was no ordinary supper.

Across the table, Molly took the girls' hands and bowed her head, awaiting grace. Something incomprehensible and powerful flickered to life within him as he felt the impact of her gaze. He did not know what it was. Shaken, he bowed his head, took each of the girls' hands and began to pray.

"Show me Thy ways, O Lord; teach me Thy paths. Lead me in Thy truth and teach me: for Thou art the God of my salvation; on Thee do I wait all day. Father, thank You for Your bounty. Please bless this food on our table, and strengthen and purify our hearts. If it's not too much trouble, please help guide Penny and Prudy toward more ladylike pursuits. Amen."

"Amen." The girls were shaking their heads, apparently not at all surprised by the blessing.

"Amen." Molly released the girls' hands and opened her eyes.

Sam had never seen a more perfect blue. While he had been praying, he should have asked God for help. Molly had an odd effect on him. He had never been fanciful in the company of a woman before. He grabbed the platter of sliced chicken and forked a few slices onto his plate before handing it to Penelope.

"Miss Molly? Do you like tree forts?" Penelope asked.

"It's really a stump," Prudence clarified, "but we pretend it's a tree fort."

"Yes, my little brother and I had our own tree fort in a cottonwood grove in the Big Bear Mountains." It was as if she were discussing something completely ordinary like the weather, instead of make-believe dwellings. Molly took the platter Penelope offered her and added a thick slice of chicken to her plate. "We fended off attacks from renegade bands and many very bad outlaws."

"We defeated the entire cavalry last week—"

"—and now we are in the middle of a siege."

Clearly, this could not be judicious, endorsing silly stories, but Sam could not look away from Molly as she held the platter for Prudence.

"A siege. How exciting." When Prudence was through dishing up chicken, Molly set the platter in the center of the table. Amusement played across her lovely face as she caught him looking at her. "Sam, I hope you think defending a fort from lawless bandits is a proper way to spend time."

"If you are a soldier or a sheriff."

"Apparently we have differing opinions. It's my mother's fault. She indulged my love of stories at an early age. That's helped with my tendency toward imagination, I'm afraid." She added a biscuit to her plate, again holding the bowl for Prudence. "My earliest memories are of sitting wrapped up in a quilt on my ma's lap. The potbelly stove was roaring, snow was tumbling like a white waterfall on the other side of the windows while Ma read from one of her novels."

"My pa would read Shakespeare." His voice deepened, the tone vibrant with emotion too layered to label. "Every winter evening after supper when the last of the work was done, he would draw his chair up to the stove, light a lamp and open his volume of plays. My sister and I would listen, captivated by the powerful words. We were too young at first to understand, but we would listen. As the years passed, we came to love the plays and, later, read the different parts with Pa."

"It sounds like a wonderful way to grow up." She broke her biscuit in two and buttered it, but her attention remained on the man seated across from her. A man she could see embodying the young Prince Hal, the beleaguered Julius Caesar or the heartbroken King Lear.

She did not tell him that she had read those plays, too. Alone, and only to herself. She did not wish to deepen the tie she felt to him, an emotional link that drew her closer when she should be moving away.

Molly set the last pile of plates on the counter. "Did you know that Sukie is at the window?"

"Okay, troublemakers." Sam set a collection of glassware and steelware next to the pile of plates. "Outside right now and get Sukie into her stall."

"She's out again?" Penelope swiped at her forehead, in exaggerated shock.

"She wants dessert, too." Prudence cut a piece of apple crisp from the baking plate. "Maybe then she'll stop chewing through her rope."

The pair loped out the back door, while the heifer craned her neck farther into the room to keep better sight of them. Her protesting moo expressed her opinion when they—and the apple crisp—disappeared from her sight.

"You really want those two to change?" Molly leaned against the counter.

"Life is hard. I want to prepare them for it." The reserve was back, now that they were alone.

"What was it you thought I could do for them?"

He glanced around, scanning the cleared table and the dirty dishes, which would be left for Mrs. Finley in the morning. "Interest them in needlework. I didn't know you had a disreputable past as a make-believe fort dweller, too."

"The things you don't know about me, Dr. Frost."

"I'm afraid to know more. You looked mild-mannered when we first met."

She couldn't tell if he was jesting or serious. She only knew that the kitchen appeared to shrink as he took one single step closer. He filled her view, making it impossible to ignore his dark, dashing handsomeness, the dependable set of his wide shoulders and his muscled arms that looked strong enough to soothe any pain, if only they would enfold her.

What thinking! She blushed, heat racing to her cheeks and making her nose strawberry red. Afraid he would notice, she spun away to retrieve her sunbonnet from the peg by the door. Her heels rang loudly, punctuating the silence between them.

"I've offended you?" His question came low and flat, as if without emotion.

But she could see some of the layers of this man, the granite outside, the tender father inside. The scholar, the physician, the widower, the brokenhearted man. Layers that lured her feelings like the moon on the tides, pulling at waves within her, layers of herself she tried to hide.

"No." She shook out the bonnet's ties. "Your daughters are wonderful. If I were you, I would love them as they are. They will grow into more ladylike interests when God wishes them to. Trust me."

"I wish I could."

"You are not a trusting man, are you?" She watched his reserve deepen, taking over. The faint ring of joyful laughter drifted in through the window. "Trust me anyway. I was not so different. I loved climbing trees and riding my pony bareback and helping my pa with the livestock. I managed to learn needlework and become fairly ladylike. They will, too."

"I'm not reassured." He jammed his fists into his pockets, hesitating as if caught between coming closer and staying away. "You are almost as bad as they are."

"I'll take that as a compliment."

"You do have a calming effect on them." He strolled her way. "If they happen into your yard again, would it be too much to show them a stitch or two? Let them see what you are sewing?"

"I would be happy to. Even if Sukie makes another appearance."

"Let's pray she doesn't break anything else." He opened the door to the pleasant breezes. The low slanting sunlight felt welcoming, and the dancing leaves and busy birds almost reminded him there was more to life than work and responsibility. More to living than clinging to the plan and patterns that had gotten him through his grief and raising two small children alone.

"The new vase is safely out of the window's reach," she reassured him.

"Unless Sukie comes in the door."

"Goodness!" She sidled through the threshold, taking care to leave plenty of space between them. As if she didn't want to risk coming too close to him, to the curmudgeon unwilling to trust any female too much. To the man captivated by her wholesome charm and whimsical sweetness completely against his will and better sense.

She passed ahead of him on the brick pathway, her skirts swishing against the overgrown flowers and shrubs. It seemed to him as if the dappled sunlight followed her, and the lark song grew more cheerful as she passed by the apple tree. Lilacs rustled, casting out a handful of tiny purple petals to float behind her on the wind.

You're seeing her with your heart, man. He tried to stop it, to force his mind to see the world as it really was—she, as she really was. Impossible. The squeak of the garden gate did not bring him back to reality. The crunch of his shoe in the grass, the whisper of the breeze against his face or his iron-strong will. Nothing could change the beautiful way he saw her, like first light come to a new world, as she glided through the long pearled rays of the sinking sun, laughing at something he could not see.

"What are you two doing? You are going to spoil my mare even more than she already is." Molly swirled to face him, her movements a graceful waltz. "Ruth loves apple crisp."

Surely he hadn't heard right. "Apple crisp can't be good for her digestion."

"She's used to sweets. I feed them to her all the time."

Why wasn't he surprised? The evening felt surreal as she danced away from him, the music of her alto joining the high sugary notes of his daughter's voices.

Dimly he saw the girls and Sukie at the trough, one twin feeding the mare, the other the cow.

"I'm gonna tell Mrs. Finley to make lots more." Finished, Penny washed the stickiness from her hands in the cool trough.

"That way we can come visit Ruth." Prudy stroked Ruth's brown nose with adoration. "She's awful nice."

"Real nice." Penny wiped her hands on her skirt. "It must be *real* fun to have your own horse."

"*Awful* fun."

There was no mistaking the poignant longing in the girls' tones. He wisely chose to remain silent. Not that he could trust his voice with Molly so close. He held out his hand to help her up into the cart. When her long, slender fingers wrapped around his, tenderness flared through him like a comet in the night sky. She may as well have taken hold of his heart.

"Thank you for supper, Sam." Her voice was the loveliest melody he'd ever heard. She settled on the board seat and brushed her skirts into place with no less grace than a goodly princess taking her throne. "I had the most unusual time. I'm sorry to say I had no positive effect on your daughters."

"I'm not even going to ask you to mention the sewing baskets." She had enthralled his daughters and enraptured him. Hardly the steadying, sensible influence he had hoped for. Undeniable proof she wasn't the right woman for him. He released the knot in the rope tethering the old mare. The horse primly nodded as if in ladylike thanks before she stepped forward, drawing the cart with Molly in it.

"Goodbye, girls. Thank you for the vase," she called as she rolled past.

"Goodbye!" The twins sidled up to him, each taking one of his hands. They were so small, frail, clinging to him with unmistakable need.

"I sure like her." Penelope sighed, as if making a wish on the first twilight star.

"I like her, too." Prudence leaned against him, a dear weight at his side.

Together they watched Molly drive down the road, growing farther and farther away from them, taking with her the beauty and the light.

Chapter Five

Spring thunder boomed high above town like cannon fire, startling the horses tethered at the hitching post in front of the dress shop. Molly held tight to her poke bonnet as a gust of wind twisted her skirts and puffed her back a few steps. Enormous raindrops pelted her like buckshot.

What weather! When she had started off to the bakery at fifteen minutes before five this morning, the day had been serene, the wind calm with not a cloud in the pastel sky. Spring was her favorite season, full of temperamental sunshine and exciting storms.

Lightning cracked overhead and she lifted her face toward the sky. Rain patted her cheeks and blurred her vision, but she caught sight of the last tail of a lightning bolt snaking across the turbulent charcoal clouds. Magnificent. She swiped the rain from her face, circled around the agitated horses and bounded up the steps to the boardwalk.

And felt a trickling sensation at the back of her neck. Most peculiar, as she had never felt that exact sensation before. A horse's whinny drew her around and there, veiled by gray rain and the transparent rubber sheets of his buggy, was Dr. Samuel Frost.

The explosion of thunder became silent when Sam's gaze met hers. The rain continued to fall but went mute. The horses neighing and sidestepping at the post made not a single noise. All she could hear was her pulse thump-thumping in her ears.

Sam looked equally as surprised to see her. He remained frozen on his seat, his eyes following her as his buggy sped closer. One moment became eternity as she felt her soul shift.

The rain's fury increased, stealing him from her sight. His black buggy sped on, time leaped back into rhythm and the symphony of rainfall returned.

What just happened? Puzzled, she tripped through the door, dripping as she went. The bell above her jingled, the warmth radiating from the stove wrapped around her like a favorite wool blanket, and she stared out at the street where Sam's buggy had been.

Had he felt the same jolt? She had not experienced anything of that magnitude and importance when she'd been in his house, or during the handful of days since when her thoughts had drifted to him more often than she would have liked to admit. Remembering his sense of humor and his tenderness with his daughters had made her wish he was a different kind of man. The sort to believe in true love.

But she feared true love was the last reason a busy doctor with two rambunctious children would want to marry anyone, especially her. She caught her reflection in the glass window. While she had never been a beauty, time and hardship had stolen the first blush from her face. The man certainly wasn't interested in her looks.

No, Sam had different hopes. He had hoped she would have a settling impact on his twins. That was important to him. If he chose to remarry, he would probably look for a hardworking and sensible wife, a convenient woman to mother his girls. Love would not be part of the bargain.

In her experience, marriage was far too precious to be anything short of true love. Her life had been one long string of disappointments with Fred, a man she had married hoping deep affection would come later.

She had been terribly wrong.

"Come in and warm up by the stove." Cora Sims, the owner of the dress shop and Molly's boss, set down the pencil she'd been using on the account books and rose from the small table at the far end of the tasteful store. "Why, you are drenched through. That storm is shaking the glass in the panes. There it goes again."

Lightning flashed as if directly overhead, accompanied by thunder. The floorboards beneath Molly's soggy shoes shook while the windows shuddered in their wood casings. The stove lid rattled when a gust of wind sent smoke back down the pipe. Molly peeled off her raincoat and hurried, dripping, toward the back room.

"You'll get a chill back there." Cora held out a dainty tea cup, steaming with freshly poured tea. "I'll hang that up. You sit by the stove. Was that Dr. Frost I saw passing by?"

She took the china cup, surprised that it rattled in its saucer at the mention of Sam's name. "Yes."

"My Holly goes to school with his little girls." Cora

tapped through the shop, weaving around the notions display case and the summer silks table in the center of the store. "Am I right in thinking the Frosts live across the main road from you?"

Her cup rattled violently a second time. Goodness, how could one rather reserved man bring forth such a response in her? She hardly knew him. She wasn't sure if she would see him again, or even if she wanted to. Why, then, did it feel as if the storm was raging within her as well?

Because you like him. That terrible truth took the rest of the strength from her knees, so she slipped into one of the wingback chairs positioned comfortably near the stove.

Cora hung up the raincoat and returned with a second tea cup, watching her curiously.

"The Frost property borders my cousin's land, yes." She tried to answer as if she wasn't in turmoil. As if she hadn't just discovered she liked a man who, according to his daughters, didn't believe in love.

"Rumor has it that you had dinner with the doctor and his children the other evening." Cora settled into the neighboring chair, her cup steaming and curiosity sparkling in her eyes. Her smile seemed all-knowing. "Samuel Frost is strikingly handsome, don't you think? Holly came down with a sore throat in March, and he was wonderful. Courteous, brilliant, and kind. I wonder why he has never remarried."

"It is a mystery," Molly agreed, the tea in her cup sloshing over the brim. She did her best to steady her hand. "A widower almost always remarries right away if there are children to raise. That's my observation, anyway."

"I've noticed the same. Dr. Frost hasn't been in any rush to find his daughters a new mother. I believe he's been widowed many years. Five, perhaps more." Cora sipped her tea, leaving a silence between them.

Five years was a goodly length to remain alone with two small daughters. Molly leaned back in the chair, the bracing crisp scent of the tea steaming her face while her mind traveled backwards to the evening spent with Sam. She'd gotten a glimpse of his good humor and tenderness, and how much he wanted what was best for his daughters.

The man had a compassionate heart. Perhaps that was why she liked him. Why her hand trembled and her soul noticed when his eyes had locked on hers. Yes, she liked him more than she should. Much more than was smart.

"I'm nearly finished with the basting work you sent home with me." She firmly changed the subject, took a sip of tea and ignored the regret within her for a wish that could never be.

If only he could get the image of the woman out of his head. Sam paced down the dark hall, restless and unsettled, unable to erase the image of Molly lifting her face to the rain, watching the roiling storm with the kind of joy and wonder he hadn't felt since he was a boy. As a little guy, he remembered spinning with both arms out as the rain pelted over him and thunder crashed overhead. That is, until his mother had called out for him to come in and be sensible.

Why was he remembering such things? There was more—the cave in the hillside he had claimed as his fort, the pony who had been his best friend, his anticipation as Ma and his sister Sara finished the supper dishes while Pa lit his pipe and paged through the big volume of Shakespeare's plays.

Life was not a story. He fisted his hands, arriving at the girls' room, where the lamplight framed them as if with an angel's touch. He froze in place outside the doorway, love creeping endlessly into every place, every fracture, every shadow in his soul. The girls in matching white flowered nightgowns and caps knelt beside their double bed, heads bowed and hands clasped in prayer.

Maybe, he conceded. Just maybe part of life was as fanciful and as captivating as anything made up. His daughters certainly were.

"…and please bless Miss Molly, cuz she's awful nice and pretty and has a horse—"

"—and she said she'd take us in a heartbeat—"

"—an' no one ever says that about us. Amen."

"Amen."

The suspicion that the twins knew he was there was confirmed when both girls opened their eyes and shared unspoken looks. A floorboard squeaked beneath his boot as he shifted his weight. Yep, those two were nothing but trouble, but he was very fond of trouble.

"Into bed, both of you."

"Hi, Pa." Synchronized, they hopped onto their feet, hems swishing.

"Maybe you could put Miss Molly in your prayers, too," Penelope began as she climbed beneath the covers.

"Because we like her," Prudence finished as she

dashed around to her side of the bed and jumped into it with a creak of bed ropes.

Molly. She was emblazoned in his mind, an image of purity and elegance standing in the rain. A dream he could not let himself believe in.

"Good night, dear ones." He tucked the covers beneath their chins, brimming over with emotion too tender to measure. "Sleep tight."

He blew out the lamp, sorry when the flame died for it stole his little girls from his sight. As he shut the door behind him, he heard their whispers and a single shared giggle. Emptiness followed him down the stairs to the parlor where the day's newspaper and his Bible awaited him. The fire in the hearth snapped and crackled, echoing in the stillness. He could not deny that his thoughts went to Molly, who was also alone in her house and lonely in her life.

He wished he could keep his thoughts from her, but he could not.

The best thing about a storm was that it did not last. Molly drew back the curtains from her window and took delight in the soft light before dawn. A clear sky turned lavender at the horizon and promised a fair morning. Flowers nodded reverently in the calm breeze and birds sang gloriously in anticipation of the sun rising.

Behind her the morning dishes dried in the drainer and the fire was banked in the cook stove. She swallowed the last of her tea, doing her best to ignore the silence surrounding her and the emptiness. Gone were the mornings filled with a gurgling baby girl chewing on her baked biscuits while Molly hurried to get breakfast on the table. Gone were the sweet times when Merry had beat pots against the floor while Molly had baked bread, or accompanied her to town to shop for groceries, or played with her toes in the clean grass while Molly knelt nearby at the washboard.

God knew best in taking little Merry. That Molly had to trust. But nothing had been able to fill the empty mornings or the hole in her heart. She longed to love again, but would it ever be? There would be no more babies and that meant gone was her only chance for a family.

What a blessing the job at the bakery was. There was no more time to remember. She grabbed her shawl from the row of wooden pegs by the door, slung it over her shoulders and threw open the door.

The shadows and half light greeted her. A lark on the ground gave her a shocked look before taking flight. Something dark on the top step caught her attention. She stopped short, staring at the bouquet of freshly picked flowers, the buds closed tightly. The soft fragrance of lilacs made her smile.

Lilacs. She thought of the garden outside Sam Frost's kitchen door.

Could these be from Sam? She knelt down to gather the long stems. Who else would have given her flowers? The bouquet had been tied with a ribbon. She ran her fingertip over the stems. The leaves felt like dried velvet, the delicate cones of blooms like the finest French silk. Memories assailed her, the lilac bushes outside her childhood home making the house smell luxuriously for most of May, planting a lilac bush outside her shanty with new little baby Merry watching, bundled safely in her basket. The scent of the blossoms reminded her of home, of love, and most of all, of hope.

Sam Frost had left these for her? Tears lumped in her throat and scalded her eyes. The man hardly liked her. She'd seen the look on his face when she'd told him about her long-ago fort. While he hadn't been horrified and she hadn't known quite how to label his confused countenance, she was certain of one thing. Sam Frost had sorely regretted inviting to dinner a woman who knew how to climb trees and fend off pretend bandits.

For a moment, just one long moment as she found a tall jar and filled it with water from the pitcher, she dreamed. What if Sam had been smitten by her? What if he'd cut these flowers with love? What if he'd left them here, hoping it would make her smile? That his regard would brighten her day and lighten her load? That when he gazed upon her, endless love filled him up, real love, the incandescent, perfect kind?

But wasn't that just a wish? Molly set the jar on the counter, closed the door behind her and hurried through the pre-dawn shadows. Sam didn't love her. He had brought his offering to delight her, sure, but because he had decided his girls needed a mother. It was a practical decision on his part, nothing more.

If her disappointment felt as large as the sky and as shadowed as the ground at her feet, she did her best to ignore it. She hurried through sleeping wildflowers and whispering grasses to the barn, blind to the beauty as dawn came.

Sam stumbled into the kitchen, blinking against the too bright light. He felt one hundred years old and soul-weary as he dropped his medical bag on the bench by the door and shucked off his coat. The sun was well up. He had no notion as to the time. Bless Kathleen for the fresh pot of coffee on the stove and the scent of bacon in the air. Must be a breakfast plate for him in the warmer.

"There you are." Kathleen bustled into the kitchen with a broom in hand. "I thought I heard the door close. You've been up since the wee hours."

"Mr. Markus is going to make it. His heart gave him a scare." Sam wrapped his fingers around the back rung of his chair. Maybe it was a trick of the mid-morning light, or his weary mind, but a shaft of sunlight sliced through the window and landed directly on the extra chair at the table, the one Molly had used the other night.

Molly. Thinking of her stirred up all kinds of tender feelings and all sorts of sensible reasons not to acknowledge those feelings. He didn't like her. He wasn't going to like her. He intended to stay in absolute control of his emotions.

Kathleen set a cup of hot coffee in front of him and the plate from the warmer.

"Bless you." He surely appreciated his housekeeper. He felt less exhausted basking in the aroma of crisp bacon, scrambled eggs and blueberry pancakes. "Where are the girls?"

"Out weeding the garden like I told them. They have that vase to work off, although it's my opinion—" Kathleen took a deep breath like a general preparing for battle. "I don't think it's right they work off the vase."

"Their cow broke the vase. They need to learn responsibility."

"Yes, I agree. But it might not look right from Miss Molly's view." Kathleen set the small pitcher of maple syrup and the butter dish on the table. "You just think about that. There hasn't been one woman in these parts brave enough to have supper with you. Those twins are a blessing, but a passel of trouble, too. A wise man wouldn't ask questions. He wouldn't hesitate. He wouldn't look left or right. He would marry that woman. Because if you don't, it might well be an eternity before another woman comes along who's partial to your girls."

Yes, that was exactly what he needed right now. Now, when he was too tired to think straight. He was seeing double. He blinked again. Maybe triple. "I don't want to get married."

"You might consider those young ones. Out there trying to impress you and Miss Molly. They need a mother's love."

He reached for the sugar jar and tipped it into his coffee. The fog in his head cleared a tad. "The girls weren't out in the garden."

"Sure they were. They were right—" Kathleen peered out the back window where the vegetable garden was visible beyond lawn. "Where did they get off to?"

Not again. Sam pushed away from the table. "Keep that warm for me. No telling how long I'll be."

Tired to the bone, he climbed to his feet. A father's work was never done. If a tiny voice in his head reminded him that Kathleen was right, that his girls obviously needed more than he could provide, he didn't want to admit it. He had been denying that voice for years.

He stumbled out of the back door and hadn't gone two feet before he realized something was different. No overgrown branches smacked him as he marched down the walkway. The overgrown lilacs had been trimmed.

Excellent. The girls were showing some improvement, after all. Maybe what they needed was time and firm, loving guidance. Kathleen was wrong.

She had to be.

"Miss Molly!"

Startled, she glanced up from her work at the bakery's front counter, wrapping dinner rolls, bread and a dozen cookies for Mrs. Worthington's afternoon pickup. She lost count of the cookies. The Frost twins tromped through the doorway, dressed in matching pink calico dresses and innocent faces. *Too* innocent faces. What were the girls up to?

"This is a pleasant surprise," she greeted. "What are you two doing here?"

"Oh, we got real hungry for a cookie."

"Real hungry."

At ten in the morning? Quite unusual. She considered her little customers. "I can't remember you two coming by the bakery before this."

"That's because we didn't know you."

"We do now."

"Uh-huh." Not that she wasn't delighted to see her little friends, but she had learned a thing or two about the pair. "What about your pa? Does he know where you are?"

Both girls shook their heads slowly. Puppy dog eyes and downcast faces.

Adorable. She did her best not to let them see her smile. "Did you girls come to town on your own?"

"It wasn't much of a walk—"

"—it didn't take much time at all. We can go back—"

"—if you want us to."

"You don't, do you?"

What did she do with them? As cute as two peas in a pod and twice as dear. She thought of the flowers at home on her kitchen counter, a gift from their father. A courting man left flowers. No doubt about that. Her stomach tightened, as if filling with too many conflicting emotions. Hope and despair, wishes and reality, faith and fear.

"We were weeding the carrots—"

"—which is really hard."

"We have to get every single weed in the whole garden—"

"—except we got hungry."

Was Sam Frost going to come courting her? Why did that question make the children standing on the other side of the counter suddenly more precious to her? Her hand shook as she recounted the cookies in the bakery box and added two more to make a baker's dozen.

They cannot be your children, Molly. She had to be careful. She had to remember that a child could not fill the void in a marriage when love did not thrive. With a flick of her wrists, she closed the box lid and secured it tightly. "Let me understand this. You two are so hungry you had to walk a quarter of a mile into town instead of going to the cookie jar in your own kitchen?"

"Oops." Penelope blushed.

Prudence bowed her head. "Maybe we wanted to see you, Miss Molly."

"Maybe I want to see you, too, but promise me something." She swept around the counter and brought both chins up to meet her gaze. "You tell Mrs. Finley or your father before you surprise me again. All right?"

"Yes'm." Both girls smiled, little beauties with hearts of gold.

Okay, so she was sweet on them. She nodded toward the table at the large front window, where the day's delicious specials were on display. A chocolate layer cake, a pan of cinnamon rolls, fresh loaves of rye bread and big plates of iced cookies. "Now, each of you pick out one thing. It will be my treat."

"Thanks, Miss Molly." They chimed together, twice the sweetness as they raced ahead of her. They had wanted to see her. Enough they had walked all the way here on a Saturday, when they had any number of fun activities to keep them amused at home.

Their question from the first day they met flitted into her thoughts. *Do you want to get married? You could marry Pa. Then he wouldn't be cross anymore. Or lonely. So, do you want to?*

Longing filled her, the longing of a mother who had empty arms and no child to love. The floor felt shaky beneath her feet. She grabbed onto the counter, holding on. It would be so easy to start caring too much. To let her affection for the girls influence how she felt about their father. She wanted a family with all of her soul, so much she ached with it.

More than that, she did not want to make a mistake.

To trade the dream of true love and happiness for the reality of uneasy silences and discord.

Do not start loving them, Molly. She willed strength back into her knees and resolve into her heart. Still, it was hard not to adore the girls. Penelope and Prudence in their matching pink dresses and bonnets, their straight black braids and shiny black shoes leaned carefully over the pretty table covered with delicious treats, considering their choices.

The door swung violently open, sending the jingle bell over it ringing with alarm. A man's dark frame filled the doorway, wearing a black Stetson, black attire and a granite-set look of disapproval. Sam's gaze collided with hers and she felt the wave of his unhappiness like a sucker punch as he pounded into the bakery, his boots striking angrily on the floor.

"Girls! What did I tell you?" His hazel eyes darkened, a formidable man of steel and cool temper.

Molly watched in horror as the startled twins turned from the table, Penelope's shoe caught the table leg, she stumbled and there was a deafening crash.

Chapter Six

Dread cascaded through him at the boom of exploding glass. Wood crashed to the floor. A porcelain plate hit the ground with a ring. One sugar cookie rolled like a wheel toward him, hit the counter and broke into three pieces.

His girls—his adorable, troublemaking girls— were in the middle of the shattered glass, splintered wood and ruined baked goods. Prudence stood with her hands to her face, her eyes round with horror. Penelope was in the rubble down on one knee, cradling one hand with her other. Fresh blood seeped between her fingers.

He didn't remember crossing the floor. Suddenly he was crunching across the debris, fear driving him.

"We're real sorry, Pa." Penelope's bottom lip trembled.

"We didn't mean it." Tears pooled in Prudence's eyes.

"Don't move. Not a step." He lifted Penny from the rubble, hating the sight of that blood. It didn't look too bad. With a kiss to her forehead, he set her safely away from the shards of glass. "I'll be right back, sweetheart. Let me get your sister."

Penny sniffed and nodded, cradling her cut hand, and he swooped Prudy into his arms. Glass and cookies ground beneath his boots as he turned, and the sight greeting him nearly toppled him. Molly knelt in front of Penelope, examining her injured hand. He lost awareness of everything—the child against his chest, the adrenaline coursing through his veins, fear that his daughter was in pain. He felt weightless, buoyant with emotion.

"It's not bad at all. I'll get some water to wash this with." Pure concern shone like a pearl's luster as she gently wiped a tear from the girl's cheek. "Come over here and sit for me, okay, love? It's going to be all right."

Penny nodded with another sniffle. "It only hurts a little bit."

His good girl. Chin set, more tears hovering but not falling, trying so hard to be brave. Vaguely he was aware of lowering Prudence to the floor. Somewhere in his befuddled mind he knew he should be the one to tend to the wound, but for the life of him he could not seem to move. Two things became crystal clear. The gentle tug against his hand as Prudence wrapped her fingers in his, and Molly as she returned with a bowl, pitcher and cloths.

"Come sit over here." Pure compassion, the woman took Penny's elbow and guided her the few steps to the long bench meant for customers. She helped Penelope to sit, her murmur spoken so low, the words were lost to him.

The little girl relaxed, her gaze taking in every de-

tail of the woman's face. Molly held the little hand to
the basin, poured water over the wound and dabbed
carefully, checking for bits of glass and debris.

He felt a tug on his hand and met Prudy's worried
face and plea-filled eyes. She hadn't been harmed by
the broken glass, but she was hurting from something
different, something harder to see.

"She's just like our list, Pa." She whispered, sidling
up against him, so it was just the two of them. "She's
nice in every way."

She certainly is. His windpipe thickened, but it was
no medical malady that made it hard to draw in air.
It was this woman kneeling before his child, with her
delicate golden curls and kindness. There was no pretense. No social decorum. Nothing but concern for the
child. Like a mother, she inspected the raw edges of
the small cut, speaking soothingly in low tones, trying
to tease a smile from the girl to reassure her.

It was almost as if Molly were a mother, for she
knew just what to do, how to comfort, how to care.

"You hold that still for me, okay, darling?" Molly
took the bloody cloths and rose with a rustle of her
skirts. She cradled Penny's chin with her free hand.
"I'll look to see if Mrs. Kraus has a salve in the medicine cabinet. Then we'll get that wrapped up good so
you can have a cookie. Maybe you had better have two
cookies. It will help you heal faster."

He watched, amazed. As she smiled down at his
daughter, she changed in the same way a bud opened
into a blossom. The same way dawn became morning.
Everything about her bloomed. Her eyes, her face, her
spirit. Pure radiance. In that light he saw something
kindred, the sorrow he'd read in her before. But this

held a joy, too, a memory and a love so powerful, he knew. He knew.

Bless her, Lord. Please look after her, for all she has been through.

Sorrow beat at his carefully controlled will. His resolve not to like or to care about Mrs. Molly McKaslin crumbled like a cookie, leaving strong, vibrant emotion. He wanted to think it was sympathy for her lonesomeness he felt, and that's what he was going to tell himself. He could not love her. He *would* not love her.

"I've got some salve in my medical bag in the buggy." He moved woodenly toward the door, his emotions oddly disconnected as he grasped the brass knob and bolted into the warm, bright day, refusing to let himself wonder why he was running so fast.

As Molly wrapped up two cookies each for the girls, she tried not to watch the girls and their father. The girls sat side by side on the bench while Sam knelt on the floor, bandaging Penelope's hand.

She gathered up both little packages and by the time she'd circled the end of the front counter, she made sure she had a smile on her face.

"This should make both of you feel a little bit better." She presented the bundles to Prudence. "Perhaps you could carry this for your sister?"

"Yes'm. Thank you so much, Miss Molly."

"Yes, thank you." The intensity of Penelope's smile had changed.

Everything had changed. Molly swallowed hard, trying to ignore the rawness in her midsection. She gave a tug on each girl's sunbonnet brim. "It was a pleasure seeing you two, but I hope the rest of your day is less eventful."

"Me, too. I only got one other hand." Penelope wiggled her good fingers. "I can't climb into our fort."

"Or lasso Sukie if she runs off."

"Or climb over the rocks at the creek."

"I guess you two will have to stay home with Kathleen for a few days until this heals up right." Sam winked at them. "You'll have to be proper. Maybe learn needlework."

"My hand, Pa?" Penelope showed him the bandage as a reminder.

"I know. Sewing is out of the question, but a father can have hope. Maybe you can sit with me in the library."

"You could read the plays to us." Prudence, hopeful, sidled close to her twin, gazing adoringly at her strong, gentle father. "The one with Viola—"

"—the girl that dresses up like a boy." Penelope finished, all hope.

"*Twelfth Night* it is." Sam rose to his six-foot height. Hard not to be impressed by his dependable shoulders and stalwart kindness. "Molly, thank you for all you've done for my daughters."

He may have been talking about cleaning Penelope's cut and comforting the girl, or perhaps sweeping up the mess in front of the window, but she suspected he was thanking her for more. Much more.

She felt a pang of hope in her heart. A hope she could not simply give in to. Maybe there was a chance his courting was sincere. Maybe.

"Helping your girls was my pleasure." She opened

the door. Fresh May sun streamed in like a celebration of life and love. "I hope you feel better, Penelope."

"I do. Now." Although the child walked by and did not reach out, her need was like a small hand grasping the strings of Molly's heart.

"I'm real sorry my shoe got caught on the table leg."

"I'm real sorry about the cookies."

Impossible not to love those darling girls just a little bit more. "I'm glad you both are all right."

"I apologize." Sam hesitated, taking the weight of the door, close enough that she could see the texture of his morning stubble whiskering his lean jaw. "Calamity finds them."

"Those two are catastrophes in calico." And the dearest. She steeled her mother's need to love those girls, refusing to catch a glimpse of the two through the window, where they waited on the boardwalk for their father.

"If the money I left with you doesn't cover all the damage, you will have Mrs. Kraus bill me?"

"She isn't going to be happy about it. Just a warning." Molly forced her thoughts to the incident, a safe topic, one that would not tear her emotions apart. "I'll do what I can to calm her."

"I appreciate it." Again, it seemed as if he was saying more as he tipped his hat. "I would hate for the girls to be banned from the bakery."

"I would, too." They shared a smile, but it felt like more. It felt like a tender recognition, like two lonely souls finding their match. "Goodbye, Sam."

"Goodbye, Molly." When he said her name, his tone deepened, as if with great meaning, with high regard. No longer reserved, no longer frosty, no longer keeping his distance, Sam brushed by her, and she felt the weight of his shadows and the spark of hope.

You will not fall in love with him, she ordered. She closed the door, watching as the man she did not want to love caught each girl by the hand. They walked toward his awaiting horse and buggy together. Their shadows trailed behind them, as if there was nothing but sunshine and good days ahead.

Alone, Molly turned her back, feeling every drop of emptiness in her soul and every impossible wish.

The image of Molly kneeling before his daughter and tending her wound stayed with him through the afternoon. So did the picture she had made in the bakery's window, with her arms wrapped around her middle, forlorn and lost as he'd untethered Stanley from the hitching post.

Sam set two glasses of lemonade on the table next to the back porch swing. It had been a good day. He had read to the girls early on. His afternoon rounds had gone well, and if no one needed a doc for the rest of the day, he would have a quiet evening at home. "Mrs. Finley says that's all you get before supper."

"Pa?" Penelope's toy horse, clutched in her good hand, froze in mid-gallop on the flowered cushion. "Do you know what?"

"We've got it all figured out," Prudence added, all innocence as she trotted her wooden mustang across the arm of the swing.

"I'm afraid to know what you girls have planned now." He leaned against the porch railing and crossed his arms over his chest, braced for the details of their next scheme. "Does this have to do with the Nevilles' pony?"

"Well, we would like to have Trigger as our very own—"

"—we surely would."

"But this is more important."

"—a *lot* more important."

More than the Nevilles' pony? This ought to be good. He braced himself for it. Perhaps it had something to do with how doting they had been to Molly's mare. Most likely the girls wanted a little more excitement than a placid old pony could bring to their lives. What else could make the girls study one another, as if silently bolstering up their courage to ask? They had never had a problem asking for what they wanted before.

Penelope squirmed, put her horse down and laid her bandaged hand on her lap. She looked vulnerable, as she had after the bakery display table had come crashing down. "Miss Molly was awful nice to us."

"She didn't yell." Prudence swiped the flyaway strands from her braids out of her face with a nervous brush. "Not even once."

"And when I almost cried, she wiped away my tears. She didn't even scold, because I'm too big to cry." Penelope's voice thinned, and on her dear face showed a world of hurt. Of need. "She's awful nice, Pa."

"And she gave us cookies after—"

"—after I wrecked everything." Tears pooled in Penelope's eyes.

Prudence's lower lip trembled.

A terrible feeling gathered behind his solar plexus. A tight coil that would not relent. His daughters were hurting. So little and delicate. "What are you two trying to say?"

"We like her, Pa."

"A whole bunch."

"We want you to marry her."

"With a ring and everything."

He squeezed his eyes shut, attempting to hold more emotions than he could handle. *Oh, Lord, help me say the right thing. Please guide me now because I'm afraid I will make a mess of this.* His girls, for all their bluster and charm, were frail at heart, as anyone was. Love made everyone vulnerable, especially children. He opened his eyes, trusting that God would help him find a way to make this right.

"We were praying too, Pa."

"So that maybe you would like Miss Molly."

"Really like her."

"So she could be our ma."

This is where he had always failed before. Sam pushed away from the railing and knelt before his daughters. The wind chose that moment to gust, sending the most lyrical scent of lilacs, as soothing as any lullaby. A few stray purple petals floated by.

He had spent so much time keeping everyone at an emotional distance. Necessary for a doctor, but it had become his way of coping. First when his marriage felt like a battleground and second when he'd found himself a grieving widower with a pair of three-year-olds to raise. He'd been terrified of failing again. Of letting his girls down. Of not raising them right.

But something had changed. Someone had changed him. He thought of Molly and her loss, the richness of her heart that had known great love and great sorrow.

He brushed a tear from Penny's cheek and a stray curl from Prudy's face. "I thought you two understood. I'm not likely to get married again."

"But it's what Mrs. Finley says you need."

"She says it all the time."

He saw right through their words to the needs of two motherless girls. They were the ones who needed him to marry. They were the ones in love with Molly McKaslin. How did he handle that? He couldn't deny the woman's beauty and kindness or the fact that he liked her.

Truth be told, he more than liked her. But marriage? The tightness coiling in his gut twisted taut. No, he could not build a marriage on love again. His heart hadn't recovered from the last attempt.

At a loss, he dug deep for the right answer. He felt the Lord's reassurance like a touch to his soul, and understood. He gentled his voice, although it remained scratchy, letting his shields down instead of putting them up, letting the wash of emotions hit him instead of denying them. "Do you really want to do that to Miss Molly? Look at me. I'm old."

"Not that old, Pa. You don't have gray hair yet."

"Or wrinkles."

So sincere. He tried again. "Sure, but I'm hardly handsome. Molly might not want to marry an almost-homely man."

"Nun-uh. Your nose isn't *too* big."

"And you have all your teeth."

"That I do." He bit his lip. His adorable girls. "I'm sure Molly wants to marry someone with all his teeth. But you know I tend to be surly."

"You don't scowl nearly as much, Pa."

"You only got cross once today."

"But I work all the time. A lot of nice ladies don't like that in a husband. They want them around to have supper with and to read alongside in the evenings."

"You could find another doctor to help you, Pa."

"That way you could have more suppers at the table."

"You girls have this all figured out, don't you?"

"We've got a list, Pa."

"Not just for us, but for you, too."

A list. He should have expected that. They had always been precocious for their age. Perhaps he would leave the rest of the argument for another time. "I'm going out to help Abner with the barn work. You girls want to come—"

He didn't get to finish his question. A cow mooed behind him near the fence, perhaps announcing a newcomer. The squeak of a wheel and the clop of horse hooves brought him to his feet. He was already striding through the garden without thought, expectation filling him. The rising dust obscured the driver from his sight, but he didn't need to see her face to know it was Molly. He knew because of the rise of emotion moving through him like the tide through the ocean.

"Miss Molly!" The girls clamored behind him through the garden gate and onto the lawn. Sukie rushed up, charging on all four feet, mooing in delight. The excitement was nothing compared to the riot of feelings within his heart for the woman who gave her first smile of greeting to him.

Chapter Seven

"Miss Molly! You came!" In unison, footfalls padded against grass. With Sukie tailing them, Penelope and Prudence hurried toward the cart, bright and shining.

"I had to come see how you were, Penelope." Molly didn't bother to hide her delight as she eased Ruth to a stop in the Frosts' driveway. "How's your hand?"

"Lots better. I can't believe we get to see you twice—"

"—all in the same day!" Prudence finished breathlessly, wrapping her fingers along the top rail of the cart. "Did you come to see me, too?"

"Absolutely. I can't adore one of you without adoring the other." Molly laughed when Sukie skidded to a halt behind the girls, and Ruth gave a low nicker of disapproval. What decorum! She patted Ruth's flank reassuringly. "It's very good to see you, too, Sukie."

The bovine lowed, lifting her head to sniff and gaze dotingly at the bakery box on the seat. Smart girl.

"You smell cinnamon and apples, don't you?" Aware of Sam staying back against the white garden fence, she handed the bakery box to Prudence. "I made this during my lunchtime just for you all."

Penelope leaned against the cart, careful of her bandaged hand. "Apple crisp. I can smell it."

"It smells good." Prudence carefully took the box. "Thank you, Miss Molly."

"Do we have to wait for dessert time—"

"—or can we open it now?"

"It's up to your pa." She allowed her gaze to find him and to linger, and offered a small smile. He clung to the shadows against the house, looking stoic and reserved and handsome. Decidedly handsome. Without a hat, his thick black hair swirled over his forehead to fall at his collar. His pensive look made his angled face appear stronger and deeply masculine. Gone was the morning's stubble, and his smooth jaw was set as if in stone. Her fingertips tingled with the urge to trail the cut of his jaw line.

You are not going to fall for this man, remember? She steeled her spine, determined to be strong. Just because her emotions for him had changed and her regard for him deepened did not mean she had to be sweet on the man. She did not intend to set her cap for him. She could hold back her need to be a part of a family again, to love and the hope to be loved.

"You girls take that into the kitchen first, so you don't spill whatever it is."

"Pa, we'll be careful."

"Real careful."

"Sure, but look at what happened this morning. Calamity strikes when you two are near." He stepped into the fall of sunlight, coming closer. "Go to the kitchen and have Mrs. Finley help you."

"Yes, sir." The two trotted off the way they came, and Sukie trailed them through the garden gate and disappeared from sight.

"Is she going to follow the girls into the house?"

"It's been known to happen." He held out his hand to help her down. "When Sukie was a calf, I would find her in the house at least once a day. She would find her way in through a door or a window."

"She does love your daughters." Molly placed her fingers on his palm, the lightest of brushes. This time it felt significant, like a bolt of lightning in a blue sky. As she swung off the seat, the sensation jolted through her spirit and soul, and for one brief moment she was airborne, buoyed as if by love. Then her shoes touched the ground, Sam withdrew his hand and yet the feeling of lightness remained.

"One morning I came in from a late night call, and there she was, sleeping in the kitchen next to the warm stove." Sam did not look in the least affected as he walked slowly at her side. "Sukie was curled up looking as pleased as could be with herself, and the cinnamon rolls Kathleen had baked for the morning were gone and the pan on the counter licked clean."

It took all her discipline to focus on the words of his story. Her hands had gone damp. Her limbs tremulous. Her entire being quaked as if she would never be the same again. "And what was your reaction?"

"I lit the stove, boiled a pot of tea and took the calf outside. She was back in the house by the time Kathleen started breakfast."

"She was letting herself into the house?"

"A mystery that was never solved." Sam appeared different. Warmer, less guarded. He stopped at the gate and held it open, but shook his head when she went towards it. A hint of dimples framed his grin. "It's my theory the calf used the pass-through hatch for the coal. She grew bigger and couldn't get in anymore. I thought letting the girls get a pet cow would teach them responsibility, but I was wrong. You already knew that, didn't you?"

"Maybe because I grew up in the country. I've had a few pet cows of my own." Yes, that was it. Concentrate on anything except Sam Frost.

"So, you've always lived in the country?"

"No. Scarlet fever took my baby daughter four years ago. Then it took my husband, and I fell sick. My mother came to tend me and she died. After that, I couldn't keep the farm running by myself. I lost the house and the land, so Ruth and I moved into town. All the hustle and bustle made me forget. It was the noise. I was always reminded I was among other people, that my old life had vanished and things were different. Somehow it made it easier to move on. At least partly."

"I'm sorry for your loss, Molly." Rich, his words, deeply intimate his tone. His sympathy touched her, as if they shared that in life and more. He moved closer, and not merely physically. "I pray there will be more children for you one day."

"I had a very hard time having Merry, and my doctor assured me there would be no more babies. Now you know why I think your twins are a blessing. I don't understand why God chose to take my only child, but in losing my daughter I know the value of a child's life and the richness of a child's love." She changed the subject. "How did you lose your wife?"

"Cancer. I did a similar thing when Paula died. I

moved from the town into the country. I worked so much, so I could stay numb from any more pain life had to offer."

"It's no way to live. Eventually you have to rise to the challenge of living and loving again, or miss what is greatest in life."

"Wise words." He had recently come to understand that.

Kathleen's voice carried from the open window. "Get out of my kitchen! Shoo! You girls take that cow outside right now."

"But she loves us, Mrs. Finley—"

"—she wants to be with us."

"Honestly! Does my kitchen look like a barnyard to you? Shoo!"

Beside him, Molly's laughter was part amusement, part tears. Was she remembering her losses? He wanted to ask her about what had happened, about her buried child. But he could not hurt her in that way.

"What a good life you have, Sam." Amusement chased away the traces of sorrow from her lovely face, the loveliest he'd ever seen.

"I know that, too." She made him different. He wanted to thank the Lord for sending the lustrous sunlight because when it glowed, it turned her blond hair to pure gold. He wanted to give thanks for the way his heart came to life, full of melody and harmony and notes in between. For the frightening vulnerable feeling of trusting a woman again.

A clatter arose in the flower garden. A lilac bush rustled and Sukie emerged on the path, a daisy hanging from her mouth. Liquid brown eyes twinkled with mischief as she loped just ahead of her little girls. Molly hopped out of the way, bringing her dangerously close to his chest and to his arms. She smelled like sugar cookies and icing and spring. Being near her was like waking up and finding a dream.

The girls dashed past, pink sunbonnets hanging down their backs by the strings, their black braids bouncing with their gaits. "Sukie!"

The heifer, as if eager to play tag, took off into the field, her tail swishing. Penny and Prudy followed, their laughter like merry bells.

"As you can see, neither is worse for the wear. Everything is back to normal." Everything except him. He sidestepped, resisting the urge to pull her against his chest, to hold her sweetly enfolded in his arms. She definitely appeared more beautiful than when he had last seen her and somehow ever more precious and wholesomely feminine. Stubborn tenderness took root within him, refusing to do anything but flourish.

Don't love her. That would be an enormous mistake. But what he heard was his daughters' pleas. *We were praying, too, Pa. So that maybe you would like Miss Molly. Really like her. So she could be our ma.* What he felt was their unquenchable need. It could not be his own need to love and care for her that made him reach over the picket fence and pluck one long stem of fragrant lilacs.

His voice was raw and gruff when he spoke, his throat oddly aching as he picked another spray. "Was Mrs. Kraus very upset?"

"I believe she will recover once she receives the rest of the payment for the bill she intends to send you."

"In other words, yes."

"I'm glad Penelope is feeling well enough to play. It

could have been more serious." She grew radiant, lustrous from the inside out. The sunshine followed her and the wind moved just to caress her hair and rustle her skirt hem. "Your twins are—"

"—trouble?"

"No. I'm searching for the right word."

"—calamitous?"

"Perfection." She almost won his heart with that one pronouncement.

"I think so, too." He plucked one more cone. Do not fall in love with her. Do not read too much into this. Do not start making a list of all her amazing attributes. No doubt, a woman like Molly wanted more than he could give.

And if a tiny voice within him wanted to argue, he refused to listen. He held the flowers out to her, the lush green leaves, dainty purple flowers and romantic fragrance. "Stay. Come join us for supper."

"I can't. I'm expected at my cousin Noelle's house within the hour." Her fingers closed over his, as soft as sun-warmed silk.

"Maybe another evening?"

"Perhaps." She studied him, as if seeing him for the first time. "Yes, I think I would like that."

"Excellent." He drew back his hand but did not step away. "Thank you for the apple crisp. I'm glad you came by."

"Yes." She breathed in the lovely aroma, the velvet petals tickling her chin. It seemed to her there was a deeper meaning to his words, a deeper meaning in her feelings for him. She clutched the lilacs in one arm and let him help her into the cart. The door to her affections opened wider, as she placed her hand in his.

You cannot love him, she told herself.
She feared it was too late.

Sam could not sleep. Having a headache hadn't
helped him to drift off, and it didn't put him in a better temper now. He felt as dark as the night, as troubled as the shadows. The lamp's single flame tossed a
pool of light on the kitchen table as he pored over his
Bible. He had need of wisdom, but not one verse he
read seemed to guide him in the direction he wanted to
go. He flipped the thin pages, stopping in Ecclesiastes.

*Two are better than one; because they have a good
reward for their labour. For if they fall, the one will
lift up his fellow: but woe to him that is alone when he
falleth; for he hath not another to help him up.*

Molly. She was the reason he had tossed and turned,
unable to make his mind calm down. He kept seeing
her everywhere, even on the back of his closed eyelids,
her lustrous kindness, her enthralling gentleness, the
silken softness of her face. She loved his girls. They
loved her. He trusted her, and he believed she trusted
him. Wasn't that enough?

His throat felt scratchy, almost sore and he took
another sip of honeyed lemon tea. The tart-sweetness
made him grimace, but soothed the discomfort. When
it came to Molly, how did he stop seeing her beauty
as something lyrical, like a romantic sonnet or a tender hymn? How did he stay sensible, for whenever he
looked at her it was with the eyes of his heart?

He drew his finger down the page. Maybe an answer here would guide him.

...how can one be warm alone? And if one prevail

*against him, two shall withstand him; and a threefold
cord is not quickly broken.*

Fine, so he would try another book. He thumbed
back a few of pages and pressed the book open.

*Hope deferred maketh the heart sick: but when the
desire cometh, it is a tree of life.*

That wasn't reassuring him. He rubbed his forehead, aching from too much thought and worry. Was
Molly the right woman for his girls? He believed she
was. He could make a list a mile long of all the ways
she would be good to his daughters and for them. He
could make another equally long list of all the quali-
ties Molly possessed that would make her a good wife.
She was hardworking, honest, fair, compassionate and
loyal. She was also the only woman who could make
him fall in love with her, completely, totally.

How did he keep that from happening? Could he
be strong enough? And if she was good for his daughters…

What do I do, Lord? He bowed his head, reaching
out for the right answer, for leading he desperately
needed. *Show me Your purpose in all this. It can't be
to lead me back to an unhappy marriage, can it? Or
is my girls' happiness of far more importance?*

No answer came in the still of the night. Just a panicked knock at the kitchen door. Work, always work.
Wearily he pushed away from the table, leaving his
troubles for another time. When he saw Mr. Gornecke
on his doorstep, he grabbed his bag without a word
and expected the worst.

"Aiden, stop the surrey." Cousin Joanna touched her
husband's arm and stood to get a better look through

the tall grasses. "Molly, I believe there is something on your doorstep."

"Oh?" She resisted every urge to leap to her feet and see. Had Sam left another bouquet of flowers? And why was she so blissfully happy about it? A woman ought to be wary of a widower's motives, especially when he had young girls needing a mother. He might be starting this courtship because he needed a wife, not because he was in love with her. Although, last night did make her hope.

Maybe there was a good chance Sam loved her. The spark of his touch was as if to her soul, and—

"Molly, perhaps you would like to be left off here." Joanna's voice interrupted.

She shook her head, realizing she had drifted off in thought. Her cousins were watching her with delight. The children on the cushions beside her were curious as to why they had stopped.

"If I were you, I would want to know what that note says." Aiden nodded toward the shanty.

"Note?" She had to ease off the seat in order to see what her cousins were smiling about. She spied the spray of lilacs tied with a ribbon on her top doorstep, anchoring a blue piece of parchment.

"Yes, perhaps I'll get off here. Thank you for the ride to church." Woodenly she turned around, angling her hoops between the seats, and dropped too hard to the ground. Dazed, that's what she was, remembering the intimate warning of Sam's tone. *Maybe another evening.*

She had not expected an invitation so soon.

The surrey jostled away, and she hardly noticed the dust rising up around her. Every step took her closer to the note. Closer to the wonderful, maybe terrible truth. Her right toe bumped into a rock. She stumbled, unable to take her gaze from the flowers, exactly like the bunch Sam had cut for her, exactly like the bouquet left on her step before.

Please, Lord, let him be in love with me. The prayer lifted from her with all the hope she had left. She knelt on the bottom step, her hands trembling.

This was it, what she had been dreading and hoping for. Sam's image filled her mind, his capable shoulders, his gentle hands, the closeness she'd felt in his presence. Ribbons of affection curled within her as she gathered the lilacs into her arms and shook open the note.

Come dine with me tonight.

Happiness lifted her off the doorstep. She felt as airy as those pure puffy clouds sailing across the crystal blue sky. Maybe this was what it felt like when the most disappointed hopes were on the verge of coming true, when impossible prayers were about to be answered.

Chapter Eight

Sam. The moment she saw him rising from the front porch, where shadows dappled the fresh-cut lawn, her affections took flight like a butterfly. Never had she known such a yearning to see a man. To wait with anticipation for his smile to brush his lips. To be eager for the gentle caring in his voice, in his eyes, in his touch.

She drew Ruth to a halt and didn't wait for Sam to come help her. She practically floated to the ground. Her skirts swished around her ankles and she wobbled, finding her balance. Fine, she may be excited but she was nervous, too. This was the start of a dream come true—maybe.

Please let this be my dream. She hoped and prayed, waiting while he closed the thick volume he'd been reading and set it on the bench.

Delight tasted like sugar on her tongue. How good it was to see him. She'd missed the low rumble of his voice, his easygoing humor, his dependable honor. As he came toward her, her soul seemed to lean toward him, as if a sign that they were meant to be together.

That true love was already blossoming between them. She wanted nothing more.

"Good evening." Sam strode toward her, appearing rather informal for a dinner date. He did look striking in a white muslin shirt and denims. "This is a surprise."

"A surprise?" No, that couldn't be right. "You're joking again."

"Uh, no. If you've come to see the girls, they were in the house a while ago charming apple crisp from Kathleen." His smile dazzled her. When he gazed upon her, he made her feel as lovely as a princess and twice as precious.

Was she blushing? She pressed her gloved fingertips to her cheeks. Yes, she was definitely overly anxious. Being courted was no easier the second time around. She drew in a calming breath. "I didn't know the girls would be dining with us as well, but you know that's fine with me."

"Dining?" His brow furrowed. "I didn't know you were coming to supper. No one said anything to me."

"No, that can't be right." She couldn't have heard him correctly. Then again, she hadn't imagined the note. She had re-read it a dozen times since she'd come home from church. "You invited me to have dinner with you. You left the flowers."

"The flowers?" He rubbed at his forehead. Why did he look so confused?

"The lilacs on my doorstep."

"I didn't leave anything on your doorstep. I gave you lilacs when you were here yesterday, but—" The confusion slid from his face. He shook his head once, scattering his thick dark hair. "You have a suitor."

A suitor? Wasn't it him? No, she realized, her mind

spinning. He would have remembered leaving the note and flowers.

"No, I think I have no one interested in me." The first strike of disappointment hit. She set her chin and fisted her hands, but that didn't stop the hurt. He hadn't left anything for her. He had not been courting her. He was not courting her now.

The second beat of disappointment hit harder than the first, but she kept her head up. Tried with all her might to keep the pain from showing. "I was mistaken about supper. Please tell the girls hello for me. I'll head home."

"But, wait—"

Her vision kept blurring regardless of how fast she blinked. She spun on her heels, focusing on the brown blur that was Ruth and the cart and kept going. His footsteps padded behind her, but she ignored them. How could she turn to him now? She had been wrong. Desperately wrong. Sam wasn't falling in love with her. He hadn't even been beauing her. He had no notion how deeply she cared about him—

No, she didn't simply care about him. She loved him. That's why when the third blow hit, it hurt enough to have cleaved her soul in two. To leave her in pieces forever. She tripped over her shoe, and Sam's hand curled around her elbow, keeping her up, holding her in place.

"What's wrong, Molly?" His tender tone cut her to the core. "Please tell me why you're crying."

"It's nothing." There were no truer words. She sniffled, remembering she'd left her reticule in the cart. Great. She had no handkerchief to dry her tears. Her stupid, revealing tears.

His grip felt like iron on her arm, holding her in

place. Any moment he was going to put the pieces together and know how foolish she'd been. How romantic and foolish, wishing for a man's love, a man who did not love her in return. Humiliated, she swiped at her eyes.

"Here. Let me." Could his voice be any more caring?

She squeezed her eyes shut so she wouldn't see him drying her tears. She felt the soft cotton dab against her skin, drying her cheeks, catching each tear as it fell. It was not sweetness she felt, really. Nor did she feel an iota of tenderness. This wasn't a loving gesture on his behalf. This was one neighbor being kind to another. Friendliness, nothing more.

"Are you going to be all right?" he asked, his voice raw and wounded.

His kindness felt like torture. She broke away, wiped her remaining tears with her sleeve and tried to take a step.

"It was the girls, wasn't it?" His words were roughly spoken, heavy with regret. "They made you think I was courting you, didn't they?"

She nodded. The temperate winds stirred around her, swirling her skirt ruffles, tangling the curls around her face, perfuming the air with flowers and sunshine. How could she be breaking and the world be so perfect and whole? She couldn't speak. She didn't trust her voice. She fought back her last tear.

"I see it now. The proposal. The disappearances. They mysteriously prune half the garden. Their list. They keep a list with all their qualifications for a new mother. You meet every one."

A dagger to her already wounded heart. The girls. She would never be their stepmother now. Loss crashed through her, taking her last drop of hope with it. She'd had too many losses already. "Goodbye, Sam."

"No, Molly, wait." He stood between her and her cart, barring her escape. "Everything the girls did, the flowers, inviting you here, trying to bring us together, that was wrong. But I can't say I'm sorry. I care for you. More than I think is safe."

"I know what you mean."

"Maybe you should stay." He rubbed the pad of his thumb on her cheek, but no more tears fell. "Let's see what's for supper. It's my suspicion Mrs. Finley is aware of this plan and perhaps has aided and abetted. There might be a very good meal waiting for us."

"Oh Sam, I've been in this exact position before, mistaking caring for love." Sheer pain twisted her features. "I can't stay."

"Not even if I ask you to?" He hated every single tear she had shed. He despised that she was hurting. Molly, gentle-mannered, caring Molly did not deserve this. The valiant tilt of her chin, the steel of her spine, the dignity she struggled to keep broke him apart. Tenderness drowned him, and helpless, he took her hand.

"The girls haven't done anything I haven't thought to do myself." Honesty, opening himself up to rejection, took the last of his pride. He felt like he'd jumped off nearby Angel Falls, the highest waterfall in the territory, and was tumbling to certain death. But he kept going. Her hand felt fragile within his own, trembling with broken disappointment and needs. He could feel every one of them. She needed to be cared for. She needed to care for others. She had deep love to give with no one to give it to. She would make a very fine wife.

Just do it, Sam. Head pounding, throat tight and achy,

fear beating at him, he got down on one knee, watching her gasp in realization. Yep, that was just about how he felt, too. Surprised and scared and afraid of another marriage hurting more than it helped. But this time, it would be different. He would make sure of it.

"Molly, I'm hoping you would do me the honor—"

"Oh, Sam, please don't ask me this." Her bottom lip was trembling, and she looked suddenly too young and vulnerable. He had never seen her so clearly. Her goodness, her love, her wounds. She tore her hand from his and dashed around him, skirts swaying.

He didn't remember hopping to his feet or following her. Only that he was by her side. "Please don't go until you hear me out. Until you know what you mean to me."

"Oh, I can see it." She looked angry now.

Even he could tell that was only a mask. She was hurting beneath. He was, too, feeling the strike of her rejection. "You won't marry me?"

"I can't marry you." She looked ready to break apart. "You are thinking about your daughters. That's why you are proposing to me. You think I'm useful. That I'll be a solution to your problems."

"I'm thinking about my girls, yes—" He caught her in his arms. She was so tiny, for the great power she had over him. He would climb mountains for her, swim the ocean, leap to the moon if that's what she wanted. Affection filled him up like a wellspring, refreshing and overflowing. Heaven help him. It could not be love in his heart. This was a convenient proposal, nothing more. "Penny and Prudy are getting older. They will be young ladies in a matter of years. They will be putting up their hair and letting down their hemlines. What good will I be to them, then? They love you, Molly. You love them. I've seen it. Go ahead and deny it."

"But you don't love me."

I don't want to love you. How could he say the words that would hurt her? That would drive her away forever? "What I'm offering you is security. You'll have a comfortable life here."

"Security and comfort? That's wonderful, but a marriage has to be more." Her voice broke. "I need it to be more."

"I'll respect you. I'll treat you right. I'll do my best by you, Molly, if only you would honor me—"

"No." She shook her head slowly, sadly. "That's not what I want."

"I care very much. That has to be enough."

"It's not even close." She choked on a sob, waiting for her words to sink in. Realization swept across his face and he released his hold on her. Freed, she stumbled, unable to orient herself. Even though she was standing upright, she felt as if she were falling down. Maybe it was because of the pain of loss and longing she'd seen in his eyes. She still felt it as she turned from him.

"Doc!" A man's voice broke the silence between them like a gunshot. A horse and rider galloped into the yard, the horse lathered, the rider panicked. "You've got to come quick. It's Mr. Gornecke. He's taken with scarlet fever now and it's real bad. Hurry."

"All right, Jerry." Sam hung his head, his frustration palpable. "Molly, I want to talk about this some more."

"No, I can't bear it. Your heart isn't going to change. It's over, Sam." Aware of the stranger watching, she ducked her head, heading in the direction of her cart.

His voice haunted her. *What I'm offering you is security. You'll have a comfortable life here.*

She was walking away from a real chance for a family. To be a mother again. Part of her wanted to go back. She hated such weakness, that she would consider his offer, even secretly, even against her better judgment.

But what about accepting his proposal? No. She did not want to live the rest of her days watching and counting all the ways Sam did not love her. Because she loved him. She had the shards of her foolish heart to prove it.

Ruth nickered in comfort. Molly patted her old friend's neck before climbing onto the seat. She felt drained, hollow. As if the emptiness that had shadowed her for years had become permanent. She gathered up the reins and cast one last look at the man she loved, the man she feared she would always love. He stood with his shoulders straight, his hands empty, the apology plain on his face.

It had been her mistake, nothing more. She snapped the reins and let Ruth carry her home.

It was near midnight when Sam locked the kitchen door behind him and dropped his bag on the bench. At least Mrs. Gornecke was improving, and he had hope for her husband. A rustle in the darkness told him he wasn't alone. A second rustle told him the twins had tried to wait for him and had fallen asleep on the window seat.

Ignoring his pounding head, he paced to the table. Every muscle he owned ached something fierce. Probably from having his heart broken. Worse, he had not faced the truth. He had stayed on the sensible path instead of telling Molly that he was in love with her.

Not that he could do anything about it now. She would be asleep, and he didn't know if she would still want him. He didn't want to build a marriage and a life on a flimsy foundation. Yet the love he felt for Molly was stronger than steel. But was it strong enough?

Maybe the real issue was his fear. He was afraid to let her close. He was afraid to trust in any woman's love, even hers.

"Pa?" Penelope sounded sleepy.

"What are you girls doing out of bed?"

"We tossed and tossed."

"We couldn't get to sleep."

"I'm not surprised." He felt hot, so he shucked off his jacket. "Where did you two go off to when Molly came?"

"Our fort."

"So you could fall in love."

Love. There was that word again. He groped around on the shelf for the tin. When he struck a match, the flame cast a dancing glow on the table set for two with the good dishes and the crystal candlesticks.

Another piece of the puzzle revealed. He lit one of the candles, listening to the drag of the girls' stockinged feet as they came to face him.

"You girls know what you did was wrong." His voice croaked, sounding harsher than he intended.

"We know, Pa." They chorused mournfully. "When we came back and Mrs. Finley said you had a house call—"

"—we figured it was ruined." Prudence sighed, a sorrowful sound if there ever was one.

"Could we have Miss Molly for supper tomorrow?"

"Mrs. Finley could serve the pot roast again."

His head pounded. Sweat broke out on his fore-head. He'd never felt so terrible. Maybe because he had lost more today than he'd had in many, many years. Maybe because he was more in love with Molly than he cared to admit even now, when he had hurt her terribly. When he feared he had destroyed any faith in him she had.

A droplet of sweat hit the table as he poured his tea. His hand wasn't steady. Something was wrong. A sore throat. Possible fever. Headache. He set the pot on the table and unbuttoned his sleeve cuff. He only had to roll the fabric once to see the tiny red bumps on the inside of his arms. No, it couldn't be.

He sank heavily into the nearest chair. The bumps hadn't disappeared. They were still there, proof of his illness. He'd never had scarlet fever. He'd been around patients suffering from it since medical school. Why now? Why tonight? His head thrummed too painfully to think anymore.

"Girls, I want you to go straight to Mrs. Finley's room and wake her. You stay there. Have Abner come to me right away. You hear me?"

"Yes, sir." Wide-eyed, the twins froze for one moment, perhaps sensing his fear before they broke into a run, clattering down the hall and up the stairs.

If he had been paying better attention, if he hadn't been so enamored with Molly, he might have caught this earlier. *Before* he had exposed his daughters. Heartsick in more ways than he could count, he lowered his head, clasped his hands and prayed.

Chapter Nine

"Rumor has it you've been spending time with our local doctor." Aunt Ida's nimble fingers plucked at the weeds among the green beans in the pleasant evening light. "Is it merely a rumor, or is there more to the story?"

Days had passed since she had driven away from Sam. She had returned to her empty home, tucked away her devastation and gone on with her obligations. One of them was right here, helping out her extended family, which she intended to do as if Sunday evening had never happened. As if Sam Frost had never admitted that he didn't love her.

Hardly a simple thing. She ignored the sting behind her eyes and the hollow feeling within her and tugged a dandelion seedling from among the little lettuce plants.

What did she say to Aunt Ida? The woman was patiently waiting for an answer.

"I'm certain the rumor is much more interesting than the truth." She patted the earth back into place and used the hand trowel to uproot a thistle start. "I met Sam's daughters when their cow ran away and decided to visit me."

"Those girls are as cute as buttons." Ida wisely did not ask anymore about the rumors she had heard. "Molly, when the Good Lord closes a door, He always opens a window. The trouble comes when we forget to believe in the window."

Just how much had Aunt Ida guessed? She tossed the thistle and the dandelion into the waste bucket. "It's over now, and it's for the best. I've had a marriage without love. I don't want another."

"Yes, the greatest is love." Aunt Ida stopped weeding to study her a moment. "I know you well enough to wonder why you're here, as calm as could be. Helping with the bread baking and the cleaning and washing little Graham's diapers."

"Why? Where else would I be?" Speaking of the baby, Molly could see mother and child as they walked in front of the windows, crossing through the parlor. Cousin Noelle looked blissful as she cradled her son, just as it should be. She was happy for her cousin. She would not think of the family she could have had. The man she still loved. "I'm here to help. It's why I have the shanty to call home."

"That's not what I meant, child." She took off her gardening gloves. "Surely you heard about the doctor? About the illness?"

"No. Are the girls sick? Are they all right?" Alarm shot through her. She loved those children. If anything happened to them—

"No, dear, it's not the twins."

Not the twins? Her brain stuck on those words, as

if unable to move past them, because then that would mean—

"Doc Frost came down with scarlet fever. Don't know when. I only heard it in church this morning. His case must not be severe if you're here. That's all I meant."

"Scarlet fever?" The trowel dropped from her fingers. Scarlet fever. Now her mind couldn't move past that terrible thought. She tore off her gardening gloves, suddenly unable to draw in enough air. No. Not Sam. It couldn't be. Aunt Ida had to be wrong. "Surely he's been ill with that before. He's a doctor."

"Molly." The older woman left her weeding, stepped over the baby beans and into the potato row. Her hands were gnarled from age but warm with love as they cradled Molly's face. "This morning at my Ladies' Aid meeting, we said a prayer for his recovery."

Then it was true. The strength seeped from her bones. The thought of Sam lying in bed suffering— She closed off that image. It was one she couldn't stand. She reached out in prayer. *Watch over him, Lord. Please spare him. Please see him safely through.*

"Are you all right, Molly?"

"Yes." She had to be. "What about the girls?"

"As far as I know they're fine. Kathleen Finley was at the meeting and she said they were showing no symptoms. I believe they are all staying at a hotel."

"Then who is caring for Sam?" She wasn't aware of the tears on her face. Only the fear that she would never see him again. The man she loved. The man who had proposed to her, offering her everything he had—family, marriage, home, hearth and children— everything except his heart. Scarlet fever was a serious illness. If she lost him. If he died with the way things were between them—

"I have to go." She bounded to her feet, in a dither, panic thick in her blood. The sun was setting. It was all she could think. Time was running out.

"Then go, dear. I'll finish here. Go to him, this man you love."

She thanked her aunt and ran for the barn amid the darkening shadows.

He was caught in shadows. They clung to him like smoke, blotting out everything. He couldn't see the trees or the sky or one single color. Where were the girls? He worried about his daughters. Were they lost, too? Feverish, he tossed and turned, searching for them. The smoke thinned, and he was able to see them, running merrily through gray fields. But he was still worried. He couldn't stop searching. There was someone else lost in the shadows.

A cool cloth brushed against his brow, dabbing blessed relief against his fever. He wasn't sure if he opened his eyes or if it was part of the dream. A beautiful woman gazed down at him, her rich golden hair down in braids, her sculpted oval face wan with exhaustion, and her eyes the most beautiful blue he had ever seen. Perhaps because of the love he saw there, pure and true, as sincere as a Shakespearean sonnet.

It seemed to him the shadows disappeared. The smoke released its hold on him and slinked away. The world around him became fuzzy. He lifted his head from the pillow, trying to see more. He recognized the blurry shape of the bedside lamp, and his four-poster bed. The opened curtains let in a blinding splash of sunlight. Had the sky ever been that clear? The grass so green? He could not remember noticing before.

"Lie back, Sam." The tone of her voice was his most cherished sound. He drank in the notes of it. He hadn't realized how much he would miss her gentle alto.

He let her push him into the pillows, the effort to lift his head had exhausted him. He panted, his body trembling with weakness. "You're here."

"Yes, I had to help." Sadness dimmed her like a candle in a harsh wind. "The doctor from Newberry says you are going to be all right. The worst has passed."

"Good to know." It didn't feel past. He hated he was too weak to do more than lay his hand on hers. The simple touch enriched him. She was the reason for the color in his life. She was the reason to believe in love again. "You came."

"I had to. The way we left things—" Regret marked her pretty features. She shrugged her slender shoulders, a gesture of helplessness or maybe, just maybe, despair. "Abner needed help tending you."

Yes, he saw her clearly. This time without the shadows of his experience and the smoke of his fears. He wrapped his fingers through hers, holding on tight. "There's something I didn't tell you before. When I asked you to marry me."

"Sam, I nearly lost you." Tears pooled in her eyes. "But for the life of me I cannot marry without—"

"—love," he finished for her. His throat hurt, his head pounded, he could barely breathe. But he had to say this. He did not want to close his eyes and become lost in the shadows again. He did not want to live without her. He wasn't afraid anymore. A woman who would sit by his side through the illness that had taken her daughter and her loved ones was someone who would stay beside him forever.

"I love you, Molly," he rasped. "I have loved you all along. I will love you through all the days of our life together if you let me. If only you will—"

"—marry you?" She finished his thought, his question. A single tear rolled down her soft cheek. "I'll only do it for love."

"For love," he agreed. He closed his eyes with a smile on his face and love in his heart.

Epilogue

One year later.

Molly McKaslin Frost felt watched as she sat in her cushioned rocking chair in the sunny parlor with her latest book in hand. She paused in the middle of Edward's offer of marriage to Elinor and looked around for the cause of the disruption.

A cow with a white blaze down her face poked her head further across the sill, reaching as far as she could with her tongue. Her gentle brown eyes focused on the half-eaten apple crisp on the end table just out of reach.

"Do the girls know where you are?" Molly set down her book and held the plate for the cow. Two slurps and the dessert disappeared. Sukie licked her lips and gave a moo, presumably a bovine word of thanks.

"Sukie! There you are!"

"Bad Sukie! You got away again."

Molly set the plate aside just as the twins rode into sight on their pony. Trigger sniffed the air, apparently unhappy he was a few seconds too late for the apple crisp. Love filled her up until she glowed as she studied her daughters. Penelope wore a blue calico dress and Prudence wore green. Happy, the girls waved at her.

"Ma! Can we get more apple crisp?"

"We're preparing the fort for a siege."

"Then it's important you have adequate dessert. I'll bring some out to the garden gate."

"Thank you!" The twins chimed in unison. Prudence grabbed Sukie's halter lead, Penelope snapped the reins and they rode off together, her little band of soldiers.

In the kitchen, Mrs. Finley looked up from her church paper. "The pot roast ought to be done soon. I suppose I should put on the potatoes."

"If you want to wait a few minutes, I'll be free to help you." She quickly found two plates, choosing ones that had already been chipped on previous fort sieges, and sliced into the apple crisp pan. As she worked, she could hear the girls through the open window.

"Pa! Pa! You're home."

"Surprise. Having a second doctor around these parts sure does help." Sam sounded chipper, as if his rounds had gone well.

A lot was going well these days. They had married last June, and every day of their marriage had been bliss. True love made the difference, for it was the kind of love that endured.

She hopped outside into the lilac-scented air. She felt weightless as she bounded down the garden path. When Sam came into sight, her heart soared, her soul uplifted. Her husband was home. "Hello, handsome."

"Howdy, pretty lady." He tipped his Stetson in greeting. "Any chance that apple crisp is for me?"

"It's for us, Pa!"

"Us and Sukie and Trigger."

The twins thanked her for the dessert and rode off, bouncing on the pony's broad back. Sukie followed happily, tail swishing.

"Come here, beautiful. I missed you." He unlatched the garden gate and held out one hand.

"I missed you, too." She laid her fingers against his broad palm, and the connection that sparked between them was pure loving sweetness. Just as in all the books, this was her ever after, her storybook ending. She let her husband draw her into his strong arms and hold her against his iron chest. She savored the comfort and joy. She tipped her face up to look at him, this man of her dreams.

"Have I told you lately how much I love you?" He brushed a kiss to the tip of her nose.

"Not lately, no. This morning, yes. After lunch, yes. But not since."

"I'm remiss." Tenderly, he kissed her, sweet and slow. "I love you, Molly."

"I love you." She went up on tiptoe to kiss his chin. What an amazing man. His love had changed her life. He had given her his heart and his daughters. He had made her a wife and a mother again. He had given her more happiness than she could hold. God was truly gracious indeed. "I think we are going to be very happy forever."

"I think so, too, my love." He kissed her again, as gently as any romantic hero.

My love. She held him tight, savoring the sweetness and the joy.

* * * * *

Victoria Bylin fell in love with God and her husband at the same time. It started with a ride on a big red motorcycle and a date to see a *Star Trek* movie. A recent graduate of UC Berkeley, Victoria had been seeking that elusive "something more" when Michael rode into her life. Neither knew it, but they were both reading the Bible.

Five months later they got married and the blessings began. They have two sons and have lived in California and Virginia. Michael's career allowed Victoria to be both a stay-at-home mom and a writer. She's living a dream that started when she read her first book and thought, *I want to tell stories*. For that gift, she will be forever grateful.

Feel free to drop Victoria an email at VictoriaBylin@aol.com or visit her website at victoriabylin.com.

Books by Victoria Bylin

Love Inspired Historical

The Bounty Hunter's Bride
The Maverick Preacher
Kansas Courtship
Wyoming Lawman
The Outlaw's Return
Marrying the Major
Brides of the West

Visit the Author Profile page
at Harlequin.com for more titles.

HOME AGAIN

Victoria Bylin

Sons are a heritage from the Lord,
children a reward from him. Like arrows in the
hands of a warrior are sons born in one's youth.
—*Psalms* 127:3–4

For my mother, Darlene Bylin McLeary.
Mom, you're the best… I love you lots!

Chapter One

Guthrie Corners, Colorado May 1890

Cassiopeia O'Rourke had been named for a constellation, but Heaven couldn't have been further away as she stepped inside the Guthrie Corners sheriff's office. Behind the steel bars sat her twelve-year-old son, looking not the least bit sorry he'd thrown a rock through a window. The *church* window, Cassie reminded herself. She couldn't think of a better way to fan the fires against them.

Since coming home a month ago, she'd wondered every day if she'd done the right thing for Luke. They'd been living in a poor Chicago neighborhood in a tiny flat, one she could barely afford on a bookkeeper's salary, when she'd received a letter informing her she'd inherited her father's mercantile business. The day before, she'd caught Luke in the alley lighting trash on fire. The day before that, he'd been disciplined at school for foul language. Where he'd learned such words, she couldn't imagine. And before that... Cassie sighed. The list went on for a mile.

She'd hoped that moving to Guthrie Corners would give Luke a second chance, that by taking him away from his so-called friends she'd find the sweet boy who'd enjoyed her hugs. Judging by the visit she'd received from Pastor Hall a few minutes ago, she'd been wrong…again.

As she looked around the sheriff's office, her regrets were legion but none were greater than the regrets concerning Deputy Gabe Wyatt. He stood in front of her now with a glint in his eyes and his arms loose at his sides. Dressed in brown trousers, a dark blue shirt and a leather vest, he seemed stronger than ever. His face had a familiar calm, but his hair, wavy and the color of tarnished gold, looked as if he'd raked his hand through it. If he'd been dealing with Luke, he probably had.

Cassie forced herself to hold his gaze until his eyes darted from her face to her toes, then back up. There was nothing personal about his perusal, no sense of the past and kisses they'd shared. He'd taken her measure as if she were a stranger. With her son behind bars, he'd doubtlessly found her lacking as a mother. Fine, Cassie thought. Let him judge her. Others had. Right or wrong, everyone in Guthrie Corners had an opinion on Cassie Higgins O'Rourke.

What kind of mother lets her child run wild like that?

As if she could keep Luke in a cage.

What kind of mother doesn't volunteer at church?

One who ran her own business, a failing one thanks to gossip and grudges.

What kind of woman would leave Gabe Wyatt at the altar?

A stupid one.

As Cassie raised her chin, Gabe crossed his arms over his chest. Fourteen years ago she could have had those arms around her. She could have been his wife. She wouldn't have traded Luke for anything, but she deeply regretted her marriage to Ryan O'Rourke. A long time ago she'd chased after a lie. Instead of settling down with Gabe, she'd run away to Chicago to become an actress. The stage…excitement…freedom. She'd found two of the three. She'd acted in one play and had been swept off her feet by Luke's father, but freedom had eluded her.

Between her wretched marriage, empty pockets and troubled son, Cassie felt as trapped as the constellation for which she'd been named. A vain queen, Cassiopeia had been chained to a chair in the night sky. No matter how the earth turned, she sat with her neck bent in shame. Cassie lived with the same disgrace. She didn't want to look Gabe in the eye, but she had to be strong for Luke.

As she raised her head, he lowered his chin. "Hello, Cassie."

"Good afternoon, Deputy." It didn't seem right to call him Gabe. She'd lost that privilege.

His eyes narrowed with irritation. "I take it Reverend Hall spoke to you."

"Yes."

"So you know why Luke's here."

"I do." Her insides started to shake. The longer she looked at Gabe, the more she wanted to beg for his forgiveness. She'd tried to apologize when she'd first arrived. She'd sent a note asking him to come by the store, but he'd ignored it. Looking at him now, she saw a rock wall. She would have blurted her apologies, but she couldn't speak to Gabe in front of Luke. Gabe deserved as much privacy as she could give him, and Luke needed her undivided attention. She turned to the cell where he lay sprawled on the cot with his hands behind his head, one leg bent and the other stretched as if he didn't have a care in the world. The pose struck her as vain. The boy had inherited Cassie's looks, but he had his father's arrogance.

She doubted he'd obey, but she had to try. "Luke, sit up. This concerns you."

He made a snoring sound.

Cassie made her voice stern. "This *isn't* a request."

Luke grunted. For an instant she thought he'd obey, but instead he switched the position of his legs and sighed.

Her cheeks flamed with embarrassment. What could she do? Take away his allowance? She'd already cut it to nothing. Resort to spanking? Hardly. Cassie knew how it felt to be hit and couldn't abide violence. Besides, Luke had grown four inches this year. He could look her in the eye and probably outweighed her.

With her mouth in a firm line, she turned to Gabe. "I apologize for my son. Of course we'll pay for the window."

"Fine," Gabe said. "But there's no 'we' here."

Cassie stiffened. "What do you mean?"

"Luke broke the window. He's the one who has to pay."

"Of course, but he's a child."

Gabe eyed her thoughtfully, then shot a glance into the cell. Her son made another snoring sound.

Cassie's cheeks flamed. "Luke! Stop that."

As soon as the order left her mouth, she regretted it. She'd just waved a red flag in front of a bull. Just as she feared, Luke let out a belch that would have made Henry VIII proud. Embarrassed to the core, she looked at Gabe. Instead of judgment in his eyes, she saw a twinkle. Cassie saw no humor in the situation at all. She started to speak, but Gabe gave a tight shake of his head.

Winking at her, he called out to Luke. "Nice job, kid. But it's going to cost you."

She opened her mouth to ask what, but Gabe put his finger to his lips to silence her. Cassie bristled. She didn't take orders from anyone, especially not from arrogant men, but she sensed Gabe's wisdom. Besides, she had nothing to lose. The situation with Luke couldn't get much worse.

She nodded her agreement, then looked at her son lying like a lump on the gray blanket. He drummed his fingers on the wall, then burped again. Cassie bit her lip. Twenty seconds later, Luke belched a third time. Mortified, she turned to Gabe. Before she could speak, he silenced her with a look.

Cassie didn't like being treated like a child. Even more upsetting, she couldn't bear the quiet. Growing up in the Higginses' household, she'd endured family meals where no one said a word. She'd learned to despise silence, especially at night when she looked at the stars. She'd long ago stopped praying for herself, but every night she asked the Lord to look after her son. In those dark hours, she heard nothing.

Now, to her amazement, she heard a wealth of sound…the rasp of Gabe's breath, the beat of Luke's fingers on the wall. The clock ticked and a wagon rattled by. Calmer, she risked a glance at her son. To her amazement, he'd raised his head and was staring at Gabe. The lawman didn't move a muscle.

Luke finally broke the silence. "What's it going to cost me?"

"On your feet, kid."

To Cassie's amazement, he complied. He moved like a snail and he didn't look happy, but he stood up.

"That's good," Gabe said. "Now apologize to your mother."

More silence.

This time Cassie enjoyed it. She knew how patient Gabe could be. The only time he'd rushed her had been about their wedding. She'd been seventeen and had wanted to wait a year. He'd been eager and had pushed for June. She'd said yes to please him, but in most matters Gabe had the patience of Job. The thought sent a pang from her head to her heart. How long had he waited for her at the church?

Luke must have sensed Gabe's stubbornness, because he turned to her. "Sorry, Mother."

Her heart ached with fresh pain. She didn't want to be *Mother*. She wanted to be "Mama" again, or "Ma" because it fit his age. The way Luke said "Mother," she felt like a shrew.

Gabe glowered at the boy. "You got the words right. Now say it like you mean it."

Cassie saw the hard set of Gabe's jaw and knew he'd stand here all day.

Luke must have realized it, too. He looked at his feet, then raised his head. His hair, dark and lanky, hung across his eyes. She'd tried to take him to the barbershop, but he'd fought her on it. He'd insisted he was too old to have his mother take him and that he'd go himself. He still hadn't done it.

To her relief, he looked sheepish. "I'm sorry, Ma."

In a five-minute standoff, Gabe had worked a miracle. Cassie's heart soared as she looked at Luke. "I accept. We'll talk more at home."

The boy, expecting to be released, looked at Gabe.

Instead of opening the cell door, Gabe hooked his thumbs on his belt. "Sit down, Luke. We're not done."

"Of course," Cassie said. "We—Luke—has to pay for the window."

"That's not enough," Gabe said.

"*And* he has to apologize to Reverend Hall," she added.

Gabe ignored her.

Confused, she followed his stare to Luke and saw what she'd come to call "the look." The boy stood with his neck slightly bent and an innocent expression pasted to his face. He looked as sweet as pie, but a smirk lurked behind his eyes. She'd seen that arrogance in Ryan O'Rourke when he'd come home after a night with another woman. She'd seen it in Luke, too. If her son thought he could get away with breaking the window, he was dead wrong. She had to make him understand, but how? What more could she do?

She was searching for an answer when Gabe faced her. "I'd like a word with you, Mrs. O'Rourke. In private."

"Of course."

She gave her son a look that promised a talking-to later, then followed Gabe out the front door.

She still smells good.

That was Gabe's first thought as he led Cassie to a patch of grass behind the jailhouse. He'd have preferred speaking to her out of public view, but he didn't want Luke to hear what he had to say. Neither did he want to be alone with her, but it couldn't be helped. Until now, except for an occasional glance through the window of Higgins Mercantile—part of his job, he told himself—he'd steered clear of Cassie O'Rourke.

The visit from Reverend Hall had changed everything. The minister had caught Luke throwing rocks at the church. He'd broken just one window, but judging by the arsenal at his feet, he'd planned to break them all. Luke had outrun Reverend Hall, but by a stroke of luck, fate or God's hand—Gabe believed in the third—the boy had plowed into him. The Reverend had caught up to them and Luke had landed in jail.

Now here he stood with Cassie. One look at her told Gabe the truth he'd fought for fourteen years. She'd wounded him to the core, but he hadn't stopped loving her.

Blinking, he flashed back to their so-called wedding day. He'd worried for a full hour before Reverend Hall had pulled him into his office and told him that Cassie was missing. When he'd gone to the house he'd built for her, he'd found the note she'd penned on fine stationery.

I'm sorry, Gabe. I just can't do it.

Why he'd kept the note, he couldn't say. But he had it tucked in the Wyatt family Bible, the one where he'd already written their names. Looking at Cassie now, he asked the question that had plagued him for fourteen years.

Why, Cassie? What couldn't you tell me?

The question hung in his mind like a hawk soaring against the wind. It just hung there, working hard but going nowhere. He wanted to ask it now but he wouldn't. Only a fool stuck his own head in a guillotine. He'd have ignored Cassie forever if it hadn't been for Luke. Gabe had a soft spot for fatherless boys. He'd been one himself…which got him to wondering. What had happened to Mr. O'Rourke?

Don't ask.

For the second time that day, he raked his hand through his hair. He couldn't let Cassie get close, but neither could he turn his back on her son. It would cost him to befriend Luke, but so would doing nothing. If he didn't do his best for the boy, Luke would keep getting into trouble and Gabe would have to deal with even bigger problems. He'd also be up all night with a guilty conscience. When push came to shove, he didn't have a choice in how he treated Luke. He hoped Cassie would go along with his plan.

When they reached the grass, he indicated the bench under an oak. The spot was next to the town library and a well-meaning soul had made it inviting with daffodils now in bloom, the stone bench and a swing hanging from a thick branch.

Cassie stayed on her feet. Either she hadn't seen his gesture or she'd ignored it. Looking nervous, she faced him. "Luke's not a bad boy. He's just—"

Gabe held up a hand to stop her. He heard the same speech every time he dealt with a fatherless kid like Luke.

He's really a good boy.

He didn't mean to do it.

Gabe didn't begrudge Cassie's defense of her son. That's how mothers loved their children. They saw the best and believed the best. Only now, with Luke throwing rocks, she had to face facts. Broken windows led to bank robberies, prison, even death at the end of a noose. He had to get her attention.

"Mrs. O'Rourke, your son's in trouble." He thought of her as Cassie and always would, but earlier she'd called him "Deputy." It had rankled him.

She looked put off. Gabe wondered if the formality irked her the way it irked him, then chastised himself for the thought. It didn't matter how she reacted. She clearly didn't love him. If she had, she wouldn't have left him at the altar twiddling this thumbs with a gold band in his pocket. He didn't mean to scowl at her, but he'd never gotten over the embarrassment. Half the town had been in the pews. The pity had just about killed him.

Cassie looked down at the grass. "Luke has problems. I know that."

Her voice dropped so low, he barely heard her. "When did the trouble start?"

"A while ago."

"Before you came to Guthrie Corners?"

"Yes."

She was still staring at the grass. He wanted to tell her to look him in the eye, but he feared the shine of tears. He settled for looking at the crown of her head, where her dark curls were twisted into a knot. In the sunlight he saw strands of red and remembered thinking she had pretty hair. She still did.

Fool! He had to keep his mind on Luke and off the boy's mother.

Cassie dropped down on the bench. Instead of meeting Gabe's gaze, she stared at the bars marking Luke's cell and spoke to the wall. "Luke's the reason I came home instead of selling the store."

He'd figured as much, though part of him had wondered if—even after all this time—she'd come for him. Did she think of him at all? Apparently not.

"We lived in Chicago," she continued. "Luke made new friends—the wrong kind, if you know what I mean."

Gabe knew very well. "It happens."

"Maybe, but not to *my* son." Cassie finally raised her chin. "I'll do anything for Luke. I know he's in trouble. I see it in his eyes. He's—" She looked down, pressed her hands to her cheeks and gulped air. As her shoulders swelled and shook, he thought of a flustered bird trying to protect itself.

In his line of work, Gabe dealt with lots of crying women. He knew the power of a strong shoulder and often played the big brother. It came with the job, but this was Cassie and he didn't feel the least bit brotherly. Even so, how could he leave her to weep? He couldn't. Wise or not, he sat next to her and put his arm around her shoulders. The next thing he knew, she'd pressed her cheek against the top part of his vest. Nothing but leather, muscle and bone separated her tears from the very heart she'd broken.

She was trying to talk, but Gabe couldn't make out the words. Nor did he want to. She'd broken his heart once and could do it again. He had to keep his distance. He had to remember that day in church and the months that followed. They'd stretched into long, lonely years. He wanted a wife and had done some courting, but no one had measured up to Cassie. He'd loved her that much. He still did, but he hated what she'd done to him.

Forgive her.

The command came from his conscience. He knew that Jesus had died for him. Like every other sinner on earth, he was an imperfect man with imperfect thoughts. Christ had died for Cassie's mistakes, too.

Gabe knew that truth in his marrow, but common sense told him to let sleeping dogs lie. As the saying went, "Once bitten, twice shy."

He waited until her sobs eased, then he lifted his arm from her shoulders. As he stood and walked to the cottonwood, Cassie removed a hankie from her drawstring bag and dabbed at her eyes. "This is embarrassing. I don't usually cry."

I know. Before today she'd never cried on his shoulder. During their courtship, he'd admired her strength. Now he wondered what she'd been hiding from him. He clamped his jaw tight and leaned against the smooth bark of the tree. He had to focus on the business at hand. "It's understandable. You're worried about your boy."

"More like panicked," she said ruefully. "I've disciplined him every way I know, but nothing works."

"That's because he's mad at the world."

She sighed. "And especially at me."

"That's a good sign," he replied. "It shows you're trying."

"I am, but nothing helps. I'm at a loss."

"I'm not," he said confidently. "Luke wants to be a man. He just doesn't know how."

Her eyes widened with understanding. "I hadn't thought of that."

Gabe didn't want to ask the next question, but he needed to know for Luke's sake. "It's none of my business, but where's the boy's father?"

"I don't know and I don't care." She bit off each word. "He's not a part of our lives."

Questions swirled in Gabe's mind, but only one answer mattered. Whoever he was, this O'Rourke character had hurt Cassie. For years he'd taken comfort in the notion she'd found happiness. Apparently not. O'Rourke had left her with a son and a mess to clean up. Gabe knew all about boys, messes and broken glass. He crossed his arms over his chest. "Luke broke the law. That means I'm involved."

"Of course."

"Here's the plan." He spoke with deliberate authority. If Cassie reacted like most mothers, she'd cringe at what he had to say. "Luke spends tonight in jail."

"Jail!"

"That's right," he insisted. "Locked behind bars with nothing to do but think."

"But—"

"He needs a taste of the future he's chosen."

Cassie's breath whooshed from her chest. "But he's so young—"

"He's old enough to break windows," Gabe said dryly. "My deputy usually stays the night when we have a prisoner, but if it makes you feel better, I'll stay myself."

Her eyes clouded. "I just don't know—"

"Cassie." Her name slipped out unbidden. "Luke isn't a boy anymore. The more you baby him, the angrier he's going to get. If he wants to play rough, fine. We'll play rough."

Her brows snapped together. "What do you mean by *rough?*"

The question irked him. "Nothing physical. You know that."

"I do." She twisted the hankie. "I just wish—"

"Don't waste your breath." He didn't want to go down any road that led to the past. "Tomorrow's Sat-

urday, so there's no school. I'll have him apologize to
Reverend Hall, then we'll fix the window. I'll show
him how, but he's going to do the work himself."

She looked resigned. "I should pay for the glass."

"I'll get it from the hardware. Luke can do chores
around the church to pay me back."

Her eyes filled with relief. "How can I ever thank
you?"

By telling me why you left. Except he didn't want to
know. "I'll tell Luke he's been sentenced to a night in
jail, fixing the window and chores, but there's something important *you* have to do."

"What's that?"

"Stay away from the jail. Don't bring him supper or
even his school books. Nothing. Do you understand?"

She looked miserable. "He's growing like a weed.
He'll be hungry."

"I'll see that he eats." He'd get meat loaf at Millie's. Dessert, too. If Luke behaved, he'd eat like a
king. If he didn't, he'd miss out on the best chocolate
cake in town. "Don't interfere, Cassie. It's called jail
for a reason."

When she nodded with understanding, he wondered
what jails had held *her*. Those places might not have
had bars, but he felt certain they'd been dark and cold.

He indicated the building. "I better get back."

As they left the grass, Cassie walked at his side. It
would have been the most natural thing in the world
to put his hand against her back to guide her. Instead
he kept his arms loose at his sides...loose and ready,
though he didn't know for what.

Chapter Two

Cassie walked the four blocks to Higgins Mercantile with her head high, but the effort made her neck ache. People stared as she passed, but no one smiled or said hello. She knew why. She just didn't know what to do about it. Maude Drake, an old rival, had been spreading rumors. Cassie had her faults, but she didn't cheat her customers. Neither had she lived in sin with Luke's father as Maude had implied.

The thought made her furious. She'd been innocent when she'd married Ryan O'Rourke. Stupid, too. She'd confused charm with character, a mistake she'd never repeat. Gabe had both. Once she'd seen his reasoning, leaving Luke in his care didn't worry her at all. Her reluctance came from a sense of debt. She already owed him amends for jilting him. Today, when she'd broken down, she'd tried to apologize but he'd cut her off. How could she put the past behind her when it weighed on her every thought?

Sighing, she unlocked the front door of her shop. When she'd first arrived, the display areas had been full of the same clutter she recalled from her childhood. She'd moved it to a storeroom and written to the merchandiser at Russell's Department Store in Chicago, the place she'd worked as a bookkeeper. The buyer for Russell's had been enthused about her venture and had approached Jacob Russell himself. The end result had been a business arrangement where Cassie sold Russell goods on consignment. If she succeeded, she and Luke could live comfortably.

Looking at the displays—pretty dishes, shiny cookware—she had dark visions of having to return it unsold. She'd had two customers in a week, but only if she counted both Pastor Hall and Thelma, his wife. Out of habit, Cassie looked at the window where her father had put a chalkboard showing the time he'd be back whenever he left the store. With business so slow, she hadn't thought to put it up. She ached to go upstairs to her apartment, but instead she took a feather duster from behind the counter and headed for a display of thimbles.

As she swished the ostrich feathers, the doorbell jingled. She looked up and saw Thelma. The minister's wife had been like a sister to Cassie's mother. When Bonnie Higgins had died of apoplexy, Thelma had taken Cassie under her wing.

The older woman paused at the dish display. "These are beautiful."

Cassie loved the fine china. With only Luke at her table, she couldn't justify buying a set for herself, but she sometimes closed her eyes and imagined a table set for the husband and children she'd never have.

"They're practical *and* pretty," Thelma added. "If the women in this town had a lick of sense, they'd ignore Maude and look for themselves."

"I wish they would." Cassie gave the shelf a last flick with the ostrich feathers, then faced Thelma. "I'm sorry about the church window."

"Of course, you are."

"Luke will make it right, I promise."

Thelma's lips curved into a sad smile. "It's not easy being a mother, is it?"

"No." Cassie choked up. To hide her eyes, she went back to dusting.

Thelma came to her side. "I know you love your boy, Cassie. Deep down, he knows it, too."

With anyone else, she could have managed a brazen lift of her head. With Thelma, she could only be herself. "I'm so ashamed."

"You shouldn't be." The minister's wife put iron in her voice. "You're doing your best."

"I don't understand," Cassie continued. "He *knows* what he's doing is wrong."

Thelma squeezed Cassie's shoulders as if she were little again. "You're not alone, sweetie. There's not a mother in the world who hasn't lost sleep over a child. I hear the boy's spending the night with Gabe."

"Yes."

"That'll be good for him," Thelma said. "Now we need to take care of *you*. Let's go to Millie's for tea."

Cassie nearly wept at the thought. She couldn't remember the last time someone had made her a meal or poured her a cup of something hot. She steeped her own tea with the cheapest leaves, but it usually went cold while she did other things. The idea of sitting at a table and being served touched her to the core, but she saw a problem.

"I don't know," she said. "Millie and Maude are friends."

Thelma got a glint in her eye. "Never mind them. I want tea and you need it."

She also needed to talk. Seeing Gabe—speaking with him—had filled her with questions. Why hadn't he married? Was he happy? When she'd come home, she'd expected to find him with a wife and children. Instead she'd found a bachelor living in the house meant for her.

"Tea sounds good," Cassie replied.

She left the feather duster on the shelf, followed Thelma out the door and locked it behind her. Like before, she left the chalkboard blank. As they walked to the café, they passed a dozen people who'd been her father's customers. Most of them had been in the church when she'd jilted Gabe. She forced a few smiles but gave up after the third cold stare. Thelma greeted every person they met. A few remarked on the weather, but no one treated Cassie with warmth. As much as she wanted a cup of tea, she wished she'd stayed in the store. That feeling doubled when they walked into Millie's Café and Thelma made a beeline for a table in the front window.

"Let's sit in the back," Cassie said.

"Nonsense," Thelma answered. "It's a lovely day and you need the sun."

"But, Thelma—"

"Cassie, trust me. People need to see you."

But Cassie didn't want to be seen. She'd had enough hard looks today, but how could she say no to Thelma? By taking Cassie for tea, the minister's wife was waving a banner of love for the world to see. Determined to be worthy of the kindness, Cassie sat in the chair facing the door. She'd smile at everyone who walked by her.

When the waitress approached, Thelma ordered tea and a tray of petit fours. Cassie's mouth watered. Millie could be mean, but she knew how to bake.

"Now," Thelma said with an arch of her brow. "Tell me about the past fourteen years."

Cassie had visited with Thelma twice since coming home, but she'd been vague about her life in Chicago. She gave a rueful smile. "That would take all day."

"Then start with Luke," the older woman said softly. "Where's his father?"

Cassie blinked and recalled the night she'd left Ryan O'Rourke. He'd come home drunk and smelling of perfume. When she'd protested, he'd struck her. She'd fallen and hit her head. Barely conscious, she'd seen him heading for Luke's room and had cried out. The distraction had worked and Ryan had beaten her instead. Hours later, when he'd passed out drunk, she'd packed one bag and left with Luke in the middle of the night. It wasn't the first time Ryan had struck her, but it was the last. The next morning she'd hired an attorney and petitioned for divorce.

"It's an ugly story." She lowered her eyes. "Ryan turned violent. I left him for my sake but mostly for Luke's."

Thelma's mouth thinned to a line. "You did the right thing."

"I hope so, but Luke doesn't understand." Cassie felt a headache coming on. "We divorced seven years ago. Luke's never had a father and he blames me."

The waitress brought the tea and two pretty cups.

Thelma filled the first one for Cassie, laced it with sugar and handed it to her. "You're strong, Cassie. Your mother would be proud."

As Cassie raised the cup to her lips, she thought of mornings she'd sat at the breakfast table, drinking tea with her mother after her father had gone to the store. She'd been Luke's age when Bonnie Higgins fainted in the kitchen and died a day later. Cassie had been too young to know her mother as a woman. Now, as a woman herself, she missed her more than ever.

"I don't know," Cassie said as she pondered Thelma's question. "What would she say?"

"She'd tell you to hold your head high." The older woman sounded sure. "She'd also love Luke to pieces and spoil him rotten."

Cassie could see it. "She'd have read him Bible stories at bedtime."

Thelma smiled. "Boys like the ones about Pharaoh and frogs falling from the sky."

Cassie made a face. "Not me."

"You would if you heard Gabe tell it."

At the mention of his name, Cassie curled her fingers around the warm porcelain and thought about the day she'd clapped eyes on the handsome new sheriff. He'd come to town from Texas, a former cavalry officer and a bachelor to boot. They'd met at her father's store and she'd been smitten. She'd also been seventeen, practically a child. She'd loved him, but she had wanted to wait to get married. Her father—and Gabe—didn't see the point. Shuddering she recalled the night before her wedding. She'd been a wreck. Then her father had brought the journal written by her mother...

"Cassie?"

She looked up and saw a tray of petit fours. Thelma put a bite of cake with white frosting on a plate and handed it to her. "You looked a hundred miles away."

"More like fourteen years." She lifted her fork. "Gabe never married, did he?"

"No."

Cassie feared the answer, but she had to ask. "I wonder why."

Thelma's brows lifted. "Until now, I figured he hadn't met the right woman."

Until now... To avoid the trail of Thelma's thoughts, Cassie took a bite of cake. Their wedding cake would have tasted exactly like the frosting melting in her mouth. Millie had already baked it and friends had left gifts at the house Gabe had built for her. She knew from the one angry letter from her father that Gabe had returned each one personally. No wonder he'd never married...she'd hurt him that deeply.

She wished she hadn't gone down this road, but she couldn't turn around. Thelma was watching her like a hawk.

The older woman put down her fork. "Do you know what I think now?"

She couldn't bear the memories. "No, and I don't—"

Leaning closer, Thelma whispered so that only Cassie would hear. "I think Gabe's been waiting for you."

"Don't say that, Thelma."

"He loved you, Cassie. I know him. He's loyal."

"But I hurt him terribly."

"You were a scared, motherless girl," she said gently. "How old were you? Seventeen?"

"Old enough to know better." Cassie set down the fork. Her tea had gone cold and the cake made her sad.

"It *was* awful," Thelma replied. "But Gabe doesn't hold grudges. I saw his face when he learned Luke belonged to you. He seemed—"

"Bitter?" Cassie said.

"I was going to say tender."

He had been tender with her on the bench. He'd been wonderful with Luke, too. If he'd let her apologize, maybe they could be friends. But he'd slammed that door shut. She felt buried alive.

"I don't know what to do." She felt trapped at the table, stuck to her chair. "I've tried to talk to him, but he won't listen."

Thelma freshened Cassie's tea, then her own. "That's the problem with apologies. They're hard to make and hard to accept."

"Maybe," she said. "But I feel so guilty."

Before Thelma could reply, the door to the café swung open. In walked Maude Drake with her husband and son. William Drake owned the bank. Billy Drake had a new haircut and a smug gleam in his eyes. The meeting couldn't have occurred at a worse time. Talk of Gabe had left Cassie reeling.

Thelma turned to the Drakes. "Maude, William. It's nice to see you. You remember Cassie, don't you?"

Bless her good intentions, but Thelma was out of her mind. Next to Gabe, Cassie had hurt Maude more than anyone in Guthrie Corners. They'd been the same age, competing for the same boys. Cassie had been a beauty and she'd flaunted it. Maude had a simple prettiness, but Cassie had called her "Mule Face." For a while, the name had stuck. She'd have blurted an apology now, but she felt certain Maude would cause a scene.

The Drakes gave Thelma a curt nod, exchanged quiet words and left the restaurant. Millie let out a loud sigh, put her hands on her hips and glared at Cassie. "What you did in Chicago ain't none of my business, Cassie Higgins. But—"

"It's O'Rourke now," Cassie said. "*Mrs.* O'Rourke."

Millie snorted. "It should have been Mrs. Wyatt! What you did to Gabe—"

Thelma intervened. "Millie, stop it."

"And that boy of yours! He's a *brat.*"

Cassie pushed to her feet. "You can insult me all you want, but I will *not* tolerate you calling my son names."

"Fine," Millie declared. "But whatever you do, keep him away from my café. *Windows* are expensive."

So the news had already spread. Cassie felt weak in the knees. Thelma stood and put an arm around her waist. "Both of you," she said. "Shouting doesn't help anyone."

"It helps me," Millie declared. "Why that—"

The door opened again. When Cassie saw Gabe, she thought she might be sick. Ashamed and trembling, she ran for the door.

Twenty minutes later, Gabe set the picnic hamper on his work desk. It held covered dishes from Millie's cafe, but what he wanted most—answers—didn't fit in a wicker basket. Why had Cassie run away at the sight of him? It was none of his business, but he'd smelled trouble the instant he'd opened the restaurant door. When he'd asked Thelma and Millie if anyone needed help, they'd clammed up. They'd also given him two distinct but familiar looks. Millie had given him the "poor Gabe" look. It usually came with whispering behind his back. *Poor Gabe... Did you hear? That foolish girl jilted him!*

Thelma's eyes had held pity, too. But she'd been focused on Cassie. When she'd turned to Gabe, he'd seen what he called the "Mama" look. That particular spark belonged to mothers of marriage-minded daughters. Thelma didn't have a daughter of her own—she'd raised three boys—but she kept an eye out for the single women at Guthrie Corners Church. She'd given up on Gabe a long time ago, but today she'd looked inspired again.

He refused to think about why. Neither did he want to think about Cassie fleeing the café with her face in a knot. She was none of his concern. Luke, on the other hand, needed his full attention. Tonight he'd get it.

Gabe had left his deputy, Peter Hughes, filling out the daily journal while he fetched supper. He turned to the desk across from his bigger one. "Go on home, Pete."

The young man shoved to his feet. "Don't mind if I do. The wife's making chicken and dumplings."

A newlywed, Pete bragged every day about his wife's cooking. He'd invited Gabe for supper a few times, but those evenings had been tedious. Married couples, especially young ones that gawked at each other, reminded him of Cassie and the life he'd been denied.

As Pete walked out the door, Gabe looked into the cell. He saw Luke on the cot on his back, still staring at the ceiling. Gabe had often thought of writing a message up there, maybe a Bible verse or just "Caught you looking." He had a plan tonight. If Luke minded his manners, he'd get dessert. If he acted like a mule, he wouldn't. Gabe wanted to make it easy for the boy to behave, so he used his friendliest tone.

"Hey, Luke," he called. "Are you hungry?"

"Nope."

So the boy wanted to play tough... Fine, Gabe thought. He was older, wiser and he'd once been a twelve-year-old boy with a bottomless pit for a stomach. Luke was armed with only a bad attitude. Gabe had an arsenal of meat loaf, mashed potatoes, gravy, corn and chocolate cake. He spoke to the boy through the bars. "Let me know if you change your mind."

He opened the basket, put the food on his desk and unwrapped the napkin from his plate. In the drafty jail, the aroma would reach the kid in seconds.

Next he jangled the silverware. "If you get hungry, Luke, you need to wash up. There's a full pitcher on the shelf and a washbowl under the cot."

His own hands were clean enough, so he sat down and took the first bite of meat loaf. He usually read the Guthrie Corners Gazette while he ate, so he snapped it open now, folded it back and set it down so he could eat and read at the same time. Three bites later, he heard the trickle of water from the pitcher, looked up and saw Luke filling the washbowl. The sight of the kid's narrow shoulders and gangly arms filled Gabe with memories.

I want kids, Cassie.

Me, too.

She'd looked solemn as she'd replied. He'd attributed her reaction to shyness at the thought of babies being conceived. Now he wondered if something else had made her reluctant.

Fool!

He had to stop wondering about the past. With Cassie's son ten feet away, the challenge bordered on impossible. In order to help Luke, he had to get to know the boy. The effort meant listening to him, even asking questions.

How did you like Chicago?

Tell me about your friends.

What happened to your father?

No way would Gabe ask that last question. It was the most important, but the answers needed to come from Cassie, not a confused boy.

When Luke finished washing, he faced Gabe. The boy had his mother's dark hair, the shape of her face. His eyes, though, had come from his father. They were brown and held a glint. Judging by Luke's age, it hadn't taken long for Cassie to latch on to another man. Had O'Rourke charmed her? Or had she truly been in love? He didn't know which would be easier to forgive—foolishness or sincerely loving another man.

Gabe thought of inviting the boy to sit at the desk but decided against it. Freedom would taste sweeter after a full night behind bars. He put Luke's meal on a tray—no cake yet—bent down and slid it through an opening in the grate at the bottom of the cell. The boy looked at the food on the floor and glowered. No man liked to bend down. Neither did twelve-year-old boys, but humility was part of Luke's lesson. Even so, Gabe didn't believe in embarrassing a man. To give the boy some dignity, he turned his back and walked to his desk. As he sat, he heard Luke lift the tray and carry it to the cot.

Some jailhouses fed prisoners gruel as punishment, but Gabe didn't see the benefit. He'd locked up men of the worst kind, but most were trail trash who hadn't eaten a square meal in days. A full belly reminded a man of what he'd traded for thievery, whiskey and bad habits. He kept a Bible in the cell, too. More than a few hardened souls had cracked it open. One had wept like a baby and asked Gabe to pray with him. It had been a humbling experience for them both.

As he ate his supper, Gabe scanned the newspaper. The words blurred into nonsense, mostly because he kept hearing Luke's fork against the tin plate. Judging by the eager scrapes, silence and hunger had softened the boy's attitude. Gabe had already told him about his "sentence," but they hadn't talked about putting in the window.

He pushed his plate aside. "So Luke, what do you know about carpentry?"

The boy shrugged. "Nothing."

"Ever build anything?"

"Like what?" He sounded suspicious.

"I don't know." Gabe had built lots of things. He'd been the man of the family from the age of ten. "I made a rifle rack when I was your age."

Luke scraped the last of his gravy, then looked up with a scowl. "I don't know how to do nothin' like that."

"*Anything* like that," Gabe corrected.

"I know." The kid sighed. "My ma's always telling me stuff like that."

"She's a good woman." He hadn't meant to go down that road, but Luke had gone first.

"She's all right," the boy said. "It's just…"

"Just what?" Gabe prodded.

"I miss my pa."

Gabe did *not* want to hear about the man who'd given Cassie this child. Anger coursed through his veins—at her, at O'Rourke—but he tamped it down. Only Luke mattered. If he had to bear a few lashes from the whip of jealousy, so be it.

"What happened to him?" he said quietly.

The boy shrugged. "I don't know."

As much as Gabe wanted to let the subject drop, he couldn't leave Luke twisting in the wind. The boy had a haunted look that Gabe knew all too well. The "whys" of life couldn't always be answered, but neither could they be forgotten. For Luke's sake, he decided to push.

"Did he leave you and your ma?"

The boy shook his head. "We left in the middle of the night. I didn't get to say goodbye."

So Cassie had left her husband the same way she'd left him, suddenly and secretly. He wondered how long ago she'd left, but he had no business quizzing Luke about his parents' marriage. On the other hand, Cassie had answers…all of them. She also had a son who bore scars. Luke, he decided, had been in jail long enough.

Gabe shoved to his feet, fetched the key and opened the door. "We've got chocolate cake for dessert. Want some?"

"Yeah!"

Just as he'd hoped, he'd taken the kid by surprise. Even four hours in a cell was enough to make freedom sweet. Luke put his plate on the tray and carried it out of the cell. He could have been at home clearing the table after supper. Gabe had no doubts about Cassie's commitment as a mother. Luke was a troubled boy, but he knew right from wrong. He had good manners and spoke as if he did his homework.

Gabe indicated the chair across from his own. As the boy sat, Gabe passed him the cake and a fork. As they ate, they talked about hammers and nails, glass, glue and how to use a saw. Gabe had a good time, but he knew that tonight, as he dozed on the cot and listened to Luke's soft snores, he'd be thinking of Cassie. Until now, he'd denied his need for answers. He'd learned to live without them, but for Luke's sake, he needed to ask about her husband.

For his own, he had to know why she'd left him at the altar. This Sunday after church, he'd ask.

Chapter Three

The last place on earth Cassie wanted to be on Sunday morning was the church where she'd jilted Gabe, but she had to bring Luke to the service. As part of his "sentence," he had to put away the hymnals and sweep the floor under Reverend Hall's supervision.

Getting Luke up for church had been a battle, but she'd had an even harder time getting herself ready. After Friday's embarrassment at the café, she'd stayed hidden in her store. Today she'd have to face Millie, Maude and worst of all, Gabe. She had to thank him for helping Luke. She dreaded getting a cold shoulder, but it had to be done. By doing the repair on Saturday, he'd spared her the humiliation of sitting in church with a broken window covered by boards.

As she and Luke walked into the sanctuary, her son pointed to the window he'd repaired. "There it is."

Cassie knew the value of praise. "You did a good job."

"Gabe showed me what to do."

Cassie could have wept at the pride in her son's voice. Even if Ryan O'Rourke had been a decent human being, he wouldn't have taken the time for Luke. He'd been obsessed with his stage career...not to mention young actresses. In an afternoon, Gabe had given her son more than Ryan ever had.

With her head high, she guided Luke to the pew next to the new glass and sat. Sunlight fell across her green dress, turning it as pale as dry grass. The warmth loosened the muscles in her neck and she wondered if someday she'd feel forgiven for her mistakes. As she studied the altar, she saw a heavy table carved with grapevines and an empty cross high on the back wall. If she hadn't been desperate to avoid hostile stares, she'd have looked away. It was too easy to picture Gabe in a suit, standing in front of the table with a ring in his pocket...her ring.

Her cheeks flamed with the memory. What would it be like to hold up her head without an effort? To stop being Cassiopeia pinned to the sky with her neck bent in shame? Her throat tightened. She wanted to pray but didn't know where to start. Instead she listened to the murmur of voices as the congregation took their seats. Behind her, she heard the tap of boots coming down the aisle between the pews and the window. She didn't dare look up for fear of the man wearing them. She wanted to be composed when she faced Gabe, not struggling for an even breath.

The boots stopped at the edge of the pew. As a shadow fell across her lap, she heard Gabe's deep voice. "Good morning, Luke. Hello, Cassie."

"Good morning," she said.

"Hi, Gabe." Luke scooted over to make room for him. The boy had assumed Gabe wanted to sit with them. Cassie had no such presumption. Instead of moving closer to her son, she looked at Gabe.

He indicated the pew. "May I?"

"Of course." As she slid across the wood, Gabe lowered his tall body on to the seat. He had a well thumbed Bible in hand, the same one he'd owned for years.

He leaned forward and spoke quietly to Luke. "The window looks good."

"Yeah," said the boy.

Cassie searched for something hopeful to say. "It's a lot cleaner than the others."

Luke grimaced, but Gabe smiled. "Luke's next job is cleaning the rest of them. Isn't it, partner?"

The boy groaned. "I need a ladder."

"I'll get you one," Gabe said easily. "Rags, too."

Could reaching Luke be this simple? She'd known for years that he needed a father, but she'd learned a valuable lesson from Ryan's abuse. No father was better than a bad one. Sometimes she thought about remarrying for Luke's sake, but how could she? Deep down, she still loved Gabe. She always would, but she'd learned another lesson from her marriage. Never again would she depend on anyone. People changed, sometimes for the worse. Sometimes, like her mother, they died unexpectedly.

As the pianist struck the first chord of a hymn, Gabe tipped his head to the side and murmured so only she could hear. "I'd like to speak with you, Cassie. Right after church."

"About Luke?"

"No." His breath touched her ear. "It's about us."

Her stomach did a flip. At last she could apologize to Gabe. She couldn't think of a more fitting place for making amends than the church where she'd left him waiting. She nodded, then faced straight ahead. So did Gabe. The hymn, an old one called "Peace In The Valley," calmed her nerves. She had no hope that the slate could be wiped clean, but maybe today she could find peace of her own. Maybe they could be friends.

Gabe sang the hymn and read the Bible verse aloud with everyone else, but he didn't hear a word of Pastor Hall's sermon. It could have been about the weather for all he knew. Sitting next to Cassie had shot him back in time to the day she'd left. He'd stood in the church for an hour before Pastor Hall pulled him into his office and told him Cassie had gone missing. When the Reverend left to tell the congregation, Gabe's best man, a fellow deputy, had offered to buy him a drink. Gabe had said no. Whiskey numbed a man's misery, but it didn't cure it. Instead he'd gone alone to their future home where he'd found the note she'd slipped under the door. Sitting next to her now, he thought of the question he'd wanted to ask for fourteen years.

Why, Cassie? What made you leave?

Soon he'd have his answer, but what happened then? Her presence stirred the embers of an old dream, but he'd be a fool to breathe life into those feelings. If she ditched him again, he'd be the town laughingstock. Gabe had his pride, but he also loved Cassie and always would. He cared about Luke, too. They'd worked shoulder to shoulder fixing the window and he'd enjoyed himself. At times, he'd felt as if Cassie had never left and Luke were his son.

When Reverend Hall gave a loud "Amen," Gabe came to his senses. He'd made arrangements with the

Reverend to watch Luke while he spoke with Cassie in the man's office. It seemed fitting.

At the end of the last hymn, the three of them remained seated until the crowd cleared. When the sanctuary was close to empty, Gabe stepped into the aisle. Cassie, looking nervous, passed him. He put a hand on Luke's shoulder. "Reverend Hall will show you where the broom is."

The boy furrowed his brows but didn't fight.

Cassie paused and murmured to Luke. "I need to speak with Deputy Wyatt. I'll find you when we're done. Don't leave without me."

"All right, Ma." The boy turned and rolled his eyes at Gabe, as if to say, *See, she treats me like a baby.*

Disrespectful or not, the gesture was an improvement over outright rebellion. Gabe knew boys. They reached an age where, now and then, they needed to be treated like men. He clapped a hand on Luke's thin shoulder. "I know how it is," he said. "But mind your manners."

Grinning, Luke followed his mother.

Cassie reached Reverend Hall first. After praising the sermon, she thanked him for helping Luke. The Reverend clasped her hand. "My pleasure, Cassie. Please come back."

Instead of replying, she stepped into the vestibule. Reverend Hall greeted Gabe with a handshake, then led Luke to a closet to fetch a broom.

Gabe pointed Cassie down the hall to the Reverend's office. When they reached the closed door, he opened it and guided her inside. He'd been in the room a few times since their wedding day—when a man stumbled, he did well to admit it and move on—but today the space looked exactly as it had all those years ago. Dust motes floated in the light coming through the window, and the bookcases were still bursting with odds and ends in addition to leather-bound volumes of wisdom.

Gabe indicated one of the two chairs in front of the desk. "Have a seat."

With her back to him, Cassie touched the arm of the chair. As he moved to pull it out for her, she turned abruptly. Their eyes met across a distance of inches. Neither moved. Neither breathed. Fourteen years melted like ice in July.

"Why, Cassie?" The words rasped from his lips. "Why did you leave like that? Not even a word—"

She pressed her hands to her cheeks. "I'm so sorry, Gabe. What I did to you is unforgivable. It was the worst mistake of my life. I—"

"Don't do this," he said with a rumble. "I just want an answer."

"But—"

"*Why*, Cassie? What did I do wrong?

"It wasn't you, Gabe. It was me. I…" She dropped down on the chair and looked at the rug. "I was stupid."

"That's not good enough and you know it." He didn't mean to sound harsh. He'd promised himself he'd be matter-of-fact, but looking at Cassie now— smelling her hair, seeing the tiny mole high on her cheek—his blood pounded in his ears.

As she knotted her hands into fists, her knuckles turned as white as his anger. If he'd been alone, he'd have punched the wall. Instead he walked to the window and looked at a field of swaying grass. He thought of the Shepherd's Psalm and lying in green pastures by still waters, valleys and shadows, and finally goodness and mercy following him all the days of his life. At the moment, he felt neither good nor merciful.

Behind him Cassie took a breath. "I didn't plan to leave. It just...happened."

Gabe clamped his jaw. "I need more than that. I *deserve* more."

"Yes, you do." Her skirt rustled as she stood. He felt her eyes on his back but didn't turn as she cleared her throat. "The night before the wedding, I was so scared."

He'd been scared, too. "Everyone gets cold feet."

"Mine had turned to ice." Her voice wobbled. "What happened next didn't help. My father gave me my mother's diary. I felt as if she'd walked into the room, but then I started to read."

They were getting somewhere. "What did it say?"

As she peered over his shoulder, the glass caught a faded image of her face. She bit her lips, but they stayed gray as she spoke. "When I opened the book, I expected to hear my mother's voice in stories, maybe prayers. Instead she'd written in verse. Poems I guess, except they weren't pretty. She wrote about how much she regretted her life. She poured her misery into that book."

Gabe frowned. "That diary was personal. Your father had no business giving it to you."

"Maybe not, but he meant well."

"So you read the book and got scared," he said simply.

"Not exactly." Her eyes found his on the glass. "I read the book and realized I was seventeen years old.

I'd lived here my whole life. Like my mother, I felt trapped. I had dreams, silly ones but they mattered at the time. Getting married felt all wrong. It was too soon, too…everything."

Gabe dragged his hand through his hair. How many times had Cassie suggested they wait a year? At least three that he recalled. Instead of listening to her worries, he'd cajoled her into a short engagement. And why? Because he'd been tired of waiting for the privileges of marriage. Like most celibate men, he knew all about the burning coals in the book of Proverbs. Instead of waiting twelve months, his impatience had cost him fourteen years.

"I should have told you to your face," she said. "But I was afraid you'd talk me into staying."

He turned and looked into her blue eyes. "I would have tried, that's for sure."

"And I'd have crumbled."

In more ways than one… She'd have stayed and felt forever trapped. She'd have stopped being Cassie and he wouldn't have understood.

Standing straight, she held his gaze. "Thelma expected me to get dressed at the parsonage. My father wanted to walk me to the church, but I told him I was meeting my bridesmaids first. Instead of going to Thelma, I left that horrible note at the house and took the next train."

There it was…a pushy groom, a nervous bride and a bad case of cold feet. From the distance of time, he saw his part in it. "It wasn't all your fault, Cassie. I pushed you too hard."

"Even so—"

"Don't punish yourself," he said gently. "It's over."

She swallowed hard. "Can you ever forgive me?"

He already had. "We both made mistakes. I'm sorry for being impatient. Let's forgive each other and move on."

"Thank you, Gabe." She dabbed at her tears with her sleeve. "It doesn't matter now, but I want you to know... Leaving was the stupidest thing I've ever done."

Leaving Guthrie Corners or leaving *him?* He didn't know, but he wanted to wipe her tears with his thumb. Before he could decide what to do, she squared her shoulders. "You've been great with Luke. I can't thank you enough."

Mention of the boy pulled Gabe back to the problems at hand. "He's a good kid. I've been wondering what happened to his father."

Her eyes blazed. "He's not in the picture."

"I figured that." He counted it as good riddance. "For Luke's sake, I'd like to know more. The boy misses him."

"How do you know?"

"He told me."

Cassie frowned. "I don't want to talk about it."

Neither did Gabe, but he needed the whole story. According to Luke, she'd left O'Rourke the way she'd left Gabe—in secret and without a goodbye. Had she been justified, or did she always run at the first sign of trouble? Gabe had to know. If she'd changed, they had a chance at a future. If not, he'd be her friend and nothing more. He didn't like using Luke to pry, but the boy had a stake in her answer.

He kept his voice low. "I can't help your son if I don't know what happened."

With a quiet dignity, she raised her chin. "Ryan O'Rourke was a philandering two-bit actor. He charmed me like a snake and I fell for it. We got married at City Hall and I count it as the second worst mistake of my life."

They both knew what the first one had been. "You left because he cheated on you?"

"No," she said, drawing out the word. "I left because he hit me."

"Oh, Cassie—"

"He threatened Luke, too."

When she walked to the window and touched the glass, he imagined a moth trapped in a jar, spent and still. He wanted to pound Ryan O'Rourke into the ground. The man wasn't fit to walk this earth, let alone claim Cassie for his wife. A good woman was God's most precious gift. A smart man cherished her. He lived for her and he'd die for her, too. And Luke... What had the boy witnessed?

Two steps brought Gabe to Cassie's side. Without a second thought, he put his arm around her shoulders. "You were smart to leave."

"Was I?"

"Yes." Adultery. Assault. Ryan O'Rourke had thoroughly broken his vows. "How can you even doubt?"

A shudder raced up her spine. "Even with the infidelity, I'd have stayed for Luke's sake. You can see how much he needs a father."

"How old was he when you left?"

"Barely five," she said wistfully. "Ryan didn't fight the divorce, but only because I didn't ask for alimony. I worked as a bookkeeper to make ends meet. A neighbor watched Luke after school, but then he made new friends."

"And you came home to get him away from them."

"Exactly."

With his arm still around her, she tilted her face up and to the side. At the same instant, Gabe looked down. When her mouth parted in surprise, he trailed a finger down her cheek. Her breath caught and so did his. He wanted to kiss her… He wanted to go back to a week before the wedding and do things differently. Did Cassie share the same hope? He didn't know, but a kiss would reveal her answer.

Slowly, giving her time to say no, he angled his head above hers. When she stayed still, he cupped her chin. When her eyes drifted shut, he knew…then, suddenly a rock shattered the window.

Chapter Four

Broken glass…shattered dreams. Cassie pulled away from Gabe with her heart pounding and her eyes wide with shock. She'd almost kissed him. For a moment she'd gone back in time and been young and unencumbered. The broken glass at her feet was a sober reminder of Luke, why she'd come home and the sorry state of her reputation. She had nothing to give Gabe Wyatt except grief and public scorn, a point made clear by the glass sparkling at her feet.

As Gabe bolted through the office door, Cassie ran after him with thoughts of Luke flooding her mind. She wanted to believe the best of her son, but who besides Luke would break a window? She didn't think for a minute it had been an accident. Rocks didn't sprout wings and fly. Boys threw them.

Cassie caught up with Gabe as he trotted down the church steps. "How could he do that!" she cried. "After all you've done for him—"

"Don't jump to conclusions, Cassie."

To her, the evidence seemed overwhelming. Luke had become resentful after cleaning the church and retaliated. Or worse... Maybe he'd seen them about to kiss. Her stomach knotted. How would she explain *that* to her son? Had anyone else seen them? It seemed unlikely. The bright sun would have turned the glass into a mirror. They'd been in the shadows, but perhaps someone had seen them slip alone down the hall and had jumped to the wrong conclusion.

As they crossed the churchyard, Cassie scanned the path to town for Luke but saw nothing, not even dust. She turned to the meadow stretching north and saw only waving grass. To the west lay rolling hills that turned into distant, insurmountable mountains. She felt as if Luke were lost to her forever.

Pastor Hall approached from the side of the building with his black robe billowing behind him. He had his hand on Billy Drake's shoulder. Behind Billy, Cassie saw Maude and her husband dressed in their Sunday best, a black suit for Mr. Drake and a prim gray gown for Maude. They looked as polished as silver candlesticks. Cassie, dressed in a green frock with leg o' mutton sleeves, felt like a peacock.

Maude's gaze shot from her to Gabe and back again. Her lips quirked into a haughty half smile Cassie recognized from their youth. Maude looked ready to accuse her of everything from low morals to being a bad mother.

Cassie opened her mouth to apologize to Reverend Hall for Luke, but Gabe took command of the conversation. He hadn't worn his gun to church, but he had his badge and a natural authority.

He looked straight at Billy. "What happened?"

Billy had a chin as haughty as his mother's. "Luke broke the window. I saw him do it."

Gabe made a humming sound. "That's funny."

"Why?" Billy asked.

"Because I was looking out the window."

Cassie sealed her lips. Gabe had been looking at *her*, though she supposed a lawman was allowed to bend the truth in the course of seeking it.

Billy shrugged. "He threw the rock. You must have blinked or something."

Cassie held back a cringe. *Or something* would include nearly kissing her. His lips had been an inch from hers. She'd seen gentleness in his eyes, then a question and an offering of sorts. She'd been ready to grab that gift and hold tight, but the rock had brought her to her senses. People in Guthrie Corners hated her, especially Maude who looked as smug as a debutante in her new hat. Cassie recognized the haughty look because she'd seen it fourteen years ago in her own mirror. Back then, she'd thought she owned this town. Not anymore. She'd never hold her head high again.

She refocused on Gabe. He was looking at Billy with a flat expression that belied nothing. "What exactly did you see?"

Billy shrugged. "He picked up a rock and threw it."

"I wonder why?" Gabe asked.

"I dunno."

If Luke had spoken in that tone, Cassie would have told him to answer Deputy Wyatt's question *right now*. Maude, though, glared at Gabe as if he'd called Billy a liar.

Gabe didn't seem to notice. "It just seems odd. When someone throws a rock, there's usually a reason."

"Maybe he was mad."

"At what?" Gabe sounded conspiratorial, as if he were including Billy in a secret. Cassie flashed back to the jail where he'd used silence to break Luke. Billy had a different personality and different motives. Gabe, she realized, had become an expert in setting verbal traps. She'd have to be careful. If she didn't watch her words, she'd end up telling him that she still loved him.

Billy seemed eager to help. "I don't know why he got mad, but I saw him break the window. I told him to stop, but he ran away."

"What exactly did you say?" Gabe asked.

Billy's cheeks turned from pale to pink. Looking down, he played with the grass with the toe of his shoe. "I just said, 'Stop.'"

Cassie knew a half truth when she heard one.

So did Gabe. "Just stop, huh?"

"Yeah." Billy sounded defiant.

Gabe crossed his arms. "So you *saw* Luke throw the rock. And you said 'Stop.'"

"That's right."

Gabe stared straight into Billy's eyes. "You know what I can't figure out?"

"What?" Billy sounded defensive.

"Why would Luke throw a rock when you were standing right there? Unless *maybe* something else happened."

Billy's face raised his chin. "I *saw* it. I swear it!"

Whenever Luke talked like that, Cassie knew he was hiding the truth. He'd inherited his father's flare for drama. She glanced at the Drakes and saw nothing but pride. Reverend Hall hadn't said a word, but she looked at him now and saw the sad expression of a wise man. He, too, suspected Billy of lying.

Gabe's eyes glinted. "You need to 'fess up, Billy. Now."

Maude broke in with a shrill voice. "My son is *not* a liar, Gabe. You know that!"

The three of them went back a lot of years, but Maude's use of Gabe's first name struck Cassie as out of place in front of Billy. It undercut Gabe's authority. It also put Cassie in her place. *I know him... I belong here.* Cassie no longer belonged in this town, but she'd do anything for Luke. Right now, that included standing shoulder to shoulder with Gabe.

Ignoring Maude, he turned to Mr. Drake. "Sir, I believe your son is holding back."

The man's eyes glinted. "Perhaps you should speak to *Miss* O'Rourke's son—"

"It's *Mrs.* O'Rourke," Cassie insisted.

Maude lifted her chin. "Of course, it is."

Her words dripped like honey, sweet but sticky enough to cause a mess. Cassie wanted to tell Maude to jump in a lake, but antagonizing the woman would do no good. Cassie had made mistakes, but she'd done her best to clean up the mess. Why couldn't Guthrie Corners give her a chance?

Gabe stayed focused on Mr. Drake. "I'll speak to Luke, but I was hoping Billy could provide some information."

Mr. Drake opened his pocket watch, read the time, then shut it again. "Speak to him if you must, but we don't have all morning."

"I do," Gabe said easily.

With those two small words, Gabe had announced

he'd do whatever it took to find the truth. Until now, no one had ever believed in Luke or in Cassie. It felt good.

With her chin up, she followed Gabe's stare to Billy. She guessed the boy to be Luke's age, but he was maturing faster. Luke had grown two inches since Christmas, but he still had the stick-like body of a boy. Billy was taller, heavier and far more confident. In a fight, Billy would win hands down. He also looked just like his mother, a fact Cassie tried to overlook.

Gabe kept his voice mild. "Where were you standing when you saw Luke throw the rock?"

"By that tree." He pointed to a cottonwood.

"Why?"

"My mother told me to wait for her. She had to speak with Mrs. Hall about something important."

Cassie heard Maude's arrogance in the boy's voice. There'd been no need to inform them of his mother's importance. Everyone knew Maude ran Guthrie Corners. Cassie felt sorry for Billy. Someday he'd learn that not everyone is impressed by a high-and-mighty attitude. Cassie had learned that lesson herself. In a blink she'd gone from a promising actress to a lowly bookkeeper.

Gabe kept pressing Billy. "Did you two speak at all?"

Billy paused. "Sort of."

Cassie could hardly stand the silence, but Gabe let it build until the tension crackled. Billy looked ready to break, but Maude interrupted. "Boys will be boys. There's nothing more to say."

"*And* we have a luncheon engagement," her husband added.

Gabe's expression went from blank to hard. "I'm done with Billy. You folks go and enjoy your meal."

Right in front of them, he touched Cassie's arm with reassurance. "Don't worry. I'll find Luke."

His eyes met hers with the intensity she recalled from fourteen years ago…from fourteen minutes ago when his mouth had come within an inch of hers. He'd used her first name, too. It was a claiming of sorts, a statement that she belonged as much as Maude did. Cassie wanted to accept that gift, but she feared it. Maude hated her. William Drake owned the bank. They had the power to make Gabe's life miserable.

Looking at Gabe now, she felt the weight of every mistake she'd ever made. She couldn't bear the thought of causing this good man any more grief. For his own good, she had to keep him at arm's length. She stepped back, breaking his touch but not her gaze. "Thank you, Deputy."

The corners of his mouth lifted, but the smile stopped short of a grin. "You're welcome, Mrs. O'Rourke."

Reverend Hall broke in. "Thelma always has refreshments after church. Cassie, you're welcome to join us. Maude, William… I know you have an engagement, but a cup of tea wouldn't spoil your meal."

The couple traded a look, then Mr. Drake shook his head. "No thank you, Reverend. Not today."

Not today had meant not with *her*. Cassie didn't want to sip tea with Maude any more than Maude wanted to share an hour with her. She had intended to make her own excuses and she still did. She needed to look for Luke.

Reverend Hall looked pointedly at Maude. "Another time, then."

"Of course." Her voice dripped with cool disdain. After a glance at her husband, she slipped her hand in the crook of his elbow and looked at Cassie as if she were dirt. "Have a nice day, *Mrs*. O'Rourke."

The Drakes walked down the path to town with Billy at their side. When they were several feet away, the boy looked over his shoulder with a smirk. Cassie saw red. Gabe and Reverend Hall traded a look but said nothing. The arrogant look on Billy's face reminded Cassie that she had a job to do as a mother.

"I should go, too." she said to Reverend Hall. "Luke might have gone home and the apartment's locked."

"I'll check for you," Gabe said.

"No, I'd rather—"

"Stay here, Cassie." The invitation came from Reverend Hall. If anyone had cause to judge her, it was this elderly minister with yet another broken window. Cassie could hardly look him in the eye. "I'm sorry about Luke and the window. I just don't know what to do."

Gabe interrupted. "I do."

"So do I," said the reverend.

Cassie gave a small laugh. "I'm glad, because I don't know my son at all right now."

Both men chuckled. She didn't see the humor, but the deep rumbling gave her comfort. Reverend Hall smiled at her. "Thelma and I raised three sons. Luke's being a boy. Granted, he's troubled and bitter and can't go around breaking windows, but he's not a bad seed. No child is."

"Especially not Luke," Gabe added. "I'll find him and we'll have a talk. My gut tells me Billy left out a few details."

"Mine, too," said the Reverend.

These men, both strong and honorable, believed in her son. A lump pushed into Cassie's throat. She'd never felt such acceptance. When she looked at Gabe, she saw the man she'd almost kissed. He'd be a good father, but in the next breath she called herself a fool. She had no right to such a thought.

His expression stayed neutral. "I'll find Luke and bring him here. Wait for me."

"All right," she answered.

Gabe bid the reverend goodbye, then strode down the path to town. Cassie couldn't take her eyes off his straight back and wide shoulders. Dressed in his Sunday best, he cut a fine figure of a man. She couldn't help but wonder why he hadn't married. She'd hurt him, but surely he'd healed with time. People learned to live with their scars. Cassie had. Those marks were deep and she'd never marry again because of them, but she'd made a good life for herself and her son.

Reverend Hall touched her back. "Let's have some of Thelma's lemon cake."

"I'd like that," Cassie replied.

As they crossed the yard, Cassie took in the whitewashed porch and the pots of geraniums on the steps. It looked picture-perfect, but Thelma had often been candid with Cassie's mother and Cassie had heard their conversations. This house had known the heartache that came with a rebellious child. Thelma's middle son had settled out West but not before running wild. He'd even done jail time in the Laramie Territorial Prison.

Walking with the reverend, Cassie thought of his words about children and bad seeds. He'd voiced her deepest fear. Luke had his father's blood and his looks, even his taste for sweets. Did he also have his tendency to deceit? Cassie's biggest mistake as a woman had been jilting Gabe. Her biggest mistake as a mother had been choosing Ryan O'Rourke to father her child.

She lifted her chin and looked at the reverend's profile. Gray hair crowned him with wisdom. The hint of a smile gave her hope.

"Do you believe what you said, Reverend? That no child is a bad seed?"

"I do."

"Even when they do bad things?"

He chuckled. "That's when I believe it the most. If love covers a multitude of sins—and I believe it does—then the lack of it leaves those sins uncovered. They fester. I don't know what happened to Luke's father—"

"He turned violent," she said simply. "I left him for fear of our lives."

"So Luke's confused and angry."

"I try, but—"

"You're succeeding, Cassie. Believe that."

"I wish I could."

They'd reached the bottom of the porch steps. Instead of going up to the house, he stopped and faced Cassie, waiting in silence until she raised her face and looked into his eyes. They were silver like his hair, faded with time but bright with kindness. "Imagine where Luke would be without you."

She thought of the trash can he'd lit on fire, the day he'd been sent home from school for fighting. Shivering with dread, she took a breath. "He'd be running wild in Chicago."

"But he's not, is he?"

"No." She smiled at the irony. "He's running wild *here*."

"Where we can all watch him," the reverend said. "Luke is missing his natural father's love, but yours is strong. So is the love of the Lord for his children. That love covers everything—Luke's sins, your mistakes. Whatever you need."

"I want to believe that—"

"So do it," he said with force. "God brought you home to us. He's not going to leave you now."

Oh, how she wanted to believe this elderly man… The thought of being home—a place where she had friends and hope, even love—made her eyes sting with unshed tears. Standing by the steps, she smelled Thelma's lemon cake. Grass rippled in the distance and she imagined lying down in it and resting in the sun. She longed to set down the weight on her shoulders but couldn't. She had a store to run and a boy to raise. She'd made a mess of her life and had to live with it.

"I wish I could believe you," she said to the reverend.

"Why can't you?"

"Because I've hurt people. I don't deserve—"

"Pshaw."

He'd come as close to cussing as she'd ever heard a preacher come. Startled, she looked into his eyes and saw a fire she didn't expect. "This isn't about what *you* deserve, Cassie. If God gave *me* what *I* deserve, I'd be staked to an anthill and left to die in the sun. I've hated. I've lied. I've committed murder in my heart."

When she looked shocked, he gave an impish smile. "And that's just since this morning."

"I don't understand—"

"Sin is sin," he said easily. "To God, it's all the same. There aren't big ones and little ones. We *all* fall short and don't you ever forget it. We're also God's children. What keeps us safe is love—our heavenly Father's love—and a mother's love here on earth. You're doing that for Luke."

"Am I?" She clutched her reticule. She needed the hankie but didn't want to acknowledge the tears.

"Absolutely," the reverend said. "Now come sit with Thelma and me. I have a story for you about another mother, a woman in the Old Testament named Rizpah."

"Who is she?" Cassie had never heard the name.

"She was one of Saul's concubines."

As Reverend Hall guided her to a chair, Cassie thought about what that meant. As a concubine, Rizpah could have been used and abused. She wouldn't have had a husband. "Did Rizpah have a son?"

"Two of them." He sat at a right angle to Cassie. "But she saved five others as well as her own."

"From what?"

The door opened and Thelma came out with a tray of refreshments. As she set it on the low table, Cassie stood and they hugged.

"I saw the window." Thelma grimaced in sympathy. "Where's Luke?"

"He ran off," she replied. "Gabe's looking for him."

With a final squeeze, Thelma released her and they both sat, taking chairs that faced the path to town where they'd see Gabe—and hopefully Luke—returning to the parsonage.

Thelma gave an indignant sigh. "They better show up soon. Lemon cake is Gabe's favorite."

Cassie hadn't known. In the days of their courtship,

she'd made him an apple pie for a picnic. He'd told her it was the best he'd ever eaten.

Reverend Hall leaned forward, lifted the teapot and filled all three cups. Without a word, he added a spoonful of sugar to his wife's cup and handed it to her. "I was about to tell Cassie about Rizpah."

"That's a hard story," Thelma replied.

"Tell me." Cassie raised the steaming cup to her lips. She didn't think a Bible story could lift her spirits, but she needed a distraction. She wished now that she'd gone looking for Luke herself. Not with Gabe... She could still feel where he'd touched her arm. Sitting with the Halls made her think of the things she'd never have...a husband who knew how she took her tea, someone who'd see her with gray hair.

Reverend Hall set down his cup. "Rizpah gave Saul two sons. Frankly, I don't think he was the best leader. He got into it with the Gibeonites, and it was left to King David to make things right. For retribution, the Gibeonites asked for the death of seven of Saul's sons."

"Oh, no." Cassie whispered.

"That's right," the reverend said. "Rizpah's boys were in the lot. So were the five sons of Merab. The Gibeonites put them to death and hung up their bodies for the buzzards. Do you know what Rizpah did?"

Cassie knew what *she'd* do. She'd have cut down the bodies and given them a decent burial, but Rizpah had lived in a different time. She'd been a concubine, a woman at the beck and call of others.

"Tell me," she said to the reverend.

"For five months, she stayed by those seven bodies. Every minute of every day, she chased away the buzzards until David finally buried the bodies. That's love,

Cassie. Those bodies stank. They were repulsive and decaying, but that's what a mother does... She loves her children when they're at their most unlovable."

Thelma spoke in a hush. "When our boy was in Laramie, I wrote him every week. Even when he didn't write back, I sent letters."

The couple shared a sad look, then the reverend smiled. "Those were hard days, but do you know where he is now?"

"California," Cassie replied.

Pride lit the reverend's eyes. "He's in Los Angeles, married with a couple of kids. He runs a grocery business."

Thelma smiled. "They sent us photographs for Christmas. He's got two little girls who look just like him."

Cassie thought of her worries about bad seeds. Maybe the reverend had a point. "I'm happy for him," she said.

Reverend Hall cleared his throat. "I want to say one more thing about Rizpah and it's this... She didn't protect just her own sons. She protected all seven of those bodies."

He paused, giving Cassie time to think. She flashed to Billy's smirk as he looked over his shoulder. It gave her chills. "You mean Billy."

"That's right," the reverend said. "He's on a crooked road. It looks straight to William and Maude, but it's not. I'm hoping you'll do something for me, Cassie."

"What's that?"

"While you're fighting the buzzards for Luke, say a prayer for the Drakes."

Why should she pray for Maude? The woman had started the untrue rumor that Cassie had never married

Luke's father. She'd also insinuated that Cassie cheated her customers. "I'll pray for Billy," she said diplomatically.

The reverend raised his silver brows. "*And* Maude."

Cassie sat in silence. Thelma's cup clinked on the saucer. A bird chirped. The breeze stirred in a low hush until she sighed. "All right, I'll try."

"Good," said Reverend Hall. "Let's eat that cake."

As Thelma sliced into the rounded edge, Cassie stared down the path to town. A man appeared in the distance and she recognized Gabe. Luke was nowhere to be seen, yet she still wanted to run down the path…to Gabe. She thought of what the reverend had said about love covering a multitude of sins. Thanks to Maude, Cassie's sins were laid bare to everyone in Guthrie Corners. Until she made peace with the town, she had nothing to offer Gabe except a bad reputation, heartache and a boy who broke windows. She'd never succeed as a businesswoman. She'd be dependent on him, a thought she couldn't abide under any circumstances.

If she loved Gabe—and she did—she'd be wise to cover up her feelings until she could stand on her own two feet. Holding back a sigh, she watched as he neared the parsonage. If it weren't for Luke, she'd have excused herself and gone home. Instead she sat straight in her chair. For Luke, she'd do anything… even eat cake with Gabe Wyatt.

Chapter Five

Gabe knew every inch of Guthrie Corners, but he hadn't found Luke. A boy who didn't want to be found could hike a mile in any direction and disappear into the land. Luke had been in town long enough to know about the cave south of town, the one by the stream where Gabe had proposed to Cassie. If he'd gone west, he'd find an abandoned house with a missing roof.

Gabe considered saddling his horse and taking a ride, but then he'd thought of Cassie and had another idea. If he borrowed the reverend's piano buggy, they could ride together. Knowing Cassie, she'd want to hunt for Luke. The ride would also answer the question hanging in his mind. After all these years, did she still love him? Had that near-kiss been about forgiveness alone, or had it been about the future?

Looking at her as he neared the parsonage, Gabe took in the tightness of her mouth and tried to read her thoughts. He couldn't discern them with his eyes, but he knew that a kiss would tell him what he wanted to know. He'd never stopped loving Cassie, but he'd tried. For a while he'd gone to socials and church picnics.

He'd kissed his share of women and had courted one with thoughts of marriage. He'd ended it when they'd kissed and he'd found himself aching for Cassie.

His lips hadn't touched hers in Reverend Hall's office, but Gabe had felt the wanting. Did he want to risk the heartache? What would she do if he invited her to supper?

He had the engagement ring she'd left at the house. He had a kitchen table big enough for eight.

He still had the dreams of a man in love. What he didn't have was a lick of common sense. Crazy or not, he wanted Cassie for his wife. Fourteen years was long enough to wait for the only woman he'd ever loved. As he climbed the porch steps, his pulse rushed at the sight of her stiff shoulders. In the reverend's office, she'd gone soft in his arms. The woman looking at him now had turned hard again. It made him love her all the more.

"You didn't find Luke," she said.

"No, but I have a few more places to look." He dropped down on the chair at a right angle to hers and looked at the reverend. "I'd like to check out the cave south of town. Would you mind if Cassie and I borrowed your buggy?"

"Not at all," he replied.

She let out a sharp breath, a sign that she recalled that spot as well as he did. He'd proposed to her by the rushing water on a day as bright as this one. It seemed like a fitting place to test the waters.

Thelma shoved a plate of lemon cake into his hand. Gabe accepted it but left it untouched. Instead he turned his head to Cassie. "What do you say?"

She twisted her fingers into a knot. "When Luke comes home I should be there."

Gabe saw her point, but he wanted an answer to his question. He also thought it would do Luke good to be locked out for a while. Being hungry and alone inspired a boy—and a man—to ask himself the questions that made a difference.

"We'll be gone an hour," he said to her.

Their gazes met in an understanding that put them back in the reverend's office. Gabe had made his move by asking her to go for a ride with him. The next step belonged to Cassie. With the aroma of lemon cake tickling his nose, he waited for her to speak. As the seconds ticked by, he counted to fourteen and knew the waiting had just begun.

How long would it take him to win her heart? A lot longer than fourteen seconds or fourteen minutes. Not even fourteen hours would be enough… Fourteen days might do the trick, but it didn't matter. If she kissed him at the creek, he'd wait fourteen months for Cassie to trust him, even fourteen more years. But first she had to say yes to the buggy ride.

Cassie couldn't stand the sight of Gabe holding the plate of uneaten cake. Did he cook his own supper in the house he'd built for her? Or did he take all of his meals at Millie's? Watching him with his favorite dessert, denying himself for her sake, sent fresh waves of guilt from her heart to the tips of her fingers.

It broke her heart to think of that spot by the stream, yet it seemed like a fitting place to address unfinished business. Fourteen years ago she'd left Gabe with a wedding kiss hanging between them. She'd never leave him hanging again. When they reached the stream, she'd tell him the near-kiss had been a mistake. She hoped they could be friends for Luke's sake, but the future held nothing more.

"Eat," she said. "We'll go when you finish."

"I'm done." He set down the plate and stood.

Cassie rose and hugged Thelma. "I should help with the dishes."

"Nonsense."

The older woman released her with a nudge that sent her following the men to the stable. In minutes they'd hitched the reverend's gray mare to the buggy and Gabe had handed her up to the seat.

Neither spoke as they drove down the road behind the church. As they passed the poplar tree, she thought of Rizpah chasing away buzzards from the bodies of her sons. Cassie had the same passion for protecting Luke. Without it, she'd have never accepted Gabe's offer to return to the spot where he'd proposed. Did he really believe Luke would hide in the cave, or had he picked it today for another purpose?

When they reached the bend that put Guthrie Corners out of view, Gabe spoke in a low tone. "Try not to worry, Cassie."

"I can't help it."

"I know," he said easily. "But mark my words. Luke'll show up for supper."

She wanted to believe him, but Luke—like his father, like her—had an impetuous streak. "How can you be so sure?"

"Because he's a growing boy. They get hungry."

So did grown men…hungry for lemon cake and home-cooked meals. Hungry for companionship and the things she'd taken from Gabe when she'd fled to Chicago. In the distance she saw the outcropping of rocks that marked the cave. In spite of rain and snow, ice storms and hot summer days, the spot hadn't changed a bit. Neither had the man sitting next to her, staring straight ahead with a quiet strength she envied.

She could almost believe they were kids again, untouched by mistakes…except she had a wayward son, a heart full of guilt and a tarnished reputation. The buggy rattled over dry earth. The horse snorted and she heard the rippling of the stream as it came into view. Craning her neck, she searched for a sign of Luke but saw nothing.

"Let's check the cave," Gabe said.

He stopped the buggy on a patch of grass that sloped down to the stream, then came around and helped her down from the seat. Side by side, they walked along the rushing water until they reached the pile of boulders that formed a cave of sorts. As she peeked into the shadows, Cassie saw ashes, a whiskey bottle and cigarette butts, but no sign of her son. She didn't know whether to be relieved or dismayed.

She stood straight and looked back down the stream. "He's not here."

Gabe touched her arm. "We'll keep looking."

His touch shot her back in time to the day he proposed. She'd packed a picnic, but he'd been too nervous to eat. Like today, he'd left his dessert untouched. Instead he'd taken her hand and pulled her to her feet. He'd led her to the edge of the rushing stream where she'd perched on a rock. As she'd looked up, Gabe had dropped to one knee. A ring with a milky white opal, her birthstone, had gleamed between his fingers.

I love you, Cassie. Will you marry me?
Yes!

She'd wept as he'd slid the ring on her finger. He'd pulled her to her feet and kissed her until she'd been blind to everything but him. Over the next few months, she'd gotten her sight back and been afraid of what she'd seen. A future like her mother's…forgotten dreams and silent meals.

Cassie was afraid again—not of being hurt or feeling stifled—she feared for Gabe. The Drakes would make his life miserable. People would shun him as they'd shunned her. She knew how much it hurt to be a pariah. She also knew that Gabe valued his badge and the respect it earned. She couldn't take it away from him, so she faced him with the intention of never kissing him again. As his brown eyes searched her face, she almost lost her will. He looked both lazy and bold, as if he could read her confused thoughts and loved her anyway. For the first time in years, she felt beautiful and loved. He touched her arm and she felt weak all over. She didn't deserve this man's devotion, but she wanted it.

When he angled his head above hers, watching her to see what she'd do, she came to her senses. "We can't."

"Can't what?" he said lazily.

"You know *what*." She stepped back to put air between them. "What happened in Reverend Hall's office, it was a mistake."

"Who says?"

"I do." Using all her strength, she raised her chin. "We were caught up in the past."

"I wasn't."

They were two feet apart, nowhere close to touching but she felt pinned in place by his eyes alone. This was the man she'd left fourteen years ago, the one who scared her with his determination. The one who could break her will with a look alone. Not now, she told herself. Not anymore. Ryan O'Rourke had given her both bruises and a backbone.

"I mean it, Gabe. We can't."

"Can't what?" he repeated.

We can't be in love.

Except she'd already fallen for him. She couldn't deny her feelings any more than she could stop being Luke's mother. The stream rushed in the distance. She felt the heat of the sun on her back. She had to stay strong. "My mind's made up. I hope we can be friends, but it would be a mistake to pick up where we left off."

His eyes took on a hard shine. "How do you know?"

"I just do."

The stream chortled over the rocks. She heard the chirp of a bird, then the scuff of Gabe's boot on the dirt as he put his hands on his hips. Dressed in his Sunday best—a dark suit, a starched collar—he reminded her of a picture she'd seen of a gunfighter. He had the same glint in his eye and the same unmoving lips. To stop herself from talking, she turned her back.

An instant later, she felt his hands on her shoulders. Their shadows blended into a gray puddle, but she felt no pressure from his grip to turn around. She could smell his shaving soap and the sun's warmth on his coat. Every fiber in her being cried out for this man. She wanted to rest in his strong arms, but at what cost? She'd lose her independence and he'd suffer the shame of loving a pariah. Eventually he'd resent her. Blinking, she thought of Rizpah chasing away the buzzards from people she loved. Cassie had to chase the town crows away from Gabe, and she had to look him in the eye to do it. In a single motion, she pivoted and stepped back.

"I'm not worth it, Gabe."

His eyes hardened. "Who says?"

"*I* say."

She braced herself for a harsh retort, but the lines around his mouth softened. As his expression shifted from hard to wise, he let his hands fall loose at his side. "You made that decision for us once before. I didn't like it then, and I don't like it now."

"We don't have a future." She had to be firm, but the words had a tender ring.

"Is that what you want?"

"It is."

She'd lied and she'd done it boldly. Guilt flapped its ugly wings. Her neck hurt and she felt heavy all over. Gabe didn't budge. If he'd crowded her, she could have stepped back. If he'd touched her, she could have acted indignant. Instead he stood like an unmovable rock, one that held the heat of the sun and offered shelter from storms. She wanted to weep for all she'd given up and for what they couldn't have. Instead she raised her chin. "What do you want from me?" she said in a hush.

"I think you know."

As much as she hated silence, Cassie hated the truth even more. She knew exactly what Gabe wanted from her. Love. Trust. A future. She still loved him and she always would, but at what cost? After enduring Ryan's abuse, she'd never lean on anyone again. She wouldn't give up her independence for anything…or anyone. The silence spoke for her. What he wanted, she couldn't give.

Gabe let out a long sigh. "I guess that's my answer."

The stream rippled behind her. She felt like a rock buried in the mud, doomed to endure years of drought and flood. She couldn't move her feet.

His eyes faded with disappointment, but he still held out his hand. "Come on," he said gently. "I'll take you home."

Looking at his outstretched arm, she longed for a different future. Today he'd shown her nothing but goodness. He'd defended her son and forgiven her for the past. He'd offered her a future and accepted her rejection without a hint of pressure. Looking at him now, she felt like a sparrow being tempted by bread crumbs. A home… Love… A father for Luke. She'd never known such generosity, but her longing had to be denied. Ignoring Gabe's outstretched hand, she led the way to the buggy where she gathered her skirts to climb in. Gabe touched her elbow, lifting her with an easy strength. Cassie settled on to the leather, then faced him. "Thank you, Gabe. For everything."

"You're welcome."

Their eyes stayed locked. Her breath caught and he gripped her hand for one last time. Warmth seeped into her fingers and flowed all the way to her middle. Gratitude flooded to her heart and she wanted him to know how much he meant to her. With her heart overflowing, Cassie leaned to the side and sweetly kissed his cheek.

She'd kissed him. Eight hours had passed, but Gabe could still feel the tickle of her lips, the brush of silk against his cheek. The spot she'd kissed had grown stubbled as he'd walked around town searching for Luke in the places a boy would hide. Gabe had walked for hours. He wanted to find Luke for Cassie's sake, but mostly he'd needed to sort his thoughts. Just when he'd given up hope for their future, she'd kissed him. It hadn't been the kiss they'd started in Reverend Hall's office, but Gabe had the answer to his question. Cassie still loved him.

So why had she turned cold again? As he checked alleys for Luke, he'd thought about Ryan O'Rourke. The man should have been horsewhipped for beating his wife. He hadn't broken Cassie's spirit, but he'd left scars that ran deep. It made sense that she wouldn't trust easily. He'd have to work to earn it and that meant going slow and respecting her worries. While walking around town, he'd passed William Drake's bank. He'd been reminded of Maude and the ugly rumors she'd spread. If Cassie couldn't make a living, she'd be forced to leave Guthrie Corners…and him.

"Fool woman," Gabe muttered as he neared the sheriff's office. Didn't she realize he'd take care of her?

Worn out and hungry, Gabe went through the door, lit a lamp and saw a napkin-covered tray on his desk. He wondered if Cassie had left it until he raised the linen and saw Thelma's lemon cake and a hearty sandwich. She'd also left a note that said, "We're praying for you both."

"We need it," he said out loud. Twice he'd walked by Cassie's store. Both times she'd been standing in the window and had shaken her head, an indication that Luke hadn't come home. He'd resisted the urge to knock on her door. He could help her most by finding Luke, and he had to respect her request for friendship and nothing more. Once her situation settled down, he'd start courting her. Until then, he'd be wise to avoid the temptation to rush her.

Instead of saying grace over his meal, Gabe bent his head and prayed out loud for Cassie. "Be with her tonight, Lord. Keep her boy safe and guide me in my search for Luke. Grant me wisdom, Lord. And patience."

Gabe groaned at the last word. Patience tested him like nothing else. After a heartfelt plea for Luke's safety and for Cassie to know peace, he said, "Use me, Lord. Amen."

He ate the sandwich in silence, thinking of the hard ways God sometimes used a man. Men died for people they loved. Jesus had suffered a cruel and haunting death. Gabe would have willingly died for Cassie to spare her pain of any kind. He was doing it now… dying to his desire to go to her…dying to his own need for companionship so he could meet *her* needs for time and understanding.

I love her enough, Lord. I'll wait.

As he cut into the lemon cake, Gabe heard a train whistle. He stopped with the fork in midair. The Denver Special arrived every evening at ten o'clock and left after boarding new passengers.

"That's it," he said out loud. Luke wasn't just licking his wounds somewhere. He was planning to run away. Pushing back from his desk, he raced out the door for the train station.

Chapter Six

When the night fell and Luke still hadn't come home, Cassie put a lamp in the window with the hope of attracting him like a moth to flame. It hadn't worked. The mantel clock had struck every hour since dusk, each time adding a chime until it struck nine times. She had to face facts. Luke wouldn't be home tonight.

Shaking inside, she pulled her shawl tight around her shoulders. After leaving Gabe, she had walked through Guthrie Corners herself. She'd asked everyone she'd met if they'd seen Luke, but no one had. She'd even visited Miss Lindstrom, the schoolteacher, to ask about any boys Luke might have befriended. Just as she'd suspected, he didn't have anyone but himself.

Neither did she. She had nothing but the store. If business didn't improve, even that comfort would be taken from her. She'd have to sell the building and move back to Chicago. Her stomach filled with moths beating their wings. To Luke, the noisy city was home. He knew every inch of their neighborhood and had friends, disreputable or not, who'd take him in. Earlier she'd checked Luke's room. Nothing had been touched.

She was certain he hadn't come into the apartment, but she hadn't checked the store. Her son knew exactly where she kept the cashbox. It didn't hold enough money for train fare to Chicago, but the contents would feed a stowaway.

Cassie snatched the lamp, hurried down the stairs and went to the desk where she kept the cashbox in the bottom drawer. As the light spread across the floor, she saw that someone had left that same drawer ajar. She didn't need to open the cashbox to know Luke had stolen from her, but she opened it anyway. Instead of bills and coins, she saw a single greenback, as if he'd left it out of concern for her.

Cassie blew out the lamp, then raced to the street. The Denver Special passed through town every night, signaling its arrival with a warning whistle. When she and Luke had ridden the train west, he'd been interested in everything—the route, where the lines switched. He'd have no trouble finding his way back to Chicago. If he hopped on the Denver Special, she might never find him. She had to get to the station *now*.

With her shawl whipping behind her, she sped down the boardwalk to the east side of town. The train station was situated a half mile away if she took the straightest path, but decent men and women drove their buggies down a road that skirted the block of saloons and questionable boardinghouses. Desperate for Luke, Cassie chose the straightest path.

As she neared the first saloon, she heard raucous laughter and women singing bawdy lyrics to the tune of a piano playing "Turkey In The Straw." Cassie crossed the street to avoid the open door, but she couldn't escape the smells of liquor and cloying perfume. Above her the stars burned bright, but she saw only Cassiopeia with her neck bent in shame. Thelma and Reverend Hall believed in God's mercy, but Cassie had her doubts. She desperately needed a break, but between Maude's gossip and another broken window, no one in this town would give her a second chance… except for Gabe.

As her heart cried out, she heard the thud of boots on the boardwalk. Startled, she turned and saw a man striding in her direction. He looked big, tough and mean. He also resembled Gabe, though she couldn't be sure. Guthrie Corners had its share of ruffians, and the shortcut to the train station had taken her to a place she would never have gone. To avoid the man, she picked up her pace.

So did he.

She started to run, but her skirts got in her way. She caught her toe on a warped board and stumbled.

"Wait up," the man called.

Cassie knew that voice, that bossy tone. It belonged to Gabe. He reached her in five strides, clasped her arms to steady her and raked her face with his eyes.

"What are you doing here?" he demanded

What did he think? That she'd come here for fun? "I'm looking for Luke," she snapped. "What else would I be doing?"

"Getting yourself hurt, that's what."

His fingers tightened on her biceps, then loosened to gentle circles of warmth. His eyes held hers, lingered, then filled with a jealous possession that made her feel both loved and lonely. She couldn't lean on this man, but she had to find Luke and he could help.

She stepped back. "Luke stole money from the cash box. I think he's running away."

Gabe's jaw tightened. "To Chicago."

"Yes."

He hooked his arm around her waist and hurried with her down the boardwalk. In the distance she saw the station, a low building with lanterns illuminating an empty platform. Her gaze rose to the train where she saw a man in a derby looking for a seat. The train had already boarded. Any minute it would leave the station.

She wanted to run but couldn't in her long skirt. "Go ahead of me!" she cried to Gabe.

After a squeeze of her hand, he broke into a run. Cassie ran as fast as she dared. A boiler shot a blast of steam into the sky. She smelled hot oil and heard two toots of the whistle. The engine chugged once, twice, then began to move.

She shouted Luke's name at the top of her lungs and ran faster. Instead of climbing the steps to the platform, she veered left and chased the slowly moving train. She saw steps and an open door to a passenger car, but she didn't have a prayer of reaching it. The engine picked up speed and the clattering cars turned into a blur of tears, grit and steam. As the caboose raced by, Cassie fell to her knees and wept.

"I'm sorry, honey."

She felt Gabe's hand on her back, then his arm around her shoulders as he dropped to his knees and pulled her head against his chest. "We'll wire ahead to the next stop. If he's on that train—"

Cassie raised her head. "I want to go after him."

"I know you do, but you can't. We don't know where he is."

She looked into Gabe's eyes and saw an understanding that shot her back in time to another train, another parting. Had he chased after the train that had taken her away to Chicago? Had he watched it disappear around a bend? Had he heard the fading whistle and felt as if his body had been ripped in two? Cassie lowered her eyes in shame.

He lifted her chin. "Luke might not even be on that train."

"He is. I know it."

"Did you see him?"

No, but he had *her* blood as well as his father's. "I just know."

"I don't." His fingers slid off her chin. "Let's go see the stationmaster. He might have seen something."

Gabe stood and offered his hand. Cassie took it and let him guide her back to the station where he opened the door and ushered her into the narrow room with a counter. She recognized the clerk as Carl Martin.

Carl looked from her to Gabe. "Good evening, Deputy. What can I do for you?"

"Mrs. O'Rourke is looking for her son." Gabe described Luke and gave his age.

Carl puckered his lips. "Ain't seen no kids around. It's usually business folks takin' the evening train."

"What about earlier?" Cassie asked. Maybe Luke had gone west instead of east.

The clerk shook his head. "What'd he do? Run off?"

"Yes," she said quietly.

When the clerk grunted with irritation, Cassie

read his thoughts. *What kind of mother are you? Why weren't you watching your boy?*

Gabe touched her back, then spoke to Carl. "I'd like to send a wire to the next stop."

The clerk handed Gabe a pencil and paper.

With Cassie watching, he wrote a terse message describing Luke and asking the stationmaster to check the train for stowaways, then he signed it "Deputy Gabriel Paul Wyatt." His badge commanded a respect she couldn't have gotten on her own and she felt grateful. As he handed the paper to Carl, the clerk promised to send it right away. Gabe thanked him, then guided Cassie through the door and into the night.

The air still smelled of steam and hot oil. With her heart aching, she stared up the empty track.

Gabe put his arm around her waist. "I'll walk you home."

"No."

"Cassie, it's late—"

"I have to keep looking," she insisted. "If there's a chance he's here, I have to find him."

She pulled away from his arm, but he tightened his grasp. "Let me."

"But I'm his mother."

"That's right," he said. "For all we know, he could be home right now. You need to be there for him."

She'd never felt so empty in her life, not even when Ryan had hit her. That night she'd had a child to protect. Tonight she had nothing but empty arms. As much as she hated the thought of waiting in her silent apartment, she knew Gabe had a point. If Luke came home, she'd be ready with a meal.

"All right," she said.

"Good."

As they faced each other in the moonlight, Cassie blinked away her feelings. Earlier she'd cried in this man's arms. She'd leaned against his chest and taken the comfort she'd vowed to forsake. For a few brief minutes, she'd shared her load and it had felt good. She couldn't read Gabe's thoughts, but she knew her own and they scared her to death. She loved this man. They belonged together, but she feared the consequences of braiding their lives.

Judging by Gabe's expression, he had no such reluctance. Slowly...carefully...he drew her into his arms until his jaw scraped her temple. She felt the bristle of the whiskers he'd shaved before church, then the pressure of his hand as he tucked her head between his hard shoulder and the flesh of his neck. His breath caught the rhythm of hers. Their hearts matched in perfect time, reminding her of the past and how deeply she'd hurt him.

She'd hurt him again if she wasn't careful. Intending to step back, she raised her head. His mouth was a whisper from hers. If he turned his head, they'd be kissing. The thought made her tremble, but even more tempting was the stillness of his embrace. The man she'd left had been impatient. He'd have already kissed her breathless. The new Gabe had the patience of Job. The future, she realized, was in her hands.

Looking down, he spoke in a rough voice. "I better take you home."

"Yes," she murmured. "Luke could be waiting."

He nodded, but the look in his eyes had nothing to do with her wayward son and everything to do with a man's wayward thoughts. Or worse, the noble thoughts of a man in love, a man considering marriage, children and the holiest of commitments.

They stepped apart and turned toward town. Instead of walking past the saloons, Gabe steered her down the longer road that curved by homes and gardens. Whether he'd done it to avoid the saloons or because he wanted more time with her, she didn't know. Either way, she enjoyed walking at his side, sharing her burdens and worries with a friend... Just a friend, she reminded herself. If Luke had run away, she'd be destined to search for him forever. If—when—she found him, she'd still be unwelcome in Guthrie Corners and unable to support herself. With each step in the direction of her apartment, the future looked bleaker. It looked bleakest of all when they reached the mercantile and the stairs leading to her empty home.

"Go inside," Gabe said. "I'll come by in the morning."

She wanted to stay with him, but instead she climbed the steps, slipped into the dark room and lit a lamp. Like before, she carried it to the window and put it out for Luke. This time, though, instead of an empty street, she saw Gabe watching for her through the glass. Wordless, she touched the pane with her fingers as she thought of an old Bible verse.

But now we see through a glass darkly. But then face-to-face...

She'd been in the dark for so long... She hadn't dared to pray for herself since the day she'd left Gabe at the altar. She hadn't felt worthy and she didn't feel worthy now, but she could pray for others. With a lump in her throat, she closed her eyes. "Be with Luke, Lord. Keep him safe. And Gabe, bless him, Lord Jesus. He's a good man." In the sudden silence, she recalled her promise to Reverend Hall. "Be with Billy, too, Lord. Help Maude and me to be good mothers to our sons."

As she whispered amen, her heart pounded. She had more to say to God but couldn't find the words. Feeling weak, she opened her eyes and looked down at the street. Gabe hadn't budged. If she motioned to him, he'd come up the stairs. He'd stay until she felt strong again. Somehow she stayed still. Another minute passed, then he tipped his hat and walked away, leaving her with knotted fingers and the knowledge that she didn't want to be alone after all.

Could she have it all? Her business *and* Gabe? Could they make a family with Luke and children to come? If business picked up, she could stay and find out. If it didn't, she'd have to leave. And if Luke didn't come home, none of her plans mattered. Looking at the empty street, Cassie touched the glass. For all her hard work and good intentions, she'd been rendered helpless by her own son. Feeling bereft, she raised her eyes to the stars. She hadn't stopped believing in God, but she'd stopped trusting Him. Tonight she couldn't stand on her own. No matter how hard she tried, she couldn't save her son.

Trembling, she bowed her head so that the crown touched the glass, then leaned enough to feel the pressure like a hand. "I'm sorry, Lord Jesus. I've made so many mistakes... I've failed everyone." Tears welled. The glass grew warm against her forehead, like a touch. "Please help me, Father God. Please bring my son home. I can't do it myself."

A sob broke from her throat. She felt weak all over and more helpless than she had all night. She didn't know if God would answer the prayer of a sinful woman like herself, but she hoped He'd look out for a troubled boy.

After leaving Cassie, Gabe went home. He figured Luke had either hopped the Denver Special or holed up somewhere for the night. Gabe couldn't go looking for him without causing a ruckus, so he slept a few hours, put on fresh clothes and left the house with Cassie's worry coursing through him. He knew how it felt to be left with doubts and questions. Fourteen years ago he'd been in her shoes. *Where did you go, Cassie? What did I do? Why did you leave me?*

He never wanted to ask himself those questions again. That's why he'd left her on the steps to her apartment. Earlier, when she'd tipped her face up to his, he'd almost caved in and kissed her. Now he was glad he hadn't. She needed her son far more than she needed the confusion of an ill-timed kiss, and Gabe intended to find him.

He went first to the train station where he spoke to Carl. The stationmaster at Ellison had already wired to say he'd searched the train and hadn't found Luke. Gabe took the news as a positive sign. If the boy had holed up in Guthrie Corners, he'd be waking up hungry. Gabe thanked the clerk, then headed for Pete Doyle's livery. He'd checked it twice yesterday but not after dark. The barn and corrals sat a quarter mile down the tracks and offered a good place to hide for a boy intending to hop a train. Gabe knew Pete well. The man wouldn't mind a bit if Gabe nosed around.

When he reached the barn, he went around to the back and entered through a side door. Stepping as lightly as he could, he walked between the stalls, looking in each one until he found Luke sleeping on his belly in a pile of straw. With his hair mussed and his arms akimbo, he looked like the innocent child he was meant to be, not the boy who'd seen his mother beaten by his father and felt those fists himself.

Gabe didn't consider himself an emotional man, but his throat went tight. Luke should have been *his* son. They'd have built things together and told jokes. He'd have taken him fishing and taught him to shoot. Looking at the boy with Cassie's hair and a stranger's eyes, he felt so cheated he wanted to smash his fist against the stall. Instead he closed his eyes and prayed.

Lord Jesus, help this boy. He needs a father.

And Gabe needed a son… The answer to the dilemma seemed obvious. He'd have to win Cassie's heart before he could call Luke his own, but for now he could take the boy under his wing and teach him how to handle bullies like Billy Drake. The three of them could go on picnics and he'd charm Cassie for as long as it took for her to trust him.

Your will be done, Lord. I'm willing to wait, but Luke needs me now and I need Cassie.

As Gabe whispered amen, Luke stirred against the straw. He looked like a child, but the last thing he needed was babying. He got enough of that from his mother. Like most boys, he needed someone to push against so he could build his muscles. Young bucks with new antlers did the same thing. So did yearling mustangs and young bulls. If Luke wanted—needed—to fight, Gabe would oblige.

He planted his boots a foot apart and put his hands on hips. "O'Rourke! Get your butt up *now!*"

Luke grunted. "Go away."

"Not a chance." Gabe hadn't hollered in a long time. He hadn't had a reason but he did now. "You scared your ma half to death. The church has another broken window. And unless Mr. Doyle gave you permission to mess up his stall, you're trespassing."

Luke buried his face in his arms. "Leave me alone."

"I can't do that." Gabe dropped to one knee, gripped the boy's shoulder and rolled him over. Luke struggled, but he was no match against Gabe and his head finally turned.

What Gabe saw told the whole story. Luke had a black eye, a cut below his left ear and a tear in the knee of his pants. He might have broken the church window, but he'd done it after taking a beating from Billy Drake. Gabe hurt for him, but Luke didn't need pity. He needed to get his pride back.

Gabe arched a brow. "I hope the other guy looks worse."

"He doesn't."

The pain of that confession hit hard. No man liked to take a beating. Christ had done it for the sake of all mankind, but He'd had the last word when He'd risen from the grave. Knowing both Billy and Luke, Gabe figured the fight had started with Billy's smart mouth. Luke needed vindication.

Gabe stood tall and offered his hand. Luke looked at it, then at Gabe. "Are you going to arrest me again?"

"Nope."

"What are you going to do?"

"Fix you breakfast, clean up those cuts and take you to apologize to your ma for stealing money. While we eat, you can tell me what Billy said that made you so mad."

"I hate him!" Luke declared.

"I figured that." Gabe waggled his fingers to get Luke's attention. "Let's go. I'm hungry."

The boy's thoughts warred on his face. He had an empty belly and he wanted Gabe's friendship, but he felt guilty about everything he'd done, including stealing from his mother. Running away still appealed to him.

Gabe dropped back to a crouch. "Your ma's worried about you, Luke. But trust me…she's going to forgive you. She knows you took the money. We both thought you were headed to Chicago."

"I was." He sounded forlorn. "But I fell asleep."

"I'm glad you did." He kept his voice neutral. "Billy Drake's been bullying the kids in this town long enough. I'm proud of you for standing up to him."

He pushed to a sitting position. "Really?"

"You bet." Gabe meant every word. "I don't know what started the fight—"

"He called my ma a bad name…the worst one."

Gabe would *never* strike a woman or child, but he'd have leveled a man for throwing that insult at Cassie. He had no doubt where Billy had gotten that foul idea. Maude and her rumors had to be stopped. He gripped Luke's shoulder. "You defended your mother. That was honorable. I'm not saying you did the right thing with the window—"

"I didn't mean to." Luke looked at the straw. "I was aiming for Billy and missed. I'm sorry about the window, but I'm not sorry I threw the rock."

"I can see why."

"I'd do it again."

Gabe believed him. Luke had the instincts of a man but not the judgment. Unless someone taught him how to fight—and when—he'd break more windows.

"How about I teach you a few things?" he said to the boy.

"Like what?"

Gabe shrugged. "For starters, how to throw a punch."

"Really?"

"Sure." He'd buy a fifty-pound sack of flour, hang it from a tree and show the kid how to put his weight behind a punch. Luke could beat the stuffing out of the flour sack, but that wasn't the only lesson.

"You have to promise me something," Gabe added.

"What?"

"You have to listen to what I say. A man needs to know *how* to fight, but it's more important to know *when* to fight."

When Luke's eyes clouded, Gabe thought of Ryan O'Rourke beating on Cassie. How much had the boy witnessed? Too much, Gabe decided. Luke had ugly memories, but time and God would work for the good. Someday Luke would be a strong defender of the weak because he knew how it felt to be small.

"What do you say?" he said to the boy.

Luke pushed to his feet. "When can we start?"

"Today," Gabe answered. "But first we eat breakfast. Then I'll take you to apologize to your ma."

Luke looked chagrined. "She's not going to like it."

"Like what?"

"She doesn't like fighting. She says I should just walk away." Luke sounded disgusted.

Frankly, so was Gabe. He didn't want to undercut Cassie's authority with her son, but she was wrong about walking away from trouble. Gabe believed in turning the other cheek as much as Reverend Hall. He never started a fight and didn't fight to defend himself alone. But when danger threatened someone else, he stood ready to protect and defend. He'd been in the U.S. Cavalry and took pride in serving his country. As a lawman, he'd promised to keep the peace at all costs. Three years ago, he'd killed a man and had no regrets. If he hadn't, Betty Woolsey would have been shot dead by her crazy husband.

When it came to boys and fighting, Cassie had a few things to learn. Gabe hoped she'd understand what he wanted to teach Luke. If she didn't, they were headed for a squabble of their own.

Chapter Seven

"No!" she cried.

"But Cassie—" Gabe frowned at her.

"I said no."

She couldn't believe her ears. How dare he promise to teach Luke how to box! She abhorred violence of any kind. She'd felt the power of Ryan O'Rourke's fists and didn't want her son to follow in his father's footsteps.

Twenty minutes ago she'd wilted with relief when Gabe walked into the mercantile with his hand on Luke's shoulder. She'd run to them from the counter and they'd met in the middle of an aisle. Luke had apologized for scaring her, then he'd given her back the money with the most sincere "I'm sorry" she'd ever heard. When she'd started to fetch a beefsteak for his black eye, Gabe had stopped her and Luke had looked proud. The next thing she knew, Gabe was talking about boxing lessons and bags of flour.

Over Cassie's dead body! She understood the desire to strike back. She'd wanted to slap Maude across the face when she'd smirked over Luke, but violence begat violence. She knew, because when she'd defended herself against Ryan, he'd hit her even harder.

She looked at Luke now and wanted to hug him again. Earlier she'd tried to kiss the top of his head, but he'd drawn back from her. Gabe had looked annoyed and now they were talking about punching bags.

Gabe glanced at Luke. "Go get ready for school."

"But he's hurt!" Cassie declared. "He's tired and—"

"He can do it." Gabe motioned at the door with his chin. "Get going, Luke. And don't be afraid to look Billy in the eye."

Cassie frowned. "Stay away from him."

"I can't," Luke muttered. "He sits behind me."

"I'll speak to Miss Lindstrom," Cassie said. "She can move your seat."

The two males exchanged a look Cassie didn't like at all. It left her out in the cold.

Luke stared back at Gabe, who indicated the door to the apartment. "Go on, kid. I'll see you after school."

Her son looked at her with the defiant expression Cassie knew too well, then followed Gabe's order, leaving her speechless. When the door closed, Gabe faced her. They were in the center of the store by the fancy dishes she loved. The *empty* store…she hadn't sold a thing in days, not even to a stranger, and now her son and Billy Drake were wrestling in the dirt.

Gabe looked pained. With the plates on one side of the aisle and the glassware on the other, he looked too big for the small space. "You have to trust me, Cassie. Luke needs those boxing lessons."

"I don't want him fighting," she insisted.

"It's what boys do."

"It's what *fools* do!" She turned and headed for the

counter. "Nothing good ever comes from people beating on each other."

"This isn't about *beating* on anyone."

She slipped behind the wood, lifted a rag and wiped the spotless surface. Gabe came forward but didn't follow her to the nook behind the counter. She focused on the rag, making half circles until she couldn't stand the silence and threw the rag down. "I give up. What *is* it about?"

"Honor."

To Cassie, honor meant being fair and truthful. It had nothing to do with punching bags. She started to pick up the rag, but Gabe put his hand on hers.

"Do you know why Luke has that black eye?" he asked.

"He and Billy were fighting."

His jaw tightened. "Billy insulted you. Luke defended your honor and took a beating for it."

"Oh, dear."

"That boy stood up for you, Cassie. He did the right thing. *How* he did it is another matter. That's why I need to buy that sack of flour."

Cassie thought of Ryan's fist on her jaw. She thought of his blood coursing through Luke's veins and how her son got the same mean look his father had. She'd come to Guthrie Corners to erase that violent tendency, not to feed it.

"It's just wrong," she insisted.

Gabe opened his mouth to speak, then sealed his lips. Whatever he'd been about to say, he'd thought better of it.

"Spit it out!" Cassie ordered.

"All right," he said, dragging out the words. "You're turning Luke into a sissy."

"I'm *what?*"

"You heard me."

"How dare you—"

"I'm right and you know it." His voice deepened to a growl. "You mean well, Cassie, but you don't understand boys. Luke needs to push against life to build his muscles. Look at him… He's as tall as you and has fuzz on his lip. He's not a little boy anymore."

She'd noticed the fuzz a few days ago and wished it was dirt she could wipe away. She missed her little boy. She didn't want him to get hurt, nor did she want him rolling in the dust with Billy Drake. She had enough trouble with Maude and the rumors.

"My decision's final," she said to Gabe.

"It's also wrong."

As the side door opened, she saw Luke. He'd washed his face and tucked in his shirt, something he hadn't done unbidden in weeks. Cassie swallowed hard. Where had the twelve years gone?

The boy eyed them both, then focused on Gabe. "I'll see you after school, right?"

They'd circled back to the boxing lessons. "Not today," Cassie declared. "You have chores."

"But, Ma—"

"Don't argue, Luke. The store needs sweeping and—"

He looked disgusted. "No, it doesn't. No one ever comes in here. They hate you. They hate me, too!"

"Luke!"

He strode out of the store, slamming the door behind him. Cassie stared in horror. Her son was too tall to be a boy and too skinny to be a man. She might not fully understand boys, but she knew that fighting caused more problems than it solved.

Gabe gripped the edge of counter. "You have to trust me, Cassie. Luke needs a man in his life. He needs a father."

A father for Luke meant a husband for her. She couldn't go down that road, but neither could she force a single word from her lips. She stepped back from the counter until she bumped the stool.

Gabe's knuckles turned white against the dark wood. "He's being bullied and so are you. There's a time to turn the other cheek and a time to stand up. Luke needs to stand, Cassie. Maybe you do, too."

Her insides shook. "What do you mean?"

"Don't hide from Maude like a whipped dog. You're stronger than that. Do something."

Gabe's voice had risen and he looked furious. He wouldn't hit her, but she still wanted to cry and had to bite her lip to keep it from trembling.

He turned away, showing her his broad back with his arms loose at his sides. After two deep breaths, he faced her again and spoke in a quieter tone. "I won't turn Luke into a bully, but there's stuff he needs to know."

"Like what?" she demanded.

"For one thing, how to duck."

Cassie thought of his bruised face. Gabe was right about Luke needing a father *and* about ducking, but she saw another answer. "Why can't you teach him how to fish or something?"

"I will," he answered. "After I teach him how to defend himself."

Everything in Cassie cried out to trust Gabe's judgment, but she wouldn't lean on anyone, especially not a man who thought he knew it all.

"No fighting," she said. "It's not right to hit someone."

"It's less right to be hit."

"I know that."

Instead of pacing back to her, he froze in place to create a wall of air. "Why are you so scared? Is it because of O'Rourke?"

"Of course, it is!" She'd been such a fool. "I'm afraid Luke will turn into his father."

"That's just plain crazy."

Cassie saw red. "You don't have to be insulting."

"I'm not." He held out his hands in surrender. "He's got your blood, too. You're raising him. That counts for more than anything O'Rourke did in the past."

Cassie thought of love covering a multitude of sins. She loved her son enough to stay strong. "My decision is final," she said to Gabe. "Fighting is wrong. *Hitting* is wrong. I don't want Luke learning to box."

"Then you better lock him in his room, Cassie. He's *already* fighting. You can't stop life from happening to him."

"I can try!"

"You're going to cripple him," Gabe said with a rush.

"How dare you!"

"You're so *wrong* I can't believe it." He raked his hand through his hair, leaving furrows of frustration that matched the ones on her heart.

She glared at him. "What gives you the right to criticize me? You don't know what it's like—"

"I know boys!" he said in full voice. "I know how they think, what they need. You don't—"

"He's my son!"

"And he's destined for *my* jail!"

"Get out!" Cassie ordered. She couldn't stand arguing. She felt shaky and weak and afraid.

"Cassie—"

"Leave! And stay away from Luke!"

Fury burned in his brown irises. "That's a mistake and you know it."

He didn't want to go. She could see the reluctance—even pity—in his eyes, but he had to respect her wishes. Without a word, he walked out the door and closed it with a loud click. Cassie picked up the cloth and started to dust her empty store. When she reached the pretty dishes, she wiped them clean with tears streaming down her face.

Whether Cassie liked it or not, Gabe had promised to meet Luke after school. He wouldn't go against Cassie's wishes and neither would he criticize her to her son, but the boy deserved an explanation. Gabe had been thinking all morning about what he'd say and had decided to counsel Luke to be patient.

The irony made him snort. Patience? Yeah, right. Gabe's vow to wait fourteen months, weeks or days for Cassie to wise up had turned into a hair shirt. He'd been giving serious thought to inviting her to the next church social, but then they'd argued. He couldn't ask her now, not until they squared things over Luke.

Gabe reached the schoolhouse just as the doors opened and children spilled out, young ones first and then older ones. Near the back of the crowd he saw Billy Drake and three boys acting like goofs. One of them was making a face and wailing "waaaa" like a cry baby. Not a good sign, Gabe thought. He looked for Luke, didn't see him and felt a stone drop in his belly. When the last child left, he walked into the schoolhouse where he saw empty seats, Miss Lindstrom at her desk and Luke writing "I will not throw rocks" over and over on the blackboard.

He also saw dust on the seat of the boy's pants. Between the "cry baby" taunts and the evidence that Luke had been shoved to the dirt, Gabe felt certain he'd been provoked into throwing the rock. The boy had also gone to school with a head of steam. He didn't need punishment right now. He needed guidance and Gabe intended to give it to him no matter what Cassie said.

Taking off his hat, he walked past the desks. "Good afternoon, Miss Lindstrom."

Luke stopped writing but only for an instant. As the tap of the chalk resumed, Miss Lindstrom stood to greet him. "Good afternoon, Deputy."

She sounded friendly but not eager. Good, Gabe thought. When she'd first arrived in town, she'd made a point of sitting near him in church. He'd had to move to the back row to break her of the habit.

"I'm here for Luke," he said.

"He has fifty more sentences to go. Then he's free to leave." She spoke in a singsong Gabe found annoying.

Luke slammed the chalk into the tray and turned. "It's not fair!"

Miss Lindstrom raised her eyebrows. "I saw you throw the rock. You could have hit one of the smaller children."

"I was aiming for Billy!"

The "cry baby" chant made perfect sense. The boys had gotten into a quarrel and Luke had ended up in the dirt. His anger had leaked in tears and Billy and his cohorts had seen it. If Luke didn't do something now to redeem himself, he'd have to put up with Billy and his garbage for months.

Gabe directed his gaze to Miss Lindstrom. "It's

your schoolhouse, but I'd appreciate it if you'd release Luke to me."

Her mouth wrinkled. "I don't know. I have rules."

"So do I."

She sighed. "I suppose, but just this once."

Luke glared at Gabe but spoke to his teacher. "I won't go with him. He's not my father, so you can't make me."

Gabe had heard enough. "Get your things, Luke."

"No!"

"Fine. I'll do it for you." He snatched up the boy's book bag, gripped his shoulder and manhandled him out the door and down the steps. Luke tried to shake off his hand, but Gabe refused to let go. "I'm not in the mood to chase you down."

"Then don't."

"You're out of luck, kid. I'm in this for the long haul."

Gabe herded him around the corner of the schoolhouse to a spot where they wouldn't be in plain view. A split rail fence marked the border of the schoolyard. A meadow stretched fifty yards to the west, giving the boy no place to hide. Confident he had Luke corralled, Gabe let go of his shoulder and dropped the book bag. "What's this about throwing rocks?"

The boy ran to the fence. Gabe reached him in four strides and hauled him down from the top rail. Luke shouted at the empty meadow. "Leave me alone!"

"No way." Gabe spun him around so they were eye to eye. "We were talking about rocks."

Luke bent down, snatched up a stone and hauled back to throw it at the schoolhouse. Gabe snatched his arm. "Drop it, Luke."

"I'll throw rocks if I want to!"

"No, you won't. Now drop it."

"Make me."

Luke jerked against Gabe's grip, but he couldn't break it. He pushed forward and pulled back. He twisted. He cursed. He struggled like a fish on the end of a line. Gabe had never seen a human being as bitter as Luke. All that hurt and anger…it had nowhere to go except deeper into the boy's soul. Luke had to get rid of it.

Gabe held tight until the rock dropped from Luke's hand, then he released his grip. "You want to fight. Is that it?"

Luke's eyes blazed. "I hate you!"

Gabe figured the boy hated everybody right now including himself, so he didn't mind being a target. He challenged Luke with a smirk. "Well, whoop-de-do."

The boy lunged at him. As Gabe side-stepped, Luke's momentum forced him to his knees. The sting of the fall must have goaded him even more, because he pushed to his feet and charged again. This time Gabe stood his ground. The blow knocked him back a step and he stumbled. As he regained his balance, Luke pummeled his middle with his fists. The boy packed a real punch, but Gabe didn't stop him. Instead he held out his arms to make himself an easy target for the boy's anger. Whatever Luke had to dish out, Gabe could take.

When he landed a particularly hard punch, Gabe grunted. A female gasp came from near the schoolhouse and he turned his head. Instead of Miss Lindstrom looking annoyed, he saw Cassie with her mouth agape. Her expression shifted from shock to outrage.

Not now…not when Luke had a full head of steam.

He shook his head to warn her away. At the same instant, Luke started to cry and shout while throwing punches. He had no awareness of his mother, no sense of anything except the feelings pouring out of him. He needed this release. Surely Cassie could see it. Babying him now would be the biggest mistake she could make. He gave her a hard stare, one full of warning, then focused on Luke. His mouth was still knotted and he'd worked up a sweat. He was walloping at Gabe's torso, but the punches were losing power. Gabe spoke in the voice he'd used as a sergeant. "Keep your fists up, O'Rourke. Protect your face."

Luke seemed to come out of a fog. Gabe didn't want him thinking too much, not until they'd crossed from enemies to allies. "Hit from your shoulder, not your elbow."

Luke's next blow landed smack in the middle of Gabe's chest. He could have stayed still, but he backpedaled as if Luke had knocked him off balance.

The boy's eyes popped wide. Surprised at his own strength, he lowered his fists.

"Fists up!" Gabe ordered as he came at him. "I'm going to swing. You duck, then come at me with your right fist."

Gabe slowed the punch to nothing. Luke saw it coming, dipped his head and socked Gabe smack in the ribs that were already bruised. Air whooshed from Gabe's lungs and he moaned.

Luke looked pleased. "Did that *hurt?*"

"Of course, it hurt!" Gabe wanted to shout with pride. "You're strong."

"I am?"

"Strong enough." Gabe rubbed his side. "The trick

is to be smart about it. You can flail around like a windmill, or you can anticipate the other man's moves. I'm not hitting back, but Billy Drake will."

Gabe thought of Cassie and risked a glance at the schoolhouse. He was expecting a quarrel but saw only waving grass. She'd left, though he knew that quarrel would be inevitable. His mind drifted to the line of her mouth, the way she looked in that prim dress...

Whomp!

The next thing Gabe knew, he was on his backside in the dirt. Luke looked shocked and little afraid. "Are you all right?"

Gabe laughed out loud, a real belly laugh, low and deep. As Luke's eyes changed from fearful to proud, a grin spread across his face. Gabe stood and mock punched the boy's arm. "You rascal!"

Luke's face lit up. "I decked you!"

"You sure did, kid."

"And you're big!"

"Bigger than Billy." Gabe stood and brushed off his trousers. He and Luke had matching patches of dirt on their backsides. It struck a chord, one that sounded low and deep and showed up in his voice. "You've got a lot more to learn, Luke, including the most important lesson of all."

"What's that?"

"It's when *not* to fight." Gabe deepened his voice. "Never swing first. Never swing at someone smaller than you. And never, ever hurt a woman."

"Yes, sir."

For the next hour, they wrestled like bears. By the time they finished, the grass had been trampled, Luke's pants had holes in both knees, and Gabe imagined purple blotches on his ribs. It had been a long time since he'd burned off steam and it felt good, especially because Cassie had stoked the fire in his belly. He wanted to win her love and he intended to do it. Spent and happy, he and Luke dropped down to the grass and sat at right angles to each other, each leaning against the trunk of the cottonwood. The sun had dropped in the sky, softening the hard blue of the day but not the knowledge that Cassie would read him the riot act when he showed up with Luke.

Gabe stared across the meadow. "My belly says it's time for supper."

"Mine, too."

Gabe didn't want the day to end, but he shoved to his feet. As he reached down to give Luke a hand, the boy looked up with a peculiar light in his eyes. "I wish my dad had been like you."

Of all the blows Gabe had taken today, that one hurt the most. He answered with the deepest truth of the day. "If I had a son, I'd want him to be like you."

The boy looked chagrined. "Even if he threw rocks sometimes?"

"*Especially* if he threw rocks."

Staring straight ahead, they walked side by side to Cassie's mercantile. Luke heaved a sigh. "My ma's going to know I was fighting."

"I'll speak to her," Gabe said. "If she's going to be mad at anyone, it should be me."

Gabe clamped his jaw. He didn't like to quarrel, but some fights had to be fought.

Chapter Eight

Cassie pounded on the door to the parsonage. As soon as Thelma opened it, she blurted her only thought. "I need help."

"Come in." The older woman opened the door wide. "Tell me what happened."

"It's Luke."

"I figured."

"And Gabe."

Thelma closed the door with a click. "That figures, too."

As Cassie followed her into the parlor, she told the older woman about this morning's conversation with Gabe and the discovery that he'd gone against her wishes. When Luke hadn't come home after school, she'd gone to see his teacher. She'd heard voices behind the schoolhouse, investigated and found Luke attacking Gabe like a rabid animal.

For an instant she'd been angry with Gabe, but then she'd seen tears on Luke's cheeks. Her son had gone into a blind rage and Gabe had been taking the punches. With his arms up and bent at the elbows, he'd been the picture of surrender, even sacrifice. She'd thought of Christ on the cross and had trembled with the knowledge that she was just like Luke, flailing blindly at life. Gabe had been right about her son needing to become a man, but she didn't know what to do about it. With her business in dire straits, she felt guiltier than ever for her failings as a woman and a mother. That's why she'd run to Thelma.

With her neck aching, Cassie knotted her hands in her lap. "I'm so confused."

Thelma sat on an old cane rocker, picked up her knitting and set the chair in motion. As she lifted the needles, a pink baby blanket took shape and her lips quirked upward. "Are you angry with Gabe?"

"I want to be."

"But you're not?"

"How can I?" Needing an answer, Cassie glanced around the room. Everywhere she looked she saw photographs of the Halls and their three sons, each one as tall or taller than his father. "Gabe was right about Luke."

Thelma twisted the yarn around her index finger. "How so?"

"He says Luke needs someone to push against."

"That's part of it."

Cassie furrowed her brow. "What's the rest?"

Thelma kept rocking. "The boy needs someone to show him what it means to be a strong man. He needs a father."

And the sky is blue. Cassie held in the retort. "I know that."

Thelma stopped rocking and set the knitting in her

lap. "So what's stopping you from asking me for that lemon cake recipe? It's Gabe's favorite, you know."

Cassie knew that, too. She thought of yesterday and how he'd set it aside to help her. This morning he'd rescued Luke and this afternoon he'd rescued him again. She owed him more than a cake.

Thelma picked up her knitting and went back to rocking. The wood creaked like old bones, but the gray-haired woman said nothing, leaving Cassie to ponder her question. Why not bake that cake for the man she loved? The answer hit as hard as Luke's fists had pounded Gabe. "I can't lean on anyone, Thelma. Not after what happened with Ryan."

"I see."

"Do you really?" Cassie lifted her arm to indicate the wealth of family pictures. "Reverend Hall's a good man and a good father. Have you ever doubted that he loves you?"

The older woman held her head high. "Not once."

"Did you ever wonder where he was at night? Or smell perfume on his collar?"

"Never."

"Then you don't *see* at all." Cassie pushed to her feet. She wanted to leave, but she had nowhere to go except her empty store. Instead she paced to a window facing a field of tall grass. "Ryan hurt me, Thelma. I'll never put myself in that position again."

"Gabe's not Ryan."

"I *know* that." Cassie scowled at the tall blades. "But people change. They leave. They let you down."

"It's true that I married well." The needles clacked behind Cassie's back. "But I've had my share of trouble. I know what it's like to feel like someone's let you down."

Cassie turned in surprise. "Who?"

"Not Ben."

"Your sons?" The middle boy had run off.

"Not in the ways that matter. Ben and the boys are human beings. They've hurt me on occasion and I've been disappointed in their decisions at times, but they're human and I know that. I never expected perfection from any of them."

As Cassie watched Thelma rocking steadily, she recalled the disappointments in her own life. Her mother's death had been sudden and devastating. Her father had never been one to talk. After her mother's passing, he'd pulled into himself like the tortoise at the Chicago Zoo she'd seen with Luke. Even Luke had disappointed her, though he had the excuse of youth.

"Who let you down?" she asked Thelma.

"The Lord did."

Shivers went down Cassie's spine.

"At least that's what *I* thought." Thelma gave a small laugh. "As things turned out, He knew what was best."

Cassie turned back to the window, holding in a sigh as she stared at the empty meadow. "I've heard that before."

"I imagine so." Thelma's knitting needles kept up a steady rhythm. "You don't know this, but when the boys were little, Ben and I were so poor I worried about feeding them. He'd been pastoring a church in Nebraska and we loved it, but the elder board changed hands. The new men voted us out."

Cassie understood the sting of rejection. "That had to be hard."

"It was." Thelma rocked the chair harder. "For two years we lived like vagabonds. Ben preached wherever people would listen and we lived on offerings. When things ran short, he worked odd jobs. Those years were hard, but I wouldn't trade them for anything."

"Why not?"

"Because they toughened us up. Now when Ben preaches about God's mercy, he knows what it is. When I tell a woman I know how it feels to stretch a bag of flour, I really do."

Cassie had known hardship in Chicago, both the pain of her marriage and the fear of doing without. After the divorce, she'd skipped meals so Luke could have all the milk he wanted. "I don't feel that way about Chicago. I wish I'd never left."

As Thelma lowered her hands, the pink yarn puddled in her lap. "You've lost your faith, haven't you?"

Cassie felt as dry as sand. "I don't ever think about it." Except at night when she looked at the stars. Except when she was worried about her son. Except when she looked in the cash box and worried again. She forced herself to look at Thelma's face and not the baby blanket. "I just want a roof over my head and food and clothing for Luke. That's enough."

"Oh, Cassie."

"What?"

"*Things* will never be enough. In the blink of an eye, they can be lost forever. Only God is enough. That's why I'm so worried about you."

Cassie thought about what "enough" meant, both to herself and others. She'd taken Gabe's "enough" when she'd run away. She'd taken her son's "enough" when she'd chosen Ryan O'Rourke for a husband. Her neck hurt as she stared out the window. "No one took my 'enough.' I gave it away."

"You made mistakes."

"I did more than that." Cassie had no patience for sugarcoating. She knew how it felt to be the victim of a mistake. After hitting her, Ryan had apologized with trinkets, but she'd still had the bruises. She couldn't let Thelma excuse the wounds she herself had inflicted on others. She had to take responsibility.

"I ruined my life, Thelma. I hurt Gabe and Luke, too. I should never have left this town and I shouldn't have married Ryan O'Rourke. I knew he drank and chased women, but I married him anyway because I wanted a part in a stage play."

"That's still a mistake," Thelma insisted.

Cassie turned back to the window. A bee buzzed on the other side, hitting the pane over and over. It reminded her of Ryan's hand slapping her face and she felt the sting of tears. She turned back to the room, but she couldn't stop her feelings. They came out in a rush. "When Ryan hit me, I thought I deserved it. Now I'm a divorced woman and my son breaks windows."

Thelma lowered the knitting. "Sit down, Cassie."

"I'd rather stand."

The old woman's features hardened with determination. "That's pride talking. It's my house, and I asked you to sit."

Cassie resented Thelma's bossy manner, but she positioned herself on the divan. When the woman's eyes shone like silver, Cassie thought of swords and tea sets, the playthings of children that turned them into adults.

"Your mother's gone," Thelma said. "But I'm here and I'm taking her place. Someone has to chase those buzzards away from you."

Cassie thought of Rizpah. "What buzzards?"

"The ones that have you convinced God doesn't care about you because you've made mistakes, that He doesn't love you just as you are. Those thoughts are black and ugly and evil. God sent his son to die for you, Cassie. He knows all about your flaws. He knows about mine and Ben's, Gabe's and even Luke's. You said you wanted enough. Here it is… God's love. His forgiveness is all you need. He's promised you eternal life. Lift up your eyes and you'll get a taste of it now."

Everything in Cassie cried out with need. "I want to believe you, Thelma. I do, but…"

"But what?"

"The town hates me. Maude's spreading rumors. If business doesn't pick up, I'll have to leave. Where's God now?"

"He's right here." Thelma gave her a hard stare. "He's in Ben and me. He's in the grass and the sky. He's in the sun and the stars. You just have to look."

Cassie thought of the stars bearing her name, the queen chained to a chair with her neck bent and her spirit broken. What would it be like to look up and see glory instead of guilt? *Oh, Lord… Help me.* A cry pushed into her throat, but she choked it back.

Thelma bowed her head. "Father God, Cassie needs you right now. She's tired and afraid and she's lost her way…"

A lump pushed into Cassie's throat, then tears welled. When Thelma asked the Lord to heal her wounds, the moisture spilled down her cheeks. Still praying, Thelma crossed from the rocker, dropped to her knees and took Cassie's hands as she lowered her head. "Dear Jesus, you love your children. You love Cassie. Chase away the buzzards, Lord, every one of them. Amen."

As Thelma looked up, Cassie thought of all the buzzards in her life. Guilt topped the list by a mile. Fear came in second and it still had its claws in her. If business didn't improve, she'd be forced to leave town. Maude had been circling Cassie for weeks now, watching her struggle and waiting to pick the flesh from the bones of her store. That buzzard needed to be chased away and Cassie knew how to do it.

When she raised her face to Thelma, she felt a fire in her belly for a new challenge. "I'm going to have a sale."

"That's a fine idea," Thelma replied.

Still holding the old woman's hands, Cassie pushed to her feet and lifted Thelma with her. "I'll mark everything half off. Let's see if Maude can sabotage that!"

"She'll try, I bet."

"Let her." Cassie thought of Gabe teaching Luke to defend himself and others. She'd just learned the same lesson. "I have a boy to feed and I intend to do it."

Thelma's eyes shone with pride. "Good for you, Cassie. When is the sale?"

"Saturday. I'll advertise in Friday's paper." She had no money to spare, but her future depended on the size of the crowd. If she could support herself, she could stay. And if she stayed, she could bake that cake for Gabe. She could even invite him to supper. She took a breath. "Thelma?"

"Yes?"

"Could I have that recipe for lemon cake?"

"You sure can." Thelma headed for the kitchen with Cassie behind her. As Cassie wrote down the ingredients, she thought about Gabe. Knowing his integrity, he'd come home with Luke and confront her. Instead of a quarrel, he'd get a supper invitation. She couldn't do more until her business succeeded, but she hoped that day would come.

She finished copying the recipe, hugged Thelma goodbye and hurried to the grocer where she bought lemons. They'd been shipped from California and were expensive, but she wanted the cake to be perfect. If she hurried, she could have it baking when Luke and Gabe arrived at the apartment.

An hour later, Cassie had put the pan in the oven and her apartment smelled sweet. She'd just put her hands in the dishwater when Luke came through the door.

"Ma, I'm home. Can Gabe stay for supper?"

A deep voice came from the landing. "Hold your horses, son."

Son...eating supper as a family. Cassie's heart thumped with longing. It was too soon to encourage Gabe. First the store had to succeed, but for tonight she could show her gratitude with a home-cooked meal. It would be plain, but Gabe had always liked simple food.

She reached for a dish towel and headed for the door. "Please, Gabe. Come in. You're more than welcome for supper."

He arched one brow. "I am?"

Her cheeks flushed. "I'd love for you to stay."

He lingered in the doorway, giving her time to

change her mind. Cassie flashed to another time he'd
lingered… He'd come into her father's mercantile and
bought a set of spoons. He hadn't needed the spoons at
all. They'd been an excuse to chat with her. Smiling,
she motioned for him to come inside. "Supper won't
be fancy, but we have dessert."

His eyes twinkled. "I smell Thelma's cake."

"I hear it's your favorite." Her cheeks turned rosy.

He looked over her shoulder at Luke. "Go wash up.
I need a word with your ma."

"Yes, sir."

Luke padded down the hall, leaving Cassie agape at
his good manners. As Gabe stepped over the threshold,
she closed the door. Turning, she looked into his eyes.
"I'm sorry for what I said. You were right about Luke."

"I didn't intend to go against your word."

"It's all right." She thought of the blows he'd taken.
"You must be bruised. I've got liniment—"

"It's nothing."

"It was *something* to Luke." She wanted to touch
his shirt sleeve but didn't. "Thank you isn't enough for
what you did today, but it's the best I can do."

"It's plenty." He touched her cheek with his thumb.
"Cassie, I—"

"Not yet," she murmured.

With their eyes locked, she stepped back and smiled
shyly. As Gabe lowered his hand, Luke came down
the hall. He'd changed his shirt, combed his hair and
was carrying a box that held toy soldiers, the ones he'd
spent hours painting on wintry days. After a final look
at Cassie, Gabe followed the boy into the front room.

She went alone to the kitchen, a cramped room
meant for a single adult and not a family. As she sliced

ham and potatoes, she listened to Gabe telling stories about his cavalry days. She'd first heard them on her parents' porch, sitting with him in the swing while the sun set and the stars came out. Normally she'd have asked Luke to set the table, but she didn't want to break the mood. Instead she put out utensils herself, then dished potatoes, ham and beans from the stove.

"Supper's ready," she called.

Luke gave his usual seat—the one across from her—to Gabe, and sat between them, making Gabe the head of the table.

As he lowered himself on to the chair, he sought Cassie's gaze. "I'd like to say grace."

"Of course." For the first time in years, she bowed her head with sincerity. So did Luke.

"Father in Heaven," Gabe began. "We thank You for this meal and for the loving hands that fixed it. Amen."

Direct and honest, that was Gabe. As Cassie lifted her knife and fork, excitement bubbled inside her. "I have news about the store."

Gabe's brows lifted. "Oh, yeah?"

"I'm going to hold a sale," she said. "Everything will be marked half off for one day only. If that doesn't draw customers, nothing will."

Gabe looked pleased. "Sounds smart."

"I'll help," Luke added.

For the next half hour, they made plans. Gabe offered to paint a sign for the store window. Luke said he'd pass out handbills. By the time Cassie served the cake, they'd become a team. They also had a common enemy, one that couldn't be ignored. Gabe mentioned her first. "Do you expect trouble from Maude?"

"Probably," Cassie answered. "But I'm ready for it."

"Me, too," Luke added. "I *hate* Billy."

Gabe lowered his fork. "Hate's pretty strong, Luke. Especially when it's aimed at someone as bad off as Billy."

"I don't think he's bad off at all," Luke countered.

"I do." Gabe lowered his chin. "Billy's a bully. One of these days, he's going to get his clock cleaned and he won't have anything left. No friends. No pride. Mark my words, that day's coming."

Cassie wanted to cheer for Gabe. He'd directed her son from hate to charity while protecting the boy's pride. She gave him a look full of admiration.

Gabe countered with a look of his own. "Maude's a bully, too. Sometimes you have to fight."

"I'm going to." In addition to holding the sale, Cassie would pray for Maude and Billy when she prayed for Luke. She might not see any changes, but she would do her best. "Guthrie Corners is home. I want to stay here."

"Me, too." Luke added.

Gabe pushed his plate away. "The sale's a good idea, but there's another way to fight."

"What?" Her nerves prickled.

"The Civic Association's having a social on Friday night. Come with me."

Needing time to think, Cassie raised her napkin to her lips and pressed. The Friday night social was a longstanding tradition of the Guthrie Corners Civic Association. For many years her father had served as president. William Drake now held that position and Maude would be the hostess. The event took place in the town hall, but it might as well have been the Drakes' parlor. Buzzards flapped and cawed in

Cassie's mind. The time had come to shoo them away for good. "I'd like that," she said, smiling.

Gabe's brows shot up. She'd surprised him. She also knew that men brought their wives and children, so she turned to Luke. "We'll both go, all right?"

"Do I have to dress up like Billy?"

Gabe interrupted. "Only if you want."

"No way!" Luke declared.

But Cassie would… If she could triumph on Friday, she'd be back in business on Saturday. She could attend church on Sunday with her head held high. She smiled at Gabe, then sliced a second piece of cake and handed it to him. Years ago they'd danced at socials like this one. He'd taken her for moonlight walks and they'd stolen kisses. Her heart pounded with memories, then dreams.

"Does Pete Doyle still bring his fiddle?" she asked.

"He will this time," Gabe said with a glint in his eye. "I'll see to it."

Chapter Nine

Gabe slipped six bits into Pete's hand. "Play 'Beautiful Dreamer,' will you?"

"Sure thing, Deputy." The livery owner wedged the fiddle under his chin, then warmed up the strings with a fancy scale. As the harmonies filled the hall, Gabe strode to where he'd left Cassie with Dale Archer, owner of the feed store, and Betty Lou Baines, the best seamstress in town.

The night had been a resounding success, though he and Cassie had both been nervous when it started. Three hours ago he'd arrived at her apartment. She'd been stunning in a royal blue gown, but her cheeks had been as pale as moonlight. He knew how much tonight meant to her. Over the past five days, they'd become close again. He'd kept up Luke's boxing lessons and he'd muscled cabinets into new places for Saturday's sale. Every night she'd cooked him supper and they'd talked on the divan while Luke did his homework in his bedroom.

He hadn't kissed her for only one reason. She'd made it clear that her future in Guthrie Corners depended on the store's success. If she couldn't make ends meet, she'd be compelled to return to Chicago where she could support herself. Gabe didn't see the need. He could provide well for Cassie, Luke and babies to boot, but she had strong feelings and he had to respect them.

Tonight Cassie would sink or swim. So far she'd been swimming like a fish. In spite of Maude's cool looks, Cassie had held her head high. With Gabe at her side, she'd approached businessmen and their wives, inviting them to the store to look at her fine things from Chicago. Gabe thought of the opal ring he'd kept all these years. If the night stayed as bright, he'd be slipping it on her finger in no time.

He reached her side just as Pete played the first notes of the song. Cassie looked up and smiled at the same memory that had prompted him to ask for it. "Beautiful Dreamer" had been playing when they'd danced for the first time in this same room. He put his hand on her back, then spoke to Dale. "I believe Mrs. O'Rourke promised me another dance."

Dale laughed. "It looks like she promised you *all* her dances, Deputy. Enjoy yourself." He looked at Cassie. "I'll tell my wife about the draperies. She'll be there tomorrow."

"So will I," Betty Lou added. "I'm from Chicago, you know. I loved browsing at Russell's."

Cassie smiled like a gracious queen. "I'll see you all at the store. We open at 9 a.m."

As they turned to the dance floor, Gabe saw a glow in her eyes he'd missed for fourteen years. She'd triumphed tonight. He'd waited long enough. Before the night ended, he'd ask her—again—to be his wife. "Let's dance," he said in a gravelly voice.

"Yes."

As she swayed into his arms, he swept her into the swirl of colorful dresses and tapping feet. The way her face lit up was worth every cent of the money he'd paid Pete. He'd never seen her so happy, so alive. The blue dress matched her eyes and reminded him of a twilight sky. The sparks between them snapped like the fireflies he recalled from his southern youth. He drew her closer. "You look beautiful."

"I'm happy." Her fingers tightened on his shoulder. "Everyone's coming tomorrow. My father's old friends…women like Betty Lou. I just needed to open the door."

Gabe tightened his grip on her waist, drawing her close as he looked into her eyes. "I can think of another door that needs opening."

He meant the door to his house. He wanted it to be *their* house, but first she had to marry him. The question formed in his heart and rose to his lips. Before he could ask it, Cassie swayed fully into his embrace, keeping time with the music *and* with him, matching their steps in the slow, sweet rhythm of the song. When he looked into her eyes, he saw stars of light. He also saw fear. Before he proposed, he had to chase it away. "I love you, Cassie."

"Oh, Gabe—"

"I think you love me, too."

Her eyes glistened with hope, but she looked down at her feet. "I do, but I'm frightened."

"Of what?"

"Everything."

He didn't want to hear a protest. With the music rising and the crowd swaying, he kissed her tenderly on the lips, tasting the sweetness of their tomorrows without a hint of the bitter past. He didn't care who saw them. The kiss felt good and right, pure and so full of promise that he didn't notice when the music stopped and the crowded shifted. Nor did he hear two boys shouting from out on the street. He didn't come to his senses until Cassie pushed out of his arms.

"That's Luke!"

She lifted her skirt and ran for the door. The crowd had the same idea. Gabe elbowed through the throng and caught up to her as she raced down the wide steps. He heard shouting in the alley, thumps, bumps and a thud that sounded like a fist on a flour sack. As they rounded the corner, he saw Billy sitting in the dirt with a bloody nose and Luke looking proud.

Gabe pushed ahead of Cassie. "Wait here."

"But he's my son!"

Yes, but Luke didn't need his mother right now. He needed a father, a man who'd skinned his knuckles and knew about battles and war and honor. As he strode ahead of Cassie, he glimpsed Maude approaching from the opposite side of the alley.

Gabe reached Billy first and hauled him to his feet. "What's this about?"

"He hit me for no reason!"

Luke shouted back. "It was *too* for a reason!"

"You started it!" Billy countered.

"Both of you," Gabe bellowed. *"Knock it off!"*

The boys stopped hollering, but Cassie and Maude had reached the edges of the crowd. He could get to the bottom of this mess if the women stayed out of it, so he froze Cassie with a look. He tried the same glare on Maude, but she burst through the crowd and pulled dear, precious Billy into her arms. "How dare you question my son!"

Gabe spoke in a voice just for Maude. "Someone has to. The boy needs discipline."

"How dare you!"

Gabe scanned the crowd for Mr. Drake but saw only onlookers. "Where's your husband?"

"He's speaking to the mayor."

"I see," Gabe answered.

Judging by the pained look in his eyes, so did Billy.

Gabe spoke to Maude. "Step back now. I'll handle this."

The woman's face twisted with disgust. "No, you won't! You're all wrapped up with Cassie. You'll take her side. She's trash and everyone knows it!"

Gabe's blood ran cold. "That's uncalled for, Maude."

"It's true!" She pointed at Cassie, who'd stayed on the periphery as he'd asked. "You're cheap and foolish, Cassie Higgins! You treated me like dirt. Now you know how it feels. I promise you, *no one* with an ounce of class will ever set foot in your store. If they do, they'll pay."

Using only his eyes, Gabe urged Cassie to speak her mind. *Fight! Stand tall!* Instead she wilted like a flower with a broken stem. He couldn't stand there and say nothing, so he faced Maude. "Cassie's a good woman. This town needs her."

He scanned the crowd, matching eyes with each man and each woman, daring them to speak on Cassie's behalf. One word of support would change the tide. Instead the edges of the crowd peeled back like the skin off an orange. Dale Archer turned his back and headed down the street. So did Mary Lou, Millie and other folks who'd earlier been friendly. To-morrow the store would be empty, but Gabe clung to a single hope. Cassie had already told him that she loved him. Surely she wouldn't leave him again.

When the crowd dwindled to the three of them and the two boys, Maude hooked her arm around Billy's shoulders. With a smug look, she dabbed at his bloody nose and made baby talk. Gabe felt sick for the boy. As she led him away, he wondered what had happened to cause the fight. As much as he needed reassurance from Cassie, Luke needed him more and so he turned to the boy. "I figure you had a good reason."

"Yes, sir." Luke had a boy's shoulders but a man's glint in his eyes. "He was pestering Margaret."

Everyone in town knew Margaret and felt sorry for her. Her mother had died six months ago and her fa-ther had fallen apart. Still a child herself at the age of eleven, she was raising her younger siblings, two boys and a girl who missed their mother. She also had curly hair and freckles. Someday she'd be a beauty, but not today. If Billy had been harassing the girl, Luke had done well to protect her.

Gabe clapped him on the back. "You did the right thing, son. Let's go home."

He looked to Cassie for agreement, but she had eyes only for her son. They were misty and wide and full of love. Then she looked at Gabe and he knew... Maude had shattered her hope. Unless he could per-suade Cassie to lean on him—to let him protect and provide—she'd leave.

Expecting the fight of his life, Gabe guided them

both down the street to Cassie's apartment. Luke chattered every inch of the way, describing how Billy had pulled Margaret's braid and called her "Freckle Head." Luke had told him to stop. He'd warned him twice, but Billy had ignored him and cornered Margaret, chanting the mean name.

"That's when I pulled him back," Luke said. "He tried to push me, but I dodged just like you taught me."

"That's good." Gabe was only half listening. He put his hand on Cassie's back and she stiffened. He lowered it and felt lonely.

Luke kept chattering. "He swung first. I ducked, then I swung back. I hit him square on the nose. I don't remember what happened next, but everything you taught me, it worked really well."

"As long as you fought fair, I'm proud." Gabe glanced at Cassie. She hadn't said a word since Maude's lambasting. He'd have preferred tears to silence, but anger would have been best. They could have fought for the future together. Instead she looked as pale as a dead body.

When they reached the stairs to her apartment, she spoke for the first time. "Luke, go wash up. I need to speak to Deputy Wyatt."

The formality made his blood boil. Luke, standing straight and proud, climbed the stairs. The instant the door closed, Cassie sighed. "I'm sorry, Gabe. I can't stay in Guthrie Corners."

"Why not?" He ground out the words.

"This town hates me."

"So what?"

"If I can't make a living, I can't feed Luke."

"I can." He touched her cheek, then leaned forward to kiss the spot where a tear had trickled.

Before his lips tasted salt, she stepped back. "I can't lean on you like that."

"You mean you won't."

"I can't!" she cried. "I leaned on Ryan and he cheated on me—"

"I'm not Ryan O'Rourke!"

"Of course not," she murmured. "But I know what it's like to not have enough. You could die. You could lose your job—"

"Or we could have fifty glorious years," he insisted. "You can't let fear stop you."

She squared her shoulders. "It already has."

"Cassie—"

"If even a single person comes tomorrow, I'll stay." Moonlight shimmered on her cheeks and turned them pale. "But if no one comes, it'll mean it's time to go. This town hates me, Gabe. It'll turn on you, too. Luke will struggle every single day. I can't stand the thought!"

He saw her point but from another angle. "Luke can take it. So can I."

"*I* can't." She hung her head.

Instead of cupping her chin, Gabe kept his hands at his sides. "You have to fight, Cassie."

She raised her head but only enough to look at his chest. "Maybe people will come tomorrow. Maybe this won't be a problem."

"It already is."

Her eyelashes fluttered up. "What do you mean?"

As much as he wanted to hold her close, Gabe stood tall. Cassie had to win this fight on her own. "It's like before," he said. "You're making decisions for both of us, but not this time, Cassie. I've got a say in the future."

"Yes, you do."

"I don't care if you run your own business or not. I'm all for it," he said with complete sincerity. "What I won't do is marry a woman who doesn't trust me to take care of her. I'd take a bullet for you. I'd dig ditches to see that you had enough."

"I know." She looked at her toes. "It's just not…"

"Enough," he finished for her.

She said nothing.

Gabe felt a fury that went back to the day she'd jilted him. "I've never been enough for you, have I?"

"That's not it."

"Then what is it?" he demanded.

"I don't know." Her voice wailed.

"When you figure it out, let me know." He turned on his heels and walked away. If she called to him, he'd go back in a heartbeat. He'd take her in his arms and be strong for them both. He'd do anything for her…except be a doormat. With the silence echoing, he headed home to his empty house where he kept the Bible with Cassie's name as his wife and the ring she didn't want. Alone in the dark, he went to the bedroom that should have been theirs and sat on the mattress, worn more on one side than the other. Bereft and alone, he dragged his hand through his hair.

"She needs help, Lord," he murmured. "Show me what to do."

Thoughts tumbled through his mind. He imagined dragging in customers at gunpoint. He considered pounding on doors and making threats. *Buy from*

Cassie or you'll answer to me! But she didn't need that kind of support. She'd said she'd stay if just one customer showed up. Gabe would have gladly been that customer—he'd buy the dishes she favored—but the thought smacked of disrespect, even manipulation.

"Please, Lord. Send someone to her shop." He slid to his knees. "I'd die for her. I'd do anything—"

As he hit the floor, his boots slipped beneath the bed and nudged an old valise. His next thought lit up the moment, the future and everything in between. He'd used that valise to bring his things to Guthrie Corners. He could use it to leave with Cassie on an eastbound train.

If the sale flopped and she left, he'd be going with her. He'd lost her once to foolishness and he wouldn't do it again. He wanted to go to her now and tell her he'd buy the train tickets, but the thought of Cassie leaving with her tail between her legs didn't sit well. He understood about shaking the dust off his feet, but he also knew how the Lord felt about Pharisees and Philistines. Someone needed to put the Drakes in their place and Gabe intended to be that man. But how? The thought that came struck him as both simple and fitting.

Cassie went up to the apartment and saw Luke sitting on the divan, waiting for her with a question in his eyes.

"Are you mad at me?" he asked.

Cassie sat next to him. "No, Luke, I'm not. You were helping Margaret."

She wished someone had helped *her.* Gabe had, but the town had turned against him, too. Sitting with

Luke in the shadows, she imagined the brush of wings
on her face and the peck of beaks. Maude had eaten her
alive tonight. Cassie had wanted to fight, but Maude's
first words had wounded her so fiercely she'd lost the
will. If she stayed in Guthrie Corners, she'd face that
scorn every day. So would Luke. So would Gabe. She
couldn't bear the thought. She simply didn't have the
courage. Nor could she stand being dependent on anyone, even Gabe. At least in Chicago she'd have her
pride.

"We need to talk," she said to her son.

"About what?"

Cassie resisted the urge to smooth his hair. "What
do you think about going back to Chicago?"

"I don't want to."

"I don't either, Luke. But I have to be able to support us."

His voice rose to a little boy whine. "What about
Gabe? You like him, don't you?"

"I do, but I'm worried about money."

Luke had heard about money trouble all his life. He
took the news with a quiet dignity he'd never before
possessed. When had her boy started thinking like a
man? Since he'd known Gabe, that's when. Was she
wrong to leave? Cassie called out to God in the dark
of her soul. *I need help, Lord. What should I do? I
can't stand the mockery, but neither can I bear the
thought of leaving.*

"I have to send a payment to Mr. Russell," she said
quietly. "If nothing sells tomorrow, I can't do it."

"It's because of Mrs. Drake, isn't it?"

"She's been angry with me for years."

"I don't want to go, Ma." He stood up. "I want to stay and fight."

Gabe's influence…again. Cassie felt both proud and scared. "We need to pick our battles, Luke. I don't think I can win this one. And I have to take care of us. I have to buy food and clothes—"

"I'll work."

What a change in her little boy… She didn't want to discourage him, but who in Guthrie Corners would hire him? What did a mother do? Cassie needed to chase the buzzards away from her son, but he was becoming a man who needed to stand on his own. She'd learned from Gabe that she needed to respect Luke's pride, but she found it hard. She found it harder still to think of Gabe. She wouldn't leave without saying goodbye, but if she had to leave town to protect her son, she'd do it. She didn't doubt that Gabe would provide for their basic needs, but she couldn't bear the thought of public scorn. Gabe could lose his position, a job he loved. He'd blame her like Ryan did…

Cassie turned to Luke. "It's best that we leave."

He looked at her with wide, vulnerable eyes. "What about Gabe?"

Cassie didn't say a word.

"You like him, don't you?"

"Yes."

She watched Luke's expression, a mix of confusion and daring. Twelve-year-old boys didn't go down the road marked love, but they knew it existed. Luke raised his head higher. "Gabe wouldn't care about the store. I know it."

"No," she answered. "But I do."

"Gabe wouldn't run," Luke said forcefully. "Neither will I. Billy's a bully. I'm not sorry I hit him. He was being awful to Margaret."

"I know, sweetie."

Luke scowled. He didn't like being called "sweetie" but it had slipped out and he took it. Cassie forced herself to sound stronger, more respectful of him. "We'll have to see what tomorrow holds, okay?"

"All right," he mumbled. "I'm going to bed."

He walked down the hall, leaving Cassie to bow her head and pray for God to chase away the buzzards from her store, Gabe and especially her son.

Chapter Ten

The next day, early in the afternoon, Cassie lost all hope. She locked the door to Higgins Mercantile for the last time, then surveyed the merchandise she'd been looking at for a month. Not a soul had come to the sale, not even the Halls, though Thelma had sent a note saying they were under the weather. For a moment Cassie wondered if they'd heard about the ugliness at the social, but she decided they hadn't. If Thelma had gotten word, she'd have dragged herself to the store to show support.

Gabe hadn't shown up, either. She'd half expected him to pressure her by being that one customer she'd mentioned. Instead he'd kept his distance. The gesture made her love him all the more, but it didn't change the facts. She hadn't sold a thing and she owed Mr. Russell a payment. The buzzards had won.

Awash in despair, she headed for the back room to fetch a shipping crate. As she passed the dishes she loved, she heard a timid knock on the front door, turned and saw Margaret peering through the window. The girl probably wanted Luke, but Cassie hadn't seen him all morning. At breakfast he'd asked if he could visit Gabe and she'd said yes. The silence in the store had driven her crazy, but she'd been glad to spare Luke the humiliation of no customers.

Sighing, Cassie went to the door and opened it. Margaret always looked a little pale, but today her freckles stood out like strawberries on her ashen face. "Are you all right, sweetie?"

"I'm okay."

"Are you looking for Luke?"

The girl glanced down the street as if she was worried she'd been followed. Seeing no one, she looked back at Cassie. "I came to buy something."

Cassie wrinkled her brow. "You did?"

"Yes, ma'am."

As she motioned for Margaret to come inside, Cassie pondered the peculiar nature of her visit. Had her father sent her? But why wouldn't Ian Glebe come himself if he'd decided to show his support?

Margaret headed for the counter and the jars holding penny candy. She looked at the peppermint and licorice, the butterscotch and the gumdrops that would be dry by now, then she reached into her pocket and set two pennies on the counter. "I'd like candy for my brothers and sister."

"Sure," Cassie answered. "You'll need some, too."

"I only have two cents."

"That's more than enough." Cassie filled four brown bags with as much candy as they'd hold. When she finished, she slid the purchase across the counter.

"There you go," she said brightly. She wouldn't let her gloom show to a child.

"Thank you." Margaret started to leave, then turned

back with a solemn expression. "My father told me to stay away today, but I heard him talking to Deputy Wyatt and Luke. They said you needed people to buy things or you'd have to leave town. That's why I came."

Cassie stood speechless.

Margaret looked even more ashen. "I know two cents isn't enough, but it's all I have."

Her one customer…a child with two pennies who'd mustered her courage to help someone else. Cassie felt a sudden, humbling rush of shame. Last night Luke had chased a buzzard away from this girl. Today she'd risked everything to repay his kindness. She'd brought the best gift she had—as little as it was—to honor him. Luke was her hero, because Gabe had taught him how. Looking at the pennies, Cassie saw the biggest buzzard of all coming straight at her. Black and ugly, the vulture had a name and its name was Pride. *Her* pride. Never leaning… Never trusting anyone… Not even Gabe when he'd waited fourteen years out of the purest love she'd ever known. She hadn't trusted God, either.

Especially God, she admitted to herself. Today, in spite of her lack of faith, He'd sent that one customer. Two cents wouldn't pay Cassie's bills, but it was enough to keep her in Guthrie Corners. If Gabe would still have her, she'd stay forever.

As soon as Margaret left the store, Cassie hurried out the door. She had to get to Gabe. Three steps down the street, she recalled something Margaret had said about her father. *I heard him talking to Deputy Wyatt.* While she'd been hiding in the store, Gabe had been fighting for her. So had Luke. She sped to the sheriff's office and went inside. Blinking, she flashed on the day she'd found her son in jail. Gabe had set the boy free to be a man. He'd set her free, too. Free to love… Free to trust.

Instead of seeing him behind the desk, she saw another deputy. "I need Gabe," she said.

"He's not here."

"Where is he?"

The man shrugged. "Dunno. He's off today."

She sped out the door and ran to the house that would soon be theirs…if Gabe would have her. She banged on the door but no one answered. She considered running through the streets of Guthrie Corners in search of him, but he could have been anywhere. He could be eating lemon cake at Thelma's or fishing at the stream. He could be at Millie's or…the list went on and on. Desperate to spill her feelings, Cassie went back to the store, selected the finest stationery she stocked and penned a letter to Gabe… A love letter that told her deepest feelings. She sealed it with white wax, then took it to his house and slipped it under his door, just as she'd done fourteen years ago. This time, instead of pain and rejection, the letter held the sweetest of invitations.

"That was awful!" Luke whined to Gabe.

Gabe had to agree. They'd spent the day calling on anyone in Guthrie Corners who might have supported Cassie. People had been friendly until he'd stated the purpose of the visit. When he'd suggested Millie could use new table linens and that Cassie had them on sale, the café owner had given a firm shake of her head.

"It's not about Cassie," Millie had said. "I admire the woman for trying. But if I tick off the Drakes, I'll be hurting for business, too."

Next he and Luke had visited Dale and Jenny Archer. Mrs. Archer had looked sympathetic, even irked, but Mr. Archer had given a firm shake of his head and insisted on staying out of the tangle with the Drakes.

Betty Lou's dress shop had been locked up tight.

Pete Doyle didn't have time for fancy things.

They'd visited Ian Glebe, Margaret's father, last of all. Gabe had told the man what had happened and how Luke had come to his daughter's defense. Mr. Glebe acknowledged Luke with a curt "Thank you," then he'd been blunt regarding Cassie. "I can't help her, Deputy. You know the Drakes. I'll be next on their list. With four children to feed—and no wife—I can't risk it."

Gabe had no right to judge the man, but the decision struck him as gutless.

Last of all, they went to the bank to speak with William Drake. "Wait here," he said to Luke.

As the boy lingered on the boardwalk, Gabe walked into the building. No tellers were at the counter, so Drake himself came out of his glassed-in office.

"Good morning, Deputy," he said. "What can I do for you?"

"I'm here about Billy."

Drake looked bored. "What about him?"

Gabe deliberately kept his hands relaxed and his tone low. "Last night wasn't as simple as you might have heard. Your son was bullying Margaret Glebe. Luke stopped him."

The banker huffed. "I hardly think you're objective."

"Then speak to Margaret."

"Is there anything else, Deputy?" His tone reeked of sarcasm.

"I've done my duty," Gabe countered. "The rest is up to you and Mrs. Drake. But be warned, sir. Your son is headed for trouble."

Drake's hair, slick with pomade, shone in the light. "Boys will be boys. It's not a problem."

"It is if no one teaches them right from wrong." Gabe didn't have time for the man's nonsense. He'd said his piece and he wanted to get to Cassie. He wished the attorney well and left. Outside he found Luke and they headed for Cassie's shop. The moment of truth had come. The mercantile would be humming with customers, or it would be dead quiet.

When they reached the front of the store, Luke tried the knob. "It's locked."

Gabe peered through the window. Not a spoon had moved. The bolts of cloth sat untouched and uncut. He didn't see Cassie anywhere.

"Go on up," he said to Luke. "I need to do something before I speak with your ma." Later today he'd hand her the train tickets with the opal ring.

After Luke slipped inside, Gabe headed for the depot. He bought the tickets for two weeks' time, long enough for Cassie to close up the shop and for Gabe to give notice that he'd be leaving his job. If he couldn't sell his house, he'd rent it out. With the tickets in his shirt pocket, he headed home.

As he opened the door, he saw an envelope on the rug, face up bearing his name in Cassie's curly writing. Fourteen years turned into a mist and burned away with the heat of anger. Another goodbye… Another rejection. He relived the humiliation of standing alone in church. He felt the burning in his gut. Once again, she'd lacked the courage to face him.

Gabe stared at Cassie's handwriting for a long time. Did he really want to marry this woman? Looking at the curls of his name, large and bold and in Cassie's hand, he thought of her stubborn pride, her irritating ways…and he knew. He could stand anything except another "Dear Gabe" letter. What she had to say, she could say to his face.

He set the letter on the side table without reading it. Tomorrow after church, he'd call on her and speak his mind.

Cassie waited all afternoon and long into the evening for Gabe to come to her. She'd poured her deepest feelings into the letter and he'd chosen to ignore it. She didn't blame him. From Luke she'd learned that they'd made calls and been rejected by everyone except Margaret. Gabe had come face-to-face with the scorn Cassie had predicted, and he'd changed his mind about marrying her. She didn't blame him a bit.

By morning, she'd lost all hope that he'd come to her. She wanted to go to church, but she also wanted their next encounter to be in private. Later today she'd go to his house, but right now she had work to do. The unsold merchandise had to be shipped back to Chicago, so after breakfast she and Luke went downstairs. Together they hauled the crates from the storeroom and began clearing the shelves.

Feeling bereft, she looked at the dishes she treasured. Fragile and pretty, she'd pack them last with extra care. She and Luke worked in companionable silence, each lost in thought until someone pounded on the door. She opened it and saw Gabe. He'd worn his dark suit to church and had pulled his hat low to shield his eyes, either from the sun or from her, she didn't know.

"Hello, Gabe."

"Cassie."

She couldn't stop staring at his jaw. Clean shaven and hard-set, it reminded her of oak and marble.

"May I come in?" He'd issued an order.

"Of course."

She opened the door just enough for him to slip inside, then closed it. Luke saw him and stood straight, but he didn't speak a greeting. Instead the men—Luke had that air today—traded a look of silent understanding.

Her son headed for the door. "I'm going upstairs."

Cassie knew what the next minutes held. Gabe would tell her that he'd changed his mind about marrying her. She'd force a smile and say she understood. They'd part with a handshake and a promise to stay in touch for Luke's sake. She'd do all those things with her head high.

As Gabe took off his hat, she looked into his eyes. "You must have gotten my letter."

"I sure did." He spat the words.

Cassie didn't understand. She'd expected a hard goodbye, but it wasn't like Gabe to be cruel. "I'm sorry."

"Why, Cassie?"

He'd asked her that question in Reverend Hall's office and she'd confessed the truth. This time she didn't understand it. She'd said everything in the letter. She wrinkled her brows. "Why what?"

Gabe reached between the pages of his Bible, took out the envelope and held it out with disgust. "You could have at least told me in person."

Looking down, she studied the crisp folds of the paper and the unsmudged ink. With her fingers trembling, she took the envelope and felt the wax seal, still unbroken, against her thumb. The fool man hadn't read the letter! He'd taken it for another rejection. Her heart soared with hope, but she didn't let it show.

"You're right," she said.

His eyes stayed hard, challenging. "Read it out loud. We can both hear the foolishness."

Cassie popped the wax with her fingernail, removed the two pages and began to read.

My Dearest Gabe,

For fourteen years I've wandered this earth without you, yet you've lived in my dreams and dwelled in my heart. In those secret places where a woman keeps her truest treasure—her love, her family—I've kept those memories of you. Today they're more alive than ever. I love you. I always have and always will.

"Cassie—" his voice broke and he reached for her. She stepped back. "Let me finish." He'd waited a long time for this moment and so had she.

"Last night you told me again that you loved me. In a moment of selfish pride, I said I didn't trust you to take care of Luke and me. This morning, with the help of a child, I came to my senses. Your love is more than enough. It's everything a woman could want. If you'll still have me, I'd be honored to be your wife. Nothing would give me greater joy. I know that Luke loves you, too."

She heard his breathing, heavy and unsteady. Her own matched it with a ragged cadence. She wanted nothing more than to go into his arms, but she had to finish reading.

"I'll be waiting for you, my love. Tonight and always.
Love, Cassie."

With her heart pounding, she looked into Gabe's eyes. They had a sheen of love and a spark of possession. Knowing that she'd treasure this moment as much as he would, he kissed her with a tender vengeance. "You scared me to death!" he whispered between breaths. "I thought you were leaving again."

"Never."

With their cheeks touching, she felt him smile as he murmured into her ear. "I have a surprise for you, too."

"What?"

"I've got three train tickets in my pocket. If you want to leave town, that's fine but I'm going with you."

"Oh, Gabe."

"We'd get married first, of course."

Cassie grinned. "Today?"

"Sure."

She wanted to jump and clap like a child. "Let's tell Luke. He'll be so happy."

Grinning, he hooked his arm around her waist and kissed her again. Just as their lips touched, the front door opened. A month ago she'd have jumped to make a sale. Today she called to the customer from across the room. "The store's closed."

Gabe's eyes twinkled. "Go on. Make a last sale."

Chuckling, Cassie broke from his arms, looked down the aisle and saw Ian Glebe. After a glance at Gabe, he spoke to Cassie. "My daughter came home yesterday with enough candy for a year. It seems she has better manners than I do, Mrs. O'Rourke." He held out his hand. "I've come to say thanks to you and your son."

While Cassie stood in shock, Gabe called up the stairs for Luke. The boy raced down, saw Mr. Glebe and stopped.

Margaret's father held out his hand. "Thank you, Luke, for helping Margaret."

As they shook, the door opened again. Dale and Jenny Archer strolled in. After a friendly nod to Cassie, they ambled to the drapery display. The Halls walked in next, then Millie and a dozen old friends of Cassie's father. Cassie was back in business, but at that particular moment, she wasn't happy about it. Gabe came to her side. "What's wrong?"

She wanted to shoo everyone out of the store. "I thought we were getting married this afternoon!"

"We are."

"But—"

Gabe grinned. "Enjoy it, Cassie. We waited a long time. A few minutes won't hurt."

After two hours the shelves had noticeable holes and she had four invitations to have tea with old friends and new ones. Even Millie had come by. She'd purchased a dozen tablecloths and ordered red-checked napkins. Everyone except the Drakes had called on her today. Cassie knew what she had to do. Unless she forgave Maude, the buzzards of unforgiveness would peck at them both until they had another argument. Silently, Cassie thought a prayer. *I forgive her, Lord. I hope she can forgive me.* Tomorrow she'd visit Maude and do her best to wipe the slate clean.

Before the thought left Cassie's head, the front door opened and she saw Maude with her husband and Billy. The women studied each other from across the room. Instead of steeling herself for animosity, Cassie approached her rival with an outstretched hand. "I know we've had our differences, Maude. I was terrible to you all those years ago. If you can forgive me, I'd like to be friends."

Maude looked into Cassie's eyes, then gripped her hand in both of hers. "I'm sorry, too. I've been horrible to you. I've spread lies—"

"It's over," Cassie said.

"I came to make it right." Maude glanced at her husband, then at Billy. "Before we leave, my son will be apologizing to Luke. Thanks to Gabe, my husband had a talk with him."

Cassie squeezed Maude's fingers. "It's not easy raising a boy, is it?"

"No!" Maude laughed and so did Cassie. As mothers of sons, they had a lot in common. As the women stepped apart, Maude glanced around the shop. "You have lovely things. I need to do some shopping."

"Take your time," Cassie said, smiling.

For the next hour, people came and went. When the last customer left, Gabe touched her elbow. "I spoke to Reverend Hall when they came by. He and Thelma are waiting at the parsonage."

"What for?" Luke asked.

Cassie didn't think Luke would object, but twelve-year-old boys could be unpredictable. He didn't have a say in this matter, but his acceptance would mean a lot.

Gabe looked at Cassie, then spoke directly to the

boy. "I love your mother, Luke. I always have. I've asked her to be my wife and she's agreed."

The clock ticked. Dust settled in a shaft of light, then Luke stood tall and looked hard at Gabe. "You'll be good to her, won't you?"

"Yes, son. I will."

A lump pushed into Cassie's throat and wouldn't slide back. With tears welling, she watched as Luke kept his eyes on Gabe. "Does this mean you'll be my father?"

"I'd like that," Gabe said. "But you're almost grown. I respect that."

"I still need a dad."

"Good, because I need a son."

Grinning, Gabe held out his hand to shake. Luke took it, squeezed hard, then turned to Cassie. In his eyes, she saw the boy who'd always live in her heart and the man he'd soon become.

Gangly and awkward, he put his arms around her. "I love you, Ma."

"I love you, too."

As her son hugged her tight, Cassie looked over his shoulder at Gabe. Tall and strong, he filled her heart with joy, peace and the hope of children. Laughing out loud, she thought of the set of dishes she'd always wanted. They'd look lovely on Gabe's table, especially when their family grew. She'd love a brother for Luke, and she'd always wanted a daughter of her own. With her heart full, Cassie whispered a prayer of thanks.

* * * * *

A popular and highly acclaimed author in the Christian market, **Sara Mitchell** aims to depict the struggle between the challenges of everyday life and the values to which our faith would have us aspire. She is the author of contemporary, historical suspense and historical novels, and her work has been published by many inspirational book publishers.

Having lived in diverse locations from Georgia to California to Great Britain, Sara uses her extensive travel experience to help her create authentic settings for her books. A lifelong music lover, Sara has also written several musical dramas and has long been active in the music ministries of the churches wherever she and her husband, a retired career air force officer, have lived. The parents of two daughters, Sara and her husband now live in Virginia.

Visit the Author Profile page
at Harlequin.com for more titles.

THE WIDOW'S SECRET

Sara Mitchell

Don't call me Naomi, she told them. Call me Mara, because the Almighty has made my life very bitter.
—*Ruth* 1:20

Jesus answered her, If you knew the gift of God and Who it was that asks you for a drink, you would have asked Him and He would have given you living water…. Whoever drinks the water I give will never thirst. Indeed, the water I give will become a spring of water welling up to eternal life.
—*John* 4:10–14

For my mother, a true Southern lady
whose life exemplifies dignity, intelligence and faith.
Thanks for loving me, no matter what.

Acknowledgments

With much gratitude to the staff members
in the US Secret Service Office of Government and
Public Affairs, and the staff of the US Secret Service
Archives. Their cheerful assistance and endless
patience, not to mention the reams of invaluable
information they provided, deserve recognition.
Any errors or inaccuracies rest entirely
on the author's head.

Prologue

New York City September 1884

A bar of orange-gold sunlight poured through the windows of the Binghams' Fifth Avenue mansion, flooding the large guest bedroom where Jocelyn Tremayne had spent the past three nights. Tonight, however, she would be sleeping elsewhere. A persistent flutter wormed its way above the constricting whalebone corset; Jocelyn stood before the ornate floor mirror positioned in one of the room's several alcoves, solemnly studying the strange reflection gazing back at her. She blinked twice to see if she could pray the freckles into disappearing, at least for her wedding day.

Her prayers went unanswered.

"You look prettier than the picture in a *Harper's Bazaar* fashion catalog, Lynnie."

Kathleen Tremayne stepped around the four-poster bed and gently lifted her daughter's hands, gave them a squeeze as though to quiet their trembling. "Everything's going to be all right now," she whispered.

"Don't you worry, sweet pea. Your daddy's in the study with Mr. Bingham and the lawyer now, signing all the papers." An expression drifted through the hazel eyes, and Jocelyn launched into a flurry of words, anything to banish that expression from her mother's face.

"I'm fine, Mother. Just…excited." Nervous. Determined. But she would never admit to fear.

She might have willingly agreed to marry Chadwick Bingham, only son and heir to the Bingham fortune, in order to save her family's Virginia estate, but she wished she'd at least been allowed to wear her own mother's wedding dress, instead of Mrs. Bingham's. The white satin gown, over thirty years old, dripped with seed pearls and ruffles and Valenciennes lace over six layers of starched (and yellowing) petticoats to achieve the once-fashionable bell shape. Jocelyn thought she looked more like a bridal cake than a bride. She tried not to think about her mother's wedding gown, refashioned five years earlier into clothes for her two growing daughters.

Shame bit deep, without warning. Jocelyn was marrying a pleasant, courteous young man, but the union bore scant resemblance to her dreams. Even impoverished Southern debutantes with red hair and freckles dreamed of romance, not business transactions.

She thrust the pinch of hurt aside. Countless other Southern daughters over the past decades of Reconstruction and national recessions had married to save their families from starvation. In return for Jocelyn's hand in marriage, the Tremaynes would be allowed to live out the rest of their lives on the thousand-acre farm her great-great-granddaddy had carved out of the Virginia Piedmont two hundred years earlier. Her younger brothers and sister would still have a home until they each reached their eighteenth year, even if their heritage had legally just been signed over to Rupert Bingham.

Perhaps the payment was justified. Until the war her father, and his before him, had run the farm with slave labor.

Kathleen tugged a lace hanky from her sleeve and dabbed her eyes as she gave Jocelyn a sweet smile. "Well. It's time. Jocelyn? Are you sure…?"

"I know what I'm doing," Jocelyn promised, even as a black chasm seemed to be sucking her into its depths. "I like my husband-to-be. He's been nothing but kind. We'll be happy, I promise."

Her mother's cool hands cupped her cheeks. "Your father and I love you very much. If—" She stopped, pressed a kiss to Jocelyn's forehead. "Let's go, then. You don't need to start your new life being late for your wedding."

Hours later, the new Mrs. Chadwick Bingham surreptitiously leaned against one of the ballroom's marble columns and slipped her feet free of her shoes. An audible sigh of relief escaped before she could swallow it. Jocelyn hoped the din of four hundred conversations and music from the strings orchestra successfully masked her faux pas—until a masculine chuckle floated into her ears from the other side of the pillar.

"I agree with your sentiment, but I'm surprised to hear it coming from the bride." A tall young man appeared in front of her, a mischievous expression glinting behind a pair of gray eyes. "Don't look so mortified. I won't tell anyone." He swept her an awkward bow, lost his balance and stumbled against the marble pillar. "Oops. Sorry. My father tells me I've sprouted an inch a month over the past year, and my feet—" A tide of red spread across his face. "I apologize." He smoothed a hand over his long side whiskers, then fiddled with the end of his string-thin mustache while he continued talking. "We were introduced in the receiving line, but that was hours ago. Micah MacKenzie, at your service, Mrs. Bingham."

"Mr. MacKenzie." Frantically Jocelyn felt for her shoes with her stockinged toes. She could feel the heat in her own cheeks, which certainly must rival her hair for color. "I—I do remember you." A polite social fabrication. On the other hand, she *wished* she remembered him. As though to balance the impropriety of her sigh, her brain abruptly nudged her memory. "You were with your parents. And—and you're in your second year at college, though I don't recall where. Your father works for Mr. Bingham, I believe?"

"Not exactly." He paused, for a moment looking far older than his twentysomething years. "Never mind. May I fetch you something to drink? You look like you're about to wilt."

"I'm sorry it shows. Brides are supposed to glow, aren't they?"

The gray eyes softened. "No, I'm the one who should apologize. Again. You make a breathtaking bride, Mrs. Bingham. Your husband is blessed."

Blessed? Jocelyn thought his word choice peculiar, but then everything about this gangly young man didn't quite seem to fit the polished perfection of all the other guests. And yet, despite his lack of poised sophistication, she felt more at ease than she had in…in weeks, actually. "Are you one of Chadwick—I mean, Mr. Bingham's friends?"

"No, ma'am. I only know Chadwick through my parents." He didn't seem to know what to do with his hands; after twiddling his thumbs, he distractedly ran his fingers through his pomaded hair, then glared down at his sticky hand. "Forgot my mother insisted I look the part," he muttered half under his breath as he pulled out a large white handkerchief and wiped his hand clean. "Now that I've made a complete fool of myself, how about if I finish the job and ask if you'd permit me to help you find your way over to your husband. You've been polite long enough," he finished gently. "The guests are waiting for you to leave, you know."

"I know. I was… I mean, I thought…" Swallowing hard, she straightened away from the column. "I can't find my slippers underneath all my petticoats," she admitted with a defeated smile. "I took them off because my toes were cramping." Was it impolite for a new bride to mention her toes? "I suppose I could start across the floor and hope the petticoats drag my shoes along, but I didn't want to risk leaving them behind."

"I understand." This time his hand reached toward Jocelyn, and for the breath of an instant his fingers hovered inches from hers before he dropped his hand back to his side. "Don't move. I'll be right back." He disappeared into the crush of wedding guests.

Moments later he reappeared, Chadwick beside him. "Here she is," Mr. MacKenzie announced. "Waiting for you, I believe." He studied Jocelyn, and she suddenly felt as though he had touched a lighted match to her pulse. "You know, Bingham, I think you're absolutely right. The freckles lend her face much more character than a ho-hum rosy-cheeked complexion. Congratulations on your good fortune."

Chadwick was gawking at him as though his ears had just sprouted peacock feathers. "I…um…thank you," he finally murmured.

"Before you take her away, she requires your assistance in a small matter." Mr. MacKenzie tipped his head to one side, a half smile lifting one corner of his mouth. "God's blessings on your life together."

And before Jocelyn could frame an articulate reply, he vanished around the marble column and was swallowed into the crowd.

"What a bounder." Chadwick offered his arm. "I never said a word to him about your freckles."

"Oh." Jocelyn swallowed a stab of disappointment.

"He's certainly not part of Mrs. Astor's Four Hundred, I gather. Friendly enough, but he'd taken off his gloves, did you notice? And his trousers were—" He stopped abruptly. "It doesn't matter. He doesn't matter, does he? Too bad. Congenial sort of fellow, not like some in this crowd. Now, what's this small predicament that requires my assistance? Why, my dear, what a delightful shade of apricot. Here—" he leaned down, and the tang of his imported French cologne saturated Jocelyn's nostrils "—whisper in my ear, then. Don't be shy. We're married now, Mrs. Bingham."

Married. With a tremulous breath of laughter, Jocelyn shoved aside all thoughts save her new status, and rose on tiptoe to explain her predicament.

Hours later, she waited for her husband to enter the grand suite of rooms the Binghams had redesigned for the newly wedded couple. Hands clammy, heart thumping hard enough to rattle her teeth, Jocelyn squeezed her eyes shut and prayed with innocent fervor that she would please the young man who had vowed to care for her the rest of their lives.

"Jocelyn…"

She gasped, hands automatically clutching the crisp linen sheet even though she forced her eyes open. Chadwick stood by the bed, wearing a deep red dressing robe. Gaslight from the wall sconce limned his face, revealing the high forehead and the hooked nose so like his father's. His face was freshly shaved save for the trimmed mustache. His eyes were… Jocelyn searched his eyes, trying to interpret their emotions.

"M-Mr. Bingham?"

"Oh, for Pete's sake, when we're alone, call me Chadwick. Or Chad, if you don't mind. I've always hated my name, to tell you the truth." His Adam's apple bobbed up and down. "The truth," he repeated like an echo. "Why do you suppose the Bible claims it will set you free?"

Flummoxed, Jocelyn gathered her courage and sat up, drawing her knees to her middle and clasping her damp hands around them. Apparently Chadwick was as nervous as she was, and thought a conversation might help them both. She warmed inside at the thought of his sensitivity. "I always thought it meant telling the truth about Jesus. You know, that He's the Son of God?"

Chadwick laughed, the sound so dark and bitter Jocelyn flinched. "No wonder my parents insisted I marry you," he said. "Well, it's too bad for both of us your youthful innocence can't last forever."

He leaned over, planting his palms on the counterpane, inches from Jocelyn's quivering limbs. "The truth is, Mrs. Chadwick Bingham, that from this moment forth, you'll never be free again."

Chapter One

~e~

Richmond, Virginia September 1894

Over a dozen clocks chimed, bonged, pinged or warbled the hour of four o'clock in Mr. Alfred Hepplewhite's store, without fuss simply named Clocks & Watches. Jocelyn smiled at the cacophony of timepieces heralding the time, while Mr. Hepplewhite placidly continued to fiddle with the clasp of her brooch watch. His gnarled hands were as deft as an artist's, his eyes intent upon the task.

The store was busy today. Restless, Jocelyn wandered toward a deserted corner near the front of the shop to avoid mingling with the other customers. For this moment, she wanted to savor the freedom of being alone, a widow of independent means beholden to nobody, whose sole activity of the day consisted of enjoying the chaotic voices of a hundred clocks.

"Mrs. Tremayne? Your timepiece is ready."

Jocelyn hurried across to the cash register, ignoring a disheveled little man wearing a bowler hat several sizes too large, as well as an officious customer who insisted that Mr. Hepplewhite hurry up, he had an appointment in an hour and didn't want to be late.

"It's always a pleasure to see you, Mr. Hepplewhite," she said as she opened her drawstring shopping bag to pay.

"And you, madam." He handed her the watch, bushy white eyebrows lifting behind his bifocals when the seedy-looking customer wormed his way past the rude gentleman to stand shoulder to shoulder with Jocelyn.

"Sorry." He produced an unrepentant gap-toothed grin. "Just wanted to see them watch chains."

"Here now, I was next. Move out of the way, you oaf."

"Right enough, gov'ner." With a broad wink to Jocelyn the other man stepped back. "Fine-looking brooch watch, ma'am. Don't see many like it these days."

"No, I don't suppose you do." Jocelyn pinned her watch in place, steeling herself to fend off another impertinent remark.

Instead the man abruptly scuttled back down the aisle. After jerking the door open, he darted across East Broad, barely missing being run down by a streetcar. People, Jocelyn decided as her gaze followed the strange scruffy man, were uniformly unpredictable, which was why she didn't trust many of them.

The door flew open again before she reached it. A tall, broad-shouldered man loomed in the threshold. Blinking, Jocelyn took an automatic backward step when, eyes narrowing, he focused on her. For some reason time lurched to a standstill, all the clocks ceased ticking, all the pendulums stopped swinging because this man with windblown hair and gray eyes looked not only dangerous, but familiar. For a shimmering second he stared down at her with the same shock of recognition she herself had experienced.

"Excuse me," he finally said.

His deep voice triggered a cascade of sensations she'd buried a decade earlier, of longing and hope, and Jocelyn squelched the emotions. "Yes?"

One eyebrow lifted, but unlike most other gentlemen, this one remained uncowed by the hauteur she had perfected over the years. "A man came in here, scrawny fellow with a hooked nose, pointy chin. Clothes too big for him. Did you happen to see him?"

Cautious, Jocelyn kept her answer short. "Yes. I did see him. He left a moment ago."

Frustration tightened his jaw. Beneath a straight, thick mustache, his mouth pressed into a thin line. Despite herself, Jocelyn's heart skipped a beat, but even as she determined to push her way out the door, to fresh air and freedom, the man swept past her down the aisle, where he proceeded to make the same inquiry of the other customers.

Impatient, Jocelyn quickened her step and walked out of the store. She was behaving like a two-headed goose. Men had gawked at her all her life, even after she was married, certainly after she was widowed. Little could be gained by turning weak-kneed over one of them. His pointed questions marked him as a policeman of some kind, though he hadn't been wearing a uniform. But even if he weren't a policeman and was only trying to find a friend, his affairs had nothing to do with her. The reserved widow Tremayne did not associate with policemen or ruffians.

At what point during her marriage, she wondered,

had she allowed herself to become the self-righteous snob the Binghams so relentlessly demanded her to be?

"Mrs. Tremayne."

Her head jerked back. "How did you learn my name?" she demanded, concealing her perturbation with words. The sidewalk was filled with pedestrians she could cry out to for help, and her shopping bag, though not heavy, would serve as a weapon if words weren't sufficient. "Surely Mr. Hepplewhite wouldn't—"

"No, but one of his customers, a Mr. Fishburn, proved to be most helpful." The man smiled down at her, a smile loaded with charm and not to be trusted. His gaze lifted in a sweeping search around them. "I take it you are unaccompanied, without a maid or… your husband?"

Sometimes, usually when caught off guard, the uprush of painful memories would still crash over Jocelyn, stealing her breath as the waves sucked her backward into the past. "My life is none of your business. Please let me pass. I have an appointment. You're making me late."

"Ah." His head tipped sideways while he searched her face with an intensity that triggered a self-consciousness Jocelyn thought she'd eradicated long ago.

Then he touched the brim of his gray bowler hat, one end of his mustache curling upward as he offered a crooked smile. "Take care, Mrs. Tremayne. God doesn't always choose to intervene in our circumstances, and life on Earth isn't always kind to innocence."

Before Jocelyn could fry him with a scalding retort, he was half a block down the street.

"God doesn't always choose to intervene..." Bah! Jocelyn could have informed the man that God might exist, but He never intervened. For ten years she'd carried the awful burden of her past, and God never supplied one moment of peace. All that religious doggerel was nothing but a lie to soothe simple minds.

As for the rest of the stranger's insulting remarks, she'd been deprived of innocence long ago, and she couldn't figure out why he had made the observation.

If she ever saw him again, which she knew was unlikely, but if she did, she planned to inform him that he was an incompetent bounder, a slavering wolf disguised as a gentleman in his three-piece woolen suit and natty red tie.

On the way home, when she realized she was pondering her encounter with the mysterious gray-eyed stranger as a curative for her growing sense of isolation, she ground her teeth together, and initiated a conversation with the person sitting across from her in the streetcar.

Micah MacKenzie lost his quarry.

Frustration pulsed through him like an abscessed tooth, but he vented the worst of it by kicking over a stack of empty crates at the back of the alley where Benny Foggarty had disappeared. Benny, the glib-tongued engraver-turned-informant for the Secret Service, was now officially a fugitive, courtesy of Operative MacKenzie.

Thoroughly disgusted with himself, he retraced his steps back to Broad Street, then settled in the shadow of a bank awning. Shoulders propped against the brick wall, he tilted his bowler to hide his face, so he could survey passersby without drawing attention, and mull over his next move. Benny's dash into that store could have been deliberate, instead of a scramble to find a hiding place because something had made him bolt. After nine months, Micah thought he knew the way Benny's mind worked, but he acknowledged now that he may have been mistaken about the expression he'd glimpsed on his informant's face.

Because of one particular woman's presence in Clocks & Watches, a more thorough investigation not only of her, but of the other customers and Mr. Hepplewhite was required, regardless of Micah's personal feelings.

Decision made, he expelled a long breath, allowing his thoughts to return to the woman he'd practically abandoned midsentence when he spotted Benny.

Lord, a bit more warning would have, well, given me a chance to prepare. It was a childish lament. Aside from a miracle or two over the last millennium, life's pathways were mostly paved one brick at a time. Believers learned to call it faith. Right now, however, Micah felt like a brick had been hurled against his head. *Chadwick Bingham's wife...*

The shop owner had addressed her as *Mrs. Tremayne,* and the obnoxious Seward Fishburn corroborated hearing her addressed thus—which indicated that Chadwick must have died, and his widow remarried. Though Micah's initial shock had faded, a surprising regret boiled up without warning, catching him off guard. Once again this fascinating woman had dropped into his life, yet once again she was beyond his reach—for more than the obvious reasons.

She hadn't remembered Micah, of course, and why

should she? He'd been a gangly college boy without a shred of sophistication, invited to the wedding along with the rest of his family only because his father had been head bookkeeper at one of the Binghams' New York banks.

But as he mulled over their recent encounter, he realized that although she might not have remembered the awkward college boy, she *had* recognized Micah on some level. Her eyes, still long-lashed, a unique swirl of green and amber and nutmeg-brown, had flared wide in surprise and what he chose to hope was gladness...before she cut him off at the knees. Her frosty voice had been stripped of the soft Southern sweetness he remembered.

The Bingham family had done their job well.

Micah tucked his thumbs inside the pockets of his vest, struggling to reconcile the enchanting bride with the embittered woman on the sidewalk in front of Clocks & Watches.

Even on a cloudy day her hair still glowed with color, shot through with every hue of red in God's palette. And the freckles still covered her face, making a mockery of her chilly disdain.

Lord, of all the people in the world, she's the one I don't want to be suspicious of.

A raindrop splashed onto Micah's nose. He tugged down the brim of his hat, and set off across the street. Regardless of his feelings, and her current marital status, Jocelyn Bingham Tremayne required thorough investigation.

She would have children, of course.

Children...

For their sakes as much as hers, Micah hoped his investigation would prove her innocent. Deep in thought, he caught a passing horsecar and rode to the terminus at New Reservoir Park, where, instead of tending to his duties, he watched the sky gradually clear of rain clouds. When sunset turned the western horizon glowing red, he breathed a silent prayer for strength, then caught the last horsecar back to town.

Chapter Two

It rained once more during the night, but the next morning brought enamel-blue skies and the fragrance of fall in the air. As she patiently curled snippets of her hair on either side of her forehead, Jocelyn abruptly decided to take a drive in the countryside.

The spit curls on her forehead were forgotten as she yanked the pins out of her topknot and began twining her hair into a braid instead. Trying to look fashionable while driving an open buggy was not only vain, but ridiculous. She may have turned into an eccentric, but she would not stoop to silliness.

Katya, the day servant she employed to clean house and do the laundry, had just arrived and was filling a pail of soapy water when Jocelyn clattered down the stairs to the basement kitchen.

"Morning, Katya. I'm going for a drive in the country."

Katya smiled her crooked smile and nodded. The Russian girl had suffered some dreadful accident when she was a child, and though she could hear, she could not speak; the right side of her mouth remained paralyzed, her vocal cords somehow damaged beyond repair. Jocelyn had spent the past two years teaching her to read and write English, so for the most part communication between them remained snarl-free, but Katya was as reticent about her past as Jocelyn was. If sometimes the silence in the brownstone chafed a bit, Jocelyn could always go next door and talk to her neighbors.

"I should be back early this afternoon. I made some hot-cross buns last night, and there are preserves in the larder. Make sure you eat something, all right?"

The girl gestured to the pantry.

"I'll stop by the market on my way to the livery stable, pick up something for lunch. I can put it in my shopping bag."

Jocelyn grabbed some extra handkerchiefs to stuff inside the bag, as well, since any drive in the country included dust or, since it had rained the previous night, splatters of mud flying from the buggy wheels and horse's hooves. When she thrust the extra hankies into the bottom of the shopping bag, however, her fingers brushed against something hard and round. Puzzled, Jocelyn withdrew what turned out to be a man's watch.

What on earth?

Jocelyn laid the shopping bag on the seat of the hall tree without taking her gaze from the watch case. It was a handsome thing, made of gold, with an intricate design engraved in bas-relief on the bottom half of the lid. But when she flicked it open, instead of a timepiece, she found a piece of paper. When she unfolded it, to her astonishment it turned out to be a ten-dollar bill. Inside the bill was a ten-dollar gold piece.

Jocelyn turned the coin over and over, not recognizing its markings, knowing only that it was not like any coin she'd ever seen, or spent. As for the ten-dollar bill... Carefully she smoothed it out, turned it and saw that the engraving on the back was slightly blurred, the print not as crisp as it should be. Goodness, but she was holding a counterfeit bill! Written in a hurried black scrawl across the blurred engraving were the words "Remember to use..." That was all.

Fear crept into her mind, dark as a blob of ink staining the paper. Trembling, she stared down at the forged bill, the coin and the innocent-looking watch case until her icy fingers cramped.

She couldn't stuff the thing away in a drawer and pretend she didn't have it, nor could she pay a visit to the police station.

Nobody in Richmond, or even in the state of Virginia, knew that the widow Tremayne was legally the widow Bingham, whose husband, Chadwick, had hanged himself from the fourth-story balustrade of their Hudson River estate in New York, precisely five years and twenty-six days earlier.

A flurry of telegrams throughout the next two days left Micah exhausted, edgy and exhilarated. Chief Hazen, head of the Secret Service, had been furious over his blunder with Foggarty, yet placated by Micah's assurance that he had stumbled onto the possibility of the first solid lead in a case plaguing the Service for eight years.

Micah steadfastly refused to divulge names, or details, citing his concern over accusing an innocent civilian in the absence of definitive proof.

An express letter from Hazen arrived while Micah

was eating breakfast at the Lexington Hotel. *Your ob-fuscatory explanations are duly noted. A contradiction exists between what you deem a "solid lead," and your fears of unjust accusations. While strict adherence to Agency policy is required, obfuscation is* not *appreciated.*

As he drove the rental hack toward Grove Avenue, Micah chewed over the implications…and faced squarely that, for the first time in his eight years as a Secret Service operative, he was a hairsbreadth away from allowing personal feelings to interfere with his professional responsibilities.

He might have been alarmed, except for the anticipation singing along his nerve endings over seeing Jocelyn Bingham-now-Tremayne again.

When he arrived at the Grove Avenue address Mr. Hepplewhite had supplied, he spent a few moments studying the place while he collected his thoughts. She lived in a plainly appointed but attractive brick town house with two sturdy white-painted columns supporting its front porch, a much smaller dwelling than he would have expected, considering who her former husband had been.

The door opened. A plump young woman with dark hair and wary brown eyes appeared, swathed in a soiled apron, with a mobcap tilted precariously on her head. She smiled a lopsided smile at Micah but did not speak.

"Good afternoon. I'd like to see your employer. Mrs. Tremayne, isn't it?"

Recognition flared in the bright eyes. She bobbed a curtsy and stepped back, gesturing with her hand. After a rapid assessment Micah noted the droop in the

facial muscles on the right side of her face, the lack
of movement on the right side of her mouth when she
smiled. He revised any plans of interrogating her; his
estimation of Mrs. Tremayne rose at this evidence of
charity toward a woman unable to speak, though there
appeared to be nothing wrong with her hearing. Few
households employed servants with any sign of defor-
mity or, if they hired them, relegated them to menial
work, where they remained out of sight.

Mrs. Tremayne allowed her maidservant to answer
the door.

"Katya? Did someone knock? I thought I heard—
Oh!"

The woman who, along with the telegrams, had disturbed his sleep all night stood frozen on the staircase.
Above the frilly lace bow tied at her neck, her throat
muscles quivered, and the knuckles of the hand resting on the banister turned white.

"What are you doing here?" she finally asked.
Then, her voice taut with strain, "Who are you?"

At her sharp tone, quick as a blink, the maid darted
over to barricade herself in front of her mistress, her
gaze daring Micah to take one more step into the foyer.
Nothing wrong with her hearing, or her loyalty, he
noted with a tinge of satisfaction. Somewhere inside
the evasive and haughty Mrs. Tremayne still lived the
forthright bride he remembered, whose handicapped
servant sprang to her defense.

"I need to ask you a few questions. Nothing ominous," he answered. "My name, since we didn't get
around to formal introductions yesterday, is Micah
MacKenzie. Operative MacKenzie, of the United
States Secret Service. We're part of the Treasury De-

partment, assigned to protect the national currency by tracking down counterfeiters." After flipping open his credentials, he pushed aside his jacket to reveal the badge, also revealing his .45 Colt revolver.

Though brief, he caught the flash of raw fear before all expression disappeared from Mrs. Tremayne's befreckled face. "Are you here in an official capacity, Operative MacKenzie? Accusing me of the crime of counterfeiting?"

Hmm. Somewhere over the years, along with a patina of social smuggery, she'd also learned how to reduce a person to the level of an ant. "Depends on what you have to say, Mrs. Tremayne." Glancing at the maid, he added, "I imagine I interrupted your maid's work. She's free to go about her tasks while you and I talk."

"I'll decide for myself whether or not Katya remains." She descended the rest of the stairs. "She's my friend, as well as my housemaid. You've no right to dismiss her as you might a pet dog."

Claws, as well, and equally protective, Micah noted, irrationally pleased with her. "That was never my intention." Doffing his hat, he stepped forward, directing all his attention to the wide-eyed maid. "Katya, I'm here to speak with Mrs. Tremayne on personal as well as professional business."

"Don't be ridiculous," Mrs. Tremayne snapped. "Katya, it's all right. Go ahead with your cleaning. Mr.—I mean, Operative MacKenzie and I will talk in the parlor."

Lips pursed, Katya subjected Micah to a head-to-toe inspection that left him feeling a need to check his fingernails for dirt. Then she nodded once, and whisked out of sight down a hallway. After the maid left, Mrs. Tremayne gestured toward the room behind Micah. "Shall we?"

As he followed her into the parlor, Micah found his attention lingering on the graceful line of her spine, delineated by a seam in her day gown that ran from the back of her neck to a wide band of rich blue velvet at her waist. The glorious red hair was gathered in a severe bun at the back of her head. But she'd cannily arranged snippets of curls to frame her face and cover her ears, which not only softened but distracted.

"You may as well sit down, Operative MacKenzie." She dropped down onto an upholstered couch, leaving Micah to ease himself into an ugly Eastlake-style chair across from her. He glanced around the room. Like Mrs. Tremayne, it glowed with rich color and a profusion of textures. For some reason the plethora of trinkets and plants and pictures invited intimacy, instead of overwhelming the visitor.

Successful interrogation, Micah had learned, required a deft balance between diplomacy and intimidation. Silence either bridged a gap or spurred a confession. After a comprehensive assessment of the room, still without speaking, he trained his gaze upon the woman sitting across from him.

A pearl of moisture trickled below one of the vivid curls arranged at her temple. Her hands were clenched tightly in her lap, betraying her nervousness, and a gut-wrenching suspicion grew inside Micah. When the silence in the room stretched to the shattering point, he leaned forward.

"You seem ill at ease, Mrs. Tremayne. Is it because

you're widowed, and a strange man is sitting in your parlor?"

"Perhaps my husband is at work in the city, Operative MacKenzie."

He admired her audacity even as he shook his head at her as though she were a naughty child. "I gather information for a living, remember? The Secret Service tries to work closely with local authorities, you see. Your police department has been efficient, and cooperative. Better for everyone involved. Except for counterfeiters. Or—" he added, his index finger idly stroking his cheek "—anyone with a guilty conscience."

"If anyone should have a guilty conscience, it would be yourself, for prying into innocent lives."

"Usually my prying reveals a depressing lack of innocence."

Beneath the freckles her skin paled, and she turned her head aside. "I beg your pardon. You're right, of course." He watched as one by one she separated her fingers, focusing on the task as though her life depended on it.

Feeling like a heavy-fisted clod, Micah sat back with a sigh. "I like your home," he announced abruptly. "Though it's a home without a man inhabiting it. No spittoons, no masculine-size gloves or top hats or canes on the hall tree, no lingering odor of tobacco in the air, no photographs on your piano. You purchased it three years ago, and listed your status as widowed."

"Again, you've made your point, Operative MacKenzie. Yes, I am a widow. What of it?" The tremble in her voice leaked through her stillness; she continued to stare fixedly at the line of silk tassels fringing the drapery that covered the top of her piano. "I should have covered every inch of that wretched piano with photographs," she murmured. "But… I've never mustered the courage. I can't face the memories, and photographs serve no purpose other than to remind me of everything I've lost. And now…" She stopped, swallowed several times.

"I understand," Micah told her, gentling his voice. "It's difficult, isn't it, losing your spouse at so young an age."

"I will not discuss my husband's death. Ever."

"Death, not deaths? So you've been married only the one time, then?"

Chapter Three

The lump in Jocelyn's throat swelled until she was afraid she wouldn't be able to breathe, much less speak. This man was too quick for her, too intelligent. "Yes," she finally managed, once again picking her way through half truths. "I... I reverted to my family name, after he died." She took quick breath that allowed her to finish, "I told you I will not discuss the matter."

"I'm not asking you to. Yet." He'd been carrying a leather satchel, and now placed it on his lap. "One of the reasons I'm here today is to ask about Benny Foggarty. I have witnesses who signed affidavits that, after entering the store, he crowded next to you and Mr. Fishburn while you were standing up front, talking with Mr. Hepplewhite." He withdrew a much-handled photograph and passed it to Jocelyn. "Was it this man?"

With a concentrated effort of will she managed to keep her hands from shaking as she took the small rectangular cardboard and pretended to study its unforgettable likeness of the man who had probably ruined what was left of her life. "Yes." She passed her tongue around her lips to moisten them. "He made a comment about my watch." Instinctively, her hand cupped it. She could feel her heart frantically thudding beneath the soft linen of her shirtwaist.

"I can see why. It's a beautiful piece. A gift from your late husband?"

"My father." Pressure built inside her chest, crowding its way up her tightening throat. "He gave it to me on my sixteenth birthday. I've worn it ever since." Until she'd had to take it to Clocks & Watches to be repaired.

Life was unfair, Chadwick used to remind her. Either learn how to duck—or close your eyes and let it pummel you into dust.

"My father gave me a watch once," Operative MacKenzie said. "I'm afraid I was more entranced with its internal workings than keeping track of time. By the end of the evening, watch innards were scattered all over the table. I put it back together, but it never did keep good time." He smiled at her, uncapping the charm as though it were a potent elixir. "Made a perfect excuse to be late for chores or other loathsome tasks I didn't want to do."

She was too fatalistic to believe she possessed the strength of will to continue her resistance much longer, not when Operative MacKenzie treated her with a quixotic blend of gallantry and steely determination. Somehow that knowledge helped ease the pressure in her chest a bit. She wondered if condemned prisoners looked with the same tremulous longing upon their executioners.

Jocelyn Tremayne, you are a weak and foolish

woman. Postponing the inevitable, she asked, "How old were you?"

"Twelve. So Benny commented on your brooch watch?"

She nodded. "Then the gentleman at the counter made some rude comment, and—you said his name was Benny? Benny left. After I paid for the repairs, I did, too. And before you ask, I've not seen him since."

When was telling the truth a lie? At what point had she become so adept at it that she could sit in her parlor and not tell an operative of the United States government that she had, albeit without her consent, become a receiver of stolen goods?

"Hmm. I believe you, Mrs. Tremayne." Then he added, "About that, at least. It's a good thing your father gave you a brooch watch. They're more difficult to pinch."

Tell him. Give him the incriminating evidence and be done with it. Why not get it over with? Her thoughts spun in a maddening tornado of lurid visions of her fate, with chain gangs and rat-infested dungeons tilting her toward mental paralysis.

She opened her mouth to confess. "If Benny's nothing but a thief, why are you chasing him?" dribbled out of her mouth instead.

Perhaps she was a lost soul after all, beyond hope of redemption.

Operative MacKenzie sat back in the chair, his finger returning to trace the line of his clean-shaven jaw while he studied Jocelyn. Unable to stop herself, she stared back. He was tall; even when seated he dominated the room, with those clever gray eyes and thick tawny-brown hair whose prosaic color she envied with all her heart. As before, he was dressed in a gentleman's day wear: gray-striped trousers that matched his eyes, and a double-breasted waistcoat under his black woolen frock coat—a thoroughly masculine man comfortable enough to make himself at home in her fussy, feminine parlor.

This man was going to arrest her—and she was gazing at him as though he were her savior instead of her executioner.

But from the instant they'd met the previous afternoon, something about him had quickened feelings inside her that she thought were as dead and cold as her marriage. His deep voice washed over her, and she drifted in the currents, savoring the fleeting connection.

If only she could pray for strength, and be equally soothed by the assurance of a response.

"We don't usually chase after thieves," he was informing her, "unless they also print money from counterfeited engraved steel plates. Benny Foggarty's one of the best engravers in the business. He's also a gifted forger, taking photographs of bills, then touching them up with pen and ink. For the past nine months Benny's been…ah…helping…me track down the principals in a notorious gang of counterfeiters. If we can't put the ringleaders out of business, last year's financial woes will look like a picnic in comparison."

He paused, but when Jocelyn did not respond he shrugged, adding softly, "Life can be complicated. You're an intelligent woman, Mrs. Tremayne. But you're also…let's say, a 'guarded' woman. Makes me wonder what's happened to you over these past ten years."

She almost leaped off the sofa. Ten years? *Ten years?* What could he mean— He must know Chadwick, after all. And if he had known Chadwick ten years ago, he must know who she was. He probably also knew—

Rising, she locked her knees and struggled to breathe. "I need to…" The words lodged beneath her breastbone. She pressed her fist against her heart. "Operative MacKenzie…"

Her entire marriage had been a lie; how ironic that finally telling the truth would result in her complete destruction. She could feel the internal collapse, feel her will buckling along with her knees, until ten years of secrets and shame collapsed into rubble.

"Take your time, Mrs. Tremayne. Contrary to what some would have you believe, Service policy prohibits the use of thumbscrews on widows."

Because he didn't modulate the tone, it took Jocelyn a second to realize he was actually teasing her, as though he'd peeked inside her soul and discerned what would disarm her the most effectively. Disarm, yet somehow calm. *Chadwick had used sarcastic humor as a weapon, but never tolerated laughter directed his way—never.*

But Chadwick's image blurred, then dissipated like a will-o'-the-wisp until she could see only the commanding figure of a man with windswept hair and smoke-gray eyes…who had risen from the chair. Whose hand was stretched out as though he were about to touch her.

Prickles raced over Jocelyn's skin. She might crave his touch with a force more powerful than the longings for Parham, her long-lost family home, but she had long ago given up girlish dreams.

In a flurry of motion she sidestepped around him, practically babbling in her haste. "I have something for you, something B-Benny dropped in my shopping bag the other day. I didn't discover it until yesterday morning. I was going for a ride in the country and— Never mind. I should have told you before, but I—but I—"

His hand dropped back to his side. "It's all right, Mrs. Tremayne. Go ahead, finish it. You'll feel better for it, I promise." The kindness in his voice made her eyes sting.

"I doubt it," she whispered.

It was done. Whatever happened to her no longer mattered. Exposure, shame, condemnation—prison. Nothing mattered but that she had finally gathered the strength to do the right thing, for someone other than herself. No longer could she control her quaking limbs. Fumbling, she opened the doors to the sheet-music cabinet, tugged out the bottom drawer, her fingers scooping up the watch box. Her steps leaden, she walked back across the room to Operative MacKenzie and thrust out her hand.

"Here. This is what I found." She thrust the object into his hands. "Inside the box there is a ten-dollar bill wrapped around a coin. The bill is obviously counterfeit. I don't know about the coin."

As she talked, he opened the box, removed the bill and coin. "I gave him this case," Micah said. "He was to hide inside it the evidence he promised to bring me. Something, or someone, made him bolt into Clocks & Watches. Mrs. Tremayne, you're not going to swoon at my feet, are you?"

"Of course not!" She hoped.

"Hmm." His gaze shifted to the gold coin, and the ten-dollar bill, and Jocelyn watched, fascinated, while he examined them with narrowed eyes and deft fingers. "Excellent workmanship, but someone mishandled the printing on this bill, which indicates an entire set was likely bungled. Coin's probably bogus, as well…but this just might be the break we've been looking for." Excitement sparked in the words.

Jocelyn sank back down onto the sofa and allowed herself a single shuddering breath.

Operative MacKenzie's head lifted. "You all right?" She nodded but didn't trust herself to speak yet; his gaze turned speculative. "In my business, I've learned how to distinguish a counterfeit bill from the real one. I've also learned the same about people. Sometimes it's more difficult to discern the counterfeit from the genuine, particularly when you think you know someone. Or, in your case, when you think you *knew* someone."

Dumbfounded, Jocelyn lifted her hand to her throat, her eyes burning as she searched Operative MacKenzie's face. "Earlier…you said 'ten years.' We've met before, haven't we?" she asked hoarsely. "Before Clocks & Watches?"

"Yes. We have." He hesitated, clasped his hands behind his back and contemplated the floor for a tension-spiked second. "It was at a wedding. Yours, to Chadwick Bingham. You were leaning against a marble column, and you'd removed your shoes because they were pinching your toes."

"You're *that* young man? You said Chadwick told you the freckles gave my face character. No wonder I—" Roaring filled her ears, and a vortex sucked her inside its black maw. "Chadwick never said that. My freckles embarrassed him. And I... I wished—"

"Gently, there."

A hard arm wrapped around her shoulder, startling her so badly she jerked. "Whoa. Relax, Mrs. Tremayne. Let's lean you over a bit, hmm? I'm holding you up so you don't topple onto the carpet. As soon as I can, I'll fetch Katya. All right?"

The words washed over her, lapping at the fringes of the whirling vortex. His warmth and his strength surrounded her. If only she could trust him, if only she could lean against him, draw from his strength, savor the feel of his protective embrace. Soak up his kindness.

Kindness, she had learned through painful experience, usually covered a shark-infested sea, boiling with ugly motives.

She would never trust a man again.

Chapter Four

Micah struggled to remember that he was a federal operative, that the woman he held was not the blushing bride he'd met one evening a decade earlier, but a witness who—strictly speaking—was also a receiver of stolen goods.

He stroked his hand up and down her arm, spoke softly, as though he were gentling one of his brother's high-strung mares. Propriety be hanged—she felt like a bundle of sticks, brittle enough that the slightest pressure would snap her.

And her eyes, Lord. As Micah gazed into them, he felt as though he'd come face-to-face with himself. There were secrets in her eyes. Secrets, and pain.

As a man, Micah might yearn for the opportunity to help assuage the pain.

As a U.S. Secret Service agent, he was bound to investigate the secrets, particularly those associated with the Bingham family.

For the moment, however, the widow Tremayne was a terrified woman, one who needed a gentle hand and a reason to trust the man who had terrified her.

In the end, Micah took her for a ride in his rental buggy. Katya, who communicated through the use of a lined tablet and pencil she kept in her pocket, refused to accompany them, despite Mrs. Tremayne's and Micah's invitation. After eyeing her mistress, she wrote for a moment, then handed the paper to Micah.

She has fear, all day. Needs help. You are good man. A servant like me. I clean house, you help lady.

The maid's extrapolation of Secret Service to Secret "Servant" touched him; he wished her mistress shared Katya's wordless trust and was surprised by Mrs. Tremayne's docility, though he doubted it would last. For a few blocks they drove in silence. But the late-afternoon sun was warm, the sound of the steady clip-clop of hooves soothing, and eventually Mrs. Tremayne relaxed enough to shift in the seat, and glance up into his face.

"Katya is very perceptive, for all her youth. I'm surprised she refused to accompany us, but she's obviously taken a shine to you. Even if you were taking me to the police station to be arrested, Katya would tell me not to worry."

"I'm not taking you to the police station. I have no intention of placing you under arrest. The motive behind this outing is to banish your worries, which I'm sure you know achieve nothing but wrinkles and gray hair. A fate worse than death for a lady, wouldn't you agree?"

"Unless the lady has a head full of garish hair." At last she smiled, the rueful sweetness of it arrowing straight to Micah's gut. "But thank you all the same. I'm much better."

"God gave you a beautiful head of hair, Mrs. Tremayne. Why not celebrate it?"

He might have struck a match to tinder. Temper burned in her eyes and the words she spoke next were hurled like fire-tipped darts. "Operative MacKenzie, we may or may not have to endure each other's company in the future. If we do, please know that the next time you feel compelled to utter any divine reference, however oblique, I will leave the room. Do I make myself clear?"

"Perfectly. Since we're traveling in a buggy along a fairly crowded street, however, I'll be especially careful how I phrase my remarks."

Well, he'd known the docility would not last, but he hadn't anticipated such a violent reaction. Micah wondered who had poisoned her mind, not only about her hair color, but about God. On the heels of that question, it occurred to him that her comments might be a clever ploy, designed either to draw attention to herself or to deflect probing questions about why she had abdicated her status as a member of the Bingham family.

If she'd been a different sort of woman, the watch with its vital evidence might still be hidden in her music chest.

A stray breeze carried to his nostrils the faint whiff of the gardenia scent that permeated her house. It was a poignant, powerful scent and threatened to turn his professional objectivity to sawdust. Micah's hands tightened on the reins. "I do have a secondary motive for this drive. If you don't mind, I'd like to stop by and talk to Mr. Hepplewhite a moment. See if perhaps Benny Foggarty returned."

"Certainly." She drew her jacket tighter, but at least

her response was civil. "I'd enjoy seeing Mr. Hepple-white again myself, if only to have him vouch for my character."

Micah prayed the old watchmaker would do pre-cisely that, since his own view of Jocelyn Tremayne *Bingham* was regrettably distorted at the moment. For the next few blocks he stared between the horse's ears, excoriating himself. The Secret Service had spent years tracking the most vicious network of counter-feiters in the agency's brief history.

Operative Micah MacKenzie was not sharing a buggy merely with a distraught, vulnerable woman. He was sharing a buggy with the widow of the man whose family—eight years earlier—had arranged for the murders of three people, one of them Micah's fa-ther.

Micah glanced sideways at her profile. Sunbeams streamed sideways into the buggy, turning her freck-les a rich copper color. It was difficult to nurture sus-picions about a woman whose face was covered with copper freckles.

When they reached Broad Street, throngs of pe-destrians, buggies and bicycles choked the roadway as well as the sidewalks.

"Strange," Mrs. Tremayne commented in a warmer tone. "I've never seen such a crowd on a Wednesday afternoon."

Micah, who had spotted several policemen's hel-mets in the crowd, made a noncommittal sound as he maneuvered the buggy down a side street, pulling up in front of an empty hitching post. "We'll have to walk from here."

He helped her out of the buggy, noting with a tinge

of masculine satisfaction the color that bloomed in her cheeks at the touch of his hand. At least the attraction appeared to have buffaloed them both. She quickly freed herself and stepped onto the sidewalk—directly into the path of a newsboy racing pell-mell down the sidewalk. Boy, cap and newspapers tumbled to the ground. Jocelyn staggered, and Micah swiftly clasped her elbows, swinging her off her feet.

The feel of her exploded through him like a tempest. He managed to gently set her down on the sidewalk, then knelt to help the newsboy to give himself time to recover, no mean feat since his hands tingled, and his fingers still twitched with the memory.

Streams of people flowed around them, glancing indifferently at the boy's plight as they hurried along toward the corner.

"Thanks," the newsboy said, his voice breathless. "Didja hear what folks is saying? A murder. Right down the street! I ain't never seen nobody dead, so's I was hurrying." He gawked at Jocelyn while he stuffed newspapers under his arm, then flashed Micah a quick grin. "I never met nobody what had more freckles than a salamander, either." He grabbed the last newspaper, leaped up and scooted down the sidewalk with the agility of a squirrel darting up a tree.

Micah stood, dusting his hands, a frown between his eyes.

"I've heard less flattering comparisons over the course of my life," Mrs. Tremayne offered with a rueful smile. She glanced down the walk. "Operative MacKenzie…"

"Why don't we stick with 'Mr.'? It's less of a mouthful." Forcing a smile, he casually stepped in front of her. "Crowd's a tad unruly. How about if I take you home? I can talk to Mr. Hepplewhite another time."

"I'm not deaf. I heard what that child said. He was probably exaggerating. People don't get murdered in downtown Richmond." She darted a quick glance up into his face, stubbornness darkening her eyes. "We're already here, and I'd like to see Mr. Hepplewhite. If you want to wait in the buggy, I'll go by myself."

Micah lifted a hand, stroking the ends of his mustache to hide a reluctant smile. "I'm sure the masses would part like the Red Sea for you, Mrs. Tremayne. But my mother would nail my hide to the door if I neglected my duty." He gestured with his hand. "Shall we?"

By the time they reached the millinery shop two doors away from Clocks & Watches, the crowd swarmed eight deep, sober business suits mingling with day laborers, shop workers and a surprising number of ladies.

"Can't believe it…shocking…"

"…in our fine city…"

"…murdered…lying on the floor…"

"Who would…atrocity…such a nice man…"

Micah casually moved closer to Mrs. Tremayne, whose complexion had turned sheet white. Her lips moved soundlessly, and he leaned down, even as his gaze remained on the crowd of people hovering around the doorway of Clocks & Watches.

"Who…" She cleared her throat, tried again. "Who was murdered?"

A burly gentleman standing beside them glanced around. "The old watchmaker, I heard," he muttered.

"Here." Micah pressed his handkerchief into her

hand. "Breathe deeply. You'll be all right." Concerned, he watched her sway, watched her struggle for composure, and fail. Consigning propriety as well as his profession to the nether regions, he slipped a supporting arm about her waist, and all but carried her backward, out of the milling crowd, to the edge of the sidewalk, where he propped her against a telephone pole.

Eyes wide, unblinking, she dabbed at her temples with his handkerchief, its deep indigo-blue color a startling contrast against her red hair. After several deep breaths, a tinge of pink crept back into her cheeks. Solemnly she looked up at Micah as she returned the handkerchief. "I'm all right now. It's a dreadful shock. I behaved like a silly goose. Thank you for..." Her voice trailed away and she bit her lip.

"Violent death is always a shock—for most people." When her body shuddered, Micah debated with his conscience for the space of two heartbeats before giving in to the overwhelming urge to protect. "Come along." He took her hand, surprised by the way her fingers tensed, then clung. "There's nothing you can do now. I'll take you home. A lot has happened to you in the past twenty-four hours."

"Mr. MacKenzie? Do you believe M-Mr. Hepplewhite's death is connected with that man, the one who dropped the pocket watch in my shopping bag?"

Before Micah could scramble for an answer, they were interrupted.

"Operative MacKenzie! Been looking for you for going on two hours now." A burly policeman approached, looking annoyed. "Who's this?"

"I'll be along in a moment, Sergeant Whitlock," Micah said as Mrs. Tremayne pulled her hand free.

He watched in admiration as she metamorphosed from fright to fearlessness, spine straight and chin lifted, her lips stretching in a social smile aimed between the two men. "I won't take any more of your time. Obviously, you both have more pressing matters to attend to. Don't worry about me. I'll take a streetcar home."

"No, you won't," Micah contradicted, only to be interrupted by Whitlock again.

"Coroner's been ordered to wait until we ran you to earth. If I'd known you were out courtin', I'd have told him not to bother." His hand tightened on his billy club. "Now you're here, you git yourself inside and do your job, Mr. Government Agent, else you can whistle for any more cooperation."

"Sergeant... Whitaker was it?" The widow Tremayne focused on the police sergeant, who seemed to suddenly shrink in size. "For your information, Operative MacKenzie *has* been about his duties. He was considerate enough just now to attend to me, which is more than I can say for any other *gentle*man in this motley crowd. All of them preferred to satisfy their prurient interest in a man's death instead of coming to the aid of a lady. You may tell the coroner that Operative MacKenzie will be on his way—shortly. Now if you'll excuse us, I'd like to express my appreciation without you looming over us."

His face red as a brick, the sergeant glowered at Mrs. Tremayne, then swiveled to shoulder his way through the crowd.

"Well." Micah scratched behind his ear. "You certainly put him in his place."

"He was rude. And something of a bully. I've never

had much use for bullies." A forlorn uncertainty settled around her like a creeping gray fog. "Am I likely to be arrested now?"

"No." At least not in the immediate future. "You've committed no crime, you handed over the evidence and you have cooperated fully. However—" he hesitated, the internal debate waging a bloody war "—I think you, and Katya, should pack your bags. Until we learn the circumstances surrounding Mr. Hepplewhite's death, I'm going to need to keep an eye on you."

"You think I'm somehow responsible for his murder?"

"I've changed my mind." He reached for her hand once more, tightening his grip when she tried to wriggle free. "Apparently you can be a silly goose. Or hasn't it occurred to you that, if Mr. Hepplewhite's murder is connected to the forged currency Benny Foggarty gave you, you might be in grave danger?"

"You want... Are you saying you're trying to protect me?"

"Don't look so astonished. You're a widow, living alone, with only a mute maid who doubtless, like most day servants, returns to her boardinghouse at night. Why wouldn't I want to protect you?"

She'd looked less traumatized when she thought he might be about to arrest her. "Because—" her voice turned tremulous as a young girl's "—because the thought never occurred to me."

"Well, get used to it, Mrs. Tremayne. I don't know yet whether your involvement is by happenstance or design. But either way, you're now under my protection."

"As an operative for the Secret Service?"

"Partly." He held her gaze with his as he slowly lifted her hand until it was inches from his lips. "But also as a man." Every nerve ending in his body rioted as he fought the urge to bring her hand those last two inches. "I'll take you home, then I'll return here. I hope you and your maid are efficient packers, Mrs. Tremayne. I have a ticket on the Richmond, Fredericksburg and Potomac leaving Byrd Street Station first thing Friday morning. You and Katya will be accompanying me back to Washington."

Chapter Five

Washington, D.C., 1894

Through the window of the ladies' hotel on F Street, Jocelyn and Katya watched Operative MacKenzie swing aboard a streetcar. He was on his way to a meeting with the chief of the Secret Service, and Jocelyn's muscles were skeined together in painful knots. "Do you think he's an honorable man?" she asked Katya, who nodded with more decisiveness than Jocelyn felt. She waited in silence while the maid wrote on her tablet.

Is very good man. Likes you.

"Rubbish. He's behaved like a gentleman, but he's no different from anybody else. I'm under investigation, that's why he brought us to Washington with him." The knowledge chafed, yet not once during the six-hour train journey from Richmond had he treated her like a criminal.

Of course, neither had he accorded her the familiarity he'd extended when she'd all but swooned in front of Clocks & Watches. Since Chadwick, Jocelyn had not handled death with any degree of equanimity. Swallowing, she tried to banish the memory of the faces of the crowd, ghoulishly craning for a view of Mr. Hepplewhite's body, found sprawled in the stairwell that led to his upstairs apartment. Operative MacKenzie had refused to share any further details, but Jocelyn's vivid imagination needed no embellishment.

Katya scowled and wagged a sheet of paper in her face. *Is differernt. Sees YOU, not hare.*

"Dear Katya, it doesn't matter, especially if Operative MacKenzie's chief believes I'm involved with some notorious counterfeiting crowd." She stared blindly down to the street below, watching the soothing motion of a white-coated street sweeper pushing his broom. Perhaps if she went for a stroll…

Katya followed her, and Jocelyn sensed her reluctance to end the discussion. "By the way, you misspelled two words," she said, hoping to divert her. When it came to reading and writing, Katya was a perfectionist.

She could also be as contrary as a goat. *Don't spelling matter. He likes you. Sees more than red hare. You lissen. Be careful. Should tell me things. I take care of you.*

"I'm sorry I didn't tell you about the watch," Jocelyn retorted wearily.

She fretted over how easily she'd refused to confide in Katya, who after two years knew more about her than any other living soul. Yet with little effort Micah MacKenzie managed to wrest from her secrets she had never shared with anyone.

Of course, Micah MacKenzie was also the first adult male in ten long years to touch more than her gloved hand. Hating the sick sensation swimming about her middle, Jocelyn tormented herself by imagining his reaction had she plonked down beside him on the train seat. He would have been courteous, of course. But she would only have shamed herself and embarrassed them both, acting on that frenzied need for connection, however ephemeral, to someone other than Katya, who offered a dollop of comfort.

No doubt he'd offer that comfort when he slapped his handcuffs on her wrists, after being ordered by his chief to arrest her.

God in heaven, she longed to hurl the angry cry, *what did I ever do to make You hate me so?*

Micah took the steps up into the Treasury Building three at a time.

Nodding, occasionally speaking to people he passed in the maze of hallways, he tried to juggle his mounting uneasiness with the conviction that he would be able to do the right thing, for everyone.

Especially Mrs. Tremayne Bingham. Regardless of the mounting evidence against her, he could not bring himself to believe she was guilty of anything but an ill-advised marriage. A faint memory surfaced, something his mother once mentioned about the Tremaynes, about why an old, distinguished Southern family married their daughter off to a Yankee from New York City. Next time he visited her, he might risk asking.

A fellow operative was just leaving the chief's office when Micah reached the top-floor offices of the Treasury Department.

"You've stirred up a hornet's nest, MacKenzie," he said. "Best put on some armor."

"Thanks, Welker." Confidence dissipating, Micah stepped inside the office with a sense of impending doom.

Chief William Hazen, appointed to head the Service earlier in the year, greeted him but remained seated behind his ornate walnut desk.

"You're late, Operative MacKenzie."

"Yes, sir. Sorry."

"Humph. Well, I have a meeting in ten minutes, so let's see what we can accomplish with the time we've got." Rising, he came around the desk to stand in front of Micah. "According to your telegram last night, you confiscated the watch you loaned Benny Foggarty, along with some hopefully vital evidence. Let's see it."

Micah removed the watch case from his coat pocket, flicked it open and withdrew the bill and coin, handing them to Chief Hazen. "Bill's damaged bogus goods, as you'll see, but the front is some of the best work I've stumbled across in years. Paper's hardly distinguishable from ours, including the silk fiber. Possibly made in England, or Connecticut."

Beneath a thick handlebar mustache, Hazen's lips compressed in a thin line. "Most troubling. I believe the ten-dollar gold piece is from one of the coin mills operating out of New Jersey." He gave a mirthless chuckle. "Though the amount of gold wouldn't cover half a filling in a tooth. Most likely underneath the shiny gold surface we'll discover a blend of copper, antimony, possibly tin. Just last week we seized a sizable quantity of those materials, which, by the way, included a stack of bona fide silver dollars."

Micah nodded. "Milling's good but not top rate, and I thought the weight wasn't quite right."

"What about the handwriting on the back of this bill?"

"Obviously, it will require thorough examination

downstairs, but if you're asking my opinion..." Micah hesitated, then finished honestly, "I didn't recognize the handwriting. Benny could have forged it, or it could be the work of the person he stole the goods from. It's also possible the network has found someone new in Richmond...." His voice trailed away. No sense stating the obvious.

"A fortunate happenstance, your securing the evidence after losing Foggarty." His movements deliberate, Hazen set the watch, coin and bill on top of his desk, then turned back to Micah. "Let's talk about this woman—your telegram gave Tremayne as her name, right? Tell me about her."

Loyalty, honor, integrity and faith all clashed as Micah waged an internal battle with his conscience. Mrs. Tremayne might have resumed using her maiden name for any number of reasons. Yet the extremity of her self-imposed isolation, and her fear, struck a false note. An innocent citizen who discovered obvious forgeries would have instantly conveyed them to the local police. An innocent citizen would have greeted an operative of the Secret Service with relief, and immediately handed over the evidence.

Jocelyn Tremayne Bingham—and he could not ignore the connection—had only been willing to part with the watch, bill and coin after practically passing out at his feet from fear.

Yet a complicated personality did not make her a criminal.

Until Micah thoroughly checked out her story, he was reluctant to reveal her ties to the Bingham family. But as a sworn operative for the United States Secret

Service, he was balancing his way across a fraying tightrope.

"MacKenzie!" Chief Hazen barked. "What's the matter with you?"

"Sorry. Yes, as I explained in the telegram, her last name is Tremayne, Christian name Jocelyn." *God, forgive me for lies of omission.* "She's a widow, but lives in a comfortable town house in a well-to-do neighborhood. From my initial interview, I'm prepared to presume innocence instead of guilt. I do not believe she knows Benny Foggarty, nor had any idea that he had passed her stolen and forged goods."

"Humph. Under the circumstances I'm not sure a single visit can support such a conclusion." Face inscrutable, he tugged out his watch, checked the time and cleared his throat again. "In my brief tenure as chief, I've heard a lot about you, Operative MacKenzie. They say you have an instinct about people. Call you the dragon slayer of lies. Claim you can convince counterfeiters to forsake their evil ways and work with us instead." He steepled his fingers beneath his chin, studying Micah's discomfiture. "For the past several years you've been tireless in your pursuit of a family most everyone between here and New York would swear in a court of law are upstanding citizens. Philanthropic do-gooders whose hearts as well as pockets are lined with gold."

"Yes, sir. There were those who praised William Tweed for his contributions to New York City's railways, despite all the graft and corruption. I believe the Binghams are worse than Boss Tweed. My father—"

"I'm aware of your father's part in bringing our attention to this family," the chief interrupted testily.

"I'm equally cognizant that his murder was never solved and information he promised would clinch the case against the Binghams was never delivered. In eight years we've been unable to verify that proof ever existed."

"If we had more men working on the case now…"

"At the time of your father's murder, we did. Two of them were fired, and rightly so, for their unsavory methods." Lips pursed, Hazen contemplated Micah for an uncomfortably long moment. "My predecessor informed me that although your father's death was the primary motivation for your decision to join the Secret Service, your first allegiance has always been to the Service, not revenge. You're an exemplary agent, MacKenzie. Don't do anything rash to jeopardize my opinion of you." He crossed over to stand directly in front of Micah. "Now. Is there anything else you'd like to tell me?"

Micah squared his shoulders. "Yes, sir. Although we've never learned the details, we've known Rupert Bingham's only son and heir, Chadwick, died five years ago. We did not know, however, what became of his wife. We do now." *Lord, please give me the right words.* "Jocelyn Tremayne is Chadwick Bingham's widow. After his death, for some unknown reason— though we can conjecture several—she reverted to her maiden name. Lastly, I haven't been able to verify it, but…" The words choked his throat and he clenched his fists, until the remnant of painful emotion faded and he was able to finish. "I don't believe there were children born of the marriage. Mrs. Tremayne refuses to discuss her husband at all."

He met the older man's gaze without backing down.

"Her marriage into the family does not indicate culpability, and her reticence concerning her husband may have more to do with a reserved personality than fear of exposure."

"Fear of exposure, you say. Well, I can enumerate some of your conjectures now. The woman was married to one of the richest men in the Northeast. It's possible Chadwick Bingham was one of the malefactors. It's also possible that his wife was, as well. On the other hand, it's possible Mrs. Tremayne is innocent, and disappeared because she knows too much about her husband's family."

Micah was grateful for the twig of an olive branch, however grudgingly extended. "My point exactly, sir. We cannot rule out some strong circumstantial evidence that the watchmaker's murder in Richmond is connected to our case. The modus operandi is too similar. In fact," he added casually, "because of my concern for her safety, I insisted that Mrs. Tremayne and her maid accompany me here to Washington. She needs protection, not persecution."

"It is not the job of the Secret Service to protect civilians!" Chief Hazen exploded. Red-faced, he jerked at his silk bow tie as though it were about to strangle him. "Even if the mandate existed, the funds are not available. We're understaffed and underbudgeted, thanks to those mouthpieces down the street in Congress."

"Mrs. Tremayne insisted on paying all expenses." To the point that she refused to leave her house otherwise, Micah recalled with a faint smile. "And I believe, sir, that earlier this year after two operatives learned of suspicious threats against President Cleveland, you transferred those operatives here to Washington, to monitor them and their families. Keep them safe, same as we're trying to keep the country's currency safe? That's all I'm trying to accomplish with Mrs. Tremayne."

The chief was shorter than Micah by several inches, but at that moment Hazen loomed over him like a sober-suited Goliath. "I may concede the point, Operative MacKenzie. But, mind you, don't test my goodwill much further. Don't ever withhold information from me again, or presume to act without authorization. We've spent over a decade shining the tarnish off our badges, proving this organization is peopled with men of honor and integrity. I will not let the Agency's reputation deteriorate again, especially now, poised on the threshold of a new century."

"I understand, Chief Hazen. I give you my word it won't happen again." Sweat pooled in the small of Micah's back, and he had to force himself to stand tall, not to beg, or rush into explanations that would only sound like rationalizations. "If you meet Mrs. Tremayne, sir, I believe you'll see that my actions were justified."

The chief heaved an explosive sigh and clapped a firm hand on Micah's back. "Then bring the lady here, and be done with it. I'd like to meet the woman who turned my best operative's head."

"Sir, I—"

"However...don't let anything, including a mysterious young widow, place you in a potentially compromising position."

Each move deliberate, Chief Hazen walked over to the window and stared outside, toward the White

House, hands clasped behind his back. "I want this counterfeiting network unmasked, stripped of its tentacles and every last member in jail by next spring, Operative MacKenzie. Every principal, every shover, every engraver, every wholesaler—the lot. I want the molds, the plates, the paper, even the blamed ink! I don't care whether it's Rupert Bingham himself, his brother-in-law or nephews. I don't care if the ringleader turns out to be their butler, or the bootblack. Get these malefactors behind bars. Do whatever you have to, legally, in order to learn the identities of the persons who are undermining our country's economic stability."

Turning, he walked back to his desk, picked up a file folder, carefully wound the string around the button tabs. Then he looked across at Micah. "After this meeting I'll clear my schedule. I'll see you and Mrs. Tremayne at four o'clock. But if I detect even the slightest trace of suspicion on her part—or inappropriate regard on yours—I'll remove you from this case."

With Chief Hazen's words buzzing like mosquitoes inside his head, Micah headed for the hotel where Mrs. Tremayne and Katya were staying. If Jocelyn Tremayne turned out to be a counterfeit of the woman he remembered, the chief wouldn't have to fire him. Micah would turn in his credentials, because he would no longer trust his instincts. On the other hand, if he were forced to choose between her and unmasking the man responsible for murdering his father...

Lord, please don't force me to make that choice.

Chapter Six

"I promise he won't arrest you or threaten you."

"But you can't promise that he'll believe me." Jocelyn glanced at the man seated beside her in the hansom cab, then, clearly uncomfortable, shifted her attention to the street.

It was a dreary afternoon, the sky a dull smear of gray, the buildings stolid rows of brick and stone. Over the clatter of the wheels, a train whistle tooted a warning; seconds later the hansom stopped, and a Pennsylvania Railroad locomotive pulling several passenger cars rumbled across Maryland Avenue on its way toward the depot. Moments later, the driver flicked the whip and the hansom lurched into motion once more.

Beneath the layers of her blouse and walking suit, Jocelyn's heart fluttered like a captured rabbit. She still didn't know quite how Operative MacKenzie had persuaded her to accompany him to the Treasury Building—except she'd been reluctant to thumb her nose at a summons from the head of the Secret Service.

As though he'd been reading her mind, after the sound of the train had faded in the distance, Operative MacKenzie observed, "I can't speak for Chief Hazen, but I might make the observation that I'm not sure *you* believe me."

She jerked her head around, searching the shuttered face. The rocking motion of the cab made her queasy, and she fought the incipient panic rising in her throat. "It's difficult, when I know I've done nothing wrong. Nothing! Yet you've frightened me, hounded me, and now you've bullied me into a situation I don't want to be in. I returned your evidence, so I don't understand what I can possibly say to your chief that I haven't already explained to you."

An unexpected smile kindled in his eyes, crinkling the corners, then beneath his mustache a corner of his mouth tipped up. "If that's how you perceive me, I'm fortunate you're here at all, Mrs. Tremayne. Ah... you've placed me in an awkward position, especially after hearing your interpretation of my actions. You see, once he meets you in person, I don't think Chief Hazen will have any lingering doubts about you."

Instantly wary, Jocelyn stiffened. "And why is that? You believe someone who looks like me is far too... noticeable...to engage in criminal activities? I'm too easily picked out of a crowd? Oh, yes—I swoon when confronted by murder."

"I could pick you out of a crowd of a hundred redheads," Operative MacKenzie said, his voice deepening. "Besides which, the lovely young woman I met a decade ago still lives somewhere inside the woman sitting beside me now. Regardless of how much you may have changed in the intervening years, Mrs. Tremayne, I don't believe you'd ever knowingly be part of anything illegal." A soft pause as potent as the touch of his fingers seeped into Jocelyn. "And you didn't swoon. You're harboring a terrible fear inside you, Mrs. Tremayne. But I also see a rare strength of character, not to mention a formidable temper."

Hot color whooshed from her chin to her hairline. If she leaned sideways a scant six inches, their shoulders would touch, and she would feel again the strength of him, of muscles tensile and tough as her oak banister. An evocative scent of starch and something uniquely masculine flooded her senses. If only she'd met this man when she was seventeen, still bubbling with hope and a heart full of dreams. Instinctively, her hand lifted to press against her throat in an effort to calm her galloping pulse. "I— You shouldn't say such things to me. I don't know how to interpret them. I wish I..." She bit her lip, tearing her gaze away from Micah MacKenzie.

With a jerk the hansom came to a halt. "Treasury Building," the hack announced.

The imposing building loomed before her, its seventy-four granite columns reminding Jocelyn of massive bars on a stone prison cell. When a warm hand gently clasped her elbow, she jumped.

"It's really not the lion's den," Operative MacKenzie murmured. "But if it were, even if I couldn't close the mouths of the lions, I'd protect you with my life." When her startled gaze lifted, she discovered that despite the light tone, his eyes probed hers with an intensity that stole her breath.

With his hand supporting her, they climbed the stairs into the main entrance. Jocelyn realized with a spurt of astonishment that she actually looked forward to engaging the chief of the Secret Service in a spirited defense of her position.

Richmond

A week had passed since Jocelyn and Katya returned from Washington, and life settled back into an uneasy rhythm of sorts. For long clumps of time, Jocelyn almost forgot about the man who had burst into her life with the force of a runaway locomotive, then chugged off toward the horizon. Operative MacKenzie was somewhere in the Midwest—St. Louis? Chicago?—chasing after counterfeiters while Jocelyn struggled to believe his parting words.

"I'll be back," he promised. *"Don't think you've seen the last of me, Mrs. Tremayne."*

"You're like the wind, Operative MacKenzie," she retorted, disguising desolation with flippancy. *"Blowing here and there, and nobody can hold it in one place, or capture it inside a basket. I plan to go back to living my life as though none of the past week ever happened."*

"Mmm. I gave up playing pretend games when I was, oh, about six years old." Then he touched the brim of his hat. *"But for now, I'll leave you to yours. Be careful, please. The police are keeping an eye out, but—"*

She wondered now what words he'd swallowed back, but refused to invest much effort in an exercise that would only trigger a plethora of memories.

Tonight she was attending a musicale at the Westhampton Club with friends—an enjoyable diversion that might allow her to forget, if only for a few hours, Micah MacKenzie and the Secret Service. During the days she filled the hours with mindless activities, while the nights taunted her with their emptiness as she searched in vain for peace of mind.

There is no peace, saith the Lord, unto the wicked.
The poisonous verse slapped at her like a vindictive hand.

"I'm not wicked!" Jocelyn announced aloud, anger and pain twining her in thorny vines. "I'm not...." When her voice broke, she bit her lip until she tasted blood. Throat aching, she snatched up her gloves and evening cloak and swept out of the room, firmly shutting the door behind her.

The night was warm, more like summer than late fall. Air thick with humidity clung to trees and buildings. Despite his considerable bulk, a man walked in soundless stealth along the city's back streets until bank buildings and stores gave way to lumber and tobacco warehouses. For a block or two he followed the railroad tracks. Eventually, he reached a neighborhood where, in daylight hours, he could never risk showing his face.

He wasn't stupid. He knew this task was both reprimand, and restitution. Still, it gave him the shivers. He was a professional, but he had a few standards; he'd never snuffed a woman. He'd stolen from 'em plenty, he'd cut a few as warnings, but he'd made it plain that he wasn't after anything worse.

But a job had to be done, and he had to do it. His reputation after the last botched assignment was hanging over his head, a noose about to drop around his size 19 neck. He'd explained. Unfamiliar city, poor directions—no time to study patterns, so the old man's death wasn't his fault.

In the end, it didn't matter. Orders were orders, and money was money. And his own life was on the line.

"Find these items, and you'll be rewarded accordingly. Fail, and your usefulness might come to an end."

There. White porch, two columns. Getaway alleys on either side. At last, luck was running his way.

He slid one hand inside to make sure the knife was within easy reach. Next he fit his brass knuckles over the fingerless gloves. Ten minutes later he slipped over the windowsill and into the house's parlor.

"I refuse to stay inside this place another day!" Jocelyn stabbed hat pins in place while she glared at her obdurate maid. "It's been three days. We've cleaned everything up, nothing is missing. The police assure me they're doing everything they can to— What?"

Katya wrote with a furious speed that mirrored Jocelyn's frustration, her double chin quivering like calf's-foot jelly. *Need to wait for*—she hurriedly searched the list of correctly spelled words she kept inside her apron pocket—*Mr. MacKenzie.*

Sergeant Whitlock, the policeman who was still investigating Mr. Hepplewhite's murder, was the officer who had appeared on her doorstep to investigate her report of vandalism. More policemen had followed, as well as a nattily dressed detective wearing a dark suit and spotted yellow bow tie instead of a blue uniform.

Operative Micah MacKenzie's name had been mentioned several times. But nobody saw fit to enlighten Jocelyn as to when he would return to Richmond, or whether or not he concurred with their hypotheses that the villain who had torn her house apart was connected with Mr. Hepplewhite's murder.

Jocelyn crumpled Katya's words into a ball, stomped across to the parlor fireplace, hurled the note into the flames, then returned to the foyer where

Katya hovered like an overwrought governess. "For the last time, I doubt we'll ever see Micah MacKenzie again. What's the matter with you, anyway? No— don't answer that, it's just a rhetorical question. And before you ask what that means, a rhetorical question is one for which I don't expect an answer. They're not meant to be answered— Oh, *botheration*." Her gloves weren't cooperating with her fingers. Jocelyn gave up and threw them down. "I'm going downtown. You can either stay here and fret, or do what the police sergeant told you to do and come with me."

Katya gave her a wounded look as she wrote. *I fetch my coat.*

They walked the two blocks to the streetcar stop in silence.

"I'm sorry," Jocelyn said after they boarded the nearly empty car and sat down, side by side but an ocean apart. "I shouldn't have lost my temper, or taken it out on you."

A self-righteous sniff was Katya's only response, but when Jocelyn glanced sideways, she spied a twinkle in her maid's eyes. "Come now, confess," she coaxed. "You've been wanting to go to town as much as I have. We'll stop by the bakery, and buy some of those nutmeg doughnuts you love so much."

When Katya dug into the folds of her voluminous sack coat for her pad and thick charcoal pencil, Jocelyn almost wept with relief. The further evidence of her crumbling fortitude drained her. Her desperation for any connection with another human being, albeit through the silent scribbling on a notepad, reduced her to a tearful puddle.

Katya tugged her arm. Their stop had arrived. Jocelyn corralled her gloomy thoughts as they joined the throng of pedestrians spilling across the tracks to the sidewalk. As long as she and Katya stayed together, Sergeant Whitlock counseled her, and confined their meanderings to the busy downtown, they should be safe.

After they strolled along East Main for several blocks, she relaxed enough to point out a display of ladies' shoes in the window of a shoe store, even laughed with her companion over a man on a bicycle bumping his way down the cobbled street scarcely a dozen paces ahead of a horsecar. She lingered in front of the bookshop until Katya thrust a piece of paper in front of her face.

Bakery.

"Oh, all right."

They walked up Sixth Street to Bromm's Bakery on East Marshall. Several moments later they emerged from the shop, carrying fragrant sacks of confections. A mule-drawn delivery wagon pulled up in front of the bakery and a wiry dark-skinned man jumped down, tying the mule to the hitching post. Katya's entire face lit up as she pointed to the straw hat on top of the mule's head, its long ears poking through holes cut on either side. When she indicated that she wanted to go pet the mule, Jocelyn waved her on without a second thought.

"I'll wait for you here. I've no desire to spoil the fragrance of our doughnuts with *eau de mule.*"

Sometimes she forgot how young Katya was, she mused, watching the girl gesturing with her hands to the driver, relieved when he obligingly introduced her to the flop-eared mule.

How had Katya endured the nightmares in her short life, yet retained the capacity for joy and hope?

Chapter Seven

An hour later, by the time they left the streetcar to walk the last three blocks, they'd gobbled down three doughnuts each. Leaves swirled about their feet in a lazy shuffle, and in a burst of contentment Jocelyn waved enthusiastically to the driver of an ice-block delivery wagon as he passed by, causing Katya to roll her eyes.

Their innocuous outing had momentarily banished the ugly shadows that swirled around Jocelyn like the leaves; a lightness spread inside her heart until she had to squelch the giddy impulse to skip down the last block like a young girl.

The mailman met them as they reached the front porch.

"Afternoon, ladies. Mighty fine day for an outing. I have a letter here for you, Miz Tremayne. Y'all caught me just before I popped it into your box." He handed the envelope to Jocelyn.

"Thank you, Mr. Hobbes," she managed, giddiness transforming into a tangled mix of hope and dread. The letter might be from Operative MacKenzie. He was probably writing to tell her he'd been ordered to California or the Wyoming Territory. She glanced down and all the blood drained from her head.

"Have a doughnut," she offered the mailman automatically, while the buzzing in her ears intensified so that she scarcely heard her own voice. "They're fresh, from Bromm's Bakery."

"Why, thank you kindly, Miz Tremayne. Ma'am." He nodded to Katya, then whistled his way down the walk.

Somehow Jocelyn managed to climb the porch steps and unlock the door. She could feel the weight of Katya's curiosity pressing down on her shoulders; she dropped her cloak onto the hall tree, then wandered into the parlor, the envelope clenched in her hand.

The Honorable Augustus Brock, New York City.

Not Micah MacKenzie, but Chadwick's uncle, his mother's brother. Jocelyn's last memory of Augustus Brock and his narcissistic wife, Portia, was the day of Chadwick's funeral. Dressed in their hastily dyed mourning clothes, they'd glared at Jocelyn like two black ravens about to pick out her eyes. "He wouldn't have been driven to commit such an abominable act of shame if you'd given him the child he longed for," Augustus's wife proclaimed loudly enough for the rest of the mourners to stiffen into appalled silence.

"Don't know why Rupert agreed to let his son marry you in the first place," her husband muttered, his complexion flushed above the high shirt collar. "Who would have thought it—all that brass in your hair and you turn out to be barren. Disgrace to the whole family."

Jocelyn started violently when a hand brushed her

arm, only then realizing that Katya was beside her, waving a piece of paper in front of her face. "Sorry." She squeezed Katya's hand, but after reading the words moved away, unable to bear even the loyal maid's proximity. "It's a letter from…some people I used to know. Be a dear, won't you, and…and make us some tea?"

Satisfied to have a task, Katya nodded and hurried from the room. Jocelyn collapsed onto the sofa. Why now? She felt like a puppet whose master delighted in dangling her over a fire. One day, she thought, the flames would leap up and consume her.

Hurriedly, before she yielded to the urge to rip the letter unread into tiny pieces, she opened the envelope and withdrew two sheets of expensive vellum.

To our niece, beloved widow of Chadwick. No doubt this missive will come as a surprise after all these years. It has long been upon my heart, and Mrs. Brock's, that the family treated you most shamefully in its disregard for your health and well-being after the death of your dear husband. It is with deep regret to know that, perhaps influenced in part by our regrettably Bourbonic conduct, you felt compelled to forsake his name.

Now there was a masterstroke of understatement for you. The entire Bingham clan, including the Brocks, had disowned Jocelyn before the gravediggers finished shoveling dirt over Chadwick's coffin. One of the Brock cousins—she neither remembered nor cared which—had gone so far as to spit on her, claiming she was nothing but poor white trash, a pathetic creature whose hair and face had embarrassed Chadwick almost as much as her barrenness.

The letter crumpled in her hands. Jocelyn inhaled a shuddering breath, flexed her fingers and forced herself to read the rest of it.

After years of searching, at last we learned of your whereabouts. I thus most humbly beseech you to lay aside the acrimony you justifiably must feel, and to consider the following as an olive branch extended toward you—a gesture of our desire for reconciliation.

It is our wish for you to return to New York for an extended visit, with the express purpose of allowing this family to atone for our shameful neglect. Time has given a far more charitable heart to myself and Mrs. Brock; I plead with you to consider this invitation as one made in utter sincerity. The past, like your beloved husband, is beyond our reach. We must fix our hearts and minds upon hope of a brighter future for us all, in which we can come to better know our dear niece. Even as I write, rooms are being readied for your arrival. Enclosed, as further proof of our goodwill, please find two one-way tickets in our private Pullman, the Aurora (as you may remember) for you and an appropriate chaperone.

Your humble servant and contrite uncle-in-law, Augustus Brock.

When Katya tiptoed in with a tray some time later, she found Jocelyn sitting on the edge of the sofa, bowed at the waist with her face in her hands, the wrinkled vellum sheets lying faceup on the floor.

Micah returned to Richmond a day after the clear, cool autumn days of the past week blew into the Atlantic, driven out by another ill-tempered hot spell from the south. Indifferent to its cloying humidity, he rented a buggy from the livery stable and drove himself directly to the Third District Police Station.

"Operative MacKenzie! 'Bout time you brought your ugly self back to help us poor clods of the Richmond Police." George Firth, acting sergeant, greeted him with a congenial handshake—and the unpleasant news that "Your little redheaded widow's got more trouble than a cemetery's got headstones."

"What's happened? Has she been harmed? Why didn't someone notify me?"

The sergeant threw back his head and guffawed. "I'll be…they wuz right, about you and Miz Tremayne. And here I am telling 'em you're just a high-falutin' government man, keeping his sticky fingers in our business."

Heat crept up Micah's face. He felt like a rube, the target of public ridicule, but he counted to thirty and waited until the other man's coarse jesting finally wound down. "I've been in constant touch with your chief, the Detective Bureau and the mayor, concerning Mr. Hepplewhite's murder and its possible connection with my case. Mrs. Tremayne is part of that investigation," he stated evenly. "Now, over the past few weeks I spent three days locked in an airless room, examining approximately $100,000 in fraudulent two-and five-dollar bills, not to mention over $20,000 in spurious coinage. Less than twelve hours later, I caught a midnight train heading west, and I've been on the road going on ten days now. I came here straight from the train station, I haven't had a decent meal or a bath in—" he glanced at the large round clock on the wall across the room "—almost forty hours. So when I ask if Mrs. Tremayne is all right, you might want to let me know—at once."

"Oh-ho, tetchy today, eh? Fair enough. Now that you mention it, you do look frayed a bit around the edges. Here—Tenner! Fetch Sergeant Whitlock. We got our own gen-yoo-ine agent from the Treasury Department back in town. Fill him in, and let's watch how fast he hightails it over to the widow Tremayne's."

Micah tied the livery horse to a post three houses down from Jocelyn's home, then checked the time. Seventeen minutes. He'd driven the buggy with imprudent haste through a maze of narrow streets, dodged two streetcars, an oncoming freight train, and clipped the wheel on a curb when he took a corner too fast on the edge of Monroe Park. He'd planned to return to Richmond a week earlier, but duty, not to mention Chief Hazen, bound him with chains he could not afford to break. Sighing, he thrust the watch back in his pocket. Ah, yes. Duty.

Katya's round face lit up like a harvest moon when she opened the door. But her gestures spoke of urgency as she bustled him into the front parlor.

"Hello, Katya. You're looking fine." When the maid rolled her eyes, Micah smiled a little. "It's all right, I came from the police station. I know about the break-in. Is she home?" he asked, glancing around the room, noticing the absence of a pair of green glass paper-weights with flower etchings that had been displayed on the doily-covered table next to the window. A colorful urn in the foyer that had boasted several peacock feathers was also gone.

He started to say something else, but the words drained out of his head when Jocelyn appeared between the fringed draperies lining the entrance to the parlor. "Mrs. Tremayne."

"Operative MacKenzie."

She hovered, seemingly uncertain about whether to enter, or perhaps flee up the staircase. Her reception was so contrary to Micah's expectations that for a moment he floundered in his own swamp of indecision. Then he looked more closely into her eyes and realized that her lack of warmth stemmed from causes other than himself. "I believe we agreed that 'Mister' is less official-sounding. What's happened, besides your home being vandalized?"

"Oh... I'd forgotten. How did you know?"

With a wry look, he gestured to his wrinkled, travel-worn attire. "I went from the train station to the police station to your house as fast as I could. I'm sorry I wasn't here sooner. Katya's back to looking anxious, and you're looking—" he reeled in the words dancing indiscriminately on his tongue "—subdued," he finished, and behind him Katya stomped the floor.

"I'm glad you're here," Jocelyn said, waving a limp hand at her maid. "There's nobody else I can ask...."

Micah waited, but when she didn't elaborate, and a backward glance at the maid revealed her frantically writing in her tablet, he went with instinct. "Here." He placed his hand under her elbow, exulting in the feel of her despite the alarming fragility that hovered all around her. "Come and sit down. Tell me what's bothering you."

"I don't know where to begin."

"Anywhere you like." He sat her down on one end of the luxurious sofa, and commandeered the other end for himself. "Perhaps...what happened the other night? The police report indicated that you weren't home, so the only damage was to some of your possessions." And he thanked God for it, though not aloud.

Jocelyn shrugged. "It doesn't matter. I don't want to talk about that, not right now."

Katya thrust her paper into his hand. *Tell her we can not to New York go, do not know these people.*

"New York?" Alarmed, he searched Jocelyn's lackluster countenance. "Who is requesting your presence in New York?"

Her complexion paled further, highlighting purple smudges beneath eyes that made her look far too old. "You needn't glare as though I were guilty of a crime." Her mouth flattened. "Or have you and Chief Hazen decided otherwise, and the purpose of this visit is to finally arrest me? Did you bring your handcuffs along with your badge?"

"No, of course not." Micah better recognized now the fear driving her barbed questions. It replicated the fear she had manifested from the day they'd met again in Clocks & Watches. Since he and Chief Hazen had decided not to badger her about her relationship with the Bingham family, opting instead to wait to see how things developed, her continued anxieties over being arrested were troubling. In Micah's experience, only guilt promulgated this level of fear.

And now—New York? Stalling, he folded his arms across his chest. "Katya, has your mistress always had a penchant for melodrama?"

"She won't understand 'penchant' or 'melodrama,'" Jocelyn muttered, flushing. She shot Katya a quick look.

The maid scowled as she wrote her response. *She is afraid ever since a letter. You must help.*

"And I will, Katya." A strand of Jocelyn's hair had slipped free of its chignon and dangled behind her ear, an alluring temptation inches from the reach of his fingers. Above her ruffled collar, the creamy texture of her neck with those irresistible freckles begged to be touched. Micah blinked, then produced what he hoped was a coaxing smile. "Before I can help, first I need to understand how a letter can frighten you enough to want to flee."

"Katya, I'd like to talk to Oper—to Mr. MacKenzie alone for a few moments, all right?"

She waited until the maid reluctantly left the parlor. "Mr. MacKenzie… I know our acquaintance has been brief, but from the moment I remembered—" She closed her eyes, and when she opened them again Micah felt as though he'd fallen into a sea churning with despair. "My intention is not to take advantage of your kindness," she whispered desperately, "but I— There's no one else. I have no other choice. Chief Hazen obviously thinks highly of you, and I remembered that before you were assigned to Washington, you were the operative in charge, in New York. And… you knew Chadwick."

After an awkward pause she resumed speaking, her gaze fixed somewhere over Micah's right shoulder.

"My marriage was not a happy one. I was unable—We never had children. There were expectations. I failed. The Binghams renounced me."

She turned her head so that Micah could not see her face, but the toneless manifestation of her pain resonated inside his soul. Some griefs were harder to heal from than others, he thought, tamping more nails onto the lid of his own anguished memories.

"It's been five years since he died," she said. "I've neither seen nor heard from anyone in my husband's family. Until—" her voice wobbled, then steadied "—until I received a letter, the day before yesterday, from Chadwick's uncle. A-Augustus Brock is Chadwick's mother's brother."

She might as well have slammed a baseball bat against the side of Micah's head. "Mrs. Tremayne—Jocelyn. Whatever he said, whatever he wants, it's all right. Everything will be all right."

"Don't try to coddle me as though I were an invalid."

Despite his own shock, her reply made Micah want to smile. He resisted the urge; if his lips so much as twitched, she'd either shatter, or hand him his head on a silver plate.

If he were smart, he'd remove himself from this case—and from Jocelyn—before the sun set.

But he wasn't going to. He couldn't. Jocelyn Tremayne Bingham was in trouble, and for some reason God had seen fit to bring her back into Micah's life.

Or to bring Micah into hers.

Thanks, Lord. I think. "There's a difference between coddling and caring, you know." When she continued to stare through him, he raised an eyebrow, then tried again. "Would you like me to read the letter?"

"No. You were born in New York, you attended university there. I just want to know what you remember about the Binghams. If you ever met the rest of their family, specifically Augustus Brock."

She wouldn't want to know what he knew about the Brocks, or the Binghams, but the time was fast approaching when her lack of knowledge could cost her her life. "My family did not move in those circles," he told her, choosing his words carefully. "I believe you know that my father was Rupert Bingham's head bookkeeper?" She nodded. "Yet it wasn't your father-in-law, but Augustus Brock who wrote you the letter inviting you to come to New York?"

"Yes."

"Did he say why?"

After a protracted moment she nodded. "He said he regrets the way the family treated me. He wants to be…reconciled."

Every muscle in Micah's body clenched in anticipation; his mind flatly rejected the prospect. "So you're wondering why, after they ignored you all these years?" Moving slowly so he wouldn't startle her, he sat forward on the edge of the seat. "Your own family died in a typhoid epidemic, you told me. But surely you have someone other than Katya to whom you could turn?"

That garnered a quick look and a jerky headshake. Choosing his words, Micah continued speaking in a calm voice that belied his own perturbation. "Your husband's family renounced you, so you renounced them by taking back your maiden name. You've lived here in Richmond for three years now, but I gather nobody here, including Katya, knows of your connection to the Bingham family, and you don't want anyone to know."

"I'm the widow Tremayne," she insisted, her hands twisting restlessly. "I don't confide personal details to others. Katya is loyal, but this is not a burden she deserves, unless I decide to—" the breath seemed to stall in her throat " unless I decide to accept his offer. I didn't want to tell you, except you've been… kind. You even championed me, as it were, in front of Chief Hazen, which I know put you at risk. You already know who I am. What I…used to be, yet you went out of your way to protect me." Her eyelids fluttered, and her tongue darted out to moisten her lips. In another woman the motion would have been provocative; Jocelyn Tremayne only looked fragile, and achingly alone.

Did he know her at all? Micah wondered. Would he ever?

Not likely she would ever offer him the privilege, when he was honor-bound to expose her father-in-law and possibly her uncle-in-law as murdering scoundrels. Arrogant criminals wearing dinner jackets and diamond stickpins, who had funneled millions of counterfeit currency into the economy so they and their families could live in mansions.

On the other hand, Micah felt equally honor-bound to do what he could to protect this vulnerable woman. *After Chadwick died, she must have stumbled onto something incriminating, and run for her life.*

"I know who you married," he corrected her. "And I know what has been happening in your life over this past month." He couldn't help himself. He reached out his hand, lightly brushing his fingers over her mottled knuckles, and felt the tingle of response all the way to the marrow of his bones. "I know you're an independent woman, and a frightened woman. What I don't know, Mrs. Tremayne, is whether or not you really want me to advise you on your choices, or if you've already made up your mind on how you plan to respond to your uncle's letter."

She was staring at her hand, her lips half-parted; when she looked up, a fiery blush consumed her face. "Why did you do that?"

Well, at least she hadn't slapped him. Micah smiled at her crookedly. "Because I couldn't help myself," he admitted. When her hazel eyes darkened to jade, he added self-deprecatingly, "My mother would warn you that I'm not very polished around women. Since my wife died, I suppose I haven't invested a lot of time cultivating the proper deportment of a gentleman."

"You were married?"

Sighing, he searched for composure while he shared pieces of his own broken past. "I met Alice a couple of years after your marriage to Chadwick. I'd just graduated from college, landed my first job. At the time, I was a civil engineer. We fell in love, married six months later."

Jocelyn's head drooped, the rigid shoulders slumping. "Were you...happy?"

"Very much. Until the birth of our son. Alice died. The doctor couldn't stop the bleeding. An hour later, I lost our son. My little boy..." Micah had been holding him. Even after all the years, memories could scorch the scar until the grief ripped open, oozing pain. "My son..."

He passed a hand over his eyes, and when he dropped it to press against the sofa's soft green velvet, Jocelyn's slender fingers brushed his knuckles in a tentative duplication of his earlier gesture. "Mr. MacKenzie—Micah, I'm so sorry…"

"I buried them together. He was so small…. I can still see his hands. They were perfect." His breath shuddered out and he lost himself in the compassion shining from Jocelyn's face, the tears sparkling in her mink-brown eyelashes. "I'll never know the color of his eyes…hear the sound of his laughter. When the pain hurts too much, I imagine him and my wife, up in heaven. Taking a walk with Jesus, all of them laughing—"

"Think it if you like, but it's a lie!" She stormed to her feet, an enraged and wounded soul lashing out blindly. "I don't want to hear about God, or Jesus, or how much we're loved. If God loved you, your wife and your son wouldn't be lying in a cold grave. I'm sorry for your loss, but at least you had someone you knew loved you. At least your wife had a child—" Her hands flew to her mouth. "I'm sorry. I—I—"

Whirling, she dashed from the parlor, the sound of her choked sobs echoing harshly in the air.

Stunned, reeling from the unexpected onslaught, Micah sat motionless. He couldn't have said which hurt more—the fiery lash of his own grief, or the frigid blast of Jocelyn's rejection.

Chapter Eight

She wept, soundlessly, her face buried in a pillow. Wept until her throat burned, and the spike lodged in her chest shrank enough to allow her to breathe. Until she was exhausted, and the outrage flattened into contrition.

What a selfish, mean-spirited harpy she was, to revile Micah MacKenzie's faith. If believing in a compassionate God, if concocting pretty mental pictures of his dead wife and infant son strolling among puffy white clouds with Jesus gave Micah MacKenzie peace…well, Jocelyn had no right to challenge them.

But she'd long ago given up believing.

After mopping her face with her sodden hankie, she dragged herself across to her mirrored washstand, and shredded the woman reflected there. *Look at yourself, Jocelyn. That dead-eyed, mean-spirited creature is what you've turned yourself into.*

Perhaps she deserved her life. Perhaps, hidden within the hopeful young girl who had nobly rescued her family from homelessness and starvation lurked an evil twin. One whose secret longings required daily doses of divine castigation.

All she'd ever wanted was to re-create the happy home she had known as a child—with a devoted husband, children, the satisfaction of successfully managing her household. After Chadwick's death, the few years she'd spent as a student at the Isabella Chilton Academy had almost resurrected hope for that dream. Of course, Miss Isabella quoted scripture—endlessly—as the source of the school's credo, which was to train women to be competent wives, as well as wage earners if marriage was not God's plan for their lives.

I don't want any part of your noble credos, Miss Isabella. They were naught but foolish fancies, like Mr. MacKenzie's.

With an inarticulate moan, Jocelyn whirled away from the mirror. Indifferent to appearances, much less propriety, she flew down the stairs, not pausing until she reached the parlor. Breathing hard, her gaze swept the room. Empty. He'd left then. She couldn't even redeem herself with an apology.

She wanted to sink to the floor and pound her fists until they bled, she wanted to scream, she wanted to— She didn't know what she wanted, only that she could not bear her present life.

"Mrs. Tremayne? Jocelyn?"

She whirled around. For a moment, every thought vanished, swept away in a cascade of relief and happiness. "I thought you'd left," she managed, surprised by the hoarse croaking sound of her voice.

"I almost did."

She looked down. "I wouldn't have blamed you. What I said was ugly. Unforgivable."

"I wouldn't have put it quite that way. Painfully honest, perhaps. For both of us. But I burdened you with my life, unsolicited, so I—"

"It wasn't a burden," she blurted, frantic to atone. "I'm sorry for everything I said. I had no right, especially when I could see how much it hurt you to confide in me about your past. If I could only go back—" Hastily she strangled the sentence. "I—I wanted to know more about you."

A little pool of silence descended.

"Why?"

Because the question was voiced so gently, because the gray eyes bathed her in kindness instead of recrimination, Jocelyn melted. She couldn't remember the last time she had been forgiven with such grace, as though her childish wish had been granted and the scene in the parlor had never occurred. If she never saw this man again after today, she would cherish the undeserved gift he had given her. In the desert of her life, she would cling to the one golden moment when someone cared enough to overlook her character flaws.

Pride and disillusionment floated away. All that mattered was her need to prolong the moment. "My marriage didn't turn out the way I expected. For a little while, I used to think about you. After a few years, I stopped." She could no longer meet his gaze. "And I made myself forget. It's been ten years, yet you're still being kind, even though I don't deserve it. I no longer trust in God. I'm not sure I even believe He exists." She stopped abruptly.

"It's all right," he assured her, his eyes smiling. "I'm

listening. I won't stomp out the door in high dudgeon, spouting scripture as I stomp."

Jocelyn choked back a fresh bout of tears. "I've never known a man like you," she managed, swallowing repeatedly to clear her throat. "I'm afraid...."

The smile died. "Afraid? Of me?"

"Of what you make me feel. Of what this— I think there's something wrong with me, something about my character I've never been able to subdue, inside." Cheeks flaming, she forced the rest of it out. "From the very beginning, that day when we were sitting together on the parlor sofa, and you held me? I— Nobody has held me like that in over te—I mean, in over f-five years. And it felt so good, so safe, I wanted more. I know what those feelings imply about my character, but you deserved to know."

He was frowning now. *Why was he frowning?* She had spoken with too much candor, she had placed him in a socially awkward position, presumed upon his kindness and thus deserved nothing but his censure.

"What those feelings say about your character is that you're a human being, and a woman. A beautiful but lonely woman who for some reason shut herself off from life when her husband died."

"I'm not beautiful on the inside. If you knew..." She choked back more words, her pulse leaping when instead of repudiation, Micah MacKenzie took her hand.

Holding her gaze, he stroked the backs of her knuckles with the pad of his thumb. Shocked speechless, Jocelyn clung to the strength of his warm fingers, her heart beating a suffocating tattoo against her rib cage.

"I know about your fear, and your loneliness," he

murmured as he cupped her trembling hand in both of his. "And your lost faith. No—don't pull away. It's all right, I'm not going to hurt you."

"If I don't pull away now, I might not be able to at all."

There. Her stark declaration finally jarred him, though despite the start of surprise he still refused to release her. Jocelyn quit tugging and closed her eyes, savoring the connection even as she steeled herself against the desolation that would follow.

"That's a dangerous admission," he mused eventually. "Not one I would have expected, despite your widowhood." Still watching her, he lifted her hand and pressed the palm over his heart. Through her fingertips she could feel the beat, a hard rhythm in tune with her own runaway pulse. "Because, Jocelyn, I feel the same way about you. Someday we'll talk about it. But now is not the time."

Somberly, he released her and gestured to the two wingback chairs arranged to face the parlor's fireplace. "Right now, we need to talk about the letter from Augustus Brock, and what you're going to do."

Her earlier temper had stung his skin, but Jocelyn's candor stripped Micah's heart bare. Alice had been reticent, both in her words and her personality; outside the criminal culture, most of the women Micah had encountered since her death abided by the social credo that precluded extreme emotion of any kind. And sensuality…well, the concept simply hadn't been part of their vocabulary.

Then Jocelyn Tremayne exploded back into his life. Did she have any idea what it did to a man, to deliver that loaded confession while staring up at him with wounded eyes the color of a sun-dappled pine forest?

A log from the fire he'd stirred to life earlier shot sparks, then settled into the flames. When a man started thinking in flowery metaphors, he was in as much trouble as that log, on its way to a fiery destruction. Weeks earlier, Micah had known he was in trouble. Without hesitation, he jumped feetfirst into the fire. "Would you allow me to read the letter from your uncle-in-law?" he asked.

"Why do you want to? Unless…" Her eyes narrowed. "Is this interest personal or professional?"

"I don't know." He answered her question, picking his way through how much to tell her. "I'm not trying to avoid an answer, Jocelyn." As he hoped, his familiarity stiffened her drooping shoulders, though she didn't protest. "As Chief Hazen explained the day you met him, for the past eight years the Secret Service has been conducting an investigation of a counterfeiting network based in New York City."

"I remember. And you were the chief in charge, until he transferred you to Washington."

"Well, I was in charge for only three of those years. What he didn't share with you is the reason for my transfer to headquarters. We believe this network has expanded their operation as far south as Charleston, and west to St. Louis. Remember Benny? He's the one who indicated a new source here, in Richmond. But he got away from me before I learned where he obtained the goods."

"Wouldn't he have obtained them from this new… source, you called it?"

He could share at least that much without fear of

compromising the case, or himself. "Both the bill and the coin were manufactured elsewhere. Benny could have snitched them from their origins, in New York, or he could have gotten them from a new shover—the person who passes counterfeit goods—here in Richmond."

She thought about that for a bit. Then, "Surely you don't think Mr. Hepplewhite was part of this network!"

"It's highly unlikely, but a thorough investigation is required nonetheless, because Benny Foggarty is still at large, and Mr. Hepplewhite was murdered." She flinched a little, but her gaze upon him was steady. "Remember I told you how murder is not the normal modus operandi of counterfeiters?"

"I remember."

"Mmm. Most of the members of this class of criminals hold down ordinary jobs, along with their illegitimate pursuits. Manufacturing bogus goods takes time—and money. So they're also bricklayers, carpenters, factory workers. But some member of this motley group crossed a line when he committed cold-blooded murder. Thus far, Mr. Hepplewhite makes the third victim that we know of."

He leaned forward, propping his elbows on his knees. The firelight danced across Jocelyn's face in an evocative play of light and shadow; Micah tried not to compare the flames to her hair, which she had stuffed into an untidy knot on top of her head. Several strands had slipped free to spill unnoticed down her back. Short snippets dangled about the neat shells of her ears....

Clearing his throat, he clasped his hands and rested his chin on them. "For the past ten days I've been pursuing another lead. Took me all the way to St. Louis. I returned to Richmond as soon as I could, not merely because I needed to follow up on Benny Foggarty and Mr. Hepplewhite, but because…" He hesitated, then added quietly, "I needed to see you."

"I'm under investigation. I received bogus goods, and my former in-laws live in New York City." Her voice was dull. "It's never been Mr. Hepplewhite. It's me. You think I'm part of this counterfeiting network because my husband was from New York City."

Lord, she's going to turn every one of my hairs gray.… "No. I do not think you're a counterfeiter. I believe you're innocent, Jocelyn. Don't shake your head. Look at me, and trust me." He waited until he knew he'd gained her complete attention. "Right now, my faith in your innocence has placed me in an awkward position, but I am not going to abandon you. That's a promise, and I don't make those lightly."

"There's no need to make promises you might have to break. I understand. You don't need to explain."

"There's every need. I want to explain—because you *don't* understand."

Head tipped sideways, Jocelyn contemplated him for a long moment. "What don't I understand?"

What she didn't understand would fill the *Farmer's Almanac*. Micah sucked in a deep breath, then prayed an urgent prayer for guidance. "As I explained, counterfeiting is peopled with men whose daily lives are the antithesis of polite society. Networks are formed, and broken, much like schools of fish in the ocean. Loosely bound, easily separated, occasionally caught in a net. However, we believe the murders that have been committed have been ordered by one, perhaps two, individuals who are *not* part of what we call a criminal subculture."

Reluctant to proceed, he picked up a miniature bronze statue of a cat posed on the table where the missing glass paperweights used to be, stroking the ears with absentminded fingers.

"Well," Jocelyn prodded impatiently, "do you know who they are?"

Carefully he set the statue of the cat aside. "If I share anything else, I'm not sure if either of us will care for the consequences."

A scant smile curved her mouth. "I'm not much afraid of consequences these days."

After this, you will be. "The parties under suspicion are influential, upstanding members of society. New York society, to be specific."

Jocelyn's eyes widened. "Oh! I see now. *That's* why you want to read the letter! I could go to New York, using my uncle's invitation as the excuse. You're asking me to, ah, replace Benny Foggarty as your inside source?"

"Not only melodramatic, but possessed of a fertile imagination."

The brief smile returned, then vanished as the shadows in her eyes deepened. "I suppose. I thought I'd outgrown the bad habit. Likely it's because I'm a freckled redhead."

"You don't think very highly of yourself, do you?"

"Life is a harsher schoolmaster than you, Mr. MacKenzie."

"Call me Micah, if you don't mind. We've known each other more or less for a decade." When she opened her mouth, he interjected swiftly, "Why don't you fetch me the letter. I need a moment to sort a few things through my mind, then we'll see if we can hitch both of our imaginations to the same buggy."

She returned moments later with the letter, and the announcement that Katya would be along with a tray. During her brief absence she had rearranged her hair, scrubbed all traces of tears from her face and now more closely resembled the poised woman he remembered. He wondered how long that poise would remain intact.

They talked idly until Katya bustled in with refreshments. The maid searched Micah's face, then, nodding to herself, left without attempting to initiate a conversation, which Micah appreciated.

"She doesn't always try to run interference," Jocelyn murmured as she handed Micah an earthenware mug full of steaming-hot tea. "Only when it's someone she thinks will take advantage of me." A soft smile appeared. "For some reason she thinks I need protecting, even though she's not yet twenty."

"You're fortunate to have her for a friend, as well as a servant."

Her face clouded. "I don't ever want to treat people as slaves or even servants, no matter what the color of their skin. When I was married to Chadwick, I saw— Well, never mind."

Inhaling a deep breath, Micah set the mug aside. "Jocelyn. This part of our conversation is going to be difficult, so we may as well get it over with. There are some things I need to share with you about your husband's family."

Chapter Nine

On a brisk mid-October morning, Jocelyn and Katya boarded a private Pullman Palace car from the stately Baltimore and Ohio depot in Washington, to complete their journey to New York City. Despite Katya's continued disapproval of the "melodrama"—her new favorite word—the maid's excitement over the journey itself was contagious. By the time the Royal Blue Limited rolled out of the station, Jocelyn was able to banish the worst of her flutters and enjoy the simple pleasure of riding the rails in style.

The private car was a sumptuous affair of gleaming walnut and polished brass, with Waterford crystal chandeliers to light its interior, and deep burgundy velvet curtains draping the glazed windows. A crisply uniformed porter informed Jocelyn that he would return at noon to prepare her a luncheon in the car's private kitchen. After a sideways glance at Katya, he bowed himself into the vestibule.

But as the miles rolled by, memories of her past life as the wife of Chadwick Bingham chipped away at Jocelyn's serenity. *Over there, she could see Chad-*

*wick sprawled in the tassel-fringed chair, in the corner
of their boudoir. He was smoking, a brooding expression on his face, as she watched the scenery pass by
in a blur.*

Katya thrust a note in front of her face, and the
image evaporated as she focused on the oversize loops
and letters. *Mr. MacKenzie meet us in New York? What
if they make me stay in basement?*

"Mr. MacKenzie won't come calling until after
we're settled in. He's going to be a distant cousin, from
South Carolina. Why don't we leave him to worry over
his part, and we'll concentrate on ours." Katya only
had to be herself, of course. As for Jocelyn's role, she'd
perfected it ten years earlier: the gullible Southerner
gratefully accepting the carrot dangled in her face.
"You must not write down any part of Mr. MacKenzie's name, remember? From this moment on, we can't
trust anyone, especially the servants. You will remain
my personal maid, and I'll insist we have adjoining
rooms. I won't let them treat you poorly, I promise."

Don't want like before I work for you.

"If I see, or hear, of anyone—and I mean anyone, Katya, including the master and mistress of the
house—mistreating you in any manner, we'll be on
the first train back to Richmond."

*We have to stay. Have to help Secret Servants.
Sorry. I will be strong. Like you.*

No matter how often Jocelyn corrected her, Katya
refused to acknowledge the agency by its correct name.
Blinking back tears now, she gave the girl's mobcap
an affectionate tweak, hugged her shoulders. "Dear
Katya, I don't feel very strong, except when you're
with me." Jocelyn forced a smile, then led Katya down

the gently swaying corridor. "Come along. I'll show you everything. This end of the car is called the observation room, because the windows are clear and you can watch the scenery go by...."

By the time the train left Baltimore rain poured from a leaden sky, with raindrops pelting the windows just as uncertainty pelted Jocelyn's resolve. Chief Hazen had reluctantly conceded that her distinctive qualifications could not be duplicated even by a trained undercover operative, but it was her own insistence that won his sanction of this scheme. How confident and self-assured she had been, fueled by ten long years of hurt and resentment and anger toward a family against whom she'd been helpless.

She had nobody to blame for her present qualms but herself. Micah had objected vociferously until their last meeting four days earlier. He had been willing to place her well-being above a case that had been a thorn in the Secret Service's side for years, and it had almost cost him his job. In her entire life, nobody—including her desperate parents—had ever lifted a finger to protect her from possible harm, either to her person or her soul.

Swallowing the lump in her throat, Jocelyn fixed the image of Micah MacKenzie in her mind to banish images of her dead husband, thoughts of his malicious family and her own insecurities.

You will never be alone, Micah had promised. *Either before I officially arrive, or whenever we're not together, someone will be watching over you. Don't be afraid...* .

Jocelyn was afraid of a lot of things, but her husband's family was no longer among them. Micah's revelations about their suspected perfidy had not surprised her. Nothing about Chadwick's family could surprise her.

She was, however, terrified of what her life would be like when Micah MacKenzie was no longer part of it.

After arriving in Jersey City, Jocelyn and Katya took a ferry across the river to Manhattan, then followed a sullen but efficient baggage handler, who led them through the crush of passengers to an equally crowded street.

Aloof from the teeming masses waited a shiny dark green extension brougham, whose coachman and liveried grooms announced without a word the owner's exalted status. Resigned to her fate, Jocelyn watched one of the grooms snap to attention, then open the carriage door. A portly man with an old-fashioned walrus mustache stepped down and moved toward them. "My dear Jocelyn," he exclaimed in an unctuous voice. "At last, at last."

Jocelyn forced herself to offer her hand. "Uncle Brock."

"More beautiful than ever," he pronounced, subjecting her to an inspection just shy of offensive. "I can see I'll have to hire an army of guards to protect you from unwanted admirers. Ah, you must call me Uncle Augustus—you're going to be part of the family again."

Jocelyn drew herself up. "That remains to be seen. I've come for a visit, not a change of residence."

In the late-afternoon sunlight his florid face turned a deeper shade of red; sweat droplets gathered across his high forehead. "Mrs. Brock warned me not to expect miracles." He fiddled with the stickpin winking from the folds of his red silk necktie, his stubby fingers nervously tracing the diamond figure of a racehorse. "She meant to accompany me, of course, but was unable to extricate herself from a previous engagement."

The overblown phrases reminded Jocelyn of his letter, but instead of the pursed-lip piety she remembered, the caramel-brown eyes conveyed an earnestness she found disconcerting. She had steeled herself for a villain, and instead found herself with a heavily perspiring bear of a man who acted almost ill at ease.

"Hopefully, Mrs. Brock will at least be able to extricate herself in time to join us for dinner."

Katya's elbow dug into her back. Jocelyn belatedly remembered that her role did not include alienating her hosts within moments of her arrival. "I beg your pardon. I'm feeling a trifle disoriented, I expect."

"Was everything to your satisfaction during your journey? I trust you enjoyed traveling in the height of luxurious accommodation again." A deep-throated chuckle puffed his cheeks. "The Aurora's still a grand piece of rolling stock, isn't she? I remember the year you and Chadwick made a trip to Chicago in that car. Your benevolent father-in-law had it completely refurbished, just for the two of you."

"I remember."

"Ahem." Embarrassment flickered. He cleared his throat again. "Yes. Well, shall we go?"

Awkwardly, he handed her into the brougham; the groom practically shut the door on Katya's heels, which rekindled Jocelyn's ire. "This is my maid, and my friend, Katya. Katya, this my uncle-in-law, Mr. Brock."

Nonplussed for a moment, her uncle hesitated, his glance hovering between Katya's carefully blank face and Jocelyn. "Well, now." He laughed again, a little too heartily. "You've become more democratic than I recall, my dear."

"I like to think of it as being thoughtful. Katya cannot speak, but she knows how to write, and she knows how to listen. I expect her to be treated with courtesy. And I'll want adjoining rooms for us."

The carriage lurched into motion, joining the teeming throng. Compared to Richmond's quiet dignity, New York roared, as restless as a pride of hungry lions. With a queer little jerk, Jocelyn realized that while she'd been relieved to shed this family's ostentatious way of life, she actually missed the city itself.

"You have changed, Jocelyn. Most unexpected, I'll admit. I have to say, I've always admired a woman who can stand her ground, however quaint the choice of battles."

"Thank you. And how is Aunt Portia?" The name emerged grudgingly.

"As always, my dear wife enjoys robust health."

Augustus squirmed about on the seat, finally settling with a gusty sigh. His unselfconscious humanity disarmed her; despite her initial stage fright Jocelyn found herself relaxing into the persona she and Micah had concocted—the reserved but congenial woman prepared to resume her former position in the family. With a bit of luck the Brocks wouldn't be guarding their tongues or their habits from a grateful widow eager for reconciliation. Hopefully, over the coming weeks Jocelyn would ferret out sufficient evidence for arrest warrants to be issued.

Under any other circumstances, she might have felt some moral qualms over her duplicity.

Then she would remember what Chief Hazen had told her about Micah's father. Murdered in cold blood. *Like Mr. Hepplewhite.* While she couldn't wholeheartedly embrace Micah's conviction that Rupert Bingham was guilty, she could not gainsay the circumstantial evidence the Secret Service had compiled against the entire family.

Naturally, she would have to be careful.

Leaning forward a bit, she soaked up the views outside the spit-polished window. Over the past five years, she'd forgotten the din and rush and roar and tumultuous congestion of New York City. Buggies and carriages and wagons clattered around them, horses snorting, their hooves occasionally drawing sparks from the pavement. Instead of trees, buildings—some taller than five stories—pressed together like books on a library shelf. And the people…so many people, more than she would have thought could possibly be squeezed onto this small island. Faces of every nationality blurred together until Jocelyn shifted her gaze to her lap simply to rest her eyes.

Keeping a polite smile plastered on her face, she nodded as Augustus pointed out sights both familiar and strange—the old reservoir still in place because, he told her, the neighboring property owners were still fighting over the cost of turning it into a park; the former residence of a governor that had been converted to another hotel, and of course, the resplendent Waldorf Hotel, just opened the previous year, by "my dear friend William Astor."

Some traffic snarl brought the carriage to a standstill a block from their destination. Jocelyn glanced outside, idly surveying a piano-box buggy with the top folded back that had pulled alongside the carriage. The man driving looked across, straight at Jocelyn. His eyes were light, strangely intent. Then the Brock carriage jerked into motion once more, pulling ahead of the man driving the piano-box buggy.

Needles of uncertainty stitched an uneven path through her body. Had he merely been curious, or was she already one more bug in a sticky spiderweb craftily spun by her husband's family? Or perhaps this man was from the Secret Service, though she had learned that the agency was perpetually shorthanded and underfunded, so she doubted they would assign a nanny to the starry civilian eager to do something of value to justify her existence.

"Terrible, the congestion these days," Augustus remarked. "Mrs. Brock and I are considering having a new home built, farther north, across from Central Park. All the best families are doing so. I've also heard about plans for a new development along the Hudson, west of the Park."

Her uncle resumed his monologue; sighing, Jocelyn tried to relax her own stiff muscles. *"Don't allow your mind to wander from the role,"* Micah had warned her. *"It won't be easy. It's not too late to change your mind."* He'd gone on to observe that she was not equipped for a life of subterfuge. Jocelyn had almost laughed in his face.

As though to prove her competence, she gave the rambling man across from her an engaging smile. "Your last telegram three days ago indicated that

Chadwick's father would be arriving this weekend. Will Mrs. Bingham be joining him?"

One winged eyebrow lifted. "My dear. I forgot, you wouldn't have known." He twirled the end of his mustache in what was probably a habitual nervous gesture, then heaved a sigh. "She died, about a year after Chadwick. She never recovered from the scandal of his… ah…the manner of his death. A bitter, grief-stricken woman, I'm afraid. Mrs. Brock tried many times to reason with my sister, but the poor dear wasn't having any of it. Rupert sold most of their properties and built himself a reasonably sized cottage on Long Island. You'll find him a much-changed man, I'm afraid."

Jocelyn found she was hardly adept after all, not in the face of such callousness. One of the properties Rupert Bingham had sold in his grief had been Parham, the Tremayne family estate in Virginia.

Her uncle's face brightened. "Ah. Home at last. And it looks as though Mrs. Brock was able to juggle her appointments after all. There, you see? The family reunion for our prodigal niece has begun."

As he handed her down out of the carriage, she watched the piano-box buggy wheel past the carriage and turn the corner two blocks later.

The driver had not so much as glanced their way.

Friend or enemy? Jocelyn wondered. Then, with a fatalistic shrug, she gathered up her traveling skirt and went forward to greet her aunt.

Chapter Ten

"Going well," Alexander MacKay reported to Micah, who had been waiting in the lobby of the Brevoort Hotel where he'd checked in two hours earlier, after watching Jocelyn and Katya climb into the Brock carriage.

MacKay was an operative out of the Richmond office of Pinkerton's National Detective Agency; he and Micah had met the previous month, when one of Mr. Hepplewhite's heirs hired Pinkerton's to investigate the watchmaker's murder. An instant rapport had sprung up between the two men, fueled by their mutual faith, Scottish heritage—and a fervent dedication to their respective professions.

Casually, Micah folded the newspaper he'd been reading. "The Service appreciates your assistance— I appreciate it. It was sanctioned—" with grumblings about funding "—because we know your face won't be recognized up here in New York. Chief Hazen told me your superintendent thinks you're an independent rascal, but someone he'd trust his life to nonetheless."

MacKay shrugged.

Using the folded newspaper as a shield, Micah handed him a thin string-tied folder. "These are photos and descriptions of the Brock family, most of their staff and Rupert Bingham. They socialize, a lot, except for Bingham, who's something of a recluse these days. Shadowing them won't be easy."

"I'll do my best." MacKay deftly accepted both paper and folder. "Do I report to you here?"

"Not directly. I'll leave word with the concierge where we can meet. Most likely I'll be followed all the time, once I introduce myself to the Brocks, and it might be safer for us all if we make other arrangements. I have an assistant, a young fellow with a quick mind and a closed mouth. He'll be shadowing *me*. For some reason, Chief Hazen thinks I need looking after."

"A pair of eyes in the back of your head never hurts."

"Mmm." The two men exchanged sober looks. "I argued, strenuously," he added dryly, "against Mrs. Bingham's inclusion in this investigation, but Chief Hazen thought she offered our best opportunity in several years." Jocelyn had agreed to revert to her married name to placate the Brocks; Micah had almost learned to use it without internally flinching. The private doubts he'd battled for weeks had intensified once he'd watched Jocelyn vanish into the Brocks' carriage. In an attempt to lighten the tone, he quipped, "What's the world coming to, when the federal government relies on a female civilian and a private detective to carry out its missions?"

Alex laughed. "Hazen and the widow ganged up on you, I heard."

"There are no secrets in the Secret Service." Micah

pointed to the newspaper Alex now held under his arm. "Make sure you take a gander at the society page. There's some possibilities for you tomorrow night and Saturday."

MacKay inclined his head. "Makes a change from chasing criminals wearing sack coats and guns. You do realize you might be trying to crack open a safe with a silver teaspoon."

"Did you know God once used a talking donkey to induce a confession from a man? I might not agree with, or approve of, allowing this woman to be part of our investigation. But who knows if God didn't provide her, at just the right time, for just this very reason? We've spent years hunting for the molds as well as the bogus goods, years trying to secure prima facie evidence against the principals in this case." *And my father lost his life.* "We want to shut them down, Alex. Permanently."

"It will happen," MacKay promised, the burr in his voice more pronounced. "'Tis the waiting that tests our faith as well as our patience. But trust yourself—trust God to bring about the result, in His time."

"You're right, of course." Micah stuffed his hands into his pockets. "She's angry at God right now, Alex. So angry she's pretty much renounced her faith. I don't want her hurt any more by this business."

"So that's the way of it, hmm?"

"I don't know. I haven't been able to think about it, try to decide whether what I'm feeling is real." He paused, adding slowly, "I haven't had much practice, courting a woman, especially when the woman thinks the courtship an elaborate sham."

"You told me you lost your wife some years ago?"

Micah nodded. "I loved her, very much. But Jocelyn…she's different. She's built this facade—the independent, self-sufficient widow—yet I don't think I've ever met a more vulnerable, lonely person. Unless we're careful, I may be responsible for her ruination or worse, her death. I need to solve the case. Something isn't ringing true, but I can't figure out what. Like it or not, Jocelyn Tremayne Bingham holds the key. I have to remain objective even as I pretend to be a long-lost cousin who—" God help him "—pretends to fall in love with her."

"You'll find a way, my friend. Have the same faith in yourself as you do in God." Alex lightly punched his shoulder. "Enjoy your courtship as well as the hunt. From the little bit I glimpsed of the lass, your widow does make a striking silver teaspoon."

By the end of the second week, Jocelyn discovered that she possessed an aptitude for undercover work, despite her overactive conscience. Most of the nervous butterflies had vanished, but the effort to daily cast off a slough of self-recrimination was more taxing than she cared to admit. Occasionally, an even more depressing possibility surfaced—she was merely resuming the lie she had lived throughout the years of her marriage.

Daily she cultivated the facade, ignoring the whispers among New York society while she absorbed everything she heard, every face she saw, every nuance thickening the atmosphere. Late at night, she and Katya huddled together in an alcove in Jocelyn's bedroom to share their discoveries through voice and written words.

Before going to bed, Jocelyn diligently burned Katya's scribblings.

And every hour of every day she yearned for Micah, with a fervency she had not experienced since her debut at White Sulphur Springs when she was sixteen years old. The dangerous play they had concocted only heightened emotions struggling to break free of a decade of self-imposed restraint. After two weeks without hearing that deep voice, of not watching the gray eyes brighten to polished silver when he laughed, or darken to charcoal when he touched her fingers—those emotions were about to spill over and drown her.

The Letter had finally arrived two days earlier. Because Mrs. Tobler, the Brocks' dragon of a housekeeper, always confiscated the mail and took it directly to Mrs. Brock, Jocelyn had no opportunity to spirit Micah's debut missive away for an initial private read. Instead, when her aunt handed her the envelope, Jocelyn professed tearful astonishment at the discovery that any member of her own family, however remote the relation, was still alive. "I'll read it aloud, if you like," she suggested to Portia. "I believe this branch of my family distinguished themselves within Charleston society. You recently mentioned that Uncle Augustus had been discussing a business venture there. A relative would be a contact he could cultivate."

Portia laid aside the rest of her correspondence. Her ringed fingers gently tapped the inlaid mahogany of her writing desk. "How odd that this man should contact you only weeks after your arrival here." The china-blue eyes with their wintry chill contrasted sharply with her creamy complexion and cupid's-bow lips. Despite her advanced age—she had passed her sixtieth birthday—Portia's voluptuous shape and exquisite gowns continued to draw admiring glances even after four decades.

In her presence, Jocelyn by turns felt garish, gangly and impatient. Sometimes a longing surged through her to yank a hairpin out of her aunt's perfectly arranged coiffure, or step on the train of one of her Worth evening gowns. Thus far she had managed to quell the impulse.

"I would imagine he read my name in the papers," she suggested now. "I scarcely remember meeting him. It was only once, when I was very young." At her present age of almost twenty-eight, seventeen was barely out of leading strings. Micah, she realized, was a very good teacher of how to disguise truth with verisimilitude. "Mama mentioned his people came from Scotland. My mother was Scottish, you know."

"Mmm. Unrestrained lot, like the Irish, with a tendency to vulgarity. But I have met Mr. Carnegie, who, despite his ancestry, has distinguished himself, with something of a philanthropic bent I find most appealing." She took a sip of imported spring water from a delicate crystal goblet probably worth more than Jocelyn's Richmond town house. "That business with his steel mills in Pennsylvania, however, is most distressing. A man who can't control the mob becomes part of it, regardless of his wealth. You might want to remember that, child."

"Yes, ma'am. Shall I read the letter?"

"Please do. You have a pleasing voice, Jocelyn, despite the Southern drawl." She flicked her an assessing glance that encompassed Jocelyn from the crown of her head to the lace trim of her morning tea gown.

"Good heavens, you'd think by now something could have been invented to remove freckles. Have you tried the bleaching rinse I instructed Matilda to make for you, to tone down the excessive red of your hair? Perhaps if you watered down the rinse, it would do for a facial scrub, as well. Not that I wish to impugn your hair and face, child. You understand that, I'm sure. And in your own quaint way, you're a very attractive woman. But I know how uncomfortable it makes you, when people gawk at you as though you were an exotic creature in a zoological park."

By now Jocelyn had learned to deflect the thinly disguised barbs with a serene Mona Lisa smile. Concentrating on opening the envelope, she withdrew the single sheet of paper, and pretended she could absorb Micah's touch through the words he had written. "I'll read my cousin's letter—I'm sure you're as curious as I to hear what he has to say." That quip earned her a sharp look. Jocelyn schooled her own face to stillness and, heart thrumming, began to read.

"My dear cousin Jocelyn,
I had long since given up hope of finding other family still living, but can today thank God for unexpected blessings. On one of my business trips to New York City, at a dinner party I attended someone mentioned they had recently enjoyed an evening at Madison Square Garden with the Brocks, and the widow of their nephew Chadwick Bingham. With utmost discretion, I assure you, I inquired as to whether the widow was the former Jocelyn Tremayne. The confirmation filled me with delight. However distant

the blood tie, we may still claim kinship, which for me is worth more than gold. With these words, I formally announce my intention to call upon you and your hosts, Tuesday afternoon, at four o'clock, in order to enjoy, however briefly, getting to know a long-lost cousin."

She looked up. "He signs it, *Your servant, Micah L. MacKenzie*." The inclusion of the middle initial indicated that all was well, and they could proceed with the intended plan.

Her aunt extended an imperious hand, and Jocelyn silently handed the letter back.

"I trust you'll conduct yourself with decorum, Jocelyn. This family has suffered quite enough scandal."

Now Tuesday had arrived, bringing with it the formerly banished butterflies, and a fog of grayness that dimmed the golden autumn sunlight. "Katya, could you loosen the stays a notch? I don't care if my aunt notices and tears a strip off me later. Right now I can't breathe. I need to breathe, Katya…."

Her patient maid laid aside the brush and combs she'd gathered to arrange Jocelyn's hair. Somberly she laid a careful hand over Jocelyn's intertwined fingers. The gesture calmed—and tweaked a feeble spark of amusement.

The reserved, proper widow of Chadwick Bingham allowed a housemaid a degree of familiarity beyond the pale for any servant. Scandal indeed!

After Katya loosened the corset, while Jocelyn gratefully sucked in air and willed the grayness away, the maid wrote on her tablet. *Do not worry. You and me, we are good. HE is gooder. You be all right.*

"He's better, not gooder, but either way, I know you're right. I'm just…" She stopped. Despite the closeness they shared it was far too dangerous to confess, even to Katya, the Chinese-sparkler sensation Micah MacKenzie set off inside her. Confiding the feelings only lent them more credibility.

Heartbreak lurked over her shoulder. More likely than heartbreak, however, she'd find herself lying dead on a cold floor somewhere like Mr. Hepplewhite, and the Secret Service still wouldn't have the proof it needed.

Yet mortal danger was preferable to heartbreak.

A few moments later, as Katya fastened the last button of her gown, the parlor maid knocked on the door to announce the arrival of a visitor for Mrs. Bingham.

Jocelyn and Katya stared at one another for a suspended moment, then with a strangled sound Jocelyn clasped the younger girl's forearms, leaned forward and brushed her lips against her smooth forehead. "Thank you," she whispered. "I couldn't do this without you."

She had just opened the door when behind her Katya stamped her foot. Turning, Jocelyn waited while the girl hurried across the room with her final note.

I believe God is with you two.

For a moment the walls closed in upon Jocelyn. "I'm glad you believe that," she finally managed. "I know Micah agrees with you. And if God chose to be *with* anyone, it would be Micah MacKenzie."

Katya scowled. Her head moved in a definitive headshake.

"Don't," Jocelyn forestalled her as she dug out paper

and pencil. "I can't, Katya. Not right now. Just—" she closed her eyes, but a longing deeper than the ocean, deeper than the bowels of the earth pushed the words past her constricted throat "—pray for him. For—for me. Please."

And before her courage collapsed, she walked out into the hallway.

Micah had been shown into the formal reception room, a calculated move designed to impress first-time callers. For a shaky moment Jocelyn stood in the entrance between the French doors, soaking in the sight of the one man she could not dismiss from her mind. He looked taller than she remembered, his shoulders broader. The strong face radiated strength and restrained power. In a room designed to dwarf self-importance, Micah MacKenzie stood at ease, just as relaxed as if he were standing in the library of Jocelyn's cozy, cluttered town house.

Even her aunt was not immune to his potent masculine appeal. Cheeks delicately flushed, the graceful hands more animated in their gestures, Portia Brock carried on a largely one-sided conversation while Micah listened, his head tilted attentively. An unpleasant possibility slipped into Jocelyn's mind. What if, like almost every other man in Portia's sphere, he'd been moonstruck by her voluptuous beauty, blinded into forgetting his own role in this dangerous game?

Jocelyn's throat locked; her feet refused to move. For one terrifying instant she herself forgot every line she'd practiced in silence and secrecy the past two weeks.

Then Micah shifted, and caught sight of her. "At last. My dear long-lost cousin." He'd altered his accent, adopting the drawl of a Southern tidewater aristocrat. Striding across the room, his back to Portia, he searched Jocelyn's face with concern flickering in the gray eyes. "Cousin Jocelyn? It's been years.... Have I changed so much you don't recognize me at all? My mustache is thicker, and you may recall lamb-chop sideburns are no longer fashionable."

He stopped a scant yard away, concern deepening when Jocelyn still didn't respond. "You're more beautiful than I remember," he tried next, and executed a perfect bow.

The undertone of facetiousness finally unlocked her paralyzed vocal cords. "It has been a long time." The words bubbled forth, a little too high-pitched, a little too breathless. "You've grown into a handsome man. I'm very sorry our families lost touch over the years. How fortunate to make contact after so long."

"I was just lamenting to Mr. MacKenzie that I find inquisitiveness a deplorable flaw," Portia interposed, coming to stand beside them, her blue eyes bright, bathing Micah in warmth and the heavy scent of her French perfume. "Now I see I must forgive our acquaintances as their penchant for name-dropping has been a stroke of luck for us all. Come, sit down, shall we, and I'll ring for refreshments."

She beckoned for Jocelyn to precede her, a ruse Jocelyn had witnessed several times before, having discovered at the Brocks' first dinner party that her aunt considered other females to be archrivals, regardless of their age. As though he hadn't noticed, Micah smoothly stepped around the older woman, offering Jocelyn his arm. "Allow me, cousin." He laid his palm over her fingers, not betraying by even the flicker of an eyelash the discovery that they were chilled, and damp. "My business in New York will require much of my time. But I have already extended my stay at the hotel in the hopes that we can become reacquainted."

"I would like that very much." Jocelyn allowed him to lead her over to a striped-silk Louis XIV side chair with a decorative motif of grotesque masks. An involuntary shudder rippled through her, which she covered with a question. "How long will you be able to enjoy this magnificent city, then?"

"Oh, several weeks, I should think," Micah replied with a sympathetic smile. After he seated her he ran his fingers over the carved masks, then straightened as though he hadn't just read Jocelyn's thoughts with uncanny accuracy. "I have managers who can attend to matters back home while I conduct business here in New York."

"And what sort of business allows you the pleasure of so much discretionary time, Mr. MacKenzie?" Portia sat down, pressing the foot buzzer with a little more force than necessary. "My dear husband is seldom free, you see. He's something of a slave driver— Oh, dear! I do hope I haven't offended you, Mr. MacKenzie, seeing as how you're from Charleston."

"No offense taken. Slavery's an evil our country's well rid of, and I'm the first man to admit it. However, I no longer live in Charleston. Early last year I moved to Washington, D.C., and live in a lovely neighborhood practically within hailing distance of the White House. I've made a lot of contacts there, all of them beneficial."

"Then you're only a day's travel from Richmond, which is where I live," Jocelyn exclaimed. "How delightful, having my only living relative so close when I return home."

"But, Jocelyn, child, you must know we're hoping you'll look upon New York as your home now. There's nothing for you in Virginia. A man of Mr. MacKenzie's obvious stature in the business world can't be expected to traipse back and forth from Washington to Richmond, even for a long-lost relative. You'd do yourself and him a grave disservice, depending too much on his goodwill." Lips framed in an appealing pout, Portia leaned forward. "Perhaps you're not aware of our niece's tragic story. We don't like to speak of the scandalous death of her husband, of course. But since you're family…"

"All I know is that her husband died, some years ago," Micah said, his gaze focused solely on Jocelyn, his voice gentle. "Quite a blow, isn't it, when one is young."

"Yes. But I've made a life for myself in Richmond, and do not foresee leaving—" She stopped, furious with herself.

"You mentioned she's only been here a fortnight, Mrs. Brock?" Micah filled in the charged silence. "Two weeks is perhaps not long enough to convince my lovely Southern cousin of the advantages of living in one of the world's greatest cities. Over the past few years I've made several visits here, and only now am considering the efficacy of purchasing property. I believe you mentioned that your husband is in real estate as well as banking? A conversation with him might prove helpful as I make a decision."

"Our middle son, Virgil, handles real estate matters for one of his father's banks." Her nostrils still quivered, but by the time the maid rolled a tea cart laden with refreshments into the room, Portia was batting her eyes shamelessly at Micah. She passed him a delicate Limoges teacup the size of one from a child's play set, which Micah accepted with aplomb. "I'll arrange our calendar to include you as often as you're free, Mr. MacKenzie."

"Excellent. I'll do my best to convince your niece to change her mind about New York." He took a sip of the thick Belgian cocoa Portia loved. Jocelyn watched admiringly as without so much as a grimace he swallowed half the stuff, then slid a smile her way. "Of course, I might decide that Washington, D.C., offers her even more."

"I think I'll make up my own mind about where I choose to live, and when I choose to move," Jocelyn whipped out with just enough spirit to wipe the smile off his face. "Right now, I'm enjoying the city, and everything it has to offer. My aunt and uncle have been most generous and hospitable."

The conversation settled into ritual; twenty minutes later, at precisely at five o'clock, Micah set aside his cup and rose.

"May I escort him to the door, Aunt Portia? I know you were supposed to meet the Auckleys to attend that lecture."

"Very well." Her mouth pursed in a moue, but she acquiesced with surprising grace. "Mr. MacKenzie, I'll send a dinner invitation soon, I promise." After a final lingering look she rose and glided over the parquet floor, silk skirts rustling.

Mindful of listening ears, Micah waited until Portia had left the room before turning to Jocelyn. "You're fine," he murmured under his breath to her. "And far more beautiful than your aunt."

"Katya told me Mrs. Brock's chambermaid confided that her mistress will be sixty-three next spring. But men still fall all over themselves whenever she appears." She heard the wistfulness in her own voice and hurriedly moved toward the door. "I hope we can look forward to seeing you again soon, cousin."

"Call me Micah. The family connection was really only an excuse to reestablish the connection. I've never forgotten you, Jocelyn. And I plan to see you as often as I'm able."

"Micah," she whispered out of the side of her mouth, stiffly waving her hand around the grand hall, another monstrosity of bad taste with its marble columns and ghostly white statues. "Anyone can hear you."

"Good. Then my intentions will be clear to everyone."

Heat rushed up her neck and burned her cheeks. When he lifted her hand to his lips and pressed a lingering kiss on her knuckles, Jocelyn gawked at him like a knobby-kneed young girl, then brought her knuckles to her mouth.

Micah inhaled sharply, his eyes darkening. A muscle twitched in his jaw.

Footsteps rang on the tiled floor, and a uniformed maid scurried across from between the columns. When she caught sight of them she stopped, eyes widening before she bobbed a hasty curtsy, then scuttled away.

"Jocelyn…" Micah shook his head.

They walked in pulsing silence to the main foyer where Palmer, the stolid butler, opened the door. Jocelyn led the way down the marble steps, into a bright bar of late-afternoon sunshine. Behind them, horses and streetcars and wagons clattered along Fifth Avenue. Pedestrians strolled the sidewalk. Only after the butler closed the door did Micah speak again. "I'll be back as soon as I can. Next time, we'll go for a walk in Central Park, where we can enjoy a bit of privacy."

"There's a safe in Portia's private parlor—it's a sunroom on the third floor." Jocelyn stumbled through the words, her tongue tangling because she could only risk a moment to tell him. "And I've seen several men visit Uncle Brock. They're always taken in through a back entrance, and two times they've been carrying leather satchels—like the one you had in Richmond."

"Identical?" he questioned sharply.

"No." She searched her memory, and repeated with more assurance, "No. These were larger, more like a club bag."

He nodded, then clasped her hand, giving her fingers a gentle squeeze. Obviously, he could feel their trembling, but Jocelyn no longer cared.

"I don't trust Chadwick's cousins."

"Why? Have they been rude? Unkind?"

Touched by his instant protectiveness, Jocelyn smiled up at him. "No. Just...secretive. Julius is the youngest, Virgil the middle. Lawrence is the oldest. He lives in St. Louis now, and wrote that he won't be back in New York until Christmas. Both Virgil and Julius maintain suites here, but I think Virgil might have an apartment at the Knickerbocker, as well. As you heard, he works at his father's bank. Julius...he's something of a misfit, socially awkward. Mealtimes, when the whole family is in residence, have been interesting."

"Ah. And what about Rupert Bingham?"

"Micah, I scarcely recognized him. He's been staying here for a week, but he mentioned at lunch that he plans to return to his home on Long Island soon. We don't talk much. He spends most of his time dozing in Uncle Brock's study, or reading. I—I can't explain it, but I don't believe he's guilty of anything these days, except—" she hesitated, then added softly "—regrets."

"Mmm..." Micah replied. "I'll pass your information along in my daily report." He smiled, a slow smile that penetrated even the frozen spots inside her heart. "When I take you to Central Park," he murmured, "I think I might have to haul you behind some bushes, and kiss every one of those shadows from your sad eyes. Good day."

After another flawless bow he tipped his hat, then strolled down the brick walkway. He looked every inch the confident, wealthy gentleman, not an operative for the United States Secret Service who had taken shameless liberties with a young woman on the front steps of her uncle's mansion, in plain view of the passersby strolling along New York City's Fifth Avenue.

With a wisp of a sigh, the young woman forgot every one of the stern lectures with which she'd armed herself. Trailing her fingers over the cool marble, she wandered down the brick path that led to the gardens behind the house.

Later, she thought. Later she would remember that this was only an elaborate stage, and she and Micah mere players in a dangerous game.

And for an hour or two, Jocelyn allowed the young girl who had never been romanced a fleeting opportunity to dream about a walk in Central Park.

Chapter Eleven

A man strolled with arrogant grace across the gravel pathway until he reached a carriage. Casually, he stood beside it and began to talk. "They've been out together three times in the past week. Last night, at the horse show, she spent more time staring at him than at the horses. I don't like the implications."

"Don't do anything precipitous at this point. I've got men investigating, as well as following, him. Thus far nothing untoward has surfaced. MacKenzie is lodged at the Brevoort Hotel, an acceptable choice for conducting business in the city. My sources inform me that he's done quite well in the shipping industry. The people he's contacted locally indicate he does have plans for expansion in the New York market. For the moment, I'm inclined to believe a connection with Mr. MacKenzie might prove useful to us down the road."

"How do you know he's not the law, or some private detective, or another long-nosed sniffer spying for the Secret Service? I don't trust him, I tell you."

"Nor do I. That doesn't mean he couldn't be useful."

"So you let him romance the chit because you

think he might be *useful?* What if he's actually stupid enough to decide she'd do for a wife? I've watched her. She plays him like a professional floozy. If he asks, she'll reel him in. With her looks, at her age there won't be many proposals coming her way. Marriage proposals, that is."

"If such an event occurs—and I stress the *if*—we have several options."

An unpleasant bark of laughter was the response. "I can see from your face which of those options you prefer."

"Don't be impertinent."

"But isn't that precisely why you depend on me?" With insolent grace, he paused to strike a match on the sole of his shoe, then lit a Cuban cigar. "Shall I share a little scheme I've devised for our charming redheaded widow?"

"No. Scheme all you want, but do nothing that will pull her out of our reach. We don't need her fleeing back to Virginia. The depth of their attraction for each other is unexpected, but we can use it to our advantage. As for your 'options,' unless I give the order, I don't want her arrested."

"Now why would I want to do that after spending the past month turning her into the perfect shover? Who would suspect Chadwick Bingham's widow of passing counterfeit goods? I've enjoyed the novelty of it all."

"I trust the person making the switch is dependable."

"Indisputably. They want their family out of Five Points." He blew a ring with the cigar smoke. "I keep telling you if our little redhead had known anything five years ago, she would have told someone, not disappeared when Bingham inconsiderately hanged himself. You never should have involved her."

"Bah! She might still look the same on the outside with her brassy hair and freckled face, but she's no longer a green ingenue. Why can I make that assumption? Because the goods we gave Benny have not surfaced. We know he passed them to her."

"How do we know Benny didn't do a double-switch on us and take everything to those infernal Secret Service mosquitoes? Maybe that's why he's disappeared."

"You fret like an old woman. Those agents are overworked, few in number. They exterminate a few hustlers, expose some green-goods swindlers and think they've done their job. I've tossed a few bones their way myself—helps keep their attention elsewhere. The Secret Service is a bumbling government agency that will disappear by the turn of the century. Our present problem with Benny will resolve itself. Flexibility, as well as cunning, is a necessity in our business."

"So you say. But I still fail to understand your distrust of the widow. We only have Benny's word that he passed her the goods."

A malignant current momentarily darkened the air. "There are things about that woman I have not shared with you. I do so now because your infatuation—"

"She's an amusing toy, not a blasted infatuation."

"—is not to be tolerated. Listen to me. After her husband's cowardly suicide, when she vanished, a half-million dollars from one of our accounts also vanished."

"Legitimate dollars, not prime examples from one of our production firms?" Thoughtfully he tapped his walking cane on the gravel pathway. "So that's the real reason behind this brouhaha. What a cunning little sneak. Of course, it's far more likely Chadwick himself accomplished the theft. As I recall, he was one of the vice presidents at that bank, wasn't he? Probably transferred it overseas, or spent it, or invested it in a silver mine or something. Although it wouldn't make sense, helping himself to the goods if he'd decided to string himself from the balustrade. Perhaps his wife decided she wanted it all, and Bingham's suicide was a cleverly arranged murder."

"Murder or suicide, he's dead. She's not."

"True. What difference does it make at this point? Besides, the woman could also be the innocent rose she pretends to be."

"Don't be stupid. I've had to replace those funds with counterfeit bills, at considerable risk. *That money is mine.* Nobody steals from me. Nobody. Jocelyn Tremayne Bingham will eventually be persuaded to share all her secrets. If we'd known she'd reverted to her maiden name, we could have found her—and the money—sooner."

Silently the companion puffed on his cigar. "Have it your way. She's an unprincipled doxy and a clever thief."

"Clever enough to know a counterfeit ten-dollar gold coin and an obviously forged bill provide her with leverage. Clever enough to have hidden them well, since we know they're not in her Richmond residence, or among her possessions here in New York."

"Moving the plates and the printer to a new location is costing us $50,000 a week. You do realize you might jeopardize the entire organization over her and still not find that money. Is she worth it?"

"I'll be the judge of acceptable risks. Better than exposure, wouldn't you agree? Don't worry. We still have the means to produce enough to keep everyone in the partnership agreeably solvent. Now, the two love-birds should be strolling along in a few minutes. Unless you want them to see you, I suggest you cut across the grass and mingle with the crowds on Bethesda Terrace."

"Very well." He flicked the cigar onto the gravel path, ground out the smoldering tip, then curved his hands over the opened window of the dark green brougham. "I suggest you have the driver hurry. You wouldn't want to be seen yourself."

God had blessed them with a perfect late-autumn day, Micah decided as he and Jocelyn strolled the Mall with the other park goers. Though past their red-gold peak, the elms still formed an arched canopy above them, with an azure sky peeking through the branches. The air in the park seemed clearer, more invigorating. He glanced down at Jocelyn, and a quiet joy radiated through his bones.

"You're looking pleased," Jocelyn said.

"I finally have you all to myself for a change, and I'm liking the feeling very much."

"And all these other people are figments of my imagination?"

"Well…you do have a fertile one." Delighted with her, Micah impulsively grabbed her hand, tugging her in front of an Irish nanny pushing a wicker baby carriage. At the edge of the path, he whisked a giggling Jocelyn around one of the many park statues into the dappled shadows. "Let's see if we can find a spot somewhere even your imagination can't discover."

If he were clever enough, and blessed with a snippet of divine indulgence, the pair of lackeys who monitored every swing of his and Jocelyn's arms would instead chase themselves in circles. "As I recall, I made you a promise some time ago. Between the Brocks parading us in front of their friends, and that spate of inclement weather last week, this is the first opportunity I've had to follow through on that promise."

He felt the jolt of her reaction, heard the catch in her breath. Micah paused in the midst of a clump of evergreens to search the endearing freckled face. "Don't be alarmed. I promise to try to remember that I'm a gentleman."

"I thought you'd forgotten," she confessed, and scarlet streaked across her cheeks. "Not about being a gentleman, I mean. About…about…what you said, the first day."

"Not a chance. As for place… I think below Vista Rock. There's a thicket of rhododendrons and azaleas…perfect surroundings for us to be alone together."

"Micah…"

"Shh…this time is for us. Enjoy the moment."

"For tomorrow we die?"

He gave her a sharp glance, his jubilance faltering. "You quoted scripture, Jocelyn."

"If it shocks you so much, I promise never to do it again."

In the blink of an eye she had whisked herself away from him, reverting from the vibrant, warm and sparkling woman to a hollow-eyed shell. Micah wanted to tie his blabbing tongue in a permanent knot. "I'm sorry. I'm a clumsy dolt of a man. You caught me off guard, but I never intended my response to wound."

Slowly, shyly, life crept back into her face. "I'm sorry, too." She caught her lower lip between her teeth, then whispered miserably, "Chadwick used sarcasm like a sword, especially when he…was in one of his black moods. I don't think he meant to hurt me, but—" she slid Micah a sideways look "—I used to be very thin-skinned. I thought I was better now. Hide of an elephant."

They hadn't reached the more secluded bluff, but after a swift survey assured him that they were alone, Micah halted and clasped her forearms. Beneath his fingers the dense curly wool of her blue Persian jacket felt soft as a newborn lamb. Holding her gaze with his own, he worked his thumbs beneath the thin leather of her gloves until he reached the fragile skin of her wrist. Her pulse thundered against his searching thumb. "Your skin is perfect. And I'd rather be holding a vulnerable, easily wounded redhead than anything else on earth."

"Micah…you shouldn't say things like that. Not now, not under these circumstances." In the shadows her hazel eyes had turned a glimmering shade of forest-green. "Our courtship is supposed to be a pretense. I can't—"

"This courtship has never been a pretense, Jocelyn. Let's admit that to each other, right now." When she shook her head he cupped her cheeks. "Yes," he murmured, and kissed the pinkened tip of her dainty nose. "Yes," he repeated, his voice deepening. Inhaling the heady gardenia fragrance of her favorite perfume, he pressed light kisses on her forehead, her translucent eyelids, all the time stroking his gloved fingers over her cheeks. "I've wanted to do this from the moment I saw you at Mr. Hepplewhite's store...."

"You looked as though you wanted to skewer me."

"Well, right now what I want is to kiss you." He lifted his head and smiled down into her unguarded face. "May I? Will you share a kiss with me, little firefly?"

Wonderingly, her hand lifted to brush her own gloved fingers with the lightest of touches against his mustache. "Haven't you already?"

"Those kisses were the appetizer." Smiling softly, he tugged off first his gloves, then Jocelyn's, and stuffed them into the pocket of his jacket. "This is the main course."

He slid their bare fingers together. Watching her eyes dilate into huge mysterious pools, her lips half parting, he lowered his head. Just before he touched his lips to hers, he closed his eyes.

Heat sizzled through Micah in explosive starbursts. Before it burned him to a crisp, he tried to force himself to end the kiss, but Jocelyn herself shattered his honorable intentions. With an inarticulate gasp she pressed against him, kissing him back, their intertwined hands fused together.

Something—the distant chords of the band striking up, a childish voice raised in laughter, perhaps it was the chittering of a squirrel—finally gave him the impetus to lift his head. Breathing hard, slowly he relaxed his cramped fingers, slid them about Jocelyn's supple waist, steadying her even as he fought to keep his own balance. Her own breath was ragged, and behind the thick screen of her cinnamon-colored eyelashes, green-gold eyes shimmered with emotions.

Micah could no more stem the need coursing through him than he could stop the wind; he touched his lips to the pulse throbbing in her temple. "Jocelyn..." Her name emerged in a ragged sigh.

Slowly, she opened her eyes and gazed wonderingly up at him. "Ohhh... I never knew... I never dreamed..." A light breeze flicked over them, loosening one of the spit curls she'd arranged about her face.

The incipient panic building inside Micah evaporated. "Me, either." A crooked smile grew and built until his cheeks ached with it. "You are so beautiful to me." He lifted the dangling curl, marveling at the shades of red and gold and auburn, at the softness.

"You make me feel beautiful." In an endearingly awkward gesture she turned her head and nuzzled his hand. "For the first time in my life, I feel—beautiful."

"Jocelyn, surely Chadwick—" Instantly she froze, and would have turned away except Micah was having none of it, firmly holding her still. "No, don't hide from me. I won't pry, I won't mention him again. Let's not spoil this present moment with the past."

"The present will spoil it soon enough." She stood, still as a fawn in the meadow, her gaze turned so wistful Micah's heart cracked.

"I told you, this has nothing to do with your family, or my job. I'm not sure it ever did—not entirely." Abandoning all restraint, he pulled her close, wrapping her in his arms. "Jocelyn, whatever happens, months ago I promised that I would not abandon you. I don't make promises like that lightly. Please believe me. I know you're angry at God, that you don't trust Him or His purpose, but I do. I do." He rocked her, longing to infuse his own faith into her pores, praying in the darkest reaches of his soul that God would heal her. "I don't have any easy answers for you. I just know that, without my faith, I could not have survived these last years. Without my faith, I couldn't walk away every time I leave you at the door of a family I believe with all my heart has wickedness at its core."

Incredibly, he felt Jocelyn's arms creep around his waist, and she laid her cheek against his chest. "Micah, you are the kindest and the strongest man I have ever known. I wish…"

"What do you wish?" He could have stood in this deep glade for the rest of his life, holding her, nurturing her back to life. "If it's within my power to grant your wish, I will."

"Micah…" Against his chest she shook her head. "You know better than to offer rash proclamations like that. Besides, not even God can grant my wish."

"I don't believe that. Look at you—that's twice in a single afternoon you've mentioned His name."

He felt the sigh that shuddered through her, sensed the unbearable pain gathering strength within her that left them both bruised and breathless.

Perplexed, but not in despair. Troubled, yet not distressed. *Lord, please give her back the hope.*

"You and Katya." Her words emerged in a thin trickle he almost couldn't hear. "I cannot fight you both. I'm so tired of fighting. Tired of wishing for what will never be, tired of trying to understand why you both believe in divine mercy when nothing in my life, since I turned seventeen—*nothing* has offered me any assurance that God cares what happens to me."

She withdrew her arms and pushed against his chest until reluctantly Micah released her. "Real or pretense, this courtship has given me something I never thought I'd have, and for that you will always hold a—a special place in my heart. But it will end, Micah. Someday you'll find the proof you need, and if they're guilty the Brocks and the Binghams will pay for the pain they have wreaked upon others. And I... I will endure. I created a new life for myself once. I can do so again."

When Micah opened his mouth to protest, she grabbed his hand and pressed a fervent kiss to the palm. "It's all right, Micah. I know you never intended to hurt me. Regardless of what you said earlier, we have a counterfeit courtship. Not a real one."

"I've spent the last eight years of my life learning how to distinguish between the real and the counterfeit. You're wrong, Jocelyn Tremayne Bingham." Temper stirred, but Micah quelled the nastiness because Jocelyn didn't deserve it. "One day this case will be over, but I'm not prepared to let you enshrine yourself in a living sarcophagus again."

And with a breeze rippling through the branches and the distant sound of a Stephen Foster melody and a blue jay shrieking a raucous protest, Micah hauled Jocelyn back into his arms, and stifled her words with kisses.

He might have felt guilty if his firefly widow hadn't melted into him, kissing him back with an ardor that matched his own.

Chapter Twelve

"You seem distracted this evening, Jocelyn." Rupert Bingham took a careful sip of water, then with equal care set the stemmed crystal glass back in its proper place. It was always a shock to see Chadwick's father, with his bent-over frame and gaunt form a marked contrast to the vigorous man Jocelyn remembered. "Did you and Mr. MacKenzie have a lover's spat?"

Both cousins snickered. As usual, Jocelyn ignored them.

"Mr. Bingham, must you speak so crudely, especially at the dinner table and in front of the servants?" Portia dabbed her lips with the napkin. "I hardly think they would engage in something so personal as a quarrel, especially at this early stage of their courtship."

"Since when does length of time have to do with affairs of the heart?" Virgil said. Like his mother, he was golden haired and blue eyed. Katya had overheard gossip between household servants that Virgil was considered a prize matrimonial catch. But his clean-shaven face at twenty-nine was already marred by deep lines on either side of his mouth and nose; most of his words were colored by a pettish contempt, though Jocelyn knew he tried to moderate his tone in front of his mother. He turned sideways now, studying Jocelyn. "On the other hand, she certainly doesn't need to waste time, if she's hoping to snare herself another husband. Pushing thirty, aren't you, darling?"

"Time…" Mr. Bingham mused, as though Virgil hadn't spoken, his brown eyes assuming their now-familiar faraway cast. "How does one measure time? Your aunt and I wed after only a six-month courtship."

"Oh, do stop being such a sentimentalist," Portia snapped. "It was an arranged marriage, and your bride spent the week before your wedding in tears."

"My dear, it would be a kindness if you allowed poor Rupert to remember his wife as he wishes." Augustus speared a piece of pot roast, then gestured with his fork while chewing the morsel. "Let's hear what Jocelyn has to say for herself, hmm? Come now, child, ignore your cousins and your aunt. Tell us about your outing with Mr. MacKenzie today."

Micah had warned her that every step she took would be monitored, every word weighed, every sentence picked apart and analyzed. Because she wanted to remain open-minded—or stubborn—Jocelyn chose to attribute the solicitousness to the Brocks' earnest desire to atone for their repudiation of her after Chadwick's death. Portia reminded her of an overzealous governess offering instruction on everything—Jocelyn's day, her attire, the endless lament about her hair. Even her penmanship had been scrutinized and remarked upon.

Augustus summoned her almost every evening after dinner to pontificate on the benefits of her moving permanently to New York, in between counseling her on her finances and encouraging her to ask Virgil for funds when she ran short of pin money. She never did, of course, yet until a few weeks ago Virgil insisted on giving her money anyway, telling her his father didn't want her to feel "like a poor relation." Jocelyn found childish delight in giving the money to ragged street beggars, emaciated urchins and astonished cab drivers.

A week earlier, however, Virgil had surprised her with a wrapped box one afternoon. Inside, nestled in powder-blue satin, she found a stiletto.

"You don't want to venture anywhere on your own, you know," Virgil said, rocking back and forth on his heels while he watched her. "The streets are dangerous, full of footpads and muggers and thieves." He lifted the vicious-looking object with its thick blade and short handle. "If you tried to scream, they'd slit your throat with this."

"Are you trying to scare me, or brag about your own nocturnal proclivities?" Jocelyn had responded. Hiding her distaste, she snatched the stiletto from her cousin, dropped it and the box onto the Turkish rug, then sauntered from the room. "Your gifts are almost as sharp-edged as you are, cousin."

Since then, Virgil no longer tossed "gifts" of money her way, or even engaged her in conversation other than a verbal jab or two over meals.

Rupert, on the other hand, tagged after Jocelyn like a lost soul, quietly pleading with his eyes for her to tell him about her life, though—unlike the Brocks—he never insisted. Instead of returning to his cottage on Long Island, Rupert had settled into another of the guest suites. Daily he murmured that he must return home, though after a month he still remained at the Brocks'.

On several occasions Jocelyn tried to convince Micah that Rupert couldn't possibly be the vicious ringleader of a network of counterfeiters. Micah, polite but obdurate, requested that she not exclude anyone from the list of suspects, including a man who behaved as though he had lost his will to live.

"Come now, don't be shy, child," Augustus insisted now with an avuncular smile. "Mr. MacKenzie's a good man, with an astute grasp of financial matters. I've told him he would have made an excellent banker."

"How preposterous." Portia irritably waved a hovering serving maid away. "Mr. Brock, do try not to bore the man to death."

"My dear, you are mistaken about Mr. MacKenzie's interest. He has confided to me that he's entered the contract stage with several local shippers, including Janssen's. They're one of our best customers. I've suggested to Mr. MacKenzie that a local bank would better facilitate these transactions, even offered to oversee the financial details myself."

"Mr. Brock, I don't think—"

"Some of my friends are going to Coney Island this evening," Julius interrupted his mother. At twenty-three he was already given to pudginess that, unless he curbed his appetite, would in a few more years turn to fat. "I promised I'd meet them."

He rose clumsily, and his sleeve caught on the cutlery, sending knife and fork clattering to the floor. Red-faced, he plodded from the room, his back hunched defensively. It had been Julius who had spat on Jocelyn at Chadwick's funeral, but she felt sorry for him now.

"One of these years," Virgil observed after his brother was gone, "you're going to have to find a job for the poor clodhopper."

"Perhaps," Jocelyn put in unwisely, "he can have yours, Virgil."

"What is this? My cousin showing some claws? Feeling pretty feisty, are you? Most women do, once a man comes sniffing around."

The butler appeared in the doorway. "Mr. Virgil, there is a…person…at the kitchen door who insists upon seeing you. He refuses to leave. I've taken the liberty of placing him in the service hall, Mrs. Brock, to avoid gossip among the staff."

"Thank you, Palmer." Portia stroked her chin, idly fiddled with the ropes of pearls around her neck. "Shall I come with you, Virgil?"

"I think I'm capable of handling the man, whoever he is and whatever he wants." Virgil rose and strode from the room.

"Well, Rupert, now that it's just the two of us, shall we retire to the study?" Augustus inquired loudly.

Rupert blinked, then nodded. His gnarled, blue-veined hands neatly folded his napkin and he rose, thanking the servant who handed him his cane. "I could use a glass of port. These bones of mine are protesting the coming winter, I'm afraid." He paused by Jocelyn's chair; for a brief second he hovered, lost in thought, a frown deepening between his eyes. "Your Mr. MacKenzie—did he know your people, child?"

Caught off guard, Jocelyn thought rapidly. "Not as well as he would have liked to. The distance between the families…" *Always tell the truth if possible, without revealing more than is absolutely necessary.*

Mr. Bingham sighed, his gaze once again drifting. "I wouldn't want you to be unhappy," he murmured, and for a second his hand rested with surprising strength on her shoulder. "You're a good girl, Jocelyn. I wish…"

"Mr. Brock, take him to the study before he turns maudlin," Portia said. After the two men were gone she expelled a sigh of relief. "Now, Jocelyn, the two of us can finally enjoy a cozy chat. Tell me, when do you plan to see Mr. MacKenzie next? There. I see the rebellious flash in those eyes. You misunderstand— people do, you know." She paused, then finished, "I wouldn't dream of prying into your personal affairs, child. I—all of us—desire only your happiness. Virgil has confided to me how several of his friends think you're perhaps a trifle too aloof. Widowed so young, under ghastly circumstances, with no mother to guide you. I was hoping—"

"I believe I'm of an age—as Virgil pointed out— where I'm confident in my own counsel." Jocelyn pushed her chair back and rose. "I did not come to New York with the intention of either finding myself another husband, or allowing you and your family to procure one for me. My feelings for Mr. MacKenzie—". She faltered, struggling with the torrent of rage that had spewed up without warning, a rage that fisted her hands because she wanted to sweep the Wedgwood china and Austrian crystal off the Brocks' twenty-foot dining room table and onto their inlaid parquet floor. Rage against her life and the unfairness of it, rage against the God Who had pushed Micah MacKenzie into her arms. Rage against the God Who had made her fall in love with this man…

The thought slapped her, and she all but staggered back, away from the table.

Portia's eyes were slits of glittering sapphire. "Your feelings for Mr. MacKenzie?" she repeated, the light nasal voice sharp as jagged crystal.

"Are…complicated." What an insipid word. "I've never met a man like Micah MacKenzie."

"From what I've heard, you've not met any men to speak of at all these past five years. Naturally, the first halfway presentable gentleman who finally attracts your attention is going to give your heart flutters. It's only the two of us here, child. We can speak plainly, woman to woman." She rose, as well, stunningly beautiful in her velvet and moiré dinner gown. "Mr. MacKenzie is an attractive man, a wealthy man. An ambitious man. When he chooses a wife, he'll choose carefully. He'll need a woman with family connections, but he'll also need a woman who can take her place in society."

"Are you suggesting that I could never be that woman?"

"Oh, my dear, no! I'm actually suggesting that you let me help you become that woman. Instead of your maid, allow me to introduce you to someone who can work with your hair. Short is all the rage now, you know. By cutting yours we can minimize the vulgarity of the color. Cosmetics to disguise freckles, gowns from Paris. I'll persuade dear Rupert to give you my sister-in-law's jewelry. She has some stunning pieces." Smiling all the while, Portia reached Jocelyn's side. "You've lost weight, haven't you? That will never do. A man wants to know he's embracing a woman." She laughed, showing her small, perfectly even white teeth. "There now, I've shocked you, haven't I? I'm sorry.

With your looks, I keep forgetting how much of a proper Southern lady still lurks inside."

"Mother." They both turned toward Virgil, who was standing just inside the pocket doors of the dining room. "I hate to interrupt whatever female wiles you're weaving, but I need to speak with you. It's an urgent matter that can't wait."

"It's quite all right." Jocelyn spoke quickly. "We were through."

She strolled with cool dignity from the room while inside, rage consumed her.

Hours later, still unable to sleep, Jocelyn slipped from her bed, a massive medieval four-poster that made her feel as though she were submerged in a dark cave. For a while she gazed down into the dark gardens, lit in bright patches by an opalescent harvest moon. Abruptly, she snatched up her wrapper, along with a shawl, and tiptoed outside into the dark hallway, not wanting to rouse her faithful guardian of a maid.

It was disheartening how easily she slipped back into the habit of drifting through houses like a forlorn shadow.

Swallowing hard, she descended to the main level. At this hour even the servants should be asleep, but she avoided the patches of moonlight nonetheless. Silently she made her way to the vast solarium at the back of the house, where a pair of French doors opened onto an acre of profusely landscaped gardens. The Brock grounds were known throughout the city, supposedly having been designed and landscaped by the great Downing himself. An eight-foot serpentine brick wall kept prying eyes out, and muffled the endless din of traffic from the street. Many times over the last month Jocelyn had found solace here; tonight she longed only to feel safe, instead of trapped.

Near the back, an alcove had been created inside one of the wall's curves, where a cast-stone bench nestled beneath a climbing rose arbor, now pruned back for winter. Jocelyn hugged the cashmere shawl close and sat unmoving on the edge of the bench, indifferent to its chilly surface. Stillness was a discipline long ingrained, though tonight her mind churned madly, like crazed rats gnawing inside her head.

How could she continue this disastrous sham courtship after this afternoon? She'd wanted to explain her feelings to Micah, but the words tumbled over themselves in a nonsensical mess—they were pretending that their courtship *was* only a pretense. She no longer knew the truth, only that she was afraid to believe Micah even when he was the only person to whom she could turn to find a way through the maze. Micah somehow always read her thoughts, as though he could climb inside her mind as one might climb a tree.

So…had he kissed her because he sensed how badly she wanted him to, or had he kissed her because he was supposed to deepen the pretense…or had he been telling her the truth and had he kissed her because he really wanted to?

The kisses.

Even now, her heart twisted with longing, her breathing was reduced to shallow sighs. She felt like a chowderhead. The tangled mental musings were less alarming than this surplus of feeling, which she didn't know how to contain or express, much less control.

A cloud drifted across the moon. Darkness shrouded her, and the chilly November night slithered beneath the shawl as well as the wrapper. Shivering, Jocelyn bowed her head and buried her face in her hands. If she thought anyone would hear, she would have prayed, begging God to show her the way, to comfort her, to fill her heart with something—anything but this impenetrable thorn-infested thicket. *From the ends of the earth I cry unto you, when my heart is overwhelmed,* the psalmist had written.

A soft, dry sob escaped, the sound jarring in the tomblike silence of the Brocks' garden. Unnerved, Jocelyn froze. Nothing happened, no heavenly visions or even another chilly breeze brushing her face; wearily she rose and started back for the house.

Halfway along the brick path her ears caught the faint sound of voices, her nose the faint whiff of tobacco. Horrified, Jocelyn weighed her options. The only way back into the house was through the solarium, where she would probably encounter whoever was enjoying a smoke. One or more of the servants, or someone in the family? Regardless, Jocelyn abruptly decided that her best defense lay in the presumption of innocence.

She couldn't sleep; she'd come outside for a breath of fresh air.

That was the truth, after all.

The shawl covered her almost to her knees; her night robe lent her sufficient modesty. Perhaps she'd challenge their rationale for lurking about the garden at two o'clock in the morning. Mind set, she made her way back up the path, clenching her teeth to keep them from chattering.

The cloud passed, and a dozen paces from the French doors Jocelyn was able to pick out the dark silhouettes of two men. Something about their posture, or perhaps their very presence, sent a shiver unrelated to the cold down her spine, and she ducked behind some sculptured boxwood shrubbery. Confrontation might not prove to be a wise option after all. Call her a coward, but eavesdropping struck her as safer.

Except when the men resumed talking, she was too far away to hear more than a few words.

"…not much longer…"

"…careful…don't want the…to suspect…"

"…my cut…"

A malevolent laugh, then silence. Then came the sound of footsteps scraping softly over the bricks, headed not toward Jocelyn, but in the opposite direction.

Their words, their secrecy—meeting in the middle of the night—indicated far more than insomnia. Her personal misery was forgotten in a leap of excitement over the possibility that she might be inches away from learning the identities of at least two of the counterfeiters. Determination swept away caution. Since she hadn't been able to identify their voices, she would have to identify them visually. Jocelyn stepped back onto the path and sauntered toward the French doors as though she were returning from an evening stroll about the grounds. She caught sight of only one of the two men, who for some reason was making his way toward the back of the garden.

Jocelyn wouldn't risk following him, but if she hurried she might catch enough of a glimpse to recognize the man who had gone back into the house. But as she darted across to the French doors, the man who had headed into the garden stopped, half turning around. Moonlight streaked across his face.

It was Benny Foggarty.

Chapter Thirteen

"And I don't know whether or not he saw me," Jocelyn finished.

For several moments Micah didn't respond. Instead, troubled and silent, he watched Jocelyn sip the mug of cider he'd ordered for her in this streetside café, praying the shock of her news hadn't shown on his face.

Their day's excursion was to have been a pleasant drive in the Brocks' victoria, via the ferry to Staten Island for a picnic. By the time they neared Fulton Street, however, a bitter northeastern wind had sent the temperature plummeting into the forties, turning the sky a bleak metallic gray. Since the light phaeton wasn't equipped for inclement weather, after a final glance at Jocelyn's cold-tipped ears, Micah leaned forward to instruct the driver to return to the Brocks'. As he started to speak, a folded piece of paper was pressed urgently into his palm; after reading the note, without altering his tone Micah instructed Jones to drop them off at St. Paul's Chapel.

Moments after the victoria disappeared into the tangle of traffic, he whisked Jocelyn and himself through

the chapel and along to the busy intersection at Park
Row, a terminus for horsecars as well as streetcars.
They climbed aboard a crowded streetcar, and several
tense moments later he tugged her off, then ushered
her onto the Third Avenue El. Not until they reached
the Bowery did Micah allow himself to relax, convinced he'd shaken off the two men who had shadowed
his and Jocelyn's every move for weeks.

He had discussed their ubiquitous presence with
Jonathan Tanner, his assistant, who maintained a connection for Micah with both the Operative-in-Charge
at the New York office, and Chief Hazen. All agreed
that ignorance of the shadows remained Jocelyn's best
protection, so until now he hadn't mentioned them.

Jocelyn's revelation changed everything.

Restlessly, not for the first time Micah scanned the
sea of humanity, praying nobody would think to look
in the Bowery for the impeccable widow Bingham and
her millionaire Southern beau. A hotbed of iniquity, the
district bulged with concert saloons and bawdy houses.
Garish street signs lured the unwary into a world of vice,
while sharpers and hawkers and thieves preyed upon
immigrants and rebellious sons of robber barons alike.
Above this raucous humanity the El clattered day and
night. Counterfeiters had flourished in the Bowery for
over thirty years, though courtesy of the Service, arrests
had dramatically dropped in the past few years as word
spread: arrests led to convictions, which led to prison.

Until his transfer to the nation's capital, Micah had
tracked down a number of suspects in the Bowery. In
the process, he had discovered that even in this notorious district a flower or two like the tiny streetside
café flourished among the weeds.

With a frigid and unforgiving wind in their faces, after leaving the El he had ushered Jocelyn through the narrow doorway into Castelli's. They managed to secure a small table in a back corner, which provided a modicum of privacy.

But the intimacy Micah had hoped for had just been shattered by Jocelyn's news.

Benny Foggarty, in league with someone at the Brocks'?

"Micah?"

He managed a reassuring smile. "I heard you. I'm thinking. Sometimes it's a laborious process." Humor briefly lit her anxious eyes. "If you'll finish your cider before it's cold, and give me a few moments, we'll talk, all right?"

"All right."

Micah watched her shoulders droop, watched her hands wrap around the thick earthenware mug as though clinging to a buoy in a raging ocean. Every instinct clamored for him to hustle her as far away from the Brocks as possible.

The fact that he was thinking like a suitor instead of an operative disturbed him on a profound level.

"I need to share something with you," he finally began, and steeled himself.

"You have to leave, I know," Jocelyn put in hurriedly. "It's all right, Micah. I knew last night, when I saw Ben—" She blinked, then in a flurry of movement scooted her wooden chair closer to his. When she resumed speaking, the words emerged low and strained. "I'm concerned for you, Micah. It's too risky for you to stay in New York any longer."

A boisterous family crowded into the front of the

café. Red-cheeked and windblown, with waving hands and staccato Italian they greeted customers and the two serving girls in a wash of bonhomie that rippled through the room, except for one table in the far corner.

"In fact—" Jocelyn gestured toward the family "—now would probably be the best time for you to leave. You can slip through that group who just arrived. I know you were making sure nobody followed us here, but hiding within a crowd also seems a prudent tactic. I'll find my way back to the Brocks' while you—"

"Shh." He clamped a firm hand over hers, stilling the restless movement of her fingers. "I'm beginning to think you've forgotten who's the professional operative here." Jocelyn's expression didn't change. Micah abandoned his feeble attempt at disguising anger with humor. "What have I ever done to make you think I could waltz away to save my own hide, and leave you undefended?"

"Because you *are* the professional operative," Jocelyn pointed out with infuriating logic. "You have an important job, a vital job, to ensure these villains are brought to justice. If something happens to you, they'll be the ones waltzing away."

Outraged, he demanded, "And what about *you?*" She sat there in her elegant walking suit, the epitome of wealth, of privilege. Even her hat with its ridiculous netted veil marked her as a cultured, sophisticated woman. She didn't belong here. He never should have brought her here. He should have taken her straight to Grand Central Terminal and sent her— Where? Eyes burning, he planted his palms on the table and leaned forward. "You plan to 'find your way back'? Explain that Mr. MacKenzie's a blackguard who abandoned you in the Bowery? In the first place, they wouldn't believe you." He gave a short, bitter laugh. "The Mr. MacKenzie they know would never dream of treating a lady in such a reprehensible manner, not when he's made his intentions obvious."

"I'd think of something. I'll tell them we argued, and I left you."

"Well, you're half right. We are arguing." Shaking his head, Micah gently squeezed her rigid hand. "Jocelyn, trust me, please. Nothing is going to happen to me. But now more than ever, I'm concerned about you. You've played your part beautifully, not even a trained operative could have performed as well as you these past weeks. But now is not the time to change our script."

"I didn't change the script, as you quaintly put it. Benny Foggarty did."

"I know." Why, of all times, did Pinkerton's have to require Alexander MacKay's services elsewhere? "Remember when I told you that someone would always be watching over you, even when I wasn't with you?"

After a moment she gave a terse nod.

"That person is a private detective who agreed to help us out. But two days ago his services were required elsewhere. Due to budgetary constraints…" In the past the words had left a perpetual sour taste in his mouth, but not fear. Not until today. He finished bluntly, "We don't have the manpower to replace him." He knew his assistant would take over for MacKay, but Jonathan's reassignment would leave Micah himself unprotected…which would ultimately endanger Jocelyn even more. "Your only contact now is me."

"I thought," Jocelyn said, "when you said someone would always be watching, that you were talking about God."

No other woman in his life could flabbergast Micah like Jocelyn Tremayne Bingham. She might as well have hopped on top of the table and belted out a ribald ditty. "God is always watching over you," he acknowledged in a husky voice. "But I didn't think you'd want to hear that, much less want to know that I pray for you—every day."

She turned away so he could not see her face, sitting with the absolute stillness that always wrenched his heart. It conveyed an arid isolation devoid of human contact as well as divine. Micah wanted to remind her how faith had preserved his sanity, and healed his own loneliness. But for some reason, each time the need to open himself up reached a boiling point, where words burned his tongue with blisters, something had restrained him.

Micah rotated his head in a vain effort to relax. Not something, he reminded himself. Someone. Someone Whose timing was always perfect, Who deserved respect, and—regardless of Micah's own inclination—patience.

So once again he swallowed the words, and waited.

Jocelyn turned back around. "I haven't wanted anything to do with God," she concurred wretchedly, "because it hurts too much. I know you don't understand."

"You might be surprised by how much I understand."

He would have said more, but at that moment the jabbering family converged around the nearby tables, recently emptied, and commenced the noisy process of seating themselves. One of the women selected the chair a scant twelve inches from Micah. A baby was draped over her shoulder, swaddled in bright colored blankets. Jostled when his mother sat down, he groggily opened his eyes, lifted a wobbly head and stared straight at Micah. Drool spilled from the corner of a perfect rose-petal-pink mouth, which suddenly widened into a cherubic smile.

Oh, God. Father...the pain... Would the pain ever cease tormenting him? Catching him off guard with its randomness, its cruelty? But God understands, he repeated to himself, as he had repeated over and over throughout the past six years. God Himself had endured the death of His Own Son.

And gloried in His resurrection.

It's different, Lord. Somewhere buried within the pain, anger flashed, quick as sun glinting off a sword, then vanished. Oh, yes, he longed to shout the words, he understood more than she could possibly realize.

But his throat was locked, and the hypocrisy of his own heart mocked him.

Gradually, he realized someone had taken his hand, that someone was speaking into his ear, words whose meaning he could not decipher but whose sweetness soothed his soul. With an effort, he tore his gaze from the baby and found Jocelyn almost plastered against his side. Her lips brushed against his ear as she talked, and the soft syllables collected themselves into coherent sentences.

"...and I know the sight of a baby can still awaken the sorrow, even after all these years. Micah? It's all right. The woman's handed the baby to someone at another table. Can you look at me instead? I... It hurts me to see your face, and know that..." When she realized she had finally gained his attention, she pulled back a little but did not release his hand.

"Know what?" Micah finally managed to unlock his clenched jaw muscles enough to ask. Like a dying man he clutched Jocelyn's fingers. Instead of a tiny head with a tuft of downy black hair, he tried to focus on Jocelyn's dainty, aquiline nose beneath the annoying veil. But this time the pain would not be silenced. "How could you possibly know what it's like to lose your own child, and every time you see a baby, to remember how your own looked, waxen and still...."

Her eyelids flinched, but she did not retreat. "I can't know your pain, Micah. Nor can you know mine. How could *you* possibly understand what it's like to be a woman who will never experience the joy of having a child at all? Who is scorned and pitied because she's barren, and who'll never know whether or not it's true."

With a jerk Micah hauled himself back from the quagmire of self-pity. "Jocelyn, forgive me. I had no right to say what I did." He turned his chair so that his broad shoulders shielded them both from the rest of the patrons. Glancing down, he saw that he was still holding her hand, probably crushing it. "I'm sorry," he murmured as he began massaging her fingers one by one. "Like you, I have dark spells. Charred spots on my soul, I call them. They flare up less frequently than they used to, but I never know when one's going to scald my throat." His voice thickened. "Babies, and small children...they're precious, innocent. Gifts from God. Most of the time these days I can celebrate new life. Sometimes..." A long breath shuddered through him. "But I do know it's difficult, to keep trusting Him when— I'm sorry," he repeated.

"I am, too." She lifted her free hand and rested it on the bunched muscles of his forearm. "All these years, I've felt as if I'd been locked inside a cage and abandoned. So I raged against life. Blamed God for all the pain I'd had to endure when all I'd ever done was try to be a good person. Then I saw... I saw..." She stammered a bit before finishing in a rush, "When that baby smiled at you, I saw your face. And listening to you just now, I think you're still fighting to free yourself from your own cage, aren't you? When we first met—for the second time—your faith angered me. You were so sure of yourself, sure in your faith. Even when you told me about your wife and son, you still blindly believed God cared about you. I didn't want to like you, Micah."

For some reason the last confession lit star points inside him that twinkled in the darkness. "I never would have guessed. Now you know a struggling sinner lurks behind the self-assured believer." He thought she smiled, but the lighting was dim, their corner shadowed.

Then she said hesitantly, "I think my anger's fading a bit. I'm... I think I'm confused, instead of angry. Does that relieve you?"

If she sensed a mustard seed's width of his feelings she would not use a word like *relieved*. He brushed his index finger against a fold of the veil. "Jocelyn... will you shove this thing out of the way? I want to see your face clearly."

"What? But it's transparent. I can see...." Shaking her head, without further protest she lifted the veil from inside the high collar of her shirtwaist and pulled it over the brim of her hat. "It is a frivolous bit of fashion, isn't it? But I like the hat itself. The feather makes me smile, because the first time Katya saw it, she asked me if ostriches were really green."

The babble of voices crescendoed around them; pungent odors of fresh baked bread and garlic and oregano permeated the air; faces of half a dozen nationalities flickered through Micah's vision in a kaleidoscope of skin tones. But the only one who could light up the darkest recesses of his mind was a creamy-white face lavishly dusted with cinnamon freckles. "You're beautiful. Even when you didn't like me very much, I still thought you were one of the most beautiful women I've ever known. I wish I'd met you before your wedding day."

He was shaken when a single tear pearled in the corner of her eye. "Would it be a terrible sin to confess how many times over the past few weeks I struggled with that thought myself?"

"It's not terrible, nor even a sin, firefly." He wanted to kiss the tear, then the eyes and the mouth trying not to tremble. "I've never judged you, Jocelyn. And Chadwick has been dead for a long time."

"Other people have not been so generous."

"Would I be right if I suggested that while he was alive, your husband was one of them?" he asked gently.

A long sigh shuddered through her. Then, searching his face with the wariness of a shy animal, she nodded. "Chadwick was a tortured soul. I was never able to help him, no matter how hard I tried to be a good wife." She paused. "I know you didn't want me to come to New York at all, but I knew I could help. I *needed* to help, not only you, but the Secret Service.

Since Chadwick's death I've never done anything to make a difference. Instead of Doing Good Works, or Being a Good Steward like Miss Isabella, the headmistress of a school I attended, used to tell us, I've tried very hard these past five years to make myself invisible. I'm not a very nice person, Micah."

"Katya would disagree. So do I."

She made a face, the ever-restless hands turning her empty mug around in aimless circles.

One day, Micah promised himself, he and Jocelyn were going to have a serious conversation about her attitudes. "Fortunately for you, this is not the time to point out how wrongheaded you are," he began.

She swatted his arm.

His reserved, distrustful widow had consoled him in public, and now she was swatting his forearm. The starlight inside him spread all the way to his fingertips, banishing completely the old griefs.

No matter what the personal cost, whatever sacrifice was demanded of him, Micah would protect this woman. "Jocelyn, will you do something for me?"

"Depends on what you want me to do."

He'd known all along she was also a smart woman. "Would you let me escort you across to Jersey City right now? Put you on a train to Washington? I'll send a telegram to Chief Hazen. You'll be met, probably by him. You'd be safe."

"Don't be ridiculous!" Even in the flickering gaslight he could see the dark color swarm up her cheeks. He wouldn't have been surprised if the red hair burst into flames. "If you think for one minute you can manipulate the circumstances to remove me from this case, you're not thinking at all, Micah MacKenzie!"

Chapter Fourteen

Because she couldn't very well flounce out in high dudgeon, Jocelyn scooted her chair all the way back into the corner and ignored the man across from her. The wretch. She'd shared a deeply private piece of herself, and all he could think about was ridding himself of her presence as expeditiously as possible?

Then he leaned forward, propping his elbows on the table with a total disregard for manners. "I'm not thinking at all," he agreed. "I shouldn't have said anything. I wasn't trying to manipulate you, I assure you. My preeminent concern is and always has been your safety."

His candor mollified her bruised feelings. "Thank you. The feeling's mutual. I will certainly consider taking a train to Washington—if you accompany me. But I'd much rather we both stay here. I'm sure Chief Hazen would agree." Her winsome look merely precipitated an ironic lift of Micah's brow; her flirting skills had corroded over the years. Dropping all artifice, she added, "There's a possibility Benny wouldn't remember me. We were in each other's company less than five minutes, that day in Mr. Hepplewhite's store. You, on the other hand…"

"Are not a stunning woman with remarkable red hair, who made a scene in a store in the middle of downtown Richmond. A half-dozen customers were still talking about you and your encounter with Benny a week later. So, Jocelyn…if Benny saw you last night, you can be sure he recognized you as the woman in Clocks & Watches. His presence at the Brocks' confirms to me that you were not randomly chosen as a dupe, but were in fact his designated target."

Dry-mouthed, Jocelyn inhaled an unsteady breath. "Why? How could he have known? My uncle's letter didn't arrive until—" She choked off the rest of the sentence, unable to voice the obvious.

Micah seemed to hesitate, as though he were searching for the right words. Like a swarm of red ants, nerves stung Jocelyn's limbs so that even a burst of laughter across the room made her jump. "Your position as the prodigal niece might be irretrievably compromised," he finished, the deep voice gentle.

"Why was I allowed out of the house to go for a drive with you?"

"They wouldn't risk questions, particularly from an infatuated man who wouldn't be fobbed off by some feeble excuse of other plans or ill health. Nor would they want the servants to gossip."

"Katya!" Alarmed, Jocelyn half rose, consumed with guilt.

"Easy, there. As long as we maintain our roles, Katya should be safe. Your instincts are sound, Jocelyn. I trust them…which, in case you haven't noticed, is why I'm agreeing with you instead of yielding to my protective instincts."

"Was there a compliment buried in there somewhere?"

"Absolutely." His reciprocal smile lasted but a second. "These people are more shrewd than any serpent. They don't like risk, and they don't act on impulse. I've been after them for a long time and, though it pains me to acknowledge it, I know them almost as well as I know my own family."

"They *are* my husband's family."

"I live with that awful truth every second of every hour." A muscle twitched in his jaw, but his voice remained calm. "They're thorough, and patient. What they've chosen to do with their lives is not only illegal, I believe it is evil. Although they know their actions harm innocent people, they don't care as long as they're not caught."

"I understand why you think that way." Swallowing hard, Jocelyn forced herself to sit back, to keep her gaze level with his. "I appreciate your confidence in me but there's something you need to understand, as well. After having lived with this family for almost two months now, I'm finding it difficult to agree with all your assumptions. Yes, they're pompous and vain and venal, and Benny's presence indicates the probability of wrongdoing on their part. I'll never completely trust them. But wicked?"

Half-consciously, she began to fiddle with the appliqué embroidery on the cuffs of her walking suit. "My aunt is happily planning nuptials between us. Uncle Brock admires you. And…and Chadwick's father has changed. Rupert's *kind* to me, Micah. He wants me to be happy. Perhaps the Brocks will change, too. They all see us together, and they believe—" She stopped dead, stuck like a bug on a pin to the conundrum of their relationship.

"They believe our courtship is real?" Micah finished evenly.

"Yes." Her voice broke on the word. Stupid, silly gudgeon. All the stern lectures to the starry-eyed creature in her mirror might as well have been directed to a dressmaker's dummy. Oh, how could she, of all the women in this merciless world, have harbored an illusion of hope in her heart?

"Jocelyn…do you remember what I told you in the park the other day?"

"I remember more what you did," she whispered, ducking her head because she could feel scarlet flags heating her cheeks.

"Those memories keep me awake at night, and distract my concentration during the day," Micah said. "Don't be shy. Here—I'll say the words again. Look at me, Jocelyn. Look into my eyes and know I'm telling you the truth."

He waited until Jocelyn found the fortitude to comply. "I've pretended to be a lot of things over the years. But falling in love with you is not one of them."

She felt as though an anvil had dropped from the ceiling on top of her. In a reflexive gesture she pressed her hand to her throat, crushing the ruched collar in a vain effort to quiet her galloping pulse. "What are you saying? Is this a ploy to reassure me, so I won't break under pressure? You needn't perjure yourself. I promised to help and I will."

"Sometimes, my love—" the words sounded more

exasperated than affectionate "—you frustrate the day-lights out of me. I shouldn't have declared myself yet. I know this is not the proper moment, nor the proper place. But what about these past months has been?" A half laugh, half groan escaped. "Here I am, apologizing for trying to reassure you, for telling you the truth. I'm in love with you." He half turned, flinging out his arm in a sweeping gesture. "We should be in Delmonico's, not a café in the Bowery, surrounded by—" With a speed that left Jocelyn blinking he turned back around, reached across and tugged the veil back over her face. "Lean over as though you dropped something on the floor," he ordered with enough urgency that she obeyed instantly. "Stay there, that's it…wait…wait. All right. Sit back up, very casually, but keep your face out of the light."

"What is it?"

"A man's come inside. His name's Limbrick. Goes by 'Brick.' Among other things, he's a boodle carrier, a person who receives counterfeit goods from the manufacturer. I arrested him five years ago, caught him shoving five-dollar bills to immigrants straight out of Castle Garden. Despicable blackguard, taking advantage of them, and poor working-class families desperate to put food on the table. He and men of his ilk are like roaches, hard to exterminate. Brick only got three years—judge at the time wasn't too fond of the Service." Casually he slid a glance over his shoulder. "He's sitting down now, with a few other men I don't recognize. Fortunately, his back is to the door, and us. Jocelyn…"

"We need to leave." She would have wept except tears would not soften sharp-edged reality. The widow Bingham would never entice, much less expect, Operative Micah MacKenzie of the U.S. Secret Service to forsake his calling. Loving each other was a dangerous mistake neither could afford. "Shall I slip out first, or you?"

For a moment he looked as though he were about to argue. Then he said, his voice grim, "I'll go first. You're sure to draw attention, but as long as you don't meet anyone's gaze you should be able to exit without a fuss. Wait to leave until after I've paid the bill and gone outside. Don't worry if you don't see me. I'll be there."

Suddenly he leaned in close enough for his breath to warm her cheek. "I'll be there, Jocelyn," he repeated, and a flash of white teeth appeared beneath his mustache. "You'll get your way, if only for a moment or two."

"My way— Oh." Her own smile was a weak imitation. "You mean, you'll be slipping out unnoticed, while the red herring creates a distraction."

"Always distracting. Always a beautiful redhead. Never a red herring. Be strong, firefly. I'll see you outside."

And with the languid grace of a panther he rose and maneuvered his way between the tables. Mr. Limbrick had tossed his head back in a coarse guffaw, then gulped down a tankard of beer with the other men at the table. He never looked Micah's way.

Beneath the fine woolen skirt Jocelyn's knees wobbled. Her throat felt hot, the muscles constricted as she waited until the door closed behind Micah. Then she rose to her feet, clasping the curved back of the chair to steady herself. The Italian family beamed at her with friendly black eyes; one of the younger men said something in Italian but Jocelyn maintained a measured pace, her gaze fixed upon the red-checked curtains framing the windows.

"What's a hoity-toity lady find to do in dese parts?" a nasal voice called out loudly in a pronounced Brooklyn accent. "I know, youse must be one of them pretty waiter girls. Saw me a redhead gal just like you last night, right down da street on the waterfront."

The lout, reeking of spirits, planted himself directly between Jocelyn and the door. "I likes da way you clean up, kitten."

Heads were turning, drawing attention their way. The raucous laughter from Mr. Limbrick's table ceased and she heard murmurs ripple over the room. Fear for Micah slithered down her spine, followed swiftly by anger. "At least I know how to clean up." She advanced upon the man, whose heavy jowls dropped in surprise. A deep flush spread across his forehead. "Move out of my way at once," Jocelyn ordered, her clear Southern voice crackling through the suddenly charged air. "You're drunk, and you smell."

"Why, you little—"

Thankfully the manager shoved his way to her side, along with several men from the Italian family, all of them surrounding Jocelyn in a flurry of waving arms and loud voices. Though speaking Italian, they managed to convey a threat to the masher, and respect for the pretty lady he'd insulted. By the time Jocelyn extricated herself from their protection, the man had thrown open the door and escaped outside. With a final smile and a heartfelt thank-you, Jocelyn followed, dignity intact though her heartbeat threatened to crack her rib cage. The sidewalk was choked with pedestrians, heads bowed against the vicious wind of the mid-November afternoon. Shivering and clammy, Jocelyn resolutely stepped forward, searching the sea of top hats, homburgs and bowlers for Micah.

"Ha! I'll teach you what happens to snooty little skirts with nasty mouths."

A beefy arm wrapped around her middle in a crushing grip that stole her breath. Stunned, for an instant Jocelyn hung motionless as she was dragged through the crowd, toward one of the dark hackney carriages that waited by the curb. When her abductor yanked open the door of the cab, outrage jabbed her like a cattle prod. Twisting and flailing her arms, she struggled to find breath enough to call out to the cab driver for help. She must not, would not call Micah's name.

She was released so abruptly she tumbled forward and would have fallen except a firm hand grabbed her upper arm, steadying her until she regained her balance.

"I've got you, Jocelyn," Micah's voice spoke in her ear.

Before she could gasp out a warning his foot had lashed out, striking the masher with a hard blow to his knee. Howling, the man stumbled back and fell, his head thunking against the carriage wheel. The horses snorted, hooves restlessly stamping. Micah looked down at Jocelyn. "Are you able to stand on your own?"

Numbly she nodded.

Micah released her, then leaned down, hauled the other man to his feet and twisted his fist around the hapless attacker's collar. "If you ever so much as blink at another woman without respect," he said in a voice that raised gooseflesh, "I'll hunt you down, no matter what sewer you're swilling at, and make you regret the day you took your first drink. Do you understand?"

Choking, blubbering a stream of profanity and pleas, the man finally went limp. Micah dragged him away from the hackney, propped him against one of the El's metal supports, then stepped back. "Do you understand?" he repeated.

The man bobbed his head. Micah turned to the small crowd who had gathered to watch. "Go on about your business," he ordered them in a hard voice that yielded instant results. Then, to the drunk, "If I can still see you in ten seconds, I'll have you arrested on so many charges you won't see daylight until spring."

Without a word the man straightened, then fled, still limping, across the broad avenue to the other side of the street.

Micah turned to Jocelyn. She tried to smile, but her hands couldn't seem to stop shaking so she ceased trying to fasten her buttons and tug down her shirtwaist. "I'm all right. I'm... He didn't hurt me." A watery laugh escaped. "Perhaps you should instruct me on how to confront an intoxicated man. I'm afraid I inflamed him, when he...um...spoke to me, inside the café."

"You don't confront drunken clods at all," he muttered, his mouth a thin slash of a line. "I never should have left you in there alone. Here, let me help you...." Despite the anger still flickering across his face, his hands were gentle as he straightened her jacket, repositioned her hat, tucked the veil inside her collar.

He'd put his gloves back on, but even so the intimacy of that gentle touch scalded. Jocelyn looked up into his eyes, unable to breathe, unable to think, unable to do anything at all but give him her heart. He hadn't asked for it, and might soon spurn the words, much as she had his. Yet the awareness flooded her in a golden warmth as irresistible as sunlight on a cold winter day. *God, I know You're going to take him away from me. But at least I have this moment.*

And for the first time in a decade, Jocelyn felt something other than anger toward the Almighty.

Slowly Micah's tender ministrations stilled, until the two of them stood together in a little pool of silence, surrounded by loud conversations, milling crowds, clattering hooves and the teeth-rattling noise of trains shuddering along the tracks above them.

"Jocelyn..." His head dipped. Then he froze, stepped back, jerking his hands away to cram them inside his pockets. He gave her a crooked grin. "I'm afraid I lost my head a little, seeing that oaf manhandle you. At least this is the Bowery. If I kissed you, which I want to with every breath in my body, instead of arresting us for lewdness, an appreciative audience would applaud."

"They might even toss coins in your hat."

"As long as they aren't counterfeit."

Before she lost her courage, Jocelyn stepped close, then stood on tiptoe to brush a kiss against one hard cheekbone. "Thank you for saving me," she whispered. "I'm sorry for causing a scene."

"Not your fault. I'm sorry I wasn't with you. There wouldn't have been a scene."

Abruptly, his smile vanished. Eyes narrowed, he began a methodical visual search, memorizing, Jocelyn knew, every face that glanced their way. She watched his face harden to a stone mask.

She turned toward the café, where several customers, including Mr. Limbrick, had gathered at the window.

Chapter Fifteen

The room was dark save for the gas flame softly hissing in a wall sconce. Near a curtained window, the man sat shrouded in shadow, his face a pale blur. Somewhere in the room a clock ticked off the seconds in a monotonous rhythm.

In his hand the man held a single sheet of paper torn from an inexpensive tablet. He had read the hurriedly scrawled words twice now, his mouth set. Finally, with a foul curse he crumpled the paper, threw it to the floor, then downed his glass of whiskey in a single gulp.

After a while he stood, walked over to the crumpled note and picked it up. Each movement deliberate, he struck a match and touched the small flame to the paper. For a moment he watched the edges curl, brown, then softly ignite in a red-gold blaze. *Like her hair*, he thought viciously.

Just before the heat singed his fingers, he dropped the burning remains onto the marble hearth of the unused fireplace, ground the ashes beneath his heel and strode from the room.

* * *

Micah stared out the window of Maisie Tanner's cottage, one hand resting on the sill, the other absently rubbing beneath his chin. Beard stubble scratched his fingertips; he needed a shave. Gusts of wind had persisted into the twilight, whistling through windowpanes and rattling shutters. A leafless tree in Mrs. Tanner's minuscule backyard swayed with the breeze; through the cobweb of its branches, Micah watched the gray sky turn dark and bleak.

"But you don't know for sure that this man recognized you," Jonathan Tanner pointed out, not for the first time. He glanced down at the report in his hand. "From what you wrote here, the patrons inside the café, one of whom included Limbrick, were looking out the window, at you and Mrs. Bingham. But that doesn't mean he recognized either of you. Yes, in a crowd Mrs. Bingham's remarkable, but she is not the only redhead strolling the streets." He laughed. "New York is crawling with immigrants, several million of them Irish, or even Scots. A fair number of them have red hair."

"No other woman's hair compares to Jocelyn's." Micah leaned his forehead against the window, his thoughts as dour as the twilight. "I shouldn't have allowed her to go back to the Brocks'," he said, also not for the first time. "We can't forget Benny. We still don't know where he is, don't know for sure what he knows or what he plans to do with what he knows. However, Benny's not a murderer. If he confesses that he passed that evidence to Jocelyn at the store where Hepplewhite was murdered, he might wind up murdered himself. So I'm thinking—" praying fervently "—that Benny's kept his mouth shut, or scarpered altogether." A sick feeling swam sluggishly in his gut, and not even Jonathan's insightful observations assuaged it. Ruthlessly Micah forced his attention on what they must do next, instead of dwelling on what was already done. "The Brocks have spies everywhere. I don't know all of them by sight, any more than you do. But today I was confident we'd given them the slip—until that ill-timed scuffle in the Bowery. I'd like to believe we weren't picked up on the trip back to the Brocks', but with all the crowds, I can't be certain."

"Well, I have it on good authority that I'm worth at least half a dozen spies, sir." The assistant tucked Micah's handwritten report along with his own typewritten notes into the Secret Service envelope he would mail in the evening post. His movements were as pedantic as those of a fussy schoolmarm, though put Jon Tanner down on the docks and the lean but well-muscled young man would pass for a navvy. "If you're that concerned for Mrs. Bingham, let me take over for Mr. MacKay. I wouldn't be around to bail you out of trouble, but I could rescue the damsel in distress."

"Your humility is reassuring." Micah turned away from the window to study the younger man. The tough arrogance of youth might still dust his spirit, but if Micah could choose one man other than Alexander MacKay to guard his or Jocelyn's back, despite his youth it would be Jonathan Tanner. "Still fancy being a professional boxer when you grow up, instead of an operative? From the look of them the shoulder seams on that suit are begging for mercy."

Unoffended, Jonathan assumed a boxing stance and delivered several rapid punches to the air. "Haven't ripped them yet," he announced with a grin. "Give me another month. As for what I want to do with my life... I don't know how to answer. Sometimes I can see myself as the next Gentleman Jim, but then I think about what you're doing. And I feel, well, selfish. Vainglorious, as Aunt Maisie calls it. I know I shouldn't waste the best years of my life in the ring, but I can't see myself spending them hunched over a desk, writing reports, either."

"What are you now? Twenty-four? Five?"

"Twenty-seven. You've been too busy falling in love with Mrs. Bingham to notice, I imagine."

At twenty-seven, Micah had already buried a wife and son. His faith in God, and his dedication to the Secret Service, had saved his sanity. At twenty-seven, he'd felt as old as Moses. Now he was prattling about Jocelyn's hair, fretting over her safety, as though he were a calf-eyed sprout half Jonathan's age. Abruptly, he reached a decision. "I'm not so busy I can't add sums and come up with the correct answer. Regardless of evidence or the lack thereof, I'm removing Mrs. Bingham from this case by the end of the week. In my judgment the danger to her life outweighs her usefulness, however critical it may be. I'm going to send Chief Hazen a telegram. I'll write out what to say, but we'll maintain established protocols and let you send it." From the outset of this phase in the investigation, they'd agreed Micah could not risk visiting places a wealthy businessman would not normally be seen, which included frequent jaunts to Western Union.

"Tonight?"

"Tonight." Micah strode out of Mrs. Tanner's fussy little parlor down a narrow hall that led to Jonathan's room. Jonathan had persuaded his aunt to donate the use of her deceased husband's old rolltop desk—which could be locked—and soon after their arrival in New York, he and Micah maneuvered it into the privacy of Jonathan's bedroom. "Your aunt will be home from her quilting bee by seven, you told me," he said after they'd closed and locked the door. "That gives us almost an hour."

"Why not pull Mrs. Bingham out now, instead of sending off a telegram?"

He'd thought about it. Yessir, he'd thought about it long and hard. "Because we're close enough to spit in their faces, but not close enough to handcuff 'em. She should be safe for another day or two, because I've been invited for dinner there tomorrow night. As I explained to Mrs. Bingham, they won't risk forging a note, claiming illness or some other trumped-up reason for her not appearing."

"Because you wouldn't accept it, and ask…ah… pointed questions."

"Precisely." He added reluctantly, "On this end, however, I'm thinking it might be wise for you to use a telegraph office in another borough."

"Don't worry about me, Mr. MacKenzie," he claimed with an insouciant grin. "Remember, I know how to be invisible. Besides, I can be to the Western Union in Queens in a quarter of an hour, sir."

Grappling with a vague disquietude, Micah opened his mouth to make the suggestion an order, but hesitated. Jonathan needed to grow, needed to test his own skills as a trained operative, instead of following orders as Micah's assistant. *To become a man,* his father used to tell him, *you have to be given the opportunity to live with the consequences of your choices.*

Jonathan unlocked the desk, rolled back the top,

and from one of the slots deftly removed an unused telegram. "I'm ready whenever you are, sir."

While Micah talked to his assistant, he simultaneously prayed that the choices he had made were not about to reap disastrous consequences.

After crossing the river, Micah alternated hansoms, two horsecars and a streetcar with four stops along the Third Avenue El, eventually wending his way back to the Brevoort Hotel. A little past ten o'clock he strolled into the lobby, whistling as though he hadn't a care in the world. No strangers loitered in the public rooms, nor were any messages waiting. The desk clerk was the usual man, as were the bellhops who stood at attention and greeted him as he strode to the elevator. Hamish, the elderly elevator operator, assured him that no new guests had arrived that evening.

Marginally relieved, a few moments later Micah unlocked the door to his room and stepped inside, his gaze automatically sweeping the area. He had time only to notice the billowing curtains that covered the windows when he sensed movement in the shadows off to his left.

Even as he ducked and spun, something hard slammed against the back of his head. Lights exploded inside his skull before he hurtled into darkness.

Pleading fatigue from hers and Micah's extended outing, Jocelyn told her aunt and uncle she would not be joining them for dinner at the Waldorf Hotel. Their protests only hardened her resolve, though Mr. Bingham's disappointment stung her conscience, and her cousins surprised her with their sincerity. "You're the only woman I know with a brain," Virgil complained. Julius gave her a hangdog expression and mumbled that at least she never made sport of him. "Who else will I talk to?"

After they finally left, with Portia's glacial disapproval still frosting the air, Jocelyn requested a supper tray and retreated to her room. She longed to eat in blissful silence, but Katya filled her tablet with questions and accusations and portents.

"Katya, please don't badger me," Jocelyn protested finally, torn between anger and tears. "Things have happened. I need to think."

Not thinking when Borcks not know where are you and Mr. MacKenzie all day.

"Katya." Jocelyn gestured silently toward the pair of ladies' chairs in front of windows that overlooked the garden, where she and the maid sat every evening. The nook was also on the opposite side of the room from the door to the outside hall, so not even a servant with ears the size of an elephant would be able to overhear.

"You must listen to me," she told Katya after they sat down. "Listen, and not interrupt until I'm through."

The maid sucked in her cheeks, but after a moment she gave a stiff nod.

"Last night, I couldn't sleep. I went for a walk in the garden. And I saw the man Mr. MacKenzie has been searching for all these months. The one who was in Mr. Hepplewhite's store that day."

Katya's eyes flooded with alarm, and a quiver shuddered through her sturdy frame.

"Seeing this man proves we were right—you and I—to come to New York. It means we can finally do something to help, Katya. I needed to tell Mr. MacKenzie, but I couldn't risk sharing this information where the Brock servants—including the coachman—could overhear. That's why we were gone for so long."

Unbidden, the events of the day crashed around her; she fought to maintain a level tone of voice. "The man's name is Benny. Benny Foggarty. Remember it, but don't ever write it down in this house." Through lips that felt like India rubber, she spelled the name out to help Katya remember it. "Can you see it inside your head?" she asked. The girl nodded. "He may or may not have recognized me," Jocelyn plowed ahead, "but I'm more afraid Micah might be in danger."

The sensation of panic intensified. Jocelyn closed her eyes and tried to imagine her favorite oak tree, but all her jumbled mind conjured up was the image of Micah's face when they'd parted earlier. In the late-afternoon light, the strong bones appeared more finely drawn, the gray eyes dull as soot. He hadn't wanted to leave her. Jocelyn insisted. Their parting had been awkward, the air rife with unspoken currents.

An internal nudge, like a puff of wind blowing against the locked door inside her heart, somehow discovered a crack and before she quite realized it Jocelyn found herself praying. Begging God to keep him safe.

Not for me, but for Micah. You took his wife and his son. Don't let anything happen to him *now.* Surely divine justice as well as divine mercy would acknowledge the legitimacy of her plea. And perhaps since the prayer was not self-serving, it would engender a response.

Katya tugged her sleeve, and with a tremulous sigh Jocelyn opened her eyes.

What do we should do?

A lump formed in Jocelyn's throat. "We're going to do whatever we have to, in order to protect him. The Brocks are out for at least another three hours. With a little bit of luck and—" swallowing the lump, she added in a rusty whisper "—with a little bit of prayer, we'll…do our part."

She cleared her throat, for the first time catching a glimmer of understanding for how Micah must have felt. "We have the perfect opportunity to engage in a bit of sleuthing. Let me think. Um… I need you to watch and listen," she began, struggling to organize her thoughts. "Stand guard outside doors. If you hear anyone, you let me know so we can scoot away before we're caught in suspicious circumstances."

A thunderous frown etched across the broad forehead. *Not good plan. I can not talk. Can not run fast. Mr. MacKenzie won't like.*

"Well, it's the only plan I can think of. I have to do something. Mr. MacKenzie needs proof. This is the first time in a month I've had the opportunity to search with minimal risk." Jocelyn stood. "If you'd rather stay here in the room, fine. I'm not a trained operative, so certainly I'm not making this an order." Turning, she headed for the huge closet. "Time is passing. I need to change out of this lounging wrapper and put on more suitable clothes, something a thief would wear."

Darts of self-loathing swooped about like a flock of ravens as she tore off the wrapper, flinging it in a graceless heap onto a padded bench. No wonder Katya was repelled by Jocelyn's suggestion. What decent soul would embrace the notion of pilfering through someone else's private sanctuaries? Her face felt hot as she recalled her childish prayer. God was good, perfect. If He hadn't deigned to answer her prayers through all the years when she had tried to please Him, what on earth made her think He would respond to petitions from a woman who had become a sneak as well as a liar?

Chapter Sixteen

Moments later, Jocelyn was hastily buttoning a narrow pinstriped shirtwaist over her chemise when Katya appeared in the doorway. She thrust out her note, her eyes solemn.

I do not want you in danger. I do not want Mr. MacKenzie in danger. I do not know what to do. But I pray.

The simple words scattered like a shotgun blast the flock of ravens picking at her soul. For years Jocelyn had fought the habit of self-denigration, born from years of marriage to a man who could never love her. At last, she faced the dismal likelihood that Chadwick himself had been involved with the counterfeiting network. Perhaps the money he had bequeathed to her was as bogus as the marriage.

There was little she could do, other than try to find the truth—and protect the innocent.

"Dear Katya." She sighed, then wrapped a comforting arm about the girl's waist. "I'm sorry. I never should have brought you to New York. This is not fair to you. You're right, my initial plan was silly. I've been thinking, and I've come up with something you can do that will be far more helpful to me, but also keeps you from danger." Surely the prayers of this pure-hearted girl would fly straight to the Lord's ear. Surely He would protect Katya, as well as Micah, a devout believer struggling to rid the country of evildoers.

Taking a deep breath, she continued, "Prepare my bedchamber as you normally do, lay out my nightgown and bed robe. Then prepare a hot bath—very hot! Add my gardenia bath oil, so that the scent fills the air. If I come racing up the stairs, and shortly thereafter someone knocks on the door, you can say truthfully that I'm taking a bath. Because, as soon as I shed these clothes, I'll jump into the tub. The gardenia odor adds credibility. That means," she added with a half smile, "the person is more likely to assume I really have been taking a bath instead of roaming the house, because even though they don't see me, they can smell my favorite scent."

Katya still looked doubtful. Struggling against desperation, Jocelyn finished, "I don't know how long I'll be gone. If I know you've done what I ask, I can better concentrate, which means I might find the proof we need a lot faster."

Reluctantly, Katya nodded, then without so much as a two-word scribble, she headed for the bathroom.

Even to Jocelyn the plan sounded illogical, ill-conceived, ill-timed. Well, if she'd had more than an hour to prepare, she could have devised a better one.

If her heart didn't ache, if her mind weren't so conflicted, if her spirit didn't cringe...

If she had never met Chadwick Bingham at White

Sulphur Springs she wouldn't be in this wretched imbroglio at all.

But then she would never have met Micah. Never known what it felt like to have a man embrace her with so much passion his body trembled. Never known how faith could help a person find her way through devastating loss. Never experienced the incandescent joy of hearing him tell her he loved her, of seeing it in his face.

God? Are you listening? I'm willing to believe in You again, because of Katya, but mostly because of Micah. Please be listening. I love him. I never thought I could love anyone, or that a man like Micah could love a woman like me. Don't take this away from us. Please.

When she realized she'd once again tumbled back through the years, into beggary, her hands closed into tight fists. She dropped down onto the padded bench, then with a low groan wrapped her arms around herself in a symbolic effort to halt the whirlwind sucking her into its deadly maw. She had no right to pray such a prayer. No right to expect dispensation from the natural law of consequences.

The Almighty was *Yahweh,* the great *I Am.* God of the present and the future. But not the past.

Jocelyn remembered with bitter clarity the last time she had sought comfort, and hope, from the Bible. It was the night following Chadwick's funeral, and, come morning, Jocelyn was informed without a shred of compassion that she would be dragged forcibly from the home she and Chadwick had shared if she wasn't out before breakfast. Heartsick and wretched, she opened the small leather-bound Bible her mother had given her, the first time she had opened it in over three years, and turned to the Book of Romans, Chapter 8, its verses bursting with promise. *Neither death, nor life...nor things present, nor things to come...shall be able to separate us from the love of God, which is in Christ....*

She remembered how she pored over the words a score of times. How with each reading, another layer of chill coated her soul like hoarfrost because in all those verses, not once did the apostle Paul mention the past. *God would not change the past.* Through grace, He apparently chose to forget it altogether, so that it wasn't necessary for Him to change it.

Jocelyn, weak, flawed, helpless mortal that she was, could not forget. For the five and a half years of her marriage, she had guarded a corrosive secret, been subjected to public ridicule. For the next five years she had tried to run away, only to discover the futility of trying to hide from one's past.

What kind of future could she offer a man for whom integrity was a way of life?

After a time, she became aware that she was curled up inside her closet like a frightened child, instead of a grown woman who had spent a decade spitting in the eye of public opinion. *Coward,* she reproached herself without heat. The enervating episodes, usually triggered by awareness of her own helplessness, came upon her less frequently. She had finally learned they would pass, taking the frightened child with them as her natural stubbornness reasserted itself.

Standing, she inhaled deeply, then finished dressing in a single petticoat beneath a plain gored walking skirt, with its higher hem at the ankle. Instead of shoes or boots, however, she shoved her feet into a pair of evening slippers whose soft soles were more conducive for sneaking about.

After waving to Katya, she eased the bedroom door closed and hurried down the hallway to the wide staircase. Moments later, silent as a feather duster, she turned the ornate handle of the door to Aunt Portia's third-floor office and stepped over the threshold.

Fifteen guilt-riddled minutes later she left the office empty-handed, her nose still twitching from the heavy rose scent that clung in the air, a persistent reminder of her aunt. She had searched the writing desk, tables with drawers, even fluttered the pages of two editions of *Harper's New Monthly* magazine tossed carelessly on a side table. Cracking the safe was out of the question. Portia Brock was shrewd enough not to leave incriminating evidence lying about for someone like her duplicitous niece-in-law to find.

Besides, though her aunt might be guilty of the sin of narcissism, Jocelyn had never truly suspected Portia Brock of being a criminal.

She fared no better on the main level in the library, nor Uncle Brock's surprisingly messy study, nor the family parlor, nor even in the obsessively neat butler's pantry. Twice she was afraid that despite his rumbling snores, Palmer had spotted her from his post in the main hall's vestibule.

Over three-quarters of an hour had passed.

Dry-mouthed but determined, Jocelyn reluctantly headed back upstairs to the family bedrooms, with some vague idea of searching for another escritoire, hopefully one with incriminating correspondence inside one of its drawers.

However, she was losing the war with her conscience as well as her courage. After all her bluster, all her pronouncements about civic responsibility, she was forced to admit that she did not possess a stern enough constitution to be an undercover operative. On the other hand, perhaps Micah, and the entire Secret Service, were mistaken about the Brocks.

Don't forget Benny Foggarty.

Mouth set, Jocelyn opened the door to Rupert Bingham's suite and marched inside.

Several fruitless moments later, she was a handful of paces from the door when it opened, and the valet froze in startled surprise.

Jocelyn's mind went sheet blank. "I—I wanted to leave Mr. Bingham a personal note," she stammered at last. "I know he's leaving first thing in the morning. He's been so kind to me...but I discovered I'd accidentally left the note in my bedroom. I was about to return to my room to fetch it."

"Certainly, madam," he replied courteously. Gray-haired and glum as an old hound, the valet showed not even a flicker of curiosity after the first instant. Of course, Jocelyn had learned within a week of her marriage to Chadwick that servants were considered movable pieces of furniture, without voice or feelings. "You may leave it in the secretary." He pointed an arthritic finger in its direction. "Mr. Bingham never locks it. I'll inform him upon his return, so he won't overlook your note."

"Thank you, Ames."

Without batting an eye, the valet proceeded into the room, and went about his duties.

She couldn't do this—her nerves were practically

clawing her insides to shreds. If another servant appeared in the oppressive gloom of this silent mansion Jocelyn might disgrace herself by shrieking like a steam kettle.

Micah was depending on her.

If no evidence could be found, he would be forced to take more drastic measures because he would not give up. If she hadn't learned anything else over these past months, she had come to know—and admire—Micah's unswerving dedication to his profession.

I won't let you down, Micah, she promised him silently, garnering strength from somewhere deep inside her soul, from the dried-up stalks of faith in God, and in herself, a faith she barely remembered. She loved Micah enough not only to leave him, but to complete her part in his mission, regardless of her screeching nerves.

It was almost midnight. Another search constituted a significant risk, but as she passed by her two cousins' suites, resolve slowed her step. On the surface, Julius possessed neither the temperament nor the intellectual capacity required for criminal activity. He collected postage stamps from foreign countries, for heaven's sake.

Virgil, on the other hand...

Jocelyn thrust open the door to Virgil's three-room suite and lunged inside. Dizzily, she swept a wavering glance about the darkened room, then pressed the button which turned on a large floor lamp nearby. In its light, her gaze caught upon a beautiful box of inlaid wood, polished to a bright sheen, sitting on top of a massive chest of drawers. In a woman's boudoir, she would assume it was a jewelry or music box, perhaps even a glove box; in a man's room, however, the shape more resembled…a cash box. An expensive, ornate version of the metal container Jocelyn had seen once in Mr. Hepplewhite's store.

She marched across the room to the chest of drawers, turned on another floor lamp and dashed across to turn off the lamp by the door.

The box was locked. Nearby a small enamel tray was filled with what might be found in a gentleman's pockets—a few coins, a silver toothpick, a receipt from a tobacconist's…several matches. A small brass key.

Incredibly, the key fit the lock to the box.

A surreal numbness drifted over Jocelyn. Like a sleepwalker, she opened the box and peered inside at two neat stacks of crisp bills. One stack of fives, the other tens. She watched her hands rifle through each stack, heard herself softly counting. Watched herself lift out a bill to examine the color of the ink, the texture of the paper. She held the bill up to the light to inspect the lines, as Micah had taught her to do.

The sheer *wickedness* outraged her: no attempt at all had been made to conceal the evidence of his perfidy. She wondered if in fact the box and key had been left out deliberately, because Virgil *expected* her to snoop through his possessions. If so, her position as the reconciled widow was more compromised than Micah's role as her suitor.

Her position no longer mattered.

Though every second increased her danger, she forced herself to focus on what Micah needed her to do. The amount of currency in the box—$500—did not faze her at all. Chadwick had carried almost that much cash to his and Jocelyn's frequent social events; he tossed whatever they didn't spend into an empty cigar box. For her first Christmas as his wife, the Binghams presented Jocelyn with a velvet drawstring bag stuffed full of $250 in bills and a hundred in $10 gold pieces—an entire year's wages for one of their servants.

So much money...

Had all of it been counterfeit, like her marriage?

Humiliation prickled her skin, followed swiftly by rage, roaring through her like fire exploding from a volcano. Each movement deliberate, she selected two bills from the middle of each stack, folded them several times and stuffed them inside her left slipper. Then she closed the lid, relocked the box and returned the key to the precise position in the enamel tray where she had found it. After turning off the light, she calmly walked from the room.

When she reached the stairs she streaked up them as though pursued by a pack of wolves, and burst into her suite with scarcely enough breath to call Katya's name. Dizzy, she pressed her fist over her heart. The heavy scent of gardenia clogged her nose and terror grabbed her throat when Katya failed to appear. *She was too late. Someone, perhaps Benny Foggarty himself, had been lying in wait, he'd snatched Katya and tossed her out the window....*

She was halfway across to the windows when Katya appeared in the doorway to her bedroom. Her face was scrubbed, still damp, her hair in a half-finished braid. She mopped her face with the towel draped around her neck as she approached, quick concern deepening in the dark brown eyes when Jocelyn grabbed her hand.

"I thought..." No. She must not allow her own fears

to spill onto Katya. Somehow she managed to smile, released Katya's damp hand, then beckoned for her to follow Jocelyn all the way into the privacy of Jocelyn's closet. "I found the evidence Micah has been searching for. But…" She paused, feeling wretchedly alone, her strength too puny against the weight of everything she needed to do. "I've made so many mistakes," she whispered, then shoved away the guilt. "Katya, I must see that this evidence reaches Micah's hands, immediately, because there might not be another opportunity for us to slip away." Without being followed, or forcibly detained.

If she had not seen Benny Foggarty in the garden— had it only been last night?—how long would Virgil have perpetuated his charade? A strangled sound emerged from her throat because, for Jocelyn, the charade was over.

Katya tugged her sleeve.

"Katya… I know this sounds confusing, and fearful. But we are leaving. Tonight, before the Brocks return." Tears stung her eyes. She grabbed the younger girl's hand, squeezed it, then leaned to remove her shoe and retrieve the folded bills. Silently, she showed them to Katya.

Equally silent, Katya took one of the bills and studied it, turning it over, her expression baffled.

"I believe these are counterfeit," Jocelyn explained, rubbing her temples to calm an incipient headache. "Over the past few months Micah—Mr. MacKenzie, has been doing more than courting me. He's also been teaching me how to distinguish a counterfeit bill from a real one. Here—take this five-dollar bill, as well. Now you have two bills, and I have two, so both of us have evidence for Mr. MacKenzie. Put yours in your pocket for now. Later you can stuff them in your brogans, like I put mine in my shoes. They'll be safer." She hoped. "But right now we have to *hurry*. The Brocks could return home within the hour. And Virgil is leaving for St. Louis the day after tomorrow." *Virgil, the vermin,* she thought, revulsion thickening her voice. "I'll explain everything later. For now, move as quickly as you can. Dress in your warmest clothes, pack only your small carpetbag."

A scant fifteen minutes later Katya met Jocelyn at the bedroom door, carpetbag in one hand, a note in the other. *Am not afraid. I trust you. Trust Mr. MacKenzie. Trust God.*

"I hope your trust is not misplaced." Swallowing a lump, she jammed the note in the pocket of her walking skirt, then tugged on her gloves. She had not taken the time to change, and carried no luggage at all. Everything she owned was tainted, and as soon as she passed these bills to Micah, she would purchase a costume or two with her own money, then burn the outfit in which she was fleeing.

After turning out the lamps, she glanced over toward her bed to verify that in the darkness the hump beneath the bedcovers resembled a person. Opening the door, she peered out into the hall, urgency shoving at her with impatient hands.

Like a pair of thieves they made their way down the servants' stairs and onto the main floor, remaining in shadows as much as possible. Jocelyn had decided to escape through a door at the back entrance, though the route forced them to traverse the entire length of the main hall, not to mention the vestibule where poor Palmer maintained his vigil.

They had just reached the library when a man's voice angrily exploded through the closed pocket doors.

"...necessary to discuss Mr. MacKenzie tonight!"

Katya jumped, her throat muscles convulsing in an unvoiced gasp. With the speed of desperation, Jocelyn grabbed the maid's arm and scuttled them into the small antechamber next to the library, where servants of guests waited for the duration of a visit.

Not much larger than the closet in Jocelyn's bedroom, the room offered a safe enough bolt-hole: none of the Brocks would deign to step foot in a place decorated with cast-off furniture, where lowly servants mingled. A narrow window shrouded in heavy velvet drapery lent an oppressive atmosphere to the small space that sent fresh chills racing over Jocelyn's skin. She sat Katya down in an unattractive wicker chair, took a deep breath, then explained to her maid what she was going to do.

Chapter Seventeen

Water dripped somewhere, a slow monotonous pling. Micah would have found the noise intolerable, except it reassured him that he was still alive. After blinking several times, he attempted to lift his head again. This time, pain did not plunge him back into unconsciousness. For a while he sat, his mind emptied out, until the blinding throb at the back of his head subsided to a bearable ache.

He did not know how long he'd been unconscious, or where he had been taken. The damp, musty odor and the quality of the silence indicated a room, or building, that was abandoned. He also wasn't gagged, convincing evidence that nobody would be within yelling distance.

His abductors certainly knew their business. Though not gagged, he was bound hand and foot to a wood chair, and a cloth sack completely covered his head. The sack comforted him. Apparently their ultimate crime was not murder. At the moment, anyway. No matter how one sliced this pie, however, Operative Micah MacKenzie was effectively useless, so he contented himself with listening to the water drip and pretended he was enjoying a Mozart sonata.

Some fragment of emotion struggled to grab his attention, a disquieting chord that clashed with the simple one-note water sonata. Then consciousness drifted back into a murky swamp.

Time passed. He roused himself again, tried praying, but his thoughts remained disconnected, disjointed.

Footsteps scraped along the floorboards somewhere over his head, a muffled but audible tread that at last broke through Micah's stupor. He tensed, marking the direction of each step, of where each board creaked, his sluggish mind automatically counting seconds. A door groaned open behind him, its hinges grating in protest. The heavy footsteps approached until Micah could hear the person breathing, smell the pungent odor of tobacco, musk and a whiff of some spice—cloves? Cinnamon?

"Well. You're awake at last."

The masculine voice was stripped of any overtly recognizable accents. Training or upbringing? Micah wondered. "Barely," he acknowledged, surprised by the huskiness of his own voice. "Can I have something to drink? My throat's parched."

A thoughtful pause ensued. "Didn't bring anything with me this time. Depending on how nice you are, I'll think about it."

"Depending on how long you plan to keep me alive, you might remember that a man can live longer without food, than he can water. How long have I been here, anyway?"

"Shrewd as an alley rat, aren't you? Even got yourself a college degree. Seems to me a smart fellow would have got himself a nice job, married a nice girl, raised a family and bought them a nice house in… Queens, perhaps? I hear there's a real nice neighborhood over there."

They knew. They knew too much. And if they knew Micah's identity, if they knew about Jonathan, as well, they would automatically suspect Jocelyn. Jocelyn, whom he had left alone and unprotected because of his own pride. His arrogance. *She should be safe for another day or two,* he'd asserted confidently to Jonathan, *because I've been invited to dinner tomorrow night.* Micah shivered, raw with fear. Anger. Resolved on a visceral level to keep both reactions from showing. "Seems to me a smart fellow wouldn't involve himself in kidnapping."

An unpleasant chortle echoed hollowly in the room. "Pay's good, real good. Besides, I don't have a daddy whose employer financed his son's education. Wonder what your daddy would say, seeing what you've done with your life. Biting the hand that fed you, so to speak."

Do not let him goad you into losing your temper. With an effort that coated his skin in sweat, Micah forced his muscles to relax, forced himself to take long deep breaths. Prayed the grinding headache would distract him sufficiently from his fear for Jocelyn to match wits with his abductor. "Any particular reason you're poking at me, or are you naturally mean?"

Something hard punched into his stomach. A gasp of pain whistled through his clenched lips; nausea burned at the back of his throat. *I can…do all things… Jesus, I can bear this because You're with me….* "Naturally mean," he mumbled, and braced himself for the next blow.

The footsteps shifted, circled in a quick impatient scuffle around Micah. "It's a shame I'm under orders not to kill you. Push much harder, Mr. MacKenzie, and I might decide to come up with a new set of orders. Wait... I forgot. It's Operative MacKenzie, of the U.S. Secret Service. Someone spilled all your secrets, Mr. Operative MacKenzie. Want to know who?"

"I hope you paid him in counterfeit bills."

This time the laugh rasped Micah's nerves to the breaking point. He couldn't stop a reflexive flinch when the man, still chuckling, whispered directly through the sack, into his ear. "It wasn't a 'he.'"

Sickening silence wrapped around Micah's windpipe and squeezed.

"Go ahead," the malevolent voice persisted. "Ask me who it was. Ask me who told all about you, in her refined Southern drawl."

Jocelyn. Father in heaven, Jesus, Jesus, don't let them hurt her....

With careless brutality the man grabbed a fistful of Micah's hair through the sack and yanked his head back. White-hot agony lanced his skull and lights flashed behind his eyes. "Can't stand hearing about your sweetheart? She's a looker, all right. Always preferred my sugarcakes with golden hair and plenty of curves—till I got me a gander of all that fiery red hair. And those eyes—they can freeze a man but I bet they'd also keep him warm at night."

"Leave her and your vile speculations out of this. You want to use me as a punching bag, I can't stop you. But save your breath and quit wasting my time, telling me lies about Mrs. Bingham." *Be strong, sweetheart.* "Because that's what they are. Lies. I know her."

And she'd already experienced enough betrayal and loss for three lifetimes.

With a contemptuous growl his tormentor released his hold on Micah's hair. "Twisted your shirttails into a knot, has she? Wish I was going to be around when you learn the truth."

This ham-fisted brute wouldn't know the truth if it were announced with heavenly trumpets. "Perhaps," Micah said between gritted teeth, "we'll both be there. One of us will be disappointed, and it won't be me."

This time he managed to tighten his abdominal muscles enough to weather the next blow. Seconds later, the sickening spice odor intensified as his captor's breath huffed into his ear once more.

"You might want to think about where you are now, Mr. Not-so-Secret Service man. Think long, and hard, about what will happen to your little redbird if you're not sitting right here the next time I return."

The threat bludgeoned with more force than his fists. Micah clenched his bound fingers until bones cracked, but his will was crumbling beneath the river of fear, outrage and hatred that rampaged through him. "What are you saying?"

"I'm saying if you're not sitting right here the next time I return, or the next time, or until hell freezes over, the widow will be pushing up daisies beside her dear departed husband. Understand that, Operative MacKenzie?"

Long after the door slammed, long after the footsteps faded until only the silence screamed, Micah sat without moving, while the river of rage hurled him against the shoals in furious waves.

But eventually the flood subsided to a trickle. Head

drooped, body battered, in that moment, fear and hopelessness chained him far more tightly than the ropes keeping him a blinded prisoner on a chair in an empty room.

Micah. They were talking about *Micah.*

Jocelyn slowly relaxed her cramped fingers. Panic would help neither Micah, nor her and Katya. The same glacial numbness that had seized her when she discovered Virgil's perfidy thickened until, with perfect calm, she was able to turn to Katya and whisper, "Something might have happened to Mr. MacKenzie. I'm going to see if I can listen through the library door. You stay here. If I'm caught—" She laid a bracing hand on the girl's shoulder. "Be brave, Katya. For me, for Mr. MacKenzie. If I'm caught, hide in here until you can slip outside." Hopefully the strategy would protect Katya from a blistering cross-examination at best. At worst… Jocelyn couldn't bear to think about what the Brocks would do to this vulnerable young woman.

Nor could she renege on her promise to help Micah. Quickly, she withdrew her coin purse and grabbed a handful of coins, pressing them into Katya's damp palm. "Here. This will pay for the hansom. You need to go to the post office," she ordered in a hurried whisper. "It's at the corner of Broadway and Park Row. The Secret Service's New York office is inside this building, but do *not* write 'Secret Service' on your tablet. Write 'Post Office,' and that's all."

Out in the hall, the grandfather clock tolled the quarter hour. Time… How long since the Brocks had returned home, how long since Virgil had entered the library? Who was he talking to, and *how much longer would they remain?*

"Go ahead and put the counterfeit bills I gave you under your feet, inside your brogans," she instructed Katya as levelly as she could. "They'll be safe there. Remember—nobody but a man who has the proper identification to prove he is an employee of the Secret Service can see those bills, Katya. You're strong, and stubborn. Don't let anyone intimidate you just because you can't speak."

Katya nodded, but through the thin beam of light that shone beneath the door Jocelyn watched two tears well up, then slide down the quivering cheeks.

The promise tumbled out. "I'll be back in a few minutes, probably." She straightened, a monstrous desolation clutching at her soul.

Never make promises, Chadwick used to tell her, his sculpted lips twisted in self-mockery. *You inevitably break them. Nobody keeps their word anymore, my dear.*

She didn't want to hear that voice inside her head ever again. She wanted to hear Micah's voice, wanted to bask in the assurance of his soul-deep faith. A faith born in hope, tested through tragedy, tensile-strong against cynicism.

She hugged Katya tightly. "You'll be fine. God will be with you. Remember that, most of all." Please let it be true, she added silently.

As she raced in a soundless dash over to the library, more fragments of scripture, ignored for over a decade, seeped into her heart. *Never will I leave you...the Lord is faithful... Be still, and know....*

All right, Lord. If those verses are true, now would be a good time...

"...and the old lady, probably the assistant's relative. Vanetti says he had no choice. I don't believe him. He enjoys killing. But he told me he pinched enough to make it look like burglary. I warned you when this happened in Richmond that the affair could turn messy, that Vanetti enjoys taking life. I'm not a prude, Mother, but this makes the third murder in three years."

Mother? Virgil wasn't talking to his father, or some other vile criminal—he was talking to *Portia*. Aunt Portia, whose skill at dissembling far exceeded Jocelyn's.

She shouldn't have been surprised by anything, nor even hurt. When Portia spoke, irrevocably confirming her identity, Jocelyn's world tilted, then settled into cold resolve.

"Sometimes death is an unfortunate but necessary consequence of a life action. Men bluster and boast about their power, but most of their manly displays are nothing but a facade to hide a weakness of character. You disappoint me, Virgil, and I trust I'll not be subjected to any more squeamish outbursts. As for Vanetti, I'm fully aware of his propensities. Six years ago Rupert's bookkeeper was actually Vanetti's first assignment with us. The man had become suspicious, and far too inquisitive. So I hired Vanetti, and provided enough erroneous information to send the Secret Service buffoons into an endless maze."

"But wasn't Uncle Rupert's bookkeeper MacKenzie's"

"I don't recall his name," Portia interrupted testily. "I made a decision then, to do whatever was necessary to deflect undue attention from our business." Her voice abruptly changed to the soft coaxing tone she used to secure Jocelyn's—and anyone else's—compliance. "It was difficult, yes. But it had to be done. Virgil, you must believe me. I retain Vanetti's services only to protect my family."

"Why didn't you buy these people off? It's not as though we're lacking the resources."

"Those resources have steadily dried up in the last five years, because of the Secret Service. Why do you think your brother moved to St. Louis? Some of our best manufacturers and wholesalers have disappeared entirely from the city, all because of those interfering government agents. Don't you understand? I've had no choice but to resort to extreme measures, like Vanetti. Wipe that self-righteous smile off your face and use your brain. MacKenzie and his ilk can no longer be bought, or turned. So unless you fancy cooling your heels in the Second District Prison, you do what you're told."

"Yes, Mother," came Virgil's mocking response. "And Mr. MacKenzie's assistant? Does he suffer the same fate as his aunt?"

"That decision will be made when he is located. In the meantime, we must reexamine our own resources."

"Are you referring to Benny? He's the one who alerted us to the truth about MacKenzie. Otherwise, we'd still be sharing meals and evenings out with the two-faced—" He cut off the rest of the sentence.

"I suspect Mr. Foggarty has been playing both ends against the middle. As for those two footpads you hired from the police department…they should have discovered MacKenzie's true identity weeks ago, along with the existence of another undercover operative working with Mr. MacKenzie." She spat Micah's name as though it were an epithet.

"Very well. As always, you've made your point. I'll take care of everything."

"See that you do. Are you sure the ubiquitous Lothario is someplace safe? No chance of discovery?"

"No chance at all. You'll appreciate this, Mother. Last year, when all the banks were going belly-up, I was able to buy several acres of land a couple of blocks from the Dakota, along Seventy-second Street." A malicious laugh slithered under the door panels. "Nothing's there at the moment but the dregs of a filthy shantytown—shacks, abandoned stores, a couple of caved-in warehouses. No tenants or sharecroppers are left. I made sure of that some months ago. I have plans for that property. By the time I'm finished, the Dakota Apartments will look like a tenement housing project by comparison."

"You're a good son, Virgil, with a good head when you put your mind in it. And Mr. MacKenzie is…?"

Jocelyn swallowed against the bile swimming at the back of her throat as she listened to Virgil's bragging. "Like I told you, nobody lives there now but rats, stray dogs and Mr. MacKenzie. I was told he's been secured in the basement of a storage warehouse, near the center of the property. Can't even hear street traffic."

"Very well. Now tell me about the urgent issue that couldn't wait until morning."

"I don't trust Jocelyn. You saw what she looked like when she returned, earlier this evening. The little fool's in love with MacKenzie, and I wouldn't put it past him to try and recruit *her*. Frankly, Mother, we shouldn't have left her here unguarded. In fact, before I leave for my meeting with Vanetti, I plan to go check her room."

"Pah! Your jealousy is showing." For a moment thick silence stained the air. Her skin clammy, Jocelyn held her breath, then gingerly pressed her ear closer against the panel. "…point is well taken. MacKenzie is a dangerous nuisance. We don't need him any longer, but Jocelyn remains more useful to me alive, regardless of your suspicions. I'll quell her intractable nature soon enough."

Virgil snorted. "And what do you plan to tell my dear cousin about her missing lover?"

"She'll never know anything except that he suffered a tragic accident. Jocelyn will recover, and I will encourage her dependence upon me, which I will continue to make use of, until I persuade her to share her knowledge of the whereabouts of my $500,000. Then, if I don't have her disposed of, I might marry her off to the most decrepit, vulgar pantywaist I can find."

"How charming." The phrase, pungent with nastiness, triggered Jocelyn's fuse.

"I want Mr. MacKenzie taken care of tonight." The quick tattoo of her heels approached the sliding pocket doors.

Galvanized, Jocelyn flew across the hall and ducked back into the servant's antechamber. Katya leaped to her feet, but froze when Jocelyn held up her hand. Rage pulsed in a drumroll from her toes to the tips of her fingers. Quivering with its intensity, she waited motionless until the muffled sound of Portia's and Virgil's voices echoed faintly back down to the main hall from the second-floor landing.

Then she turned to Katya. "They've captured Micah, and they plan to kill him—tonight. I'm not going to let that happen, because Virgil made a bad mistake. He gloated to his mother, bragged that nobody could find Micah. My cousin is wrong. I'm going to find Mr. MacKenzie, and free him before they have the opportunity to carry out their evil plans."

Chapter Eighteen

Sometimes, over the ceaseless moaning of the wind, Micah heard the scuffle of mice; once he thought he heard a dog bark. The building grated and groaned in concert with the wind, but he no longer flinched every time a board creaked somewhere above him. His captor would return when he returned; Micah could wonder whether it was day or night, or speculate on how many hours he had left to live—a futile exercise because there were no answers, only present absolutes. He was bound and blindfolded, in a dark room, alone.

Thirst plagued him, and his muscles burned from the thick coils of rope that bound him in this chair. The headache at least had abated to a dull throb he could ignore, and for a while now he'd applied his sluggish thinking to the task of how to escape. Instincts aside, even the greenest rube would conclude that were Micah to obey instructions, tamely waiting like a caged bear, when his captor returned the villainous cur was more likely to slit his throat than quench his thirst.

He hoped Jonathan had managed to contact Operative-in-Charge Bagg of the New York office, though Micah nursed few illusions that he would be found alive if he couldn't escape on his own. Fear for Jocelyn gnawed unabated at his vitals. He must escape, for her sake more than his own. The threat against her had been designed to pulverize, and it had almost worked.

Except…they didn't know Jocelyn the way he knew her. She would saw off her tongue before she betrayed him, because, though she hadn't spoken the words, she was in love with him. He'd felt it in her touch, in the kisses they'd shared, seen it shining from her eyes.

He didn't want to think about what would happen to Jocelyn if he failed to escape from this foul-smelling dungeon. Seven years ago he'd wondered if he would ever recover. Back then he had clung to his faith, his family, his friends, marveling at how God could use grief to toughen the external shell of one's faith, while time softened the internal agony until it turned to acceptance. Slowly, his heart healed.

By the time he met Jocelyn again in Richmond, he had climbed out of the pit, believing without pretense or pride that he was now strong enough to handle whatever life tossed his way. He trusted God to keep His promises, to fulfill His purpose for Micah's life, to reveal plans that would prosper his spiritual walk, not harm his soul.

Jocelyn was right. He was an idealistic fool.

His reactions seven years ago simply reflected those of a man shielding himself, through denial and numbness, from more than he could bear. Time hadn't healed; time had merely made him complacent. Arrogant.

Hours of darkness eked by while Micah clung with

slipping fingers to faith that seemed to slide through them like fog. Isolation and darkness finally accomplished their work, stripping his soul of pretense: the strongest man could be broken. Faithful believers could…abandon all hope.

For his entire adult life, Micah had striven to honor the Lord, even amidst unspeakable grief. Not once, back then, had he asked the inevitable question. No, not Micah, the devout man of God with a staunch biblical name, wrapped securely in faith. Micah MacKenzie knew all the answers. God bequeathed to human beings the singular attribute—a moral conscience, with the ability to make choices based on that conscience. Which meant mankind no longer lived a perfect life in a perfect garden, having made poor choices since Adam and Eve bit into an apple. So, of course human beings lived in a fallen world, full of evil and sorrow.

Like a brainless lamb, Micah, like Job, had chosen—*ha!*—to trust in God's ultimate goodness over an imperfect mortal's lack of understanding.

Now, in this dark hole that might as well have been in the belly of a large fish, Micah confronted the detritus of his moral superiority. He was no better than aeons of believers who, albeit in sincerity, thought they understood enough to not ask the question.

He should have remembered that even the Son of God cried out from the cross: *"My God, My God, why have You forsaken me?"*

How appropriate that Micah choke down his humble pie while bound hand and foot, blind as a beggar, wondering if the next sound he heard would be his last.

Why? *I'm asking now, Lord.* Why *have You allowed*

this to happen? Why would God bring him and Jocelyn together, only for Micah to be exterminated like an insect, leaving Jocelyn forever hardened or, even more gut-wrenching, murdered with the same callousness as his father?

Jocelyn. Jocelyn...

Gradually, as hours passed and a bone-numbing cold set in, doubt metamorphosed into anger. No! By all he held sacred—including his faith, *no*. He wasn't Jesus, wasn't the Savior of all mankind. He was a man, and while he had a breath of life in his lungs, he refused to turn his cheek for death to smite its fatal blow. His captors had shackled his body, deprived him of sight.

They had almost succeeded in shackling his emotions, his mind.

Anger was a potent elixir, particularly when it shattered the last of your illusions.

I'm angry at You, God. Angry, hurt and, yes, feeling betrayed. Like Jocelyn. The cup was bitter, but Micah downed it in a single furious gulp.

There are none so foolish as those who light a candle to see where they've come from, and never see the chasm in front of them before they fall into it.

Jocelyn...forgive me.

All right, then. God had not seen fit to free Micah from his plight, so with only the power of his will as a weapon Micah set himself to the task. Muscles straining, sweat dripping from his forehead, down his back, he twisted and wriggled and jerked, ignoring the pain. If he could break the chair legs, he might get enough slack in the ropes to enable him to slide free, or use the splintered wood to saw through them. If he could—

"Micah? Are you in here?"

The faint feminine call shot a sizzling jolt of electricity through him that nearly stopped his heart. The counterfeiting networks he'd encountered were not above using women to lure the unwary into a trap. Some of those women had been innocent dupes, but they accomplished the task regardless. Micah ceased his exertions, chest heaving while he debated whether or not to respond.

"Micah!" Footsteps scurried in a whispery shuffle on the floor above. "Ouch! Oohh...there have to be stairs... He said the basement.... *Micah!* If you can hear me, please answer!"

It *was* Jocelyn.

Yelling was not wise, but Micah saw no other choice. If she'd been followed, they had little time. "Down here!" he shouted. "Jocelyn, there are stairs. Find them, but don't call out again." His struggle to free himself intensified. She couldn't defend herself for long if she were attacked.

He heard the rattle of the doorknob, and the hinges squeaking in protest. Before he could blink twice he was engulfed in the faint scent of gardenia and damp wool.

"Micah... Micah, are you hurt? What did he do? I'll kill him myself, the blackguard!"

She yanked the sack from his head. The room was pitch-dark, save for the glow of a carriage lantern next to the door. A carriage lantern? Hours in the dark had adjusted Micah's vision; he looked up into the face of his beloved, a moon-pale oval swathed in the folds of her hooded cloak. Biting her lip, she lifted her hands to his face and wiped the sweat away with fingers that shook. But as she leaned over him a thin beam of lantern light illuminated her eyes, eyes blazing with a terrible wrath.

"How could he? *How could he!*" She tore at the ropes. "Micah…the knots are too tight. I can't…"

Micah's heart swelled in admiration, and love. "Gently, sweetheart. You're here. You're all right. I don't know how, but you're here." He couldn't help the grin that felt like it would crack his face. "You're all right," he repeated, stupefied. "Except I'm supposed to rescue you. You rewrote the fairy tale."

"I quit believing in fairy tales when I was seventeen. Oh, these wicked knots!" She flexed her fingers as she glared at his bound wrists. "If I can't untie these ropes my version of the story will turn into a spectacular failure. I should have thought of this— of course they would keep you confined, unable to move. I should have filched a knife somewhere. I should have—" Her breath hitched. "There wasn't time. There's little time now. I— Micah, I know who the ringleaders are. It's Virgil, and his mother. His *mother.* Not my uncles." Her fingers fumbled at his wrists again. "P-Portia and Virgil were in the library. I heard them, through the door. They're going to kill you, he's probably not five minutes behind me. I ran, I had to leave Katya, but I knew if I couldn't find you first I couldn't bear—"

"Jocelyn, listen to me. Hush. Listen to me."

She blinked, but Micah watched in relief as awareness flickered. She straightened, pinched the bridge of her nose, then released a pent-up breath. "Sorry. I just… Seeing you like this was a shock. I'm all right now."

"Of course you are." For the first time he directed

his attention to his surroundings, a shiver of disgust rippling along his muscles. Dust and dirt coated indistinguishable lumps of boxes, crates and several long tarpaulin-covered piles of lumber with their sawed-off ends poking out. The floorboards were warped, stained, and without the filter of the empty flour sack they had used to cover his head, the putrid stench of mildew and rotten garbage made his eyes water. "We need a sharp object. Sorry to have to ask, but I'm afraid you're the only one able to search for it."

Without a word Jocelyn dashed across the room to fetch the lantern. "I paid the hansom driver with my last two dollars, to sell me this lantern," she confided as she strode undaunted across the floor to a shrouded stack of metal objects. After a cursory search she moved farther away. Micah realized that she was likely talking to divert them both from his helplessness. "I imagine he decided two dollars was safer than a demented woman threatening to have him arrested for not aiding a distressed widow." Boards clattered, and she sneezed. "I'm afraid I wasn't very ladylike."

"I think you're the most magnificent woman I've ever known." Since he couldn't help her, Micah resumed his own struggles, and had finally managed to free his left thumb when he heard Jocelyn stifle an exclamation.

"What is it?" he asked sharply.

"A dead…creature." She cleared her throat and muttered an apology.

Micah clamped his lips together to keep from yelling at her to hurry, instead redoubling his efforts to free himself.

Several moments later she exclaimed, "Found something!" and scurried back to his side. "I don't know what it is, only that the ends are sharp." She set the lantern on the floor, behind the wooden beam to which he and the chair were tied. "Hold still. I'll try to cut the rope, not you." A bubble of half-hysterical laughter escaped. "Chief Hazen would never forgive me."

Outside, the dog resumed barking again.

Micah prayed.

"Almost...there!" Jocelyn muttered, and Micah felt the ropes fall away from his wrists.

Pain streaked up his arms; Jocelyn attacked the ropes around his chest while he dangled his hands, flexed his fingers and clenched his teeth while abused muscles and nerves screamed back to life. By the time she'd sawed through the ropes that bound his torso he was limber enough to relieve her of the makeshift tool, taking over the job of freeing his legs.

"I'm sorry I couldn't find a knife."

"You did. It just looks like a whiffletree bolt."

"A what?"

With a grunt of effort he tugged the last knot free and began massaging his legs. "You found a whiffle-tree bolt—wait. Since you're from Virginia, you might know it as a swingletree bolt. They're used to fasten the crossbar, where the harness traces are fastened."

"I don't know what you're talking about." She stared down at the metal bolt, whose end curved like a bow into two sharp points.

"Someday I'll show you." The back of his neck prickled. Staggering, he used the hewn beam to lever himself up. "Right now, we need to extinguish this lantern, and hope we can escape from the building before whoever that dog is barking at enters it."

"Oh." Bending, Jocelyn lifted the lantern and snuffed the flame, plunging the room into unrelieved darkness.

"Take my hand." Micah found her fingers.

On the floor above them, footsteps moved in rapid thuds toward the corner where the stairs led to the basement. Grimly, Micah weighed their options, then tugged Jocelyn across the room toward the door. "Shh…" He situated them on the wall next to the doorway, shoving Jocelyn behind him. When the person clattering down the stairs opened the door, his gaze would be directed toward the center of the room, where Micah was supposed to be. "Get ready to run up those stairs," he whispered into her ear, his lips brushing the soft hair.

She squeezed his hand.

Seconds later a blinding spear of light filled the stairwell, followed by the solid bulk of a man, moving fast. He burst into the room, aiming the light as Micah predicted toward the center of the room—and the empty chair.

The man uttered a foul curse, obscenities that flowed unabated as he made a beeline for the chair. Micah gave Jocelyn a hard shove into the darkened stairwell; for a simmering second, time stretched, hovering forever on the brink between discretion and bloodlust. *He could take him.* Knock him senseless, then break a couple of his ribs when he was helpless. Give him what he deserved.

Instead, Micah turned away, and followed Jocelyn up the stairs.

Suddenly, they heard a bellow, and light flooded

the stairwell. "Stop! I'll kill you both!" Still swearing threats, the man stormed up the stairs behind them.

Jocelyn stumbled.

Micah wrapped an arm around her waist and lifted her off her feet, scrambling for purchase on the worn treads. They gained the top of the landing and Micah released Jocelyn, who darted out of the way, behind one of the support beams. Thin white moonbeams streamed through cracks in the boarded windows where half the boards had fallen off. "Get outside," Micah ordered. "Don't look back. I'll find you."

"Micah, no…"

"Run!" He ducked and swiveled as their would-be murderer burst into the room, a knife in one hand, brass knuckles over his other fist.

Micah lunged, tackling the bruiser who easily out-weighed him by a hundred pounds. They tumbled to the ground in a tangle of limbs, Micah seizing the wrist with the knife, slamming it against the doorpost even as he flinched away from the brass knuckles, which missed his chin by a whisker. With his thumbs he searched for and found the vulnerable collection of nerves and veins in the thick wrist and squeezed, squeezed with all his strength until with a frustrated groan, the man dropped the knife.

Retaliation was swift. Micah evaded a punch to the jaw again, but the brass knuckles caught him in a blow to his sore midriff. The air whistled from his lungs, but he managed to roll over onto the knife, then lashed out with his foot, landing a glancing blow on his assailant's head.

They both scrambled to their feet, only this time Micah held the knife.

"You'll die slow, you filthy—" He called Micah a name. "And so will the chippie."

"Not today," Micah growled. "And not by you." Moving fast, he leaped to the side, scooped up the tubular lamp the man had dropped and shone the brilliant beam directly into his face.

Yowling, the man stumbled backward through the doorway, hands lifted like a shield in front of his face—and tumbled in a resounding crash down the stairs.

Chapter Nineteen

Jocelyn had no intention of leaving Micah alone with a man the size of a barn; she grabbed a board and dashed back across the old warehouse just as the assailant plunged head over heels down the stairs.

"Micah! Are you hurt? Did he stab you? I saw the knife. I know you told me to run but I couldn't." Near-blinded by the bright light, she reached his side, scarcely noticing when Micah pried the board from her fingers and tossed it onto the floor.

"I'm not hurt," he managed breathlessly. Still holding the lantern, he manacled one of her wrists with his hand as they descended the stairs. "You might have been, had that knife been a gun."

"It wasn't, and now you have a weapon, should you need one." She felt strange, almost giddy, as though her feet were floating down the stairwell while her brain floated somewhere up in the dusty rafters. "Do you think he's dead?"

"I don't know. Can you hold this lantern? Here— wrap your fingers around the handle, that's it. Casts a strong light, doesn't it? Try not to stare directly at it. We'll have to turn it off when we go outside— Are you all right?"

"Just a trifle…disoriented, but I'm fine, Micah. Don't worry about me. Take care of that—that monster."

She caught sight of his frown before he turned and knelt beside the sprawled body. "He's alive." Standing, he pondered in silence for a second, then shrugged. "No help for it. I'm going to drag him over to that post and tie him up. Give him a taste of his own medicine. As soon as I'm sure you're somewhere safe, I'll arrange for him to be taken to the city jail. Now, if you'll shine that lamp to light our path…"

A short while later, with the captor now the captive, Jocelyn led Micah across the upper floor of the ramshackle warehouse. "We're only a few blocks from the Dakota Apartments," she told him. "Can you imagine the effrontery of my cousin?"

"Nothing surprises me much these days," Micah replied as they reached a door held in place by only one rusting hinge. "Except you, Jocelyn." She watched dreamlike as he turned off the lamp, set it on a dust-filmed barrel, then took her hand and brought it to his lips. "You've saved my life—in more ways than you can imagine."

"All I could think about, when I listened to Portia and Virgil plotting your death as though they were discussing choices on a menu, was that I'd never have a chance to tell you that…" Shyness locked her jaw.

She thought he smiled. "Time enough for declarations later. Come along, let's see if we can find our way to the El. There's a station at Seventy-second Street. Do you have any change?"

"Oh…" A spurt of vertigo made her dizzy, but Jocelyn was too aggravated with herself to pay much attention. "I wasn't thinking. I gave that cab driver everything, for the lantern…. Micah, I'm so sorry. How stupid of me."

"Hush." She gave a gasp of surprise when his arms snaked around her and he pulled her close, his lips pressing chapped kisses against her forehead, her temples. "I don't want to hear any more disparaging remarks about the woman I love, the woman who just saved my life. We'll walk. It's chilly, but the wind has died down."

The woman he loved… The strange sensation intensified, as though her spirit along with her brain had just peeled away like a grape skin from her body, and was hovering over them in a surrealistic mist. "I never thought a man would say those words to me…."

"I never thought I'd say them again myself." Micah released her, found her hand again and gave it a tug. "Come along. Let's try to escape into the city while we've got some moonlight." He helped her maneuver around rusted iron tools, a stack of empty fruit crates and a pile of crumbling bricks.

"'*East Side, West Side, all around the town…*'" Jocelyn warbled in an effort to stave off her queasiness. She couldn't remember the words of the popular song "Sidewalks of New York," and switched to humming, docilely following Micah as he picked a path along the side of the warehouse.

When they reached the end of the building, Micah stopped; Jocelyn almost plowed into him, and his arm went around her shoulders. "Steady there. Let me study the lay of the land a bit."

"Nobody's here. Used to be, but Virgil got rid of them. Like they were vermin. That's how I think of *him* now. Virgil the vermin." Vaguely she shifted her weight, wondering why her left leg seemed to be throbbing. "He bought this land—the cab driver told me it covers almost three city blocks. He wasn't very friendly, the driver, I mean. Said this was an eyesore, and no place for a lady. I had to bargain for the lamp like I was a poor immigrant."

Micah's hand gently covered her mouth. "Shh..." he murmured into her ear. Then, "Are you sure you're all right? You're not scared, are you?"

"Not anymore." She had to think a moment, then added candidly, "But I feel...strange."

"Not too cold?"

"Mmm. This is my warmest cloak, even if I didn't take time to change into walking shoes. Katya and I were sneaking out. Oh... I do have money. It's in my shoe. But we can't use it. It's bogus goods. I found the proof we've been looking for. Virgil left it in his room, I think on purpose, so I called his bluff. Here, I'll show you."

She started to lean down to remove her shoe and would have fallen if Micah hadn't grabbed her waist. "Tell me later, sweetheart, all right?" He held her a moment, but thin cloud fingers had drifted in front of the moon, and Jocelyn couldn't see his expression. She decided to watch the clouds instead, because she finally remembered that Micah had mentioned something about getting the lay of the land. But she was tired, she suddenly realized. So tired she wondered how much longer she could stand.

"Better now? Then let's go. We're going to stay in

the shadows of those buildings, then make our way across that field. There's a tree in the middle. We'll stop there for a second. All right?"

Her mouth didn't want to cooperate, so Jocelyn nodded. Micah was in charge now, she reminded herself. All she needed to do was to follow. She wasn't alone anymore.

The night enveloped them, but the wind from the previous afternoon had ceased and the air was crisp, invigorating rather than frigid. In the distance, yellow streetlamps outlined the street where Jocelyn had bargained for the carriage lamp; the rest of their little world lay in soft shades of black velvet. Star points of light glimmered, then disappeared when the moon slipped free of the clouds. Somewhere in the distance a horse neighed. The faint odor of burning peat stung her nostrils. On the other side of a jumbled mass of outbuildings, she thought she glimpsed the brighter light of a lantern— No. Was the dizziness blurring her vision? She could see lots of yellow blobs of light, and vague amorphous shapes.

Abruptly, Micah yanked her behind the darker huddle of a small shed. Easing her to the ground, he tugged her cloak firmly around her and whispered for her to keep her face down, the hood over her head. "The police are here," he murmured, his tone a low rustle of sound.

"Looking for us? Shouldn't we— No." Horrified, Jocelyn grabbed his shirt, and realized for the first time that Micah was hatless, coatless and probably freezing. "Micah, I don't know if we can trust the police here," she whispered back, the words tumbling over themselves. "Portia p-paid two of them, to follow us."

"I know. It's all right, don't worry." In the darkness she felt his hand moving up until he cupped her cheek. "Jocelyn, will you trust me?"

"Not if you plan to lure them away so I can escape without you."

Without warning his mouth covered hers in a hard kiss. "Don't be a goose. I want to sneak closer, see if I can hear what they're saying. Will you stay here, and not move an inch? Please?"

"Yes." He started to rise, but she grabbed his hand. "Micah? I—" No. Now was not the time to confess her love. Now was the time to trust not only Micah—but God.

"What is it? Don't be afraid. I promise, I'll be safe. I know what I'm doing, all right?"

"I know." She brought the cold, rough hand to her mouth and brushed a kiss of her own across his knuckles. "I wanted to tell you I'll be praying, Micah."

He froze, then she heard his breath exhale in a long sigh. "Why?" he said.

But as she watched him fade into the night, Jocelyn thought she heard a faint word echo in the frosty air, a word that didn't make sense. Frowning, she shifted until she could lean back against the rough plank siding. Her left leg hurt—she must have knocked it against something. Her face ached from the cold, even inside gloves her hands felt like frozen sausages, and the whorls of nausea persisted in annoying her. With difficulty she drew up her knees, then rested her head on her crossed arms. Stay still, keep her head covered and trust him. Well, that was simple enough, since she was worn to a nub. Rescuing people expended a tremendous amount of energy and she was more than ready for a moment of rest. But puzzlement fretted away over that little word she thought she'd heard.

Why would Micah, whose faith she had grown to admire and trust—why would Micah ask "Why?" when she confessed that she'd be praying?

By the time he crept within thirty yards, Micah could plainly hear the nasal voice of a police sergeant over the restless stamping of horses' hooves, the jingle of harnesses and the steady hiss of two dozen police lanterns. Crouched behind an abandoned subsistence farmhouse, he emptied his mind of Jocelyn, of her parting words, of the cold that threatened to sap his strength. The fight with that behemoth inside the warehouse had taxed him more than he could afford to admit.

"...and with her maidservant stole an undisclosed amount of jewelry and cash from the Augustus Brock residence on Fifth Avenue. The maidservant is a mute, but has been taught to read and write by the suspect. She may or may not have accompanied Mrs. Bingham to this site. One of the Brock servants, the housekeeper, claims she overheard Mrs. Bingham say she was meeting her lover at an abandoned warehouse, which is purportedly located near the center of this block."

The sound of the policeman's voice was momentarily drowned out by the approach of a Black Maria—the infamous wagons used by police to transport prisoners. While he had breath in his body, Micah would save Jocelyn from that fate.

"...by twos, and approach from all four sides. Right, now, be quick about it, lads."

The bevy of uniforms separated into pairs; Micah swiveled on his heel and made his way back to Jocelyn. Moments later, breathing hard, he dropped down beside her still form, almost invisible in the shadow of the shed until she lifted her head from her knees. He caught the faint upward curve of her mouth.

"Already? I was enjoying my nap...."

"Hopefully you'll soon be able to take one in a nice feather bed." Keep it light, he decided as he helped her to her feet, held her close until she found her balance. "We need to move as fast as we can, quietly," he murmured, his voice a low rumble. "If you must tell me something, use a low voice but don't whisper. The sound of a whisper actually carries farther."

She nodded. He led her around a mound of trash, toward the cover of the next building—a single-story structure minus all its windows. When they reached the edge, an open field stretched between them and the next cluster of buildings. Micah tightened his grip on her hand. "Run, but stay as hunched over as you can manage," he muttered out of the side of his mouth.

Halfway across the muddy, uneven field she faltered, and he heard a low moan. Because she was swaying on her feet, Micah grabbed her shoulders, though his gaze continued to follow the bouncing yellow lights moving toward the warehouse. "Jocelyn? What's wrong?"

She staggered beneath his hands, and would have collapsed had he not gathered her into his arms. "Sorry...dizzy..." The words emerged reed-thin. "My leg. I don't know why, but it...hurts."

Grimly, Micah calculated the distance, then set his teeth, lifted her high against his chest and set off across the field. They had five minutes or less before those policemen reached the warehouse and discovered that the man tied to a beam did not match the description of the one they were expecting.

"I'm going to be ill…."

"No, you're not. Breathe shallowly, through your nose, slowly…that's it," he encouraged her between his own labored breaths. "Just a few more yards, and we'll be out of sight again." For how long, he did not know, but at the moment his fear for Jocelyn overrode his fear of discovery.

A cluster of shanties had been built around a copse of scrubby trees, now stripped of leaves. Micah carefully set her down in the middle, where moonlight spilled narrow streamers of white between the branches; the shanties provided a screen between the police lanterns and their hiding place, allowing Micah to use the moonlight to try to find out what was wrong with Jocelyn.

"Easy now, sweetheart." He leaned her back against the smooth trunk of one of the larger trees, but when he tried to straighten her legs she gasped. "Your leg—you told me your leg hurt. Which one? Don't try to talk, just point." Her hand fumbled downward, then limply collapsed onto her left thigh.

Without another word, Micah pulled her cloak away. "I have to check," he told her, maintaining a low, calm tone as he lifted her skirt hem, telling her she would be all right, and to trust him—and the words stuck in his throat as he picked up the white lawn petticoat beneath the fine wool of her skirt.

In the pale block of moonlight, the left side of the petticoat, from the knee down, was soaked with blood.

Chapter Twenty

For Micah, it was as though he'd been catapulted back into the stinking basement of the abandoned warehouse. No matter where he directed his gaze, darkness swallowed him.

"Micah?"

The tremulous sound of Jocelyn's voice jerked him back to his senses. "Looks like you've hurt your leg a bit," he told her softly, throttling his alarm. "Close your eyes if it helps, but I need to expose your leg so I can see what's going on."

"I'm not a wilting wallflower," she mumbled as she attempted to lean forward. Her hands fumbled to pull her skirt higher. "Oh…my skirt. It's torn, isn't it? I vaguely remember yanking at it because it caught on something. But I don't remember hurting my leg."

She sucked in her breath when Micah clasped her ankle in one firm hand, while with the other he peeled back the blood-soaked petticoat to expose a long, dangerously deep gash that had sliced her calf from ankle to knee.

The shrill bleat of a police whistle rent the air.

Jocelyn flinched, but Micah tightened his hold on her ankle while he turned his head to swiftly survey their surroundings. "Likely they've discovered we're not inside the warehouse. They'll be spreading out now, to search."

"We need to—"

"Yes. But not until I bind this, try to slow the bleeding." Releasing her ankle, he retrieved the knife from the scabbard he'd helped himself to when he tied up its owner. "Your petticoat will have to do for bandages. Don't try to help me. Stay as still as you can. I'll try not to hurt you, but I'm going to have to...to handle you, with some familiarity."

"Do what you have to." He heard her swallow, and for an instant he debated whether turning themselves in would be the more prudent course. The gash was nasty, needed cleaning, possibly even stitching. She needed the skilled hands of a doctor, and another woman to offer consolation.

God...? I don't know what to do.

Jocelyn's fingers, cold and frail, brushed against his beard-roughened cheek. "You're a good man, Micah MacKenzie," she said, her voice pale as the moonbeams. "I...believe...in you."

With a choked sound, Micah covered the hand on his cheek with his own. "Then I guess I can't let you down." He planted a kiss on her palm, then gently felt her pulse and without comment curled her fingers into a ball. "Hold my kiss, hold it tight."

Somewhere a voice shouted, and the dog set to viciously barking again.

Micah worked with reckless speed, tamping down the ingrained notion to protect a woman's modesty as he used the knife to slash the front of the blood-soaked petticoat free of Jocelyn's trembling form. Full of tucks and frills and six inches of scalloped embroidery for the hem, the sodden fabric was useless. He tossed it aside, forcing himself to slow down, to treat her with gentleness because she was above all things a lady, not a seasoned warrior on the field of battle. Matter-of-factly he slid his hands beneath the skirt, behind her back, and somehow managed to untie the ribbons so he could wrest the remainder of the petticoat free. Rigid as the tree trunk she leaned against, with her breath emerging in little pants, Jocelyn neither moved nor flinched away from their enforced intimacy.

When it was done, Micah's hands were full of close to two yards of the softest lawn fabric he'd ever felt. Ruthlessly, he cut everything into strips, and laid the narrow ribbon ties aside. After putting the knife away, he plowed a hand through his sweat-matted hair. "Only another minute or two, and I'll be done. All right?" She nodded. "This will hurt," he warned her next. "Bite your fist if you need to, but don't make a sound."

"Won't…"

He folded two of the strips into a narrow but thick pad, took a deep breath, then pressed it over the gaping wound. Though her body jerked, then trembled uncontrollably, Jocelyn did not utter a sound. Micah had never loved her more. He applied pressure and counted, but knew every second they remained here increased the danger. Muscles knotted with tension, he used two more strips to bind the wound, then tied everything in place with the ribbons and stuffed the rest of the fabric inside his waistband. Lastly, he snatched up a dented pail without a handle, stuffed the bloodied remnant of petticoat inside and thrust the pail beneath a jumble of garbage inside the shed.

He would have given his left arm for that pail to have been full of water. Instead, he wiped his sticky hands in the dirt, then rubbed them together to rid them of as much of the blood as he could before turning to Jocelyn.

"I'm going to help you up, then I want to see if you're able to walk."

"I can walk." She was already trying to shove herself away from the tree, but her movements were uncoordinated, clumsy.

More voices yelled out, and another whistle shrieked into the night. From the corner of his eye Micah saw a yellow circle dip and bob like a butterfly, moving into the open field.

Somewhere beyond the cluster of trees and shanties, he heard the clatter of hooves and the grating rumble of iron wheels on cobblestone. If they could reach the street...

"Hold on." He captured Jocelyn's straining arms and hauled her up. For a dangerous moment, he held her trembling body close.

Her hands moved restlessly up and down his arms. "Why, your coat—it's gone. They took your coat. You're...freezing. Take my cloak."

"I'm fine. Later, we'll share your cloak." He shifted her to his side, one of his arms wrapped firmly around her shoulders. "We're almost on the opposite side from where the policemen gathered. There's a street at the end of these buildings, I believe. If we can cross it to the other side, we should be safe." He doubted it; the New York police were among the most efficient in the world, but he wasn't going to share that disquieting knowledge with Jocelyn.

They set off down a rutted path littered with trash and clumps of hardened clay. Within half a dozen paces, Micah knew Jocelyn's strength was gone. Another swift glance around kicked his pulse into a drumroll of urgency. He counted four of those menacing yellow circles merging—they were coming closer. As he lifted Jocelyn into his arms, from the street in front of them he heard a voice bellow out an order; off to the left he heard a responding shout, followed by two short blasts of the whistle.

His worst fears had been confirmed. They were slowly and inevitably being surrounded.

A dark shape sprang out from behind one of the trees. Desperately, Micah slid Jocelyn to the ground, hoarsely ordered her to hold on to his waist while with one hand he grabbed the knife.

"Psst. Hey, mister! Over here…" The dark shape materialized into a small boy, hovering at the corner of an old house with all its windows knocked out. "I can help," he whispered, stepping around a twisted coil of thick cables. An oblong of moonlight revealed a thin dirt-smeared face, and a wiry body poised to flee. A flat stockinged cap half covered his head. "Ya's gots to hurry. The coppers, they's everywhere."

"How much did they pay you to lead us straight into their laps?" Keeping his gaze locked on the boy, Micah adjusted his grip on Jocelyn's waist, and held the knife so the moonlight glinted on its flat blade.

The boy glared back, then spat on the ground. "I hain't no stoolie. 'Sides, if I wanted to, could've led *them* straight to *youse*."

Micah fractionally relaxed. "Good point. What's your name, son?"

"I'm not your son," he shot back fiercely. "And my name's Heinrich, but I'm *American,* now."

"Heinrich. I'm Micah, and this lady is Mrs.—" he hesitated "—Mrs. Tremayne. She's injured."

"They say she stole from some rich hoity-toities up on Fifth Avenue."

"She's a fine lady, and never stole anything from anyone. The people who said that, or told that tale to the police…they're lying, Heinrich."

The boy made a far-too-contemptuous sound for a lad younger than twelve. "Don't I know it." He twisted to look over a bony shoulder. "I'll hide you. Got no use for *politieagenten.* But we gotta to hurry."

Without warning, Jocelyn uttered a soft moan, her head flopped sideways, and she would have toppled to the ground if Micah hadn't been holding her up. She had fainted. He didn't even know if she'd been aware that their survival now rested in the hands of a young boy. *And a little child shall lead them,* he thought, the irony twisting his stomach.

"I'll follow you, but I have to carry Mrs. Tremayne, so don't move too fast." He hefted Jocelyn's dead weight back into his arms, trembling from exertion and exhaustion. "Hopefully it's not too far."

"It's not." Without another word Heinrich set off down a narrow alleyway between two buildings. Through the trees the bobbing police lanterns spread out in an ominous line stretching out on either side of the warehouse. Micah calculated that they had several moments left before one of those globs of light cut across their trail.

"Here. Over here, mister!"

Almost wheezing now, Micah plunged into the ink-blot of darkness. Once he stumbled and almost fell, then staggered forward, toward the high-pitched whisper. When he reached Heinrich, he lowered Jocelyn to the ground, breath heaving from his lungs, and glanced at the wrecked skeleton of a wood-frame building in front of him. Only two walls remained upright; the rest had collapsed inward, leaving a jumbled heap of boards, tin and stones. He passed his tongue over his cracked lips, watching dumbfounded as Heinrich carefully lifted a square tabletop minus its legs and set it to one side. Then he removed several jagged-edged planks to reveal what looked like the entrance to an underground tomb.

"Down here," he whispered. "There's steps. They're brick. You want I should help you with the lady?"

"Thanks, but I can manage. I'll leave you to cover our tracks." With a bemused prayer of gratitude, Micah somehow managed to descend into the bowels of the collapsed building without falling.

In the absolute darkness he could hear Heinrich's quick puffs of breath, sense the boy's movements, but he had no sense of space. He was, once again, blind. Helpless.

But not quite.

Heinrich slipped by him with the nimbleness of a cat. "I'll light a match so's you can see, but then I'll have to blow it out. Long as we stay quiet, they won't find us, mister."

Micah smelled the acrid sulphur as the resourceful youngster struck the match. The small flame gathered strength and supplied sufficient light for Micah to assess their hideaway. They were in a cellar, surprisingly dry, with narrow shelves still lining one of the stone walls. Heinrich lit the stump of a candle and stood in the opposite corner, holding the candle to allow Micah to see a lumpy mattress on the floor, covered with what looked like several moth-eaten horse blankets.

"She can rest better here. Is clean. My *moeder* told me clean is better." His accent was more pronounced now, and Micah realized with a pang that the boy was nervous, almost afraid.

"Thank you, Heinrich," he said, then laid Jocelyn's still-unconscious form on the pallet. He lifted a fragile wrist and counted the pulse, then carefully covered her with one of the blankets. "You've probably saved our lives."

"Shh!" He blew out the match. "I hear them. We stay still, *jah?*"

When Jocelyn forced her heavy eyelids open, at first she thought she'd died or been buried alive, so complete was the darkness. Despite the vague memory that she must remain absolutely quiet, a tiny whimper of panic escaped.

"It's all right." Micah's low voice flowed over her, reassuring and calm. "You're not alone. I'm right here, beside you." She felt his hand slide up her arm, to rest against her cheek. "We're in a safe place. Soon we'll be taking you to an even safer place, with a bit of light included in the relocation. You've been out for a while. How do you feel?"

She had to think about it. When she tried to talk, her tongue felt thick, swollen and unmanageable. "Stiff. Strange. What... Are we—are we in jail?"

"No. No, dear one, we're not in jail. But for a little while longer we have to stay in darkness. Here." She heard rustling, and a sound like milk bottles clinking? Then Micah's arm slowly lifted her to a sitting position. "Heinrich's the most resourceful fellow I've ever met. I'm thinking of hiring him. He's only ten, but perhaps Chief Hazen would make allowances." As he talked in his soothing bass rumble he held, amazingly, a bottle of water to her lips. "Easy, just a sip at the time. This is spring water all the way from France, courtesy of a hotel chef who's equally smitten with Heinrich. When you're up for it, I have beef broth for you, from said chef."

Jocelyn could almost feel life flowing back into her limbs as the liquid soothed her parched throat. After her initial thirst was quenched, Micah bathed her face and hands with surprising skill, considering that their chamber was devoid of light, as black as the inside of a cast-iron skillet.

"Can we talk?" she ventured hesitantly. "The police—"

"Heinrich's last report, about an hour ago, I believe, is that they've ceased searching the area, but have posted policemen on every corner, and every fifth streetlight, on all the surrounding streets. As long as we keep our voices low we can talk, but we'll have to remain in the dark."

"Heinrich...he's the boy who saved us? I remember when he sprang out, from behind a tree." A lingering shudder of fear rippled along her nerves. "I don't remember much else."

"Heinrich lives with his mother and sister in what I gather is a pieced-together shack over on Riverside

Drive, about half a dozen blocks from here. His father is dead, but Heinrich won't talk about it. They lost everything in the Panic last year, including the home his papa built twenty years ago, in the Kleindeutschland district, near Tomkins Square. Heinrich has spent the past year pilfering this old shantytown, trying to be the man of the family. Poignant story."

"How strange…he found us. He happened to be here…" She didn't know how to phrase the words, because it had been too long since she was willing to believe God would intervene.

"I think God sent him along," Micah finished for her, and she had never heard that tone from him. Halting. Almost…tentative.

The darkness between them seemed to throb with uncertainty.

"I think you're right," Jocelyn finally agreed.

Restoration did not burst over her in a Damascus Road experience, yet Jocelyn's heart expanded until in a shimmering wash of wonder she embraced the truth of it. "Micah, what would you say if I told you that I… that I believe I've…forgiven God, for not being Who I thought He ought to be?" She sniffed, finishing in a ragged whisper, "And I'm trying to believe that He'll forgive me, for not being faithful, like you and Katya."

His fingers brushed against her face once more, then traced a tender path down her nose, to her chin. "I'd say you're in a better place than I am."

"I thought so, earlier." The blackness inside her for so long was fading to the gray wash of the early-morning sky in the moments before sunrise.

She stirred, searching with her fingers until they bumped into a forearm hard as the post to which he had been tied. "It's worse, to suffer alone, Micah. You never know when your mind is your friend, or your worst enemy."

He took hold of her fingers, a crushing grip born, Jocelyn knew, of memories he would grapple with the rest of his life. She lay quietly, wishing she were stronger, wishing she could see, but grateful she couldn't. Ever sensitive to atmosphere, she knew some secrets that needed to be brought into the light could only be shared under the merciful cover of darkness.

Chadwick had never spoken to her of the tortures he suffered, except at night. He would drift into her bedroom, sprawl into the boudoir chair and tell her things she had promised never to reveal.

Perhaps if she had encouraged him, if she had reached out to hold his hand as she was now holding Micah's, perhaps Chadwick would still be alive.

The internal sunrise coalesced into gold-rimmed determination: it was time, time to rid her soul of secrets that had kept her in bondage for ten long years. And in revealing those secrets at last, perhaps she could help Micah find the courage to rid his own soul of nightmares.

"What happened to you in that awful warehouse?" she asked him as simply as she could. "Will you tell me?"

Chapter Twenty-One

"I'll try," Micah said, his voice hoarse. "I think it would be easier if I were doing something while I talked. Do you think you're ready to try a little broth? It's probably cold by now, but you need the nourishment."

Jocelyn heard the undertone of fear. "I have the constitution of a pair of draft horses. I'll be fine, Micah. My leg scarcely hurts at all."

"Little liar. Heinrich fetched a bar of carbolic soap from his mother. While you were unconscious, he stood watch so I could light a candle. I cleaned the gash, and bound it with the last of your petticoats. I know what I saw. Don't think you can fool a Secret Service operative."

"Perhaps you should have been a physician. It aches some, Micah. But truly, I feel much better. Some broth would be wonderful." She'd eat snake soup if it would help ease his worry. If only wounded souls could be washed out with carbolic soap to keep them from festering. If only…

Her internal struggle against inadequacy stirred.

But despite her physical enervation, Jocelyn flung the self-flagellant's whip aside, astonished when it disappeared without a flick of protest.

Micah had taught her how it felt to be loved, to be cherished regardless of glaring personal flaws. He thought she was beautiful—inside and out. All he needed was for her to reciprocate in kind. So she waited, giving him the gift of restful silence while he sorted through his thoughts.

After he rummaged about, then held an uncorked bottle filled with lukewarm but surprisingly tasty beef broth to her lips, he began to talk. "...and I reached the bottom, far beyond the grief of losing my wife and son. I felt helpless when they died, but not stripped of everything that I believed made me a man. A...man of faith. The last couple of nights...down in the belly of that stinking basement, I finally..." In the darkness he emitted a huff of a laugh. "Let's just say I finally knew how you felt all these years, why you were so angry at God. At me." He sighed heavily. "Will you forgive me, for being such a sanctimonious prig?"

"Even when I was angry I never thought you were—well, I won't even say the words, because they do not describe the Micah MacKenzie I know. You're too hard on yourself. You were never a hypocrite, Micah. I wouldn't have admitted it, but I could see you believed everything you said, believed with all your heart. You were doing the best you knew how to live by faith. At the time I didn't want to hear it. What I did want—" She stopped dead, stricken all of a sudden with shyness.

"What did you want, sweetheart?"

It was time. Her heart banged against her rib cage.

Somehow in the dark Micah had maneuvered her to a sitting position so that her back rested against her cloak, which he had folded into a cushion to place between her and the cold stone wall. He had also removed all the pins from her hair. No matter that he was cold and tired and hurting and afraid. Still he protected her, nurtured her—understood her.

Loved her.

She found herself combing her fingers through the tangled mass of hair streaming down her back and shoulders, fashioning a braid as though the prosaic task emboldened her resolve.

She might be a wilting wallflower after all.

Impatient, she tossed the half-braided hair over her shoulder. "You want to know what I wanted? I wanted your faith in the goodness of God. I wanted to hug the way I felt when you were with me as though the feelings were my favorite doll. I wanted…you." She stammered the confession but, as always, once the flow began it took on a life all its own. "From the very first time you looked at me, on my wedding day, you saw… me. Not just a gawky redhead with too many freckles, wearing a thirty-year-old gown that made her look like a moldy cupcake."

"Would you be terribly disillusioned if I told you there's a vindictive part of me that would like nothing better than to stuff every member of that family into the back of a Black Maria and send them to Second District Prison for what they did to you?"

"I should have been strong enough to believe my own family, not my husband's. No, don't say anything else, don't hold my hand right now." A watery laugh escaped. "I want to remember that I found the courage all on my own, when I say words I've never spoken to another man."

"All right." His voice was awash in tenderness.

"I thought I'd forgotten you. Then, in Richmond, that day in my parlor? The first time you touched me, I knew I would never be the same again. I was so afraid, of so many things, but most of all, I was afraid you would sense how very much I wanted you to hold me. To comfort me. To protect me in all the ways I used to believe a man shows that he cares for a woman. Ways my husband never did, but you have from the moment you put your arm around my shoulders so carefully. I've soaked up your love, and never offered mine in return."

"Don't, sweetheart. You don't have to say anything more. I can wait. Jocelyn? Do you understand? I can wait."

"Well, I can't," she snapped out, edgy in her awkwardness. "Micah, I never loved Chadwick as my husband, but—" *God? What if he doesn't believe me?* "—I love you. I do. Do you believe me?"

"And why wouldn't I, when I've seen it shining from your eyes every time you look at me, from the glow that lights up your face whenever I walk into the room." His fingertips found her face in the dark and lovingly stroked her cheeks, her chin. "And the virago who rescued me from the pit, with only her courage and a whiffletree bolt? How could I not believe how much that incredible woman loves me?"

"Oh."

He stirred, then she felt his breath and the softest of kisses fluttered against each eye. "Someday you'll have to tell me that story. But I think there's something else you need to tell me first. Something that's been eating you alive for years."

"Yes." She was never more grateful for darkness than now, when she was about to break a vow forced upon her by her husband on her wedding night, with the one man who more than anyone else on earth had earned the right to know. Yet she didn't quite know how to turn the key in a lock rusted over with shame. "Did you ever wonder why after being married over five years, Chadwick and I never had children?"

"Yes, I wondered." He gave her cheek a final pat, then settled on the lumpy mattress beside her, far enough away that they weren't touching, close enough to reassure her of his presence. "I even made some discreet inquiries. You've had a rough time of it, haven't you?"

"Everyone blamed me. They said I was barren, that I wasn't even a woman— It doesn't matter now."

"I think it matters very much, because you believed them. I don't. Why did you never have a child, Jocelyn? Go ahead, say it. Remember, nothing you reveal will surprise or shock me."

A laugh bubbled up, then all of a sudden harsh sobs ripped through Jocelyn like the gash that had ripped open her leg—deep, wrenching cries that stole her breath. She couldn't see, she couldn't breathe, and the panic clawed her insides. *"I...can't...breathe...."*

"Shh. I'm here, love. I'm here. Let it out, that's it, just let all the hurt and anger and pain come out. You've held on to it for too long...."

She heard his voice, the deep bass tones lapping over her in gentle waves, felt the calm stroke of his hand, rubbing her arm, up and down, up and down so that gradually the frantic beat of her heart slowed, the racking sobs dwindled. A clean trickle of breath seeped into her lungs, then another, until shame no longer whirled like sharp knives around her.

"I never had a child, because Chadwick and I never—" She had to clear her throat, and when Micah pressed the bottle of water into her shaking hands she gulped it down, almost choking because she needed to say the words, needed to get the confession done. "We never sh-shared a bed. He was...he was— Micah, Chadwick preferred to spend his time...with other men. Oh, God forgive me. I promised I'd never tell. I promised."

"Sweetheart, you've done nothing wrong. Nothing. I'd guessed, some weeks ago, about Chadwick. And the truth can't hurt him now."

"How can you love me? I wasn't enough of a woman to help him. He told me that, over and over again. I was his wife, but I couldn't help him. Now I've betrayed him, I revealed his secret. It was a secret, Micah."

"It was a secret he had no right to inflict upon you, Jocelyn. As for your not being enough of a woman..." She could hear the throttled anger in his voice, but the hand stroking her arm with such tenderness never faltered. "That was a desperate lie foisted upon an innocent young girl, because he was a desperate man with no other place to go. His family never knew, I take it?"

"No. I was so full of shame, and there was nobody else to go to, nobody I could trust."

"That's why he killed himself, isn't it?"

"Yes. He left a note, apologizing for ruining my life. He asked me to keep his secret so that his family wouldn't be dishonored, and told me he'd put money in a bank in Scotland for me. He left instructions and promised I should be c-comfortable the rest of my life. But he told me to keep that a secret, as well, especially from his family. I think he was afraid of what they might do. I've been living off the interest." Her throat was hot, and the wracking episode left her drained, emptied out, until all that was left was a hollow shell. "I never needed the largesse of the Binghams, or the Brocks. B-But I might have been wrong. Because I think Chadwick may have stolen that money—from Portia."

She felt the shock ripple through Micah, though he only made an encouraging noise in his throat. "If I find out it's true, I'll have to think what to do. I don't know…he stole it for me, not for himself. Micah, he wasn't an evil man, no matter what he did. Just…a tortured one."

"I'd never brand him as 'evil,' sweetheart. But ultimately he was a selfish man, living his way of life at your expense, then taking his own, leaving you to face the consequences alone."

"I was far more unhappy living a lie with him, than I was living it after he died. I was a woman of independent means, beholden to nobody, because of those funds. Now—" she gulped noisily "—Katya might have more money than I do, if we discover that those funds were stolen."

"Let's not worry about those funds right now," he said, very gently.

"You're right, of course. 'Sufficient unto the day?' Isn't it interesting? I haven't read the Bible in years, yet lately all the verses I learned as a girl keep popping into my mind." She was babbling, and with a watery sniffle gushed out the rest. "Even though he probably stole from his own aunt—and, you may as well know, I find a certain ironic justice in that, considering what Portia really is—but even knowing those funds are probably tainted, I can't be angry at Chadwick any longer. I don't want you to be, either...."

"Mmm. Well, while we're confessing, I'll share that I do feel sorry for him, for the struggles he must have faced. But you'll have to give me a while to forgive him for how the choices he made affected the young woman he had publicly vowed to love. To honor."

Moving like an arthritic old woman, Jocelyn carefully shifted her aching leg. Without a word Micah eased closer, and wrapped his arm around her shoulders. Only then did she feel the last of the tension relinquish its choke hold, and a murmuring sigh slipped out as she rested her head against the comforting bulk of his chest. "Part of the reason I turned my back on God was because I couldn't forgive Chadwick. I was so angry, for so long. I felt cheated, and betrayed. It poisoned my mind. It took years for me to realize that he, too, must have felt betrayed. He needed understanding, but—I wasn't able to offer it. So I couldn't forgive myself, either."

She paused, gathering strength from the spring-like rebirth God had breathed into her since she'd become reacquainted with Micah. "I suppose I knew forgiveness was the only way to heal. It doesn't matter whether you feel like it, or that you don't know how to go about it, or that the other person doesn't deserve it. You still have to be willing to try. Until now, I didn't care enough to make the effort. I wasn't a very nice person, Micah." She felt the growl in his chest, and hastily explained, "But I'm better now. I'm…trying to listen to God. He forgives us, doesn't He? Even for what seems to be unforgivable?"

"We'll discuss your 'niceness' later. But you're right, about the forgiveness part. Asking for it's the hard part. Or maybe…it's believing you've received it. I'll have to chew over that one myself." He hugged her. "See? I don't claim to have all the answers any longer."

He sounded so comfortable with his own flawed humanity that Jocelyn found the courage to say, "If I hadn't married Chadwick, we never would have met. And you wouldn't have an inside informer to help solve this case."

"Well, when you put it like that…"

Drowsy and almost at peace, Jocelyn closed her eyes and drifted into sleep, the steady rhythm of Micah's heartbeat beneath her ear.

Heinrich returned sometime later, rousing Micah from the light doze he'd allowed himself. His arm was stiff because he hadn't moved it, not wanting to disturb Jocelyn's slumber. Compared to the suffering he'd endured while tied to that chair, holding the woman he loved was pure pleasure. Now, as the boy lit the candle and carefully placed it in a hollow space where one of the stones in the wall had fallen out, Micah eased away from her side. She murmured a little, but didn't awaken as he lowered her into a more comfortable reclining position.

"We go soon," Heinrich whispered. "Before light. *Moeder* has readied a bed, for the lady. And… I brought a cart, so you don't have to carry her."

"The police?"

"Still there. But the one on the corner is leaning against a telegraph pole. He is asleep."

"Will you stay here, with Mrs. Tremayne, while I go have a quick look around myself? Mostly I just want to stretch my legs," he added quickly, and Heinrich's small face lost the defensiveness. "I'll be back soon. Say, fifteen minutes? If Mrs. Tremayne should wake, would you reassure her? If you talk with her like you and I have talked, I'd appreciate it." Watching the dark eyes in the candlelight, Micah offered his hand. "Agreed?" he asked, and after a moment the boy reluctantly thrust his hand out.

By his rough calculation, only fourteen minutes had elapsed by the time he reconnoitered the three-block landscape, verifying Heinrich's report. A waning moon in the now-cloudless sky shone on the policemen's ominous silhouettes. The one slacker continued to drowse against the telegraph pole. The others walked their beat, swinging their billy clubs with each step. Twice carriages rolled by on the street they'd have to cross to reach Riverside; in the distance Micah could hear the rattle and clatter of the Ninth Avenue El.

He returned to the cellar in thoughtful silence.

"Did you cover the hole?" Heinrich instantly demanded, not waiting for the answer as he shot up the steps to see for himself.

Smiling a little, Micah settled onto the floor beside Jocelyn; Heinrich returned, lit the candle and wriggled around Micah to Jocelyn's side.

"Would you like some broth?" he asked her, his gaze openly adoring. "Chef François is the best in all of New York."

"Thank you, Heinrich. I believe I would." As he

went to fetch it, she looked up at Micah with anxious eyes. "Is it safe for us to move? He warned me about the policemen."

"What do you think, Heinrich?" Micah asked, as the boy offered Jocelyn the jar of beef broth, keeping his back to Micah.

The small body visibly relaxed. "We need to go while the policeman sleeps, I think."

"I agree." Micah exchanged a warm glance with Jocelyn. "Then as soon as Mrs. Tremayne finishes her broth, we'll head out." He watched her expression soften as she thanked Heinrich for the soup, watched her praise without patronizing his courage and ingenuity.

And the thought seared into Micah's heart: *this woman was meant to be a mother.*

He loved her with every fiber of his being. But Micah didn't know if he possessed the courage to wait in fearful agony for nine months, wondering if he would be forced to watch her life bleed away, or be told that his baby was not strong enough to live.

Chapter Twenty-Two

Jocelyn remembered the journey as a series of wild fluctuations between nerve-shredding silences and noises that rattled her brain. The silent, moonlit night had become their enemy. Every creak of the crude, two-wheeled cart echoed like cannon shot, and Micah's labored breaths hurt her almost as much as the pain in her leg. When they reached the shelter of the last building, her heart sank. The magnitude of their escape route lay before them in a wide swath of deserted avenue, with a lone figure plainly visible, propped against a telegraph pole.

Micah carefully lowered the handles, then straightened and flexed his shoulders before turning to lean over Jocelyn. "All right?" he mouthed, and she nodded.

Heinrich sidled up, his face a dirt-smeared oval with a jutting chin. "If the policeman sees you, I will... will—"

Micah's hand curved over one narrow shoulder. "Divert him?" Heinrich nodded, and Jocelyn watched in bemused silence as Micah affectionately tugged the boy's cap down over his eyes. "Take care of yourself, sprout. I'll do my part."

"Two blocks straight ahead, wait just inside Riverside Park, remember? I will meet you there."

Before she could stop the gesture Jocelyn reached out, her fingers closing around an arm skinny as a broomstick handle. "Heinrich? Please be careful."

He replied with the rude sound she deserved. "They won't catch me. I will be there. Do not worry, Missus."

And he disappeared into the night.

Hands braced on either side of the cart, Micah brought his face next to Jocelyn's. "I love you," he breathed. "This next stretch is probably going to hurt even more. Hold on, firefly."

Before she could respond, he picked up the handles. When the sleeping policemen lurched upright, shouting as he pelted into the vacant lot behind them, Micah pulled the cart out of the shadows.

Halfway across the street, the policeman's whistle blew.

Teeth rattling, Jocelyn clamped her hands over the sides of the cart, bracing herself to help Micah the only way she could. Fiery darts of pain exploded throughout her body. She ignored them. Over the noise of the cart and Micah's labored pants, she heard more shouts from somewhere in the stygian depths of the abandoned shantytown.

Nobody ran toward her and Micah. Nobody ordered them to halt, or surrounded them and brandished their billy clubs in their faces.

When they reached the other side of the street, Micah did not slow down or stop. To the north, hulking shapes of half-finished mansions loomed above a stretch of flat land and scrubby trees. Jocelyn heard the mournful wail of a ship steaming along the Hudson, the distant ululation of a train whistle. Dizzy from the pain, nauseated from the cart's merciless jostling, she fixed her gaze on Micah's straining silhouette, and prayed.

An interminable span of time later, all motion and noise abruptly ceased. Jocelyn forced her frozen fingers to relinquish their death grip on the rough sides of the cart. She would have spoken, but her mouth was too dry.

Slowly, Micah lowered the cart handles, then stood, hands dangling at his sides, head bowed, shoulders slumped in exhaustion. Beyond him the river flowed silvery-black beneath a star-splattered western sky.

And there, dashing toward them in the starlight, skinny arms waving in triumphant circles, was Heinrich.

When he reached them, Jocelyn watched with tears filling her eyes as Micah lifted the boy completely off his feet, then gathered him into a ferocious hug. For a brief instant, Heinrich dangled motionless, then his arms wrapped around Micah's neck, and he laid his head on Micah's shoulder.

Dawn was tiptoeing across the eastern horizon when they reached the shanty where Heinrich lived with his mother and four-year-old sister, Elfie.

"*Moeder,* they are here!" He scampered ahead to greet the woman who appeared in the doorway. She held up a hand lamp, which allowed Micah to maneuver the cart around a variety of objects Jocelyn once would have considered trash, to the entrance of what was now her home.

"We have little. But you are welcome." Heinrich's mother introduced herself as Magda Schuller. "I have prepared a bed for the lady, and some food."

"We have caused you too much trouble," Jocelyn began, miserably aware that this woman was endangering herself and her children for them.

"It is no trouble." Sadness clung to her like gray soot. "I am sorry I have not much to offer."

Micah carefully lifted her from the cart, and Jocelyn briefly surveyed Magda Schuller's home. Scarcely larger than a gardener's shed, the structure was pieced together with mismatched boards, rough-cut logs and a tar-paper roof held in place by thin slats. A narrow length of pipe protruded from the roof, functioning as a chimney. Jocelyn ended her survey with Magda, a slight woman wearing a scarf on her head and a faded shawl tied in a knot at her waist. She stood in the open doorway, her expression carefully blank. "You are offering everything you have," Jocelyn told her, fighting to keep her voice steady. "Mr. MacKenzie and I are honored."

"See, *Moeder?*" Heinrich grabbed his mother's hand and tugged her over to them. "They are not like those *hoechnawsyich* you clean houses for—"

"Heinrich!" She cuffed the back of his head, then smashed him against her side. "I can see myself, these people. Now, go. I have laid a fire. You will please light it? The lady is injured, and needs warmth." Almost shyly, she nodded to Micah. "My son says you are in danger, with the police. They will not look for you here, I think."

"We won't be in danger much longer, Mrs. Schuller, thanks to you and your son," Micah said. "I appreciate more than you'll ever know, your taking in two fugitives."

His arms tightened around Jocelyn. "I'm not setting you down, so please stop wriggling. In my current state, I might drop you."

The night sky had faded to smudged gray, so she could clearly see that fatigue had carved deep lines on his brow, and either side of his mustache. His hair was disheveled, matted with perspiration, his collarless shirt streaked with dirt and dried blood. Equally concerned for him, Jocelyn murmured into his ear, "You're exhausted. I can feel you trembling."

His mouth curved in a breathtaking smile. "I can still carry the woman I love over the threshold. Look on it as a dress rehearsal."

Silenced, Jocelyn ducked her head, and gave herself into his keeping.

The New York office of the Secret Service was located in the post office building, in a large room divided by makeshift partitions into three cubicles. Within moments of Micah's appearance, at a little before eight o'clock in the morning, messenger boys were summoned, telegrams sent, and telephone operators were making dozens of calls—though none of them were to the police department.

Until Portia and Virgil Brock were arrested, Micah insisted on maintaining the illusion that he and Jocelyn were fugitives and that Jocelyn's surname was "Bingham." "Too many police lackeys on the Brock payroll," he said, his voice gravelly. He was beyond exhausted, buoyed only by elation, and determination.

"Don't like it," Operative-in-Charge Bagg, chief

official of the New York office, admitted. "Superintendent Byrnes resigned recently, you know. Had to—reformers created themselves a committee to investigate police corruption. So I see your point about the police, Operative MacKenzie. We certainly don't want to alert the wrong people. Until the charges against you and Mrs. Bingham are formally dropped, however, you will need to be accompanied by one of my operatives at all times, and stay out of sight."

"I agree." Micah's thoughts drifted back to Jocelyn, asleep when he'd left, guarded by a devoted Heinrich and the briskly efficient Magda Schuller. Heinrich's sister, Elfie, bright-eyed as a cricket, was enthralled with Jocelyn's hair, but when her mother instructed her not to touch it, Elfie obediently perched on a three-legged stool to maintain a silent vigil with her big brother.

For the moment, Micah could best protect them all through his absence.

"Back in October I brought an assistant with me from Washington," he said. "Jonathan Tanner. I've sent him a wire to one of our prearranged addresses. He's young, but a crackerjack bodyguard. So if you've no objections, I'd like him to resume duties as my nanny."

Operative Bagg regarded him for a long moment, his clean-shaven, youthful appearance turning sober. "The telegrapher approached me with your message, which I did not send, because your Mr. Tanner wired us late last night. His aunt was murdered in her home, the same night you were abducted. Made to look like robbery. Mr. Tanner claims the foul deed's a ringer for the one that happened in Richmond." After pondering the ceiling for a moment, he added, "Mr. Tanner further claims that there has been no police investigation whatsoever. You may well imagine his opinion of our city's police department is not…salutary?"

Dear God, how many more innocent people must suffer before You allow justice to be done? "Do you know Mr. Tanner's whereabouts?"

"He's a mysterious fellow, plays cards close to the vest. I don't frankly know where he is, only that he promised to be here by—" he glanced at a large wall clock "—half past eight. He, um, also promised to bring you a change of clothes."

"Efficient as always. I know I reek worse than a wet goat. Sorry. As soon as Mr. Tanner arrives, we'll take ourselves off to that hotel. While we're waiting…" He dug into his wrinkled, bloodstained trousers and produced a silver dollar coin, which he studied for a long moment before handing it to Bagg. "Mrs. Schuller pressed this into my hand as I was leaving. Probably her entire savings, but she knew it would be safer for me to hire a hansom, and neither Mrs. Bingham nor I had any change." He adamantly refused to take Mr. Schuller's Sunday suit, which Magda had unpacked from a dented steamer trunk. She was, Micah knew without her saying a word, hoping to have saved it for Heinrich, yet willingly offered it to a stranger.

"You can see why I risked my neck to walk a few miles instead. If we can find out how long Mrs. Schuller has had this coin, and where it came from, you might discover a trail to follow."

Operative Bagg picked up a magnifying glass from his desk. "Mmm. Looks like the work of a gang we've been trying to arrest for several years. They passed a lot of coinage. Horse Market gang, they call themselves. Either tin or copper on the inside, most likely. Decent engraving, but notice the surface isn't quite as sharp as the real thing. We've found a number of these spurious goods in the last two months, mostly turned in by shop-and saloon keepers in the Seventh Ward."

"Yessir. I'd like to replace that, if we can arrange it, with a real one, for Mrs. Schuller. It's the least she deserves." He blinked, fighting a wave of dizziness. "There's more." A plain oak straight chair had been shoved against the partition. Micah sat, then with the exaggerated care of a drunk removed his right shoe, fumbled inside the toe and at last produced the folded bills Jocelyn had given to him before she fell asleep. "Here's the proof we've been trying to unearth for eight years, courtesy of the most courageous woman I've ever known."

His face screwed up in distaste, Bagg gingerly accepted the bills and spread them open on top of his desk. He gave a low whistle. "Amazing. Some of the best counterfeits I've ever seen. Very disturbing."

"Mmm. Probably some of Benny Foggarty's finest work. But as soon as we arrest him and the Brocks, that ought to finally dry up the last of the manufacturing and wholesaling of counterfeit notes from out of New York City." He wriggled his foot back into his shoe. "Those notes, however, are my primary motivation for not alerting the police. Yes, we have proof to cut off at least two snake heads in this nest of vipers. But to cripple them beyond recovery, we're also going to need the molds and the plating apparatus…" His brain was shutting down, he realized groggily. He couldn't think of the words. "Without the identities of all their wholesalers…"

"Operative MacKenzie! Sir…" Bulging valise in one hand, Jonathan Tanner burst into the cubicle and rushed across the floor, skidding to a halt in front of Micah. The flat cap he wore was slipping, his hair beneath it ill-kempt; a streak of dirt blackened one of his cheekbones. "So it wasn't a lie. You *are* here. I wasn't sure, I've been trying to— I…" He lifted his spare hand to momentarily cover his face. "I came as fast as I could, sir," he continued, all the emotion throttled. "I'm relieved to see you're alive."

Micah scraped together what he hoped was a reassuring smile. "Yes, I'm alive, looks notwithstanding." He hesitated, then added heavily, "I wish I could think of what to say, about your aunt. I feel responsible."

The younger man shook his head with a violence that belied his subdued voice. "Maybe so. Maybe we're both responsible, for using her house. But if I'd been there, she wouldn't be dead."

Without warning he hurled the valise on the floor at Micah's feet. His hands clenched into fists. "I saw him leave. *I saw him,* but I was so concerned about my aunt I didn't follow him. And she was already dead. She never hurt anybody in her life. If I hadn't been staying with her—"

"Don't, Jon." Micah heaved himself to his feet and wrapped a bracing arm around his assistant. Jonathan shoved him away, but when Micah staggered, almost taking them both to the floor, the younger man clutched his arm in a steadying grip.

"M-Mr. MacKenzie…she's dead, and the murdering dog who killed her escaped. I let him escape." With a hoarse groan, Jonathan ceased resisting Micah's comfort and stood, shoulders shaking, while he unleashed a storm of grief.

Operative-in-Charge Bagg discreetly left the room, returning some moments later with a parcel wrapped in butcher paper tied with a string—and a bemused expression on his face. "There's a vendor on the street corner," he explained absently, glancing sideways at Jonathan, who was now sitting hunched over in the chair Micah had vacated. His eyes were red, but he was calm. "Best pretzels in the City. Thought you gentlemen could use some food."

Bagg thrust the parcel at Micah. "Hansom's waiting, manned by a driver we trust, to transport you and Mr. Tanner to the hotel. Ah…before you leave, thought you should know about a rather disheveled young woman, a servant from her dress, I encountered outside. I've detailed Operative Raynor to interrogate her. She's a mute, but literate. I tripped over her brogans just now, on the post office steps. She'd apparently been hunkered down behind one of the columns since dawn. I was set to arrest her for loitering when she caught sight of my badge, at which point she shoved a writing tablet in front of my face."

"Katya!" Gladness bounded through Micah. "She's Mrs. Bingham's maid! Is she all right? Did she give you the other two bogus bills from Virgil Brock's room?"

"Girl's stubborn, and unharmed." He unbent enough to smile a little. "And yes, the counterfeit bills have been added to the two Mrs. Tremayne gave you. Though plainly distraught over her mistress, she is being treated with all due civility. I have assured her—repeatedly—that both you and Mrs. Bingham are alive, and reasonably healthy."

Along with the smile, a twinkle appeared in his eyes. "She might not talk, but she manages to convey her thoughts adequately through pencil and tablet. She also knows how to stomp her foot to great effect. You needn't fret over the matter, Mr. MacKenzie. I have everything well in hand."

Light-headed with relief, Micah nodded. "Of course. In that case, I leave her in your capable hands." He stooped to pick up the valise, desisted when Jonathan whipped out a hand as he rose, hefting the valise with him. "One other matter," he said, looking at his assistant. "If possible, I'd like to borrow your best artist. While I clean up, Mr. Tanner can provide a description of his aunt's murderer. I'll be interested to know whether it matches the description of the man who abducted—and was returning to murder—me last night."

Chapter Twenty-Three

When Jocelyn awakened, she lay for a long time with her eyes closed, soaking in the soft sounds around her until her conscious mind accepted that she was truly safe. Blinking, she fumbled to push a dangling strand of hair off her face, and languidly studied the interior of the crude shanty.

The door was open, washing the room in fresh air and the peach-hued glow of late afternoon. A length of clothesline had been fastened with a nail to a board in the tilted wall and a rough support beam at the foot of the cot where Jocelyn lay. Pinned to the clothesline, a curtain made from a hodge-podge of stitched-together fabrics afforded her a small measure of privacy.

The scent of coal mingled with a faint medicinal aroma that she gradually realized emanated from the vicinity of her wounded leg. Experimentally she tried to move it, then lay very still, biting her lip until the shock of pain subsided.

A small scrubbed face peeked around the make-shift curtain.

"*Moeder!* The lady...she iss awake." A little girl

with red cheeks and Heinrich's dark eyes hurried over to the cot, her wide-eyed gaze never leaving Jocelyn. "Can I to touch her hair now?"

The woman Jocelyn remembered only vaguely appeared beside her daughter. "Hello. Do not be afraid. I am Magda Schuller, Heinrich's mother." Today the head scarf was gone, her hair scraped back in a bun. "This is my daughter, Elfie." Calmly, she nudged the girl aside to rest a red, chapped hand against Jocelyn's forehead and cheek. "Is good. No fever. Does your leg pain you? While you sleep, Mr. MacKenzie and I change the bandage. Is bad cut, but no sign of infection. I rub with witch hazel, to help the pain."

"*Moeder!* Can I touch her hair? You will ask her, you promised."

Magda grimaced. "Please forgive. She has not seen a person with red hair. I will not let her bother you. Elfie! You will go and stir the soup, then we will see. Do not to touch the griddle." Without fuss she removed the curtain in order to monitor her daughter.

Elfie's lower lip protruded in a pout, but without another word she trudged across the tiny room to a two-burner laundry stove, where the soup simmered in a large round pot. Jocelyn watched in amazement as the little girl, who couldn't have been more than four years old, picked up a long spoon and deftly stirred the contents.

When Jocelyn's sister, Hannah, had been four, she spent her days playing with her collection of elegantly dressed dolls and a toy china tea set from England. Jocelyn swallowed the lump congealing in her throat. "If you like, I'll teach Elfie how to braid my hair. The lesson should keep her happily occupied for hours!

Um…can you tell me how long I've been sleeping, and where Mr. MacKenzie is?"

"You haf slept much. Is late afternoon, near to sunset. Mr. MacKenzie promise to return before dark. I do not know where he went. Only that he also promise to bring a doctor, and a carriage."

Smiling, Jocelyn thanked Magda for taking such good care of her. "Mr. MacKenzie and I could not have landed in more capable hands."

The other woman shrugged, looking uncomfortable. She pressed her hands over her apron, straightened Jocelyn's cape, which was serving as an extra blanket, smoothed the makeshift curtain, then finally waved her hand jerkily in the air.

"We do not always live here, like this."

"I know," Jocelyn said, her heart going out to the stoic woman. "Heinrich told us. You lost your home, and your husband, didn't you?"

With a long-suffering sigh, Magda dabbed her face with a corner of her apron. *"Jah."* She smiled sadly. "My husband was a shoemaker, very skilled. But last year, and the year before, times are bad. Nobody could buy shoes. He went to a bank to borrow money. Then… the bank close. Some people come, say we must pay for our house, or we haf to leave. And so…we come to here. One day my Kurt goes to look for work. He never comes home. I take *da kinderen,* and we look…"

Her throat muscles quivered, but after a moment she continued steadily, "We never find him. So Heinrich say to me '*Moeder,* I am the man of our family now.'"

"Heinrich is a good son."

"He sees too much, too young. He is…not gentle, like his father was. He does not trust people."

"I'm so sorry, Mrs. Schuller."

"Is strange. He trust you, and Mr. MacKenzie." While she talked, Magda picked up a battered pan with a scattering of half-peeled root vegetables. "Heinrich tells me Mr. MacKenzie say God used him, to help." She kept her gaze on the vegetables. "I do not know what to tell my son. God would not to use a boy who is become a thief, and a beggar. Heinrich does not think I know. But I do. God does not visit people who live in places like this, or behave like my son."

Jocelyn felt Magda's bitterness as though it were a live coal, handed to her by a woman who could not have been more different from Jocelyn than a princess from a scullery maid. Yet in that moment, she knew they were sisters, joined not by the heritage of blood, but by the heritage of grief and disillusionment.

"Until lately," she said, groping for words, "I believed that God didn't visit anybody—poor or wealthy. But I'm beginning to see Him differently now." An almost-urgent compulsion nudged her hand to slide across the soft wool cloak that covered her until her fingertips brushed Magda's frayed sleeve. "Magda? God's Son was born in a place like this. And He ate a lot of meals with thieves and beggars. Please don't be ashamed of your home. There is more warmth and welcome here than I've found in the stone mansions where I lived for five years."

"You are a good woman, Mrs. Tremayne. And a kind one." In the gauzy light streaming through the door, her troubled countenance softened. "I will remember what you say to me."

"Then I hope you'll remember one more thing," Jocelyn murmured, though sleep weighed her eyelids down until she had no recourse but to close them, "Heinrich…is taking care of his family as best he can. I believe God understands." She could feel a smile curving her lips. "If I recall correctly, Jesus forgave a robber from the cross. And… He adored…children."

As she drifted back into sleep, somewhere she heard the faintest echo of what sounded like a heavenly chuckle.

Scrubbed clean, wearing fresh clothes and feeling, finally, more alive than dead, Micah tugged out his pocket watch as the carriage rolled past the large street clock next to the Fifth Avenue Hotel. His watch, like his heart, ran fast.

"It's almost six-thirty. Can we make it by seven?"

"I'll ask the driver." Jonathan glanced at Katya, sitting beside him in rigid silence. "Excuse me," he murmured, his voice gentling. He twisted to open the glass, then shouted the question to the driver.

At the next block the driver fought through the still-heavy pedestrian traffic, turning west on 25th. After steadying the horses, he snapped the whip, sending the carriage down the street at a fast trot.

"My dear chap," Dr. Aloysius commented to Micah, "I will be of little use to the young lady if we suffer a fatal mishap in the process of racing to her rescue."

"I promised to be back by sunset," Micah said. "I don't want her to be afraid."

Katya unbent enough to smack her palms together. Unable to write in the crowded carriage filled with people, and the load of parcels for Jocelyn and the Schullers she refused to relinquish, she glared across the murky interior at Micah.

"You're absolutely right," he admitted. Over the last several months he'd come to know this girl almost as well as Jocelyn. "She's a stout heart, and won't be afraid at all. Nor should you, about her. Mrs. Schuller and I cleaned the wound and bound it tight. It wasn't even bleeding when I left. The only reason I'm bringing Dr. Aloysius along is..." Stumped, he glanced across at Jon.

"Is because Operative MacKenzie himself is afraid," Jonathan finished dryly.

"Not like I was twenty-four hours ago," Micah responded without heat, understanding his assistant's own struggle.

Thirty-two minutes later the carriage rolled to a smooth halt on the broad avenue planned a decade earlier by Frederick Law Olmsted, whose vision included rolling green hills on bluffs overlooking the Hudson. Doubtless those dreams had not included clusters of shanties strung in a ragtag row behind the wooden fence lining Riverside Drive.

The driver opened the door, and Micah leaped out. "I'll let them know we're not the police," he said.

"Mr. MacKenzie!" Heinrich darted out from beneath a stack of warped window frames leaning against the side of the shanty. "It is you! You're back. You're back!" He flung himself into Micah's arms, jabbering in an excited mixture of English, Dutch and German as Micah swung him around in a triumphant circle.

"We're a little late." He gestured to the others. "These people have come with me, to help."

"I'll perform the introductions," Jonathan said. "Go ahead, go rescue the damsel in distress. We'll catch up. Heinrich?" He offered his hand to the boy. "I'm Mr.

Tanner. I was supposed to be watching over Operative MacKenzie here. He slipped through my fingers, and I understand I have you to thank for taking care of him when I wasn't able to."

Micah left them to it. With Katya on his heels, he sprinted to the front of the shanty, where Mrs. Schuller stood in the doorway, holding little Elfie. For a long moment the woman did not speak, her gaze moving between him and Katya. Then her lips curved in a grave smile. "We haf been waiting long, Mr. MacKenzie. But your lady is well. She tells me she has much faith in you." And with a dignified bow she and Elfie stepped aside.

He ducked through the doorway, and stopped dead. Jocelyn sat in a carved oak parlor chair, her leg propped on a crate. A patchwork quilt discreetly covered her from the waist down. Light from a smoky kerosene lamp hanging from a nail in the rafters illuminated her face. Moving like a sleepwalker, Micah approached her side, then fell to his knees. She reached up, touching her fingers to his freshly shaved cheek. "Do you know what I've been doing?" she whispered in a choked voice.

He covered her hand with his. "Staying safe, and sleeping?"

"That, too." Her eyes glistened. "I've…been praying. To God. For you."

His breath huffed out, and with a hoarse sound he buried his face in the side of her neck. Her arms wrapped around his shoulders, and he heard her soft voice murmuring in his ear, about love, and healing, and faith. Oblivious to their audience, Micah finally lifted his head and pressed a fervent kiss upon her half-parted lips, and the words ceased altogether.

Chapter Twenty-Four

By the time they left the shanty, Katya had written two pages of questions for Jocelyn, and four pages outlining her own exploits after she sneaked out of the Brocks' mansion at dawn. Amazingly, Heinrich and Elfie developed an instantaneous bond with the girl, communicating effortlessly with a tangled blend of words and pantomime. While Dr. Aloysius tended to Jocelyn, Heinrich answered most of Katya's questions about what had transpired with her mistress since the previous night.

"Remarkable young woman, that Katya," Jonathan observed to Micah, who had refused to leave Jocelyn's side. "And what a lucky stroke that Operative-in-Charge Bagg tripped over her on the post office steps this morning."

"I'd call it something other than luck," Micah corrected lightly. "Did I tell you it was Jocelyn who taught her to read and write?"

"Only about a dozen times." Shaking his head, Jonathan moved out of the way, his expression closing up as he propped his shoulders against one of the shanty's support beams and crossed his arms over his chest.

Someday soon, Micah promised himself, he and Jocelyn together would have to formulate a plan to help Jon heal. Tenderness fluttered beneath his breastbone like thousands of tiny butterflies. *Together.* He liked the sound of that.

"Amazing constitution," Dr. Aloysius muttered beneath his breath several times as he applied adhesive plaster to close the incision, then wrapped the leg with a roll of fresh bandages from his medical bag. "I come prepared for a feverish, half-dead woman, and instead find a clean wound healing nicely, and an alert woman with excellent reflexes and healthy color."

A light blush stained Jocelyn's freckled cheeks, though in typical Jocelyn fashion she downplayed her own strengths. "Mrs. Schuller and Mr. MacKenzie are excellent nurses." She smiled down at Micah, who was sitting beside her on the floor. "You needn't have dragged the poor doctor all the way up here."

"I wasn't willing to take any more chances with your life."

"Speaking of her life," Jonathan put in, the hard edge more pronounced, "I forgot to tell you, while you were asleep a telegram from Chief Hazen arrived. Mrs. Bingham is officially off this case, as are you. Chief Hazen indicated that the decision was his, regardless of your own wire suggesting the same. For some reason he takes offense when his operatives are abducted and used as punching bags."

"Punching bags?" Jocelyn asked.

Micah grimaced. "And how did he learn those details, Mr. Tanner? What happened to your discretion?"

Jonathan shoved away from the beam and strolled over, standing over Micah with clenched fists. "I stuffed it inside the envelope along with my last report to Washington. You should have Dr. Aloysius take a look at those bruises and your ribs. I do a little boxing, Mrs. Bingham," he told Jocelyn without a shred of shame, "so I know what I'm talking about. That brigand hit him when Operative MacKenzie's hands were tied behind his back."

"Only twice." Micah heaved a sigh and rose, rested a reassuring hand on Jocelyn's shoulder and quelled Dr. Aloysius's concern with a look. "And I'm fine. Sore, but no busted ribs, all right? Let it rest, Jon."

"He killed my aunt. He was going to kill you. And those swine who found him at that warehouse let him go. They let him go free! He could have killed again."

"But he didn't," Micah reminded the angry young man firmly, glancing at Jocelyn. "The man's name is Vanetti, which is the name you heard spoken in the Brocks' library, correct?" Jocelyn nodded. "He's on the Wanted posters of almost every law enforcement agency on the East Coast, not to mention Pinkerton's. An alert police detective, not on the Brocks' payroll, nabbed him, largely because of Mr. Tanner's excellent description. Vanetti was on the platform at Grand Central, with a one-way ticket to Chicago. Took two more officers and a baggage handler to, ah, convince Vanetti to cooperate. Now he's in jail, where in due time he'll receive the punishment he deserves for his crimes."

He looked back at Jonathan. "This part of the investigation is over, Mr. Tanner. *Over*. Let it go."

Jonathan glared around the small shanty as though he expected someone to stab him with a pitchfork.

"I was supposed to protect my aunt, and she's dead because I listened to you. I spent two blasted hours traveling all the way to Brooklyn and back to mail that telegram. I'm supposed to be protecting you, not being sent to a corner like I was a piddling puppy! Aunt Maisie's murdered and you get yourself bushwhacked, all because you try to protect everyone but your own arrogant self."

"Mr. Tanner? Jonathan? I understand how you feel." Spoken in that liquid Southern drawl, Jocelyn's voice could have melted the iron girders supporting the El's tracks. "He's not really arrogant, he just cares too much sometimes. None of us is to blame for Mr. Vanetti's actions. We're only responsible for our own."

In the fitful light, Micah watched every muscle in his assistant's body tighten, though he merely inclined his head. "I don't know that I can agree. You saved his life, after all. Not me."

"Last night perhaps. How many times over these past months have you saved him, in silence and secrecy, when only God knew?" Jonathan shook his head, lips compressed into a thin line of renunciation. Compassion filled Jocelyn's eyes. "I lived with silence and secrets for so many years I'd almost forgotten what it feels like not to be afraid. Fear, and feeling helpless, are universal to the human soul, Jonathan. Blaming yourself, blaming God only feeds the fear."

"Mrs. Bingham—"

"My name is Jocelyn *Tremayne,*" she interrupted firmly, her hand searching for Micah. "As far as I'm concerned, Mrs. Bingham died last night, outside the Brocks' library door. Please, call me Mrs. Tremayne."

"Mrs. Tremayne, I'm glad Operative MacKenzie has

someone like you at his side." He shoved away from the post. "Sir, now that Operative-in-Charge Bagg has taken over the proceedings, you won't need an assistant any longer. The search warrants for the Brocks' residence have been issued, as well as warrants to search the bank where both Virgil and Augustus have offices. Operative-in-Charge Bagg has men watching both places, with orders to follow and apprehend any members of the Brock family should they try to flee. He informed me that he thought you might want to arrest the principals yourself, and is willing to wait until ten o'clock before initiating them himself. Called it poetic justice."

Micah tugged out his watch. Eight thirty-seven. If they left immediately, and went straight to the Brock mansion, he would have the satisfaction of shackling Portia Brock in handcuffs himself, hopefully in view of all the servants. As for Virgil...

"Micah? I want to be there, too," Jocelyn announced. "They were my husband's family, not my own, but I will always feel a sense of responsibility for what their greed did to you, to your father. To our country."

"You're only responsible for your own actions," Jon muttered.

Micah scowled, and would have reprimanded him except instead of shrinking into herself, Jocelyn unbelievably—laughed. "Mr. Tanner, you're absolutely right. How about if I want to be there because I'm working to control a vindictive streak, but haven't mastered it yet?"

The corner of Jonathan's mouth twitched. He darted a quick glance of apology toward Micah. Micah, still reeling from the sound of his beloved's musical laughter, shook his head. "Well, why not? Jocelyn deserves to be present for the coup de grâce as much as anyone. Is she able to travel, Dr. Aloysius?"

The physician pondered his expansive belly, scratched beneath his neat spade-shaped beard and finally nodded. "I would prefer her to be in a bed, resting, for at least a week. Based upon my examination, however, I must admit there is no compelling medical reason, beyond prudence, that would prohibit her from a short detour?" He made a tsking sound. "'Tis a sorry day indeed, when members of one of New York's finest families stand guilty of such malfeasance."

"An even sorrier day when their actions force people like Mrs. Schuller and her children to live in hovels like this," Jonathan stated shortly. "I'll escort Dr. Aloysius to the carriage. Since Mrs….ah… Tremayne…will require extra room, I'll catch the Ninth Avenue El."

"Thank you, Mr. Tanner." Dr. Aloysius closed his black leather bag and donned his bowler.

Frowning now, Micah watched his assistant offer stiff farewells to Magda, Katya and the two children. Jonathan skimmed little Elfie's soft cheek with his index finger, bunched his hand in a fist to deliver a mock punch to Heinrich's shoulder. He complimented Magda, and told Katya he admired her bravery, then ushered the doctor outside.

A niggle of presentiment zinged through Micah. Leaning down, he murmured to Jocelyn, "Will you wait here for me a moment? Please?"

After searching his face, she nodded. "I understand, Micah," she murmured back. "Go after him. Do what you can."

He waited until Dr. Aloysius was settled inside the carriage and Jonathan had started down Riverside

Drive. "I noticed you neglected to mention your destination, after you board the El," he said, falling into step beside the other man.

"I was hoping you hadn't." For several paces they walked in silence. "Mr. MacKenzie...let me go, sir."

"I will, Jon. But it's not easy." Clasping his hands behind his back, Micah looked toward the dark water of the Hudson River while he spoke. "Last night, I came within a hair's breadth of losing my faith in God. I thought I'd endured the worst tragedies a man can suffer. I thought I survived because I believed God would give me the strength to bear whatever life tossed my way."

Memories prickled along his spine. "But I'd never been tied to a chair and blindfolded, never left alone in the dark with no expectation of rescue, and the knowledge that two more people I love very much would likely die because of me. One of those people, Jon, is you."

Jonathan's head was lowered, his face averted; Micah was unable to read his expression. But at least he was listening. "I hope I never again feel the...the physical and emotional and spiritual paralysis, that I felt last night. If I do—" swallowing, Micah finished huskily "—if I do, I will remember that I survived it once before. I'll remember that God didn't really turn His back, any more than you and Jocelyn gave up trying to find me. We all come to forks in the road of life, Jon. I'd say you're at one right now."

"I can't work for the Secret Service any longer. No matter what you say, I...can't."

"I know."

"Then...what do you want from me?"

"I want to know that you'll remember me as a Christian who faltered, who shook a fist at God and asked Him why. And I want you to remember that I chose to take the fork in the road that leads back to trust, to faith. That's all." Stepping back, he unclasped his hands, spreading them wide. "If you come to a place where you believe you have nowhere to go, I'd like to know you'll come looking for me, if you're still not ready to trust God."

Slowly, Jonathan lifted his head, even more slowly nodded. "All right. I can't deny that I have a lot of doubts right now. I—I don't know what I think, about a lot of things. Operative MacKenzie…"

"Call me Micah. You're no longer working for me."

In the purplish-black of a cloudy night, Micah barely caught his faint smile. "Thanks, then—Micah. I won't forget. Anything."

"Be careful out there, all right? Boxing's a dangerous pastime, whether against another man's fist, or at shadows."

"Yes, sir. I mean, Micah." He hesitated. "Mrs. Tremayne is right. You're not arrogant at all."

He offered a hand, and Micah shook it, feeling the hard calluses on the edge of Jon's palms, the careful strength of his grip. *Protect him from developing calluses on his soul, Lord.*

A stray current of wind blew across the Hudson, sending white-tipped ripples splashing onto the shore like the rhythmic beat of a heart. For a moment or two after Jonathan Tanner melted into the darkness, Micah listened to the water, and the wind, relishing the sounds of nature. Of life.

Then he strode swiftly back to the shanty to fetch Jocelyn and Katya. Justice was waiting to be served. He reached into his pocket, removed the five-pointed star and pinned the badge in place.

Chapter Twenty-Five

Lights blazed from every window of the Brocks' stone mansion. The carriage halted directly in front of the twin pillars that flanked the brick walkway leading to the front doors.

Almost immediately, a stocky man wearing dark clothes and a bowler poked his face inside the carriage, and touched his fingers to his hat in acknowledgment of Jocelyn before focusing on Micah. "Operative MacKenzie? I'm to tell you that Mr. and Mrs. Brock are in residence. An hour gone, Julius went with several companions to a bowling alley on East Thirteenth Street. Operative-in-Charge Bagg deemed him a person of no consequence at this time, so Mr. Julius was not detained. Virgil Brock, however, was arrested not thirty minutes ago, while waiting for the Cortlandt Street ferry in Jersey City."

"Botheration!" Jocelyn forgot her manners, but was too incensed to care. "The coward. I was looking forward to gloating over him."

The charged atmosphere lightened; both men's faces momentarily relaxed.

"You'll still have an opportunity to gloat," Micah promised.

"We'd best make haste, sir. The orders are that as soon as you and Mrs. Bingham alight, everyone will converge at the front door."

"I assume the estate is surrounded, all entrances manned by trustworthy men?"

"Handpicked, sir."

Micah nodded, then turned to Jocelyn. "Are you ready?"

"I've been ready for weeks," she declared, ignoring a sudden attack of the jitters.

Micah carefully lifted her from the carriage, steadying her with a firm grip on her waist. "This might get ugly," he warned her. "From everything you've said, Portia's not likely to surrender easily, for all she'll be surrounded by a squad of Secret Service operatives and a couple of U.S. marshals." He handed her the cane Dr. Aloysius had provided, but did not release his hold until Jocelyn proved she could stand on her own.

"I'll be fine." She gripped the cane firmly in one hand, Micah's arm with the other. "For ten long years I allowed these two families to turn me into a weak, fearful creature. Those days are over."

They started up the walk, and with every step the pain in her leg yielded to the righteous confidence running like a stream of living water throughout her body. "Now I'm ready to show them the real Jocelyn Tremayne, a woman who most definitely will never again fear the Virgil or Portia Brocks in this world." With Micah's help, she managed to climb the stairs up to the landing.

The huge front door opened, and Palmer appeared,

his dignified face cracking in astonishment. For a moment he gawked at them in stupefied silence. "Mrs. Bingham. Mr. MacKenzie," he finally managed. "We… That is to say, it was my understanding that the police…" He gulped, then passed a trembling white-gloved hand across his brow. "Mr. and Mrs. Brock are…are…"

"Inform Mr. and Mrs. Brock that we'll meet them in the library," Jocelyn announced. "At once." She stepped forward, and the stammering butler moved aside. "And, Palmer? My name is Mrs. Jocelyn *Tremayne*."

With the cane and Micah's rock-solid arm keeping her steady, and four Secret Service operatives bringing up the rear, they advanced upon the library, their footsteps and Jocelyn's cane beating a triumphant victory march on the polished marble tile.

Moments later, the Brocks strolled without any show of haste into the library, Portia clinging to her husband's arm—an affectation, of course. Jocelyn could count on one hand the number of times Portia ever permitted this show of wifely submission. They were dressed to the nines in formal attire, Portia resplendent in a creamy-white gown crusted with pearls. An eye-popping blue sapphire hung about her neck. Augustus, on the other hand, looked miserably uncomfortable in his tie and tails. Red-faced and perspiring, he studied the cluster of people gathered in the library with nothing but bewilderment clouding his mild brown eyes. Jocelyn thought with a twinge of concern that he might be ill, instead of angry.

"I am grateful you're here," Portia announced in dulcet tones, her gaze searching out every man in the room but Micah, lingering on each one until they shuffled their feet, cleared their throats or looked away. "I see you've captured my dear, misguided niece. We've spent a frightful night and day, hoping the police would be able to find her before her life was utterly destroyed by a man we esteemed very much."

She sliced a look toward Micah and Jocelyn wondered if she were the only one who sensed the malevolence swimming behind the china-blue eyes, darkened now to cobalt. "These past few years have been a trial. Jocelyn's mind, you know, has been dreadfully weakened. Such a tragic business. I was most—"

Micah stepped forward, directly in front of her. "Mrs. Brock, your lies grow tiresome. We will hear no more. The district attorney has issued warrants. I am placing you and your husband under arrest for the crime of counterfeiting. Also for the bribery of public officials, for defamation by oral utterance of an agent for the United States government and finally, for conspiracy to commit murder."

"Mr. MacKenzie…" Augustus cleared his throat several times, but his words remained hoarse. "I don't understand. Last night, Mrs. Brock informed me that our niece— Forgive me." He clumsily withdrew his handkerchief and dabbed his mouth, while his confused gaze sought out Jocelyn. "You stole my wife's jewelry. Mrs. Brock was devastated. And you, Mr. MacKenzie—" he studied Micah for another befuddled moment before shaking his head "—somehow contrived to steal a half million dollars from my bank. My son Virgil showed me the figures last evening."

The gasp escaped before Jocelyn could prevent it; her gaze flew to Portia, who was coyly batting her eyelashes at the agent standing beside her as though they were engaged in a harmless flirtation. Jocelyn turned away from the disgusting tableau as the confirmation settled inside her with a little click. *Oh, Chadwick,* she thought, not knowing whether to laugh, or cry. Such a role model he'd had in his aunt and cousin.

"And beyond the pale, appearing on the doorstep at this hour." Augustus had drawn himself up to his full height, his barrel of a chest expanding. "How dare you barge into my home, sir, with these wild accusations, distressing myself and my wife?"

A muscle in Micah's jaw twitched. With blinding speed he whipped out his credentials, thrust them in Augustus's face, then tucked the folder back inside his jacket. Light from one of the room's chandeliers caught on his badge, which set it to gleaming like polished silver. "I am, and have been for the past eight years, an operative for the United States Secret Service." Jocelyn saw him make a discreet motion with his hand, and two of the deputy marshals moved to flank Portia Brock. "Your family, and your brother-in-law Rupert Bingham, have been under suspicion for a long time, Mr. Brock. Two nights ago, Mrs. Tremayne—"

"You're an agent for the federal government?" He shook his head, and a tremor shuddered through him. "And my niece's name is no longer Tremayne. She is my nephew's widow, and you will accord her respect by referring to her by her proper name."

Quietly, Jocelyn hobbled over to stand beside Micah. "You didn't know, did you?" she asked Augustus. The knowledge settled inside her heart, along with a stirring of pity. "You've been as much a victim of your wife and son as I have."

"What manner of vulgar talk is this, speaking of 'victims,' Jocelyn? I demand an expla—" He swayed a bit on his feet, then collected himself. "I demand an explanation."

Jocelyn nodded. "You're hearing the explanation, Uncle. And so will your wife, whom I refuse to address as 'Aunt.' Everything you've heard from Operative MacKenzie is true. I haven't stolen anything, nor has he. But Mrs. Brock and your son Virgil are guilty of every crime of which they stand accused. They stood in this very room, while I listened on the other side those closed doors—" she pointed to the pocket doors behind one of the operatives openly displaying his Colt revolver "—and listened to your wife order a man named Vanetti to murder Operative MacKenzie. When I escaped from the house, Virgil was on the way to Mr. Vanetti with the order."

Augustus's face drained of color. Humiliation burned in his eyes, painful to see, and with temper goading her Jocelyn whirled toward Portia. "You're the most despicable human being I've ever known. If I had my way, the courts would reinstitute public stocks in the market square. And you would be placed in them, with an announcement written in large letters for all the world to know what a hypocritical liar you really are."

Quick as the lash of a whip, Portia drew back her arm and slapped Jocelyn's cheek. Every man in the room jumped forward, Micah with a hair-raising growl of fury. Jocelyn, her cheek throbbing, grabbed his arm with one hand and waved the men back with her cane. "You have the authority to arrest her," she said to Micah, holding on to his arm until he looked down into her face. "But I have the right to confront her. Let me."

Breathing hard, Micah slowly nodded, and stepped aside.

Righteous wrath boiled through her but instead of retaliating in kind, Jocelyn locked gazes with Portia. The weight of ten years fueled her actions as she yanked every hairpin from her head, flinging them at Portia's feet onto the thick Aubusson carpet. When the last one was removed she shook her head, and the chignon she'd fashioned at the shanty unraveled. Her hair spilled in a glorious sunset tumble around her shoulders, halfway down her back. For good measure, Jocelyn lifted her hands and skeined them through the mass. Finally, she lifted a handful and held it up, inches away from Portia's quivering nose.

"My hair," she announced, "is red. *Red.* And I'm proud of every strand, because this is the color God made it. Moreover, the man who loves me—loves me—believes I am beautiful." She grabbed Portia's ice-cold rigid hand, then pressed it to the cheek the woman had just slapped. "These freckles you abhor? There's more beauty in one of these spots than in a single inch of your powdered face."

She released her hold on Portia's hand and flung it aside. "You want to slap my other cheek? Go ahead. I'll still be more beautiful than you are, because you can clothe yourself like the Queen of England, and pretend your face can still launch a thousand ships like Helen of Troy, but inside you're a selfish, vain creature. A pathetic excuse of a woman who turned to crime to compensate for the emptiness of her soul."

"I could say the same about you." Fury palpated

through Portia, but instead of striking Jocelyn's other cheek, she chose the weapon of words. "I trained you well, transformed you from a self-effacing nobody to a woman who knows the strength of her own power. What a magnificent disdain I see in you now! We would do well together, you and I. Why don't you dismiss your pathetic suitor? Love is a tool. Use it, and when it rusts, throw it out. There's nothing he can offer I can't replace ten times over. These sedulous charges will be dropped. He has no proof. Your claim will be dismissed in court as hearsay. And I will personally ensure that Mr. MacKenzie is eviscerated."

"I don't think so," Micah drawled, coming to stand beside Jocelyn. "Operative Matthews? Would you mind enlightening Mrs. Brock?"

"Not at all, sir." He marched across the room, and withdrew several sheets of paper filled with typewritten words. "Mrs. Brock, this is the recorded and witnessed testimony of Mr. Vanetti, and your son Virgil Brock. Both acknowledge that on four separate occasions you did order without shame or remorse the deaths of four individuals, including the foiled attempt on Operative MacKenzie." He slid Micah a sideways look. "According to Mr. Vanetti, said murders commenced on the night of June 24, in the year 1887, when he was ordered to, ah, dispose of Mr. Angus MacKenzie, Operative MacKenzie's father and Mr. Rupert Bingham's head bookkeeper. Furthermore, he was to dispose of evidence that Mr. Angus MacKenzie had discovered that would implicate members of the Brock family in a counterfeiting scheme against the First City Bank of Brooklyn, New York."

Augustus sputtered an anguished protest. "Henry

Lundford was president of that bank, and our friend. Mrs. Brock... Portia..." He started for his wife. "I don't understand. Why? I gave you everything. I work sixteen-hour days, six days a week, to provide you with a life envied by even Mrs. Astor herself."

"You're nothing!" Portia said, her facade finally cracking as her words spewed into air grown thick and foul. "A pompous windbag whose tedious character I've endured for thirty years. I needed something to feel alive. A pastime more stimulating than playing whist with boring females, and presiding over your dinners. Do you understand?" Feverishly, she searched Jocelyn's face, then Micah's. "Have you any idea of the complexity required, the intelligence needed, to create a network of skilled craftsmen able to produce over five million dollars a year? To be able to command their loyalty, and their silence?"

In a dramatic gesture she lifted her arms in front of her. "Go ahead. Arrest me. I'll still have everything I need to twist every one of your Secret Service knickers in a knot, and I'll do it from prison. You think you've won, but you're wrong."

"I assume you're referring to the three sets of engraving plates? Stashed in a barn on Long Island, under the floorboards of a tenement in Jersey City, and in the back of a foundry not a dozen blocks from here?" Micah queried, casually cupping Jocelyn's elbow while he spoke and urging her out of striking range. Understanding him better than he realized, she complied.

Micah's hand fell away, but not before—without ever taking his gaze from Portia Brock—with the lightest of brushes he skimmed his finger along her reddened cheek. "We also have in our possession the printing press at the dummy printing company you own on Fifty-fifth Street, with the ink and the paper stolen from the U.S. Treasury Department three years ago. Benny Foggarty's proved to be a font of information, you see."

"You found Benny?" Jocelyn asked, slumping in relief. All right, yes, her leg hurt, but she refused to sit down on a stick of furniture in this house.

"Let's just say the Service still has a trick or two up its sleeve that even Mrs. Brock is unaware of." A wolfish smile spread across Micah's face as he produced a pair of handcuffs. "Mrs. Brock, your network has been disbanded. Permanently."

He snapped the handcuffs around Portia's wrists, and a palpable wave of relief swept through the room. "Oh, one other item I almost forgot to mention. If you're hoping to contact your eldest son for help— don't bother. He was arrested at his St. Louis home yesterday for possession of counterfeit goods discovered underneath the floor of his study." Still smiling, he glanced across the room. "Marshal O'Keefe? I believe you arranged for police transport?"

"Arriving momentarily, Operative MacKenzie."

"How fitting," Micah said, "that the Black Maria you sent along for Mrs. Tremayne and me will instead be transporting you."

Behind them, Augustus emitted a choking sound. Before anyone could reach him, he collapsed onto the rug, his arm flung in mute appeal toward his wife.

Chapter Twenty-Six

Richmond, Virginia December 1894

A light snow dusted the city like confectioner's sugar as Micah drove the buggy along the quiet Richmond streets. At one corner a cluster of boys and girls waved as he passed, their arms full of ice skates and sleds. Six inches of new snow had fallen the previous day, and the almanac was predicting a white Christmas.

Micah smiled to himself.

Jocelyn had promised to make him an apple pie, his favorite, for Christmas Eve. Not to be outdone, Katya and Magda Schuller promised to ply him with enough dishes from their native lands to pop the buttons on his overcoat.

The Schullers had settled into life in Richmond with a joy that never failed to warm Micah's heart. For the past month they'd been living with Jocelyn, but Micah knew Jocelyn had been negotiating with Mr. Ginter, a prominent philanthropist, to purchase a house for them in the rapidly developing west end of the city.

When he reached the town house, he took the steps two at a time, but Heinrich still beat him to the door.

"Mr. MacKenzie! We have been waiting. There is a visitor, to see the missus. Come—" He grabbed Micah's arm and tugged him inside. "She is crying, but she is smiling, too. I am taking Elfie, and we are going outside, to play in snow that is still white. In New York, snow turns black, very soon." He clattered out of sight toward the kitchen door.

Alarmed, Micah divested himself of coat, muffler, hat and gloves, dumping them on the hall tree. Katya appeared in the hallway and beamed at Micah, her head bobbing up and down as she reassured him with her eyes.

"Micah!" Jocelyn stood when he strode into the parlor. "You're not going to believe this. Look who's here." Her deep navy gown swirled around her ankles as she rushed to his side. In the gaslight her red hair deepened to a rich auburn; in her expression he read gladness, but her hands fluttered nervously and beneath her freckles she was too pale. "Do you remember Mr. Bingham, Chadwick's father? He journeyed all the way down here, to see me. I—" She shook her head. "I'm afraid I don't quite know how to tell you this...."

"As long as he hasn't tried to persuade you to move back to New York, you needn't be afraid of telling me anything." Hiding his concern, Micah walked over to the fireplace where Rupert Bingham stood. They shook hands. "Mr. Bingham. You've come on a long trip through a snowstorm, hopefully not for the purpose of upsetting Mrs. Tremayne."

Rupert was looking less frail than he had been a month earlier, at Portia's and Virgil's arraignment. His handshake was firm, and a pleased little smile hovered around his lips. "As with life, Operative MacKenzie, I bring sad tidings along with glad ones."

A moment of awkward silence ensued, until Jocelyn finished conferring with Katya and joined the two men.

"Why don't we all sit down?" she suggested. "My knees are still shaking."

"But your leg isn't hurting, is it?"

"No. Practically good as new." She and Micah exchanged a private look, and he settled comfortably beside her on the sofa. "Micah, Mr. Bingham's sad news concerns Augustus. He died two weeks ago. Complications from the heart attack he suffered the day we arrested his wife."

"I'm sorry. I know it's little consolation, but—" He hesitated. "I'm very sorry," he repeated.

"Quite all right, my boy," Rupert assured him. "Augustus was always a self-complacent man, but he wore his pride like a gentleman. His wife's and sons' perfidy was a blow from which he never recovered. I was the executor of his estate. I spent the week after his funeral going through his papers. In the process, I found something that I realized would mean a great deal to my son's wi—" his face pinkened as he corrected himself "—to Mrs. Tremayne. I'll let her show you."

"Micah…" Without warning tears filled her eyes. She reached for an official-looking document lying on the table, and with unsteady hands gave it to Micah. "This is the deed, to the Tremayne family estate. After Chadwick's death, Parham was one of the properties Rupert sold to Augustus. Then Uncle Augustus sold it again. But apparently in last year's Panic the people he sold it to couldn't pay their mortgage. Augustus bought Parham back from them for—for—"

"For a pittance," Rupert supplied distastefully. "Even more reprehensibly, and I have already spoken to Operative-in-Charge Bagg. I have reason to believe that it was not Augustus, but Portia, with Virgil a willing accomplice, who arranged to repurchase the property from those desperate people. Not only did they pay less than half its worth, from what I was told, they were paid in counterfeit funds."

Rage curdled inside Micah, every muscle clenching in protest. Beside him, Jocelyn visibly flinched, though she did not look surprised.

"Fortunately," Rupert continued, "Augustus's name remained on the deed."

Micah wished Rupert would stop rambling and come to whatever point he had made that had upset Jocelyn, but merely asked, "And the owners?" He took Jocelyn's hand.

"Abandoned the place last spring. Your agency has been alerted. Again, I was given to understand that if any of those bills surface, the people may be located, as well, and hopefully more of the bogus money confiscated. No success thus far, according to Operative-in-Charge Bagg. He sends his regards, by the way."

"When you return to New York, please send mine, as well."

"Yes." He shot Micah an astute look. "Well, as I was explaining to Jocelyn when you arrived, since the deed was found in Augustus's safe, and since the new will he made before he died bequeathed all his properties and monies to me, Parham technically became mine."

A clouded look drifted through his eyes, and for

a little while he contemplated the flames dancing in the fireplace. "I can never atone for the distress Chadwick visited upon Jocelyn through the manner of his death, nor the evil his mother's family inflicted upon you both. I ask Jocelyn to accept what I've offered as a heartfelt attempt to restore at least a part of her past, in the hope that it can offer a brighter future."

"He is giving me the deed to Parham," Jocelyn said tremulously. "Micah… I have my family home back. My home…"

"I have lawyers working their way through the legal thicket, but far as I'm concerned, from this moment Parham is back where it belongs, free and clear, with no encumbrances."

Stunned, Micah unfolded the heavy manila papers and scanned them. "I'm not sure I can top this Christmas present," he admitted, trying without success to swallow the knot hardening in his throat.

Rupert gave a cackling laugh and slapped his knee. "Son, from what these old eyes see, compared to what you have to offer this pretty lady, even a family estate turns to a lump of coal."

"I wouldn't call Parham a lump of coal." Jocelyn twined her arm through Micah's, her fingers lightly caressing the aging document he still held. "But you're right. I've learned that love is far more important than land. And a shanty can be turned into a beautiful dwelling, because of the people living in it."

Micah's heart commenced pounding. Carefully, he laid the deed to Parham on the table beside him, then glanced across at Rupert Bingham. The older man winked.

"I believe I caught a whiff of some of those nutmeg

doughnuts you told me Katya made this morning? How about if I sneak into the kitchen, perhaps snitch one behind her back? Or perhaps I can convince her to join me at the kitchen table and see who can eat the most."

"Mr. Bingham, you'll do no such thing!" Jocelyn sputtered, bewilderment plain in her face. "Katya will bring a plate in here, and we'll all eat them together."

"Stay," Micah finally untangled his tongue enough to say. "I think, in a sense, your presence couldn't have been timed more perfectly." *Thanks for that, Lord. But You do have an interesting sense of humor.*

Jocelyn turned back to search his face. "What's going on? Micah, I'm not sure my heart can take too many more shocks."

When her hands twined together in her lap, Micah's own nerves settled. Certainty and peace flowed over him with the warmth of fire on a snowy December afternoon. "What I brought with me won't constitute a shock," he promised, adding with a half smile, "I'm rather hoping it won't be that much of a surprise."

"Micah, please don't tell me you've quit the Secret Service. You promised you wouldn't. I never expected you to change your vocation—not for me. You're one of the best operatives, Mr. Hazen told me when we were—"

Micah silenced the words with a brief kiss that flustered her into openmouthed silence. "Pardon my indecorous display in front of you," he murmured to Rupert, an unrepentant grin deepening when the older man threw back his head and laughed.

"Best way I know to silence a good woman."

"Yes, sir." Micah focused all his attention on the woman he loved, taking both her hands in his. He sucked in his breath. "Jocelyn… I love you. I think I've loved you for ten years. I also loved Alice, and will always hold a special place for her in my heart." His voice deepened. "I'll miss my son until I die. But God has given you and me a chance few people are offered, and I don't want to lose it. I don't want to lose you. Jocelyn…" The words froze as all of a sudden he realized that if she refused him, he would have nothing. All his hard-won hopes, all his dreams for a future, would dissolve into a cold white mist.

"Micah, I love you with all of my heart. I don't want to lose you, either." Without hesitation she leaned close and whispered just below his ear, "So *ask* me, for heaven's sake! I promise to give you the answer at once."

"Ah…" All the words drained down into his boot heels, but he was smiling as he withdrew the jeweler's box from Tiffany's. The symbolic gesture infused him with courage, and the smile broadened until his cheeks ached with it. "In that case, will you marry me, Jocelyn Tremayne?"

Jocelyn nodded toward Rupert as the tears spilled over and dampened her freckles. "Yes, Micah, I will marry you. Oh—" Her eyes rounded when she saw the ring box. Micah flipped it open, and no longer cared that his hands were shaking because Jocelyn's were, as well. "I've never seen anything so beautiful," she whispered as he slid the betrothal ring on her finger.

"It's not the most elaborate. Public servants don't make a large salary, but it looks like you."

Rupert joined them, resting his hand on Micah's shoulder. "You're right. It's a perfect ring. You've a good eye, son. You don't mind if I refer to you as 'son'? You're a good man, MacKenzie. I think Chadwick would be relieved to know someone worthy of the honor has won Jocelyn's heart." The wistfulness drifted through his eyes, then faded. "I miss him, you know. But he was a very unhappy soul, wasn't he? I wish I understood...."

Jocelyn kissed Rupert's cheek. "May I share what I finally learned? Most of the time what we need more than understanding is forgiveness." She held the ring up so that the light caught on the sparkling diamond and two deep red rubies that perfectly matched her hair. "And to know that you're loved, not only by the people to whom you've given your heart, but, even more, by God."

"I've lost my entire family to death, and disgrace. What could God offer at this point in my life?" Rupert asked, and Micah heard in his voice all the bitterness he no longer heard in Jocelyn's.

With a smile more brilliant than her ring, Jocelyn looked up into Micah's face. "Everything," she promised Rupert. "God has everything to do with our lives, if we let Him, regardless of our ages. One day, Micah and I will have to share our journey with you."

"But for now..." Unable to resist, Micah clasped his beloved's waist, lifted her completely off her feet and twirled her around. "Let's find Katya, tell her the good news and have some doughnuts."

Rupert followed the joyful couple as they strolled hand in hand from the room, a stubborn mustard-size seed of hope nudging against the dry soil of his heart.

He grudgingly acknowledged that he might be interested in hearing that story.

Shoulders squared, he strolled toward the sound of their laughter.

Epilogue

Virginia April 1897

Sunset washed the spring green of budding trees in shades of orange and purple, turning the brick on the stately old house an earthy shade of rust. Golden daffodils imported from Holland dipped their heads in homage to the day. Beneath the stately old oaks surrounding Parham, shy white dogwood blossoms and bold red azaleas brightened the lengthening shadows.

Inside the central house, doors banged open, and a drumroll of footsteps scrambled down hallways and staircases, then dashed into one of the connecting wings.

"It's a boy!" Heinrich yelled, skidding to a halt in the door to Uncle Rupert's study. "Miss Jocelyn's fine, and so is the baby. Mr. Micah's— You won't believe it, but he has tears on his face. *Moeder* told me to tell everyone, about the baby, I mean, I think to give me something to do." He grinned a snaggle-toothed smile. "Now, I must go and tell the others."

A beatific glow bright as the daffodils lit Rupert

Bingham's face. He tamped out the pipe he'd been smoking in nervous silence for nigh onto fourteen hours, carefully laid his book aside and stood. His bones crackled in protest from all the work he'd subjected them to over the past weeks, but Rupert ignored the discomfort. For a moment he pondered the book he'd been reading, his hand resting on its supple Morocco leather cover. Jocelyn had given him the Bible for Christmas. "Our baby's due in the spring," she told him. "There's a story in the Bible, about a woman who cried out to God, because she was barren. One day God heard her cry, and gave her a son. If this baby is a boy, and you want to know what his name will be, read the passage I've marked."

Jocelyn, Rupert had learned, enticed a man with the subtlety of a blacksmith's hammer. Her tactics to convince him to move down to Virginia and inhabit the wing where her grandparents had lived out the last of their years had proved equally effective. Sometimes he marveled at how little he missed city life.

Must be the air here in Virginia, he decided with a self-indulgent smile as he headed along the connecting hall, into the main house.

"So it's to be Samuel Angus, is it?" he murmured aloud. "Good strong name."

Coltish legs flying, Heinrich scampered from the wing of the house where Uncle Rupert lived to the big oak tree outside, next to the porch, where Katya pushed Elfie on a rope swing Mr. Micah had fashioned for her.

"It's a boy!" he shouted, loping over to snatch his sister out of the swing. He pinched her dripping nose, then tossed her into the air with his strong young arms.

"You can see him soon, cricket." He liked the nickname Mr. Micah had bestowed upon her. "But you can't cry anymore, *jah?*"

"Is Miss Jocelyn dead?" Elfie asked fearfully, her lower lip red from being chewed on too much all day long.

"Would I be smiling, if it were so?" Scowling now, Heinrich turned to Katya, and felt his own face color up. Tears stood in the maid's eyes, and suddenly he didn't know what to say, or how to act. Katya had wanted to remain with Miss Jocelyn, but the doctor told her single young ladies were not allowed.

"Miss Jocelyn is asking for you," he told her, hoping she would not cry too much. He didn't understand why, when the baby was squalling and the doctor and *Moeder* were smiling and he had heard with his own ears Miss Jocelyn thanking God, and telling Mr. Micah how much she loved him— Why must grown-ups cry when good things happened? "She said to tell you she is healthy as a pair of draft horses. It made Mr. Micah laugh."

He grabbed Elfie's hand. "Hurry up."

"Heinrich, we have a new brother," Elfie breathed, holding on to her older brother with her grubby fingers when he snorted a protest. "Yes. Mr. Micah told me we're all family, and this baby is to be our brother." She twisted to look over her shoulder at Katya. "And you will to be his aunt. I heard Mr. Micah say so."

"The baby will be grown by the time we get to see him," Heinrich grumped.

But when Katya joined him and Elfie, he couldn't help but slant her a look. Their eyes met, and her mouth formed its one-sided smile. Together they trooped up the porch stairs and into the cool, light halls of the house.

* * *

Micah hovered over Jocelyn and his son with a blend of disbelief and jubilation. His shirt was matted with splotches of sweat, he'd rolled up the sleeves, and at some point over the last twelve hours Jocelyn had watched him rip off the collar and cuffs, hurling them in an explosion of fear into a corner of the room.

She lifted one tired hand to his face, brushed the mustache with her fingers. "I'm glad this part's over. But it really wasn't so bad, Micah. Look what came out of the pain." As though in response, little Samuel mewled in his sleep, and Jocelyn snuggled her cheek closer to his precious head. "He is all right, isn't he, Micah? Dr. Keller promised that his lungs sound perfect, and his heart…"

"He's perfect," Micah told her huskily. "And there'll never be any doubt whose son he is."

"He's got your mouth and nose. Dr. Keller says we won't know about the color of his eyes for a few days, but I think he'll have your beautiful gray eyes, as well."

"I don't care. I'm still too busy thanking God that my wife and son are alive, and well."

"Thank you, for having the courage to give me a child." Shifting a little, she pushed a fold of swaddling cloths aside to better gaze at their sleeping baby. "Are you…are you all right, with everything, Micah?"

"Give me a year or two." He sat down on the chair Magda had placed beside the bed for him, then carefully lifted his son from his wife's arms. "What do you think, Sam? Will you be a bookkeeper like your grandpapa, a banker like your grandpapa Rupert—or a boring civil engineer like your father?"

"Perhaps he'll be a heroic operative for the Secret Service."

"Only if he stays in an office and doesn't run afoul of a nasty nest of counterfeiters."

"I think, for a little while, I can leave his future in God's hands." Drowsiness descended, but Jocelyn fought the lassitude, wanting to bask in the moment with just her husband and her son. *I have a child. Thank You.*

Twilight stole softly into the room, along with a gentle spring breeze that billowed the lace panels over the opened windows.

"Micah?" Jocelyn murmured some time later. "Are you sure I'm doing the right thing, with the money?"

"Absolutely." Very carefully he laid a sleeping Samuel in the cradle before returning to Jocelyn. "Proof of Portia's claims has never been substantiated, since the documents Virgil offered were proven to be forgeries. We'll never know for sure where Chadwick got the funds he gave you, which is why you promised me—oh, going on two years now?—that you were at peace, about this."

"I just want to honor God. I spent so many years, not doing so.... I want to know I've done the right thing, for the right reasons, not just because of you and me. But because of Samuel."

"God is the God of today, not yesterday, remember. And He looks at your heart, not your bank account." He wrapped her frazzled braid around his knuckles, then tickled Jocelyn's nose with the ends. "This time, your loving silence gives Rupert a happy memory of his son, and something he can be proud of, because Chadwick took care of you. Now the money will be used to help others like the Schullers, instead of isolating you in a bitter cocoon. I understand the difference, firefly. So does the Lord. Be at peace, in your heart, and let's enjoy our son's birthday."

Rivulets of emotion rushed through Jocelyn's exhausted body in an effusive flow. She didn't know how to contain the joy—it was like trying to bottle sunlight, or hold back a spring thunderstorm. "Thank you, for restoring Parham." She let the words spill forth, knowing her husband really did understand her. "For...being willing to pursue my dream." Fumbling, she searched for his hand, sighing with contentment as she stroked the strong bones and sinews. "When you told me you were a civil engineer before joining the Secret Service, and how much you enjoyed making things work, I think that's when I knew for sure that God had engineered everything."

Micah leaned over and kissed away the tears dribbling onto her smiling mouth. "Ever the humorist, these days, aren't you, sweetheart? Except for the past seventeen hours, forty-three minutes and oh, about twenty-seven seconds, I've enjoyed turning Parham back into a home, not only for us, but for other people we've grown to love. It's been a bit of a challenge, turning slave quarters and outbuildings into livable dwellings after thirty years of neglect, but you know how much I love a challenge."

"Do you know how much I love you?"

"I believe you've mentioned it, in passing. Do you know how much *I* love *you?*"

"More than I deserve. Micah?" He rumbled an encouraging sound. "After the restoration is finished, and we've found other needy families who need a place to stay until we help them back on their feet…can we have another child? A sister or another brother, for Samuel?"

"Great glory, woman, are you trying to kill me?" He rolled onto the floor, to his knees, and planted his forearms on either side of Jocelyn's head. "Samuel's scarcely an hour old."

She smiled up into his face, loving him, and waited.

"Well…" His head lowered, and he kissed her. "It would be nice, wouldn't it, to see how many more redheads God blesses us with."

"Redhead!" Rupert roared from the doorway. "Did I just hear you say my new grandson is a redhead?"

Elfie darted beneath Rupert's arm. "My new brother, he is to have red hair, like Miss Jocelyn?" she squealed, clapping her hands together.

Heinrich ducked past Rupert on the other side, reaching his arm to snag his sister in her dash toward the cradle. "A redheaded brother," he grumped, rolling his eyes. "I will be forever having to beat somebody up to protect him."

From out in the hallway Jocelyn heard the resounding thud—Katya, stomping her foot.

"Is this the train station, that you all talk in loud voices?" Magda followed the others into the room. "You must be quiet, and not wake the *zuigeling*."

With sheepish smiles, the group converged in noisy silence upon them. Micah retrieved Samuel, holding him so that everyone had the opportunity to gaze upon his perfect little face—and a head full of flaming red hair.

Watching them all, Jocelyn lay in bed, and let the peace of God fill her heart.

* * * * *

SPECIAL EXCERPT FROM

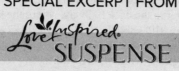

Love Inspired.
SUSPENSE

*When a guide-dog trainer becomes a target of a
dangerous crime ring, a K-9 cop and his loyal
partner will work together to keep her safe.*

Read on for a sneak preview of
Blind Trust *by Laura Scott,*
the next exciting installment in the
True Blue K-9 Unit miniseries, available
June 2019 from Love Inspired Suspense.

Eva Kendall slowed her pace as she approached the training facility where she worked training guide dogs.

Using her key, she entered the training center, thinking about the male chocolate Lab named Cocoa that she would work with this morning. Cocoa was a ten-week-old puppy born to Stella, a gift from the Czech Republic to the NYC K-9 Command Unit located in Queens. Most of Stella's pups were being trained as police dogs, but not Cocoa. In less than a month after basic puppy training, Cocoa would be able to go home with Eva to be fostered during his initial first-year training to become a full-fledged guide dog. Once that year passed, guide dogs like Cocoa would return to the center to train with their new owners.

A few steps into the building, Eva frowned at the loud thumps interspersed between a cacophony of barking. The raucous noise from the various canines contained a level of panic and fear rather than excitement.

LISEXP0519

Concerned, she moved quickly through the dimly lit training center to the back hallway, where the kennels were located. Normally she was the first one in every morning, but maybe one of the other trainers had gotten an early start.

Rounding the corner, she paused in the doorway when she saw a tall, heavyset stranger scooping Cocoa out of his kennel. Panic squeezed her chest. "Hey! What are you doing?"

The ferocious barking increased in volume, echoing off the walls and ceiling. The stranger must have heard her. He turned to look at her, then roughly tucked Cocoa under his arm like a football.

"No! Stop!" Panicked, Eva charged toward the man, desperately wishing she had a weapon of some sort.

"Get out of my way," he said in a guttural voice.

"No. Put that puppy down right now!" Eva stopped and stood her ground.

"Last chance," he taunted, coming closer.

Don't miss
Blind Trust *by Laura Scott,*
available June 2019 wherever
Love Inspired® Suspense *books and ebooks are sold.*

www.LoveInspired.com

LISEXP0519

WE HOPE YOU
ENJOYED THIS

LOVE INSPIRED®
SUSPENSE
BOOK.

Discover more **heart-pounding** romances of **danger** and **faith** from the Love Inspired Suspense series.

Be sure to look for all six Love Inspired Suspense books every month.

Love Inspired SUSPENSE

Looking for inspiration in tales
of hope, faith and heartfelt romance?

Check out **Love Inspired**® and
Love Inspired® **Suspense** books!

New books available every month!

CONNECT WITH US AT:

Facebook.com/groups/HarlequinConnection

Facebook.com/HarlequinBooks

Twitter.com/HarlequinBooks

Instagram.com/HarlequinBooks

Pinterest.com/HarlequinBooks

ReaderService.com

Inspirational Romance to Warm Your Heart and Soul

Join our social communities to connect with other readers who share your love!

Sign up for the Love Inspired newsletter at **www.LoveInspired.com** to be the first to find out about upcoming titles, special promotions and exclusive content.

CONNECT WITH US AT:

Facebook.com/groups/HarlequinConnection

 Facebook.com/LoveInspiredBooks

 Twitter.com/LoveInspiredBks

LISOCIAL2018